STAR OF ERENGRAD

EVEN BEFORE HIS comrade struck the ground, Stefan was running. He must have shouted for Bruno to surrender his horse to him, because suddenly the saddle was empty and Stefan was vaulting up. All the time he felt the eyes of the Chaos warrior upon him, fired with a hungry hatred that, Stefan sensed, burned for him alone. Fear not, he vowed, for you will have your fill of me now.

He turned Bruno's horse about and charged full on against the creature that had struck Tomas down. The two horses closed upon one another. At the moment of intersection Stefan swung his sword, and held his shield braced to receive the answering blow. Metal met metal and a shuddering jolt ran the length of Stefan's body. He had just enough time to see the visored helm of his adversary as the warrior thundered past, already wheeling around to launch another attack.

More Warhammer from the Black Library

· **THE VAMPIRE GENEVIEVE NOVELS** ·

DRACHENFELS by Jack Yeovil
GENEVIEVE UNDEAD by Jack Yeovil
BEASTS IN VELVET by Jack Yeovil
SILVER NAILS by Jack Yeovil

· **GOTREK & FELIX** ·

TROLLSLAYER by William King
SKAVENSLAYER by William King
DAEMONSLAYER by William King
DRAGONSLAYER by William King
BEASTSLAYER by William King
VAMPIRESLAYER by William King

· **THE TALES OF ORFEO** ·

ZARAGOZ by Brian Craig
PLAGUE DAEMON by Brian Craig
STORM WARRIORS by Brian Craig

· **THE KONRAD TRILOGY** ·

KONRAD by David Ferring
SHADOWBREED by David Ferring
WARBLADE by David Ferring

· **WARHAMMER NOVELS** ·

THE CLAWS OF CHAOS by Gav Thorpe
ZAVANT by Gordon Rennie
HAMMERS OF ULRIC by Dan Abnett,
Nik Vincent & James Wallis
GILEAD'S BLOOD by Dan Abnett & Nik Vincent
THE WINE OF DREAMS by Brian Craig

A WARHAMMER NOVEL

STAR OF ERENGRAD

NEIL McINTOSH

For Hanna
With grateful thanks to Neil Jones (for all the red ink)
and to Sian, for your constant support

A BLACK LIBRARY PUBLICATION

First published in Great Britain
in 2002 by The Black Library,
an imprint of Games Workshop Ltd.,
Willow Road, Lenton,
Nottingham, NG7 2WS, UK

10 9 8 7 6 5 4 3 2 1

Cover illustration by Martin Hanford

A CIP record for this book
is available from the British Library

ISBN 1 84154 265 2

Set in ITC Giovanni

Printed and bound in Great Britain by
Cox & Wyman Ltd, Cardiff Rd, Reading, Berkshire RG1 8EX, UK

See the Black Library on the Internet at
www.blacklibrary.com

Find out more about Games Workshop
and the world of Warhammer at
www.games-workshop.com

THIS IS A DARK age, a bloody age, an age of daemons and of sorcery. It is an age of battle and death, and of the world's ending. Amidst all of the fire, flame and fury it is a time, too, of mighty heroes, of bold deeds and great courage.

AT THE HEART of the Old World sprawls the Empire, the largest and most powerful of the human realms. Known for its engineers, sorcerers, traders and soldiers, it is a land of great mountains, mighty rivers, dark forests and vast cities. And from his throne in Altdorf reigns the Emperor Karl-Franz, sacred descendant of the founder of these lands, Sigmar, and wielder of his magical warhammer.

BUT THESE ARE far from civilised times. Across the length and breadth of the Old World, from the knightly palaces of Bretonnia to ice-bound Kislev in the far north, come rumblings of war. In the towering World's Edge Mountains, the orc tribes are gathering for another assault. Bandits and renegades harry the wild southern lands of the Border Princes. There are rumours of rat-things, the skaven, emerging from the sewers and swamps across the land. And from the northern wildernesses there is the ever-present threat of Chaos, of daemons and beastmen corrupted by the foul powers of the Dark Gods. As the time of battle draws ever near, the Empire needs heroes like never before.

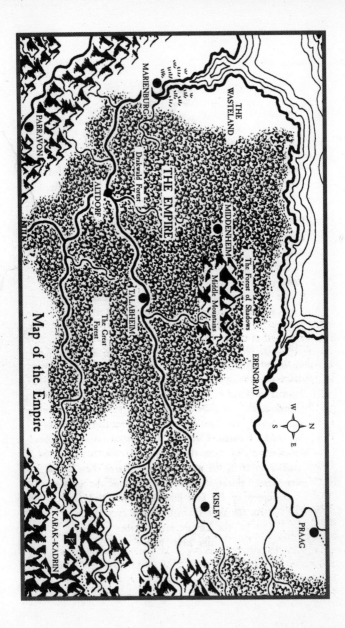

Map of the Empire

PROLOGUE
Blood of the Pure

WITH THE DESPERATION born of a creature facing annihilation, the orc lashed out at its tormentor. The green-skinned warrior was fast and powerful. Its massive bulk and daubed insignia marked it out as a chieftain amongst its kind, and it moved with the pace and purpose of a killing machine that had already sent countless foes to their graves. But today that power and speed would not be enough. Today, on the windswept Grey Mountains at the very edge of the Empire, death would turn its gaze upon the orc itself.

The creature threw back its bulbous head and released a howl of rage. The cry echoed over the land, across the snow-covered foothills that bordered the realm of man, but met with no answer. The tribe's journey of bloody plunder had reached its end. The mountain village of Stahlbergen would become their tomb.

The orc's human opponent took a step back, taunting his prey. Stefan Kumansky drew fresh, frozen air deep into his lungs, and used the stolen moment to absorb the image of his enemy. The orc chieftain was quick for its kind, but Stefan knew that he was quicker. His blade had already found its

7

mark, and blood like blackened oil was flowing from wounds carved in the creature's olive-tinged flesh. The swordsman fixed the creature with an unblinking stare, and drew himself up to his full height. A bitter smile formed on his lips.

'That's right,' he said, quietly. 'Get a good look at me. Let my face be your last memory of this world.'

The orc roared again, sensing this was its last chance of survival. It launched itself at Stefan, compressing all its remaining strength into one last attack. Stefan was pushed back onto the defensive. He thrust out his sword to parry the axe, and the collision of steel on steel sent a hammer pulse shuddering through the length of his body. He struggled to keep his foothold upon the icy slope; one slip now and the orc would have him.

He looked up as the greenskin chieftain bore down upon him. Sunlight glinted off the razored edge of the orc's axe. For an instant Stefan lowered his guard, inviting the blow. The orc's sunken eyes widened in surprise as it heaved the axe. As it fell, Stefan sprang forward, beneath the arc of the blade. Before the orc could react he stabbed out with his sword, severing the orc's hold upon the weapon.

The axe hit the ground, spattering the snow with blood. The orc tried to stop and turn, but its momentum carried it on down the icy slope until, finally, it fell. Immediately Stefan was upon it, his sword levelled at the orc's heavily built body. His lungs were pumping furiously as he fought for air on the high mountain. Stefan knew that he, too, was near collapse. His sword, as he raised it, felt heavier than he could ever have imagined.

The fallen orc gazed up at the exhausted swordsman standing over him. A look of sly animal cunning flickered in its eyes. As the orc twisted its huge body round, grasping at a final chance, Stefan delivered the blow, stabbing the sword down firmly into the monster's chest. The steel pared flesh from bone in the thickly muscled cavity, releasing a spray of putrid gore.

'That's for the dead of Stahlbergen,' Stefan shouted. He pulled the sword clear then drove it down again, tearing the leathery flesh apart. He stood back, and from somewhere found the strength to lift the sword once more, but the orc's death throes had subsided. It would never move again.

Stefan looked down and spat upon the body. 'That's for all of us,' he muttered. 'The living and the dead.'

He let the sword drop and sank to his knees, weariness pouring through him. A sudden, eerie stillness had settled upon the mountain. Up above, along the path winding around the mountain, the village lay quiet, almost tranquil in the morning sun. The peacefulness of the scene belied the carnage that had gone before.

Stefan drew down a deep breath, and ran fingers through the tangle of matted hair hanging down over his face. For a swordsman who had known barely twenty-three summers, he had already grown well accustomed to victory. But he knew that, this time, he was not yet ready to savour its taste. The orcs might have been put to the sword, but Stefan Kumansky's mission was far from ended.

His journey had begun far away, in Altdorf, at the very heart of the Empire. Stefan had been one of the band of swordsmen hired by Heinrich Krenzler. The proposition that the young adventurer had laid before them was as simple as it was dangerous: ride to the Grey Mountains and seek out and destroy the orc warband that had taken the village of Stahlbergen. Krenzler was offering a generous purse, but even without the money, this was a task that was true to Stefan's heart. He had willingly pledged his sword to the cause.

Yet he had ridden to the Grey Mountains knowing that there was another side to their mission. Stories told of a missing gemstone had been circulating for months amongst the swordsmen of the Empire. A gemstone plundered by the orcs from a sorcerer in Gratz, an all but forgotten place deep within the forest that bordered the Grey Mountains.

That it was valuable – a gem cut from rare and precious stone – was beyond dispute. But others held that it possessed darker virtues; that it was a talisman for evil, with charms that could enchant and enslave. Many of the men who had ridden to Stahlbergen had paid no heed to the story. But Krenzler had believed it, and so had Stefan. Destroying the orcs would count for nothing if the stone itself was not also eliminated.

The sound of footsteps and a voice calling his name shook Stefan from his reverie. He looked up, and for a moment his heart lifted to see Bruno Hausmann, still alive and well, emerging from the maze of wooded paths that led from the far side of the village.

Stefan scrambled to his feet, eager to share news of his victory with his comrade, but he quickly saw that Bruno was in no mood for celebration. The look in his brown eyes spoke of anguish, not of jubilation. Stefan wiped away the filth encrusting the hilt of his sword, a knot tightening in his stomach. Bruno stopped short of Stefan, his words interspersed between gasps for breath.

'Have you seen them?' he asked Stefan.

'Seen who?' Stefan demanded. 'What's happened?'

'Orcs. A group of them managed to break out. They've taken captives, Stefan. Women from the village.'

Stefan gazed around him. Despite Bruno's words, images of Krenzler and the gemstone still dominated his thoughts. 'I've seen no one,' he said after a moment. 'Where's Alexei and the rest of the men?'

Bruno motioned up the path towards the cluster of dwellings on the hillside. 'Many are dead,' he replied. 'I don't know about Alexei. I think he and a few others headed out of the village, hunting down the orcs that escaped to the north.' He broke off, still struggling for breath. 'But there were other orcs, Stefan. I saw them.' He gestured down the mountain. 'They've taken the women to the caves.'

'What about Krenzler?' Stefan interrupted. 'What about the stone?' He knew that Krenzler had gone back to the village in search of the crystal. Until they had the Gratz stone, their work was not done.

Bruno shook his head vigorously. 'Let's worry about that later,' he insisted. He caught hold of his comrade's sleeve, tugging him towards him. 'The women, Stefan! We have to find the women, before it's too late!'

Stefan turned towards his comrade. They had shared so much together. Countless battles along the road, countless victories won and sorrows borne. Sturdy and honest, Bruno was the closest Stefan had ever had to a true friend. He would gladly give his life for him.

But the warning voice would not relent. Stefan had to go back to the village.

He pulled himself free of Bruno's grasp. 'Krenzler went to find the stone,' he said, firmly. 'Destroying the orcs will count for nothing if we don't find it. Evil will only find another host. We have to destroy it.'

Bruno spread his arms wide in as gesture of disbelief. 'Didn't you hear what I said?' he implored. 'This is about more than a miserable crystal. There's people down there who are going to die if we don't do something. *Now*, Stefan.'

The two swordsmen stood facing each other, their breath frosting the crisp air. Stefan wanted to tell Bruno that his heart was torn, that he would willingly tear himself into two parts if he could. But he knew deep in his soul that the voice would allow him only one path, as it always had these past twelve years. And he knew, too, that Bruno would not understand.

In the end, no one could ever truly understand the force that drove him on.

'Take one of the others,' Stefan said at last. 'Find Alexei. I'm going after Krenzler.'

Bruno stared back at Stefan, his expression growing cold, disbelieving. The silence on the mountain fell like a curtain between them. The moment was broken by the sound of a human voice, a woman's scream rising up from the honeycomb of caves below.

Bruno's face creased with anger and hurt. 'Do what you will,' he said. 'I won't abandon those people.' He turned away from Stefan and ran towards the path leading down the mountain.

Stefan stood, watching his friend for a few moments longer, before taking his own, opposite path, back up the mountain towards the village. He had no choice; Krenzler had gone in search of the gemstone and had not returned. Stefan knew he must finish what they had begun.

FURTHER ALONG THE trail, the village of Stahlbergen began to reveal its scars. The greenskin occupiers might have been purged, but the legacy of their short and brutal reign was all too apparent. True to their reputation, the orc warband had plundered all that they could find. Anything of any value had been ripped from the heart of the village, and what could not be plundered had been destroyed. Houses lay in ruins, walls cracked and crumbling and doors broken down and smashed upon the roadway. Plumes of acrid smoke drifted up from the hearts of countless fires, curling like cruel black snakes against the white tableau of the mountain.

Most of all, the cost could be counted in human lives. At each turn in the road Stefan came across more of them: men, women and children from the village, and the bodies of his fallen comrades. More than a dozen men had ridden to the mountains with Heinrich Krenzler; only a few would make the journey home. The dead lay amongst the burning wreckage, their bodies like broken dolls. The air was thick with the sweet, sickly smell of charred flesh.

As he looked at the carnage around him, Stefan was drawn back to his memories. To the blackened shell of his childhood home; to the village of Odensk twelve years ago, the day after the Norscans had come. There was the figure, lying face-up upon the cold stones, one arm reaching out towards Stefan. That was the first time he had truly looked upon death. And death had returned his gaze, returned it through the cold, lifeless eyes of his father. That was the day that Stefan had ceased to be a child. That was the day he had set out upon the journey that was going to map his life.

He shivered and hurried on, trying to deflect his thoughts away from the past. He located the centre of the village, and came to a simple white building that had been the shrine of Sigmar. He paused outside the sturdy oak doors, still intact despite the ferocity of the onslaught they had endured. This was where the orcs had made their base, where they had hoarded their treasures. If the stone were anywhere, it would be here. Stefan pushed open the doors and stepped inside the once holy place.

The room stank – of blood, putrefaction and of death. Stefan lit the stub of a candle that he retrieved from the debris. He stepped cautiously inside the shrine, working his way through the vestibule to the main chamber. The single flame cast a pale, waxy light across the interior. The white walls had been daubed with excrement, then further defamed with foul runes painted in blood. Stefan fought back a bitter bile that rose up in his throat.

The only orcs left inside the shrine were very dead. To judge from the devastation all around, their passing had been a particularly bloody one. Scattered amongst the wreckage was what remained of the orcs' plunder – gold, silver plate, the remnants of precious icons. Some of it was from the village, but not all; some had come from further afield, from other staging posts along the way of the orcs' savage odyssey. But nowhere could Stefan see anything that might resemble the gemstone he sought.

He looked around, wondering if Krenzler had been here, if he could possibly have taken the command post single-handed. Whatever had happened here, there was no trace of the wealthy adventurer now. It was possible he was dead; that he had paid for his quest to find the ill-favoured stone with his life. It was possible, too, that he had destroyed the crystal before he himself had been destroyed. Somehow, on both counts, Stefan Kumansky doubted that it was so.

Outside, the sun still shone, indifferent to the slaughter. A wave of black carrion birds wheeled in the blue sky above, celebrating death's dominion and the feasting time to come. Stefan stepped out from under the shadows of the shrine and sat down upon the lip of a well. A stench like death itself rose up from the poisoned water. He looked away from the smoking ruins of the village, across the snow-capped mountain toward the caves below.

He thought about going in search of Bruno, but in his heart knew that it was too late. He had made his decision, and it had yielded him nothing. Stefan sank down and buried his head in his hands. Krenzler had disappeared and the gem-stone had slipped through their hands. Evil had been purged from Stahlbergen, only to be set loose upon the world once again.

CHAPTER ONE
The Altered Man

FOR MOST PEOPLE who lived their lives secure behind the walls of Altdorf, Stahlbergen had never meant anything more than the name of a distant place, far away from their everyday existence. With the passing of time, even the name was forgotten by all but a few. But one man did not forget. Stefan Kumansky had left the Grey Mountains far behind, but he remembered the dead of Stahlbergen. And he remembered the Gratz stone, the cursed crystal that had led Krenzler and his men to that lonely place.

The vanished gem was the reason that Stefan could not forget, nor lose sight of the quest that had first led him to the Grey Mountains. He knew that it came from a place of darkness, that it held a promise born of evil rather than good. Stefan knew he would not truly rest while it remained at large. From that day in Odensk, when childhood had ended and the world had turned forever, Stefan had sought out evil. Where he found it he would confront it, and where he confronted it he would fight against it, until it was destroyed. It was like answering a call from deep inside of himself, a stirring which, though he did not fully understand it, he could not deny. Over the years since Odensk it had become his defining purpose, the force that had driven him to perfect his mastery of the sword until he had no equal within the city of Altdorf, and few beyond. To pay his way in life, Stefan accepted the pay of a mercenary, for purses offered by men such as Krenzler. But it was vengeance, not gold, that stirred his soul to seek ever greater valours.

Stefan had been unable to find any trace of the Gratz stone, but he knew that if there was one man who knew of its whereabouts, then that man would be Heinrich Krenzler. But it seemed that Krenzler had vanished from the face of the world that day on the mountain, vanished as completely as the crystal that he had been searching for. Stefan had returned to Altdorf, to the mighty city at the heart of the Empire that had been their mutual home. He had scoured the inns and taverns where once Krenzler had bought the loyalty of the men who served him. But everywhere he went, the word was the same. Nothing more had been heard of the adventurer. It was as though all traces of his life had been erased, or left, like his house in Altquartier, shuttered and empty.

As the weeks turned to months, the trail grew ever colder, and Stefan's belief in the quest started to weaken. He began to wonder if a madness had possessed him that day on the mountain. A madness that had driven him to search for a crystal that no longer existed – or perhaps had never existed. He began to wonder if even Krenzler had been born of his imagination. The same madness had let him watch his comrade go alone to struggle against impossible odds. Bruno had survived, but the hostages from the village had not. The women had died that day, and Stefan and Bruno had not spoken since.

Over time, Stefan fell back into his old life in the city, his sword earning him his keep where it could. He imagined that, finally, the voice warning him of the evil within the shadows would relent. It would fade and die, and his memories of Stahlbergen, Krenzler and the Gratz stone would die with it.

But the voice would not relent. It kept whispering, quiet but insistent, keeping Stefan on his guard. Even at his lowest ebb, part of Stefan remained alert, watching and waiting, although he no longer knew what it was that he waited for.

Then, a year to the day after he had returned from the Grey Mountains, the dreams had begun.

They had begun as no more than a faint but incessant tug upon the memory of sleep. He would wake suddenly, clutching at the shape of a dream that would melt away with the breaking light. But, after time, the dream took on more solid shape, and the image of a man, a man he had never met before, started to fix itself in his mind.

At first the face had shown itself only at the very edges of his imaginings: a distant figure blurred in shadow, a passer-by in a crowd. But, as the nights passed, the stranger loomed ever larger and clearer in his nocturnal world, until his dreams were of him alone. Across the nights of troubled sleep, the dreamer began to study the face, committing every line and aspect of its features to memory.

Soon Stefan had begun a new search. A search to find the bearer of the face that now haunted him, or, rather, its counterpart amongst the living world. He roamed the streets of the city almost at random, unsure of where this new search should begin or end. Soon the face had come to dominate his waking thoughts as much as it saturated his dreams, displacing all thoughts of Krenzler. Now Stefan Kumansky began to wonder if, truly, he were not losing his sanity. He tried to shut the anonymous stranger away, banish the spectre from his thoughts, but to no avail. The image haunting him only intensified, until the picture of the rounded, well-fed face with its knowing smile filled his imaginings night and day.

Sometimes, during his travels across the city, Stefan might stop to confront his reflection staring back it him from the glazed frontage of a busy tavern. What he saw was not entirely comforting. It was the face of a man still young, dark, shoulder-length hair pushed back from a lean and unscarred face that many would call handsome. Yet Stefan himself recognised a look that marked him out from the revellers on the other side of the glass. It was a look of single-minded purpose, a look that bordered upon obsession. A look that had only hardened since Stahlbergen. A look –perhaps – of a man nearing the edge of madness.

At such times, Stefan would wrap his cloak tight around him and hurry on into the gathering night. If there was something within him that marked him as different, then that was only as it always had been. Whatever the path that destiny had chosen for him, he was surely meant to travel it alone.

Finally, and unexpectedly, his search came to a resolution. Stefan found himself one day crossing a wide boulevard somewhere in the wealthier part of the city. With a start, he realised that he barely knew where he was or how he had come to be there. Bewildered, he looked around, trying to get his bearings from the tall imposing buildings that lined the streets on either side. As he stepped into the road he narrowly avoided being struck down by a coach thundering down the centre of the street. At the last moment Stefan threw himself to one side, out of the unswerving path of the carriage.

Stefan looked up at the windows of the coach as it raced past, and found himself face to face with the passenger riding inside. The encounter lasted barely a moment, but long enough for Stefan to be sure that this was the face he had been searching for. It was the face of a man he had never met, yet something in the stranger's eyes spoke of a recognition, an old, almost buried, association. It was the eyes that held the key to his dreams.

'Come on mate!' Stefan felt hands, rough but not unkind, pulling him back upon his feet. 'You're lucky,' said the man at his side. 'That one doesn't stop for nobody.'

'Aye,' agreed a second who had come to Stefan's aid. 'That he doesn't. Though, it could be argued you're unlucky – I hear tell he doesn't venture out much at all.'

Stefan muttered his thanks to the two men. 'Tell me,' he asked them, 'who is he? Does he have a name?'

The first man laughed. 'I should think he does,' he said. 'If you don't know it now, you will before long. His name's Ernst Furstlager,' he added, 'merchant and speculator,' The man made a low, sarcastic bow. 'A rags to riches story that will be the talk of all Altdorf before long,' he added. 'He's made more money in the last year than my guv'nor has made in twenty, and doubtful if he's come by it honestly, neither,' he said. 'Leastways, that's how my guv'nor tells it.'

Stefan brushed himself down and shook each of the two men in turn by the hand. 'Thank you,' he said to them. 'Thank you very much.'

* * *

THAT WAS THE point at which the dreams stopped. Stefan Kumansky knew now that the gods had sent him a message, that his searching was finally at an end. From then on the night hours were given over to a vigil, close by the walls of Ernst Furstlager's mansion. What he learnt did not greatly encourage him. His rescuer on the street that day had been right. The merchant Furstlager might recently have grown wealthy beyond all imagining or reason, but it seemed he rarely ventured far beyond the confines of the mansion. But this night, Stefan promised himself, this night would surely prove to be the exception.

Stefan set out across the city shortly after dusk, a cloth bag slung over one shoulder. His journey took him through narrow, airless streets bordered by tall wooden-framed buildings, each path and dwelling brim full with the clamour and bustle of life. Tonight the traffic of drinkers, peddlers and dealers had a particular urgency to it. The normally drab streets were decked with banners, and garlands of sweet-smelling flowers took the edge off the usual human stench. Tonight was the first evening of Sigmarsfest, and all of Altdorf was readying itself for a week of festival.

All except one. For Stefan Kumansky, the night offered only one thing. The prospect of Ernst Furstlager at last leaving his home to spend the evening in the city. The Founders' Feast, held each year on the eve of the Festival of Sigmar, was a banquet graced only by the richest and most powerful of Altdorf nobility. Each year the founders would elect to invite as their guest of honour one merchant who had shone above all his peers. If what Stefan had heard about Ernst Furstlager was true, then this year there could be only one name upon the founders' lips. This year there could be only one guest of honour, and Stefan had made his silent wager that Furstlager would be unable to resist the chance to parade his newly-made wealth amongst them. If he was ever to get inside the Furstlager mansion, then surely it would be this night.

At length he reached the Albertschloss, the quarter of the city populated by the pinnacle of the merchant classes. A year ago Ernst Furstlager's name would have meant nothing to the feted men of commerce who had settled here. Now, suddenly and inexplicably, it was on the lips of each and every one. Furstlager – and his meteoric rise – was the talk of the city.

The dreams had begun to tell Stefan why. Now he would find out for sure.

The Furstlager mansion could only be approached from one direction: a tree-lined avenue off the main highway that led to heavy iron gates set inside a perimeter wall. Keeping well beneath the cover afforded by the trees, Stefan advanced up the avenue until he had clear sight of the house. Once he was sure he was concealed from view, Stefan crouched down, and waited.

Aside from its size and obvious trappings of wealth, there was nothing out of the ordinary about the house itself. In common with just about every other building in Altdorf that night, flags of the Empire flew from poles or from windows, fluttering gently in the evening breeze. A few lights burned in windows at the front of the house, but most of the residence seemed to be in darkness.

Stefan stayed watching, motionless, oblivious to the cold penetrating his limbs. After about an hour, the gates to the coach house at the side of the main building swung open, and the silence was broken with the sound of iron-clad wheels turning upon the paved forecourt.

A carriage flanked by at least a dozen outriders emerged from the gates of the mansion. The windows had been covered, but Stefan allowed himself a smile of satisfaction as the entourage swept past. He waited a few moments longer after the carriage had passed out of sight, to be sure that there was no other escort following. Then, one hand touching lightly upon the hilt of his sword, Stefan approached the house.

With the iron gates most likely to be guarded, Stefan edged his way around the outside of the walls, staying as far as possible beneath the cover of the trees. Once he had the back of the house in view, he pulled a climbing iron out from his bag, and cast it towards the top of the wall. Stefan drew hard upon the rope to be sure it was firm, and began to climb.

This was the point at which he would be most vulnerable. If he had been seen by any guards on either side of the wall there would be little he could do to evade capture, or worse. It was a risk he knew he had no choice but to make. If he was to get inside the house, then it was to be tonight, or never.

Stefan scaled the wall in two swift movements. He paused momentarily on top to scan the area below. The grounds of the mansion stood empty in the silver moonlight. No sign of any guards. The few lights that burned were at ground level off at one side. Stefan guessed that what remained of the guard would be quartered there, probably taking advantage of their master's absence to enjoy a pot of ale and a few hands of cards. Enjoy them at your leisure, Stefan enjoined them. I promise you, I've no intention of disturbing you.

He made his way quickly across the open grass. All the windows at ground level had been secured with iron grilles. Stefan selected a casement where the iron and brick looked weakest, and set about forcing the bars apart. He had no excuse to offer if he was apprehended – the truth was, there was none. The honest answer – that he suspected that Furstlager had somehow come into possession of the gemstone, and had used its evil charm to generate his power – would have no credibility whatsoever, and the best he could have hoped for was a spell in the Altdorf asylum. Probably, he reflected, a long one.

He bent one window bar back. A second soon yielded to the heavy iron lever, a loud crack penetrating the night air as the metal snapped in two. The locks themselves were relatively flimsy and Stefan now had the window open in a matter of seconds. He hauled himself upon the ledge and squeezed through the gap between the bars and into the house. Easy, he reflected. Almost too easy.

Stefan stood for a moment until his eyes grew accustomed to the interior gloom. Directly ahead, a flight of stairs led up to a room from where a faint light shone. Stefan had taken barely half a dozen steps towards the stair when a voice called out, cutting through the stillness inside the house.

'Stop right there! Whoever you are, drop your weapon and turn around!'

Stefan stopped in his tracks, and turned, very slowly, in the direction of the voice. A figure was dimly visible in the darkness behind him; a man of much his own build, but wearing some kind of uniform topped off with a light steel helmet.

'Drop the sword,' the voice repeated. 'Drop it now.'

Stefan hesitated, then placed the weapon carefully down upon the ground at his side. The figure moved a few steps forward out of the shadows. 'Now come over here where I can see you,' the man commanded. 'Don't try anything clever.'

Stefan did as he was bid, walking slowly, one step at a time with his hands hanging by his sides. He could see the guard's face now, and the long halberd aimed towards him. Stefan looked at the man, knowing that he wanted to find evil in his face. Knowing it would be easier that way. But all he saw was an ordinary man – barely more than a boy, in fact – struggling to keep from shaking as he faced an intruder. Just a frightened boy, trying to do his job. Stefan forced a smile of reassurance, hoping to stop the guard from doing something stupid. But in his heart he knew this could not end well for both of them.

'Listen,' Stefan began, 'this isn't what you think–'

'Shut up!' There was a tremor in the guard's voice. 'Just come over here, and keep your hands down.'

Stefan walked towards the youth, his expression neutral, unthreatening. The last thing he wanted was for the young soldier to panic. The two men were no more than arm's length apart. Light from the moons beyond the window ran the length of the halberd, revealing a lethally sharp blade. Stefan took a step closer.

'Sorry,' he said. With one hand he knocked the staff aside. With the other he grasped hold of the guard's tunic and pulled him forward until the two were all but entwined. By that time Stefan had his short knife in his hand, and was sliding it between the other's ribs. He brought his free hand up to stifle the young man's cry, and held it there until his life had ebbed away.

He let the body slide to the ground, then stooped to close the boy's eyes. 'May Morr grant you peace,' he whispered. 'You were not deserving of this.'

He stood for a moment in the darkness of the stairwell, listening. The only sound bar the few words exchanged had been the clatter of the weapon as it fell to the ground. It might have been enough to raise the alarm, but, for the moment at least, all was quiet.

He turned away from the body and climbed the stair towards the source of the dull amber light. Ahead of him, beyond an open set of heavy oak doors, lay a huge chamber almost the width and breadth of the entire mansion. Inside, shapes began to reveal themselves. The walls were decked with pictures, elaborate works in oil and ink. Statues lined

the walls each side of a long table, images of gods shaped
from bronze and marble. At the near end of the room was the
source of the light: the embers of a fire, all but dead. The glow
from the fire was glinting off something mounted upon a
plinth on the far wall, a polished stone the size of a man's
fist. The crystal glowed a sickly yellow in the firelight, a single, jaundiced eye drawing Stefan in.

He had never set eyes on the crystal before, yet he knew in
a moment that this was the Gratz stone. And he knew why
the orcs and now Furstlager had gone to such lengths to possess it. The stone radiated magic energy.

As he stood, gazing at the wondrous yellow orb, Stefan
began to wonder what gifts the stone might bestow upon a
man such as himself, if he possessed it. The answer that came,
unbidden, was that the stone could grant him powers beyond
his wildest dreams. Who knew what he might achieve, were
his swordsman's skills to be wedded to the magical proper-
ties of the stone. Who knew what–

Stefan shook his head vigorously, averting his eyes from
the insidious sulphur glow. His head cleared. He took out a
thick cloth and wrapped it securely around the stone then
placed it in his back pocket.

Suddenly, there was a sound behind him like a heavy
breath being exhaled, and then a tiny, muffled explosion. He
turned around to see the dying fire suddenly brought to
vibrant life.

He was not alone. Seated by the fire, an old and emaciated
dog by his side, was Ernst Furstlager. The merchant looked up
at Stefan and smiled.

'Stefan Kumansky, if I'm not mistaken. As you can see, you
were expected.'

Stefan gazed at the merchant. He had never before seen
Furstlager at close quarters, but this was undoubtedly him –
the face from the dreams. There was something about him –
something in his face – that tugged at another, deeper memory.

'I see there's no need to introduce myself,' Stefan
responded, coldly.

'None at all. All Altdorf knows of you, Kumansky.' The
merchant reached for a glass set upon the table at his side,
and took a careful sip. 'I can't say that your reputation is

entirely flattering.' The dog at his feet, ancient and painfully thin, stirred fitfully, moaning in its slumbers. Furstlager stroked the animal and smiled.

'Stefan Kumansky the fearless fighter against evil,' he said. 'Always chasing shadows where in reality there is only light. I knew you wouldn't be able to resist the chance to come to thieve what is legitimately mine.'

'There's nothing legitimate about the gemstone, however you came about it,' Stefan countered. 'It has only one purpose: to advance the cause of evil, and the fortunes of the men who embrace it. That's why I'm going to destroy it.'

Furstlager gazed at Stefan, indulgently. 'You're a young man, Stefan. Perhaps I should forgive your foolishness. I'm a merchant and a collector of artefacts. The stone you came to steal is just one such artefact: beautiful, but quite harmless. You'll start by putting it back in its proper place, then we'll think about what to do next.' He laughed. 'Who knows, perhaps I could be persuaded to find a place for you. With the right guidance, you might do well.'

'You won't buy or threaten me,' Stefan replied. 'I'm here for just one thing. I'm not leaving without it.' He paused. 'What have you done with him, anyway?'

Furstlager's eyes widened, his expression blank incomprehension. 'You talk in riddles now. Done with whom?'

'Krenzler. Did you pay him to bring you the stone?' Stefan looked again at the seated figure of the merchant; the well-fed face with its smooth, glistening jowls. Something about the face told Stefan that Krenzler was far from dead.

Furstlager's expression hardened. 'Return the stone,' he said, coldly.

'I don't think so,' Stefan replied.

'The stone,' Furstlager repeated, no cajoling or humour in his voice now. 'Replace the crystal where you found it.'

There was a sudden, rending sound from the shadows by the fire. Something large and powerful had started to move. Stefan glanced round. It looked as though the body of the sleeping animal had been ripped in half. From out of the torn bag of skin and bone, something else, something terrible, was emerging. The creature growled, a hungry, brutal sound.

Furstlager smiled. 'I won't repeat my request.'

'You'd be wasting your time if you did,' Stefan countered.
He spun round just as the creature launched itself at his
throat. Stefan had a momentary glimpse of two eyes that
glowed like phosphor, and a row of bloodied teeth bearing
down. The dog-monster howled as it fell upon him. Stefan
got his sword across his body just in time to fend off the
attack. The creature had its jaws locked around the blade,
grinding its fangs upon the polished steel as though it was
gnawing at a bone.

Stefan felt the creature's strength, its powerful body shaking him from side to side like a leaf. The cloth containing the
stone fell from his pocket, and the crystal skimmed away
from him across the polished floor. The dog-creature let go of
the sword, spitting blood from its jaws where the blade had
made its mark. It sprang back, and fell upon its haunches,
compressing its muscles ready for a fresh attack. As it
launched itself again, Stefan thrust his sword upwards, into
the thick knot of flesh behind the dog's neck. The creature
howled but refused to die and Stefan was pulled off his feet
by the brute force of the dog's momentum. For a moment he
was being dragged along the floor behind it, desperately trying to keep a hold upon his sword.

The dog writhed violently, twisting from side to side to free
itself from the sword, and Stefan had the chance to regain his
feet. He plied his blade with both hands and managed to lift
the creature off the ground, still impaled upon the steel. With
a mighty heave, he thrust it back, into the hot coals of the fire
behind him. The monster roared in agony as the flames licked
up around its body, and Stefan pulled the sword clear.

Furstlager wasn't smiling now. In fact, very little about him
was the same. He seemed to have sloughed off years in age,
and the fattened body of the merchant had given way to the
taut, leaner frame of a younger man. Only the eyes, those
piercing azure eyes, remained unchanged. Stefan now saw
that they were the eyes of Heinrich Krenzler, and they gazed
at him with pure undiluted loathing.

'I knew I'd find you, in time,' Stefan said, quietly. 'Where's
the real Ernst Furstlager? Did you use the stone to kill him,
then steal his identity?'

'You should have died too, back in the mountains,'
Krenzler said. 'I should have made sure of that. Consider

your escape only a postponement,' As the man lunged towards him, Stefan caught the glint of steel beneath the folds of his cloak. The stiletto was slender and light, but undoubtedly sharp enough to slice clean through a man's throat. Krenzler wielded it with a lethal speed and skill. Stefan was forced back, fending off the whiplash blows from the other man's blade. The stiletto stroked the flesh on his face, cutting the skin. Krenzler bared his teeth in a leering grin, and Stefan found the space to land a blow of his own. His sword cut through the other's guard and lodged in the base of his windpipe. Krenzler's eyes widened in disbelief as blood bubbled through his nose and mouth. As Stefan pulled his blade clear his opponent toppled back, bringing a shelf stacked high with artefacts crashing down on top of him. Krenzler lay pinned beneath the debris, and did not move again.

But, to his left, something else was beginning to stir amidst the fire still blazing in the hearth. The flames had reduced the dog-creature to a burning shell, but Krenzler's diabolic familiar was not yet dead. Stefan stood frozen with horror as the skeletal frame emerged from the fire, smoke and flame still licking around its carapace. The beast's jaw fell open to reveal its fangs, charred but intact.

Breathing fire from its scorched lungs, the creature started to crawl towards Stefan, its eyes, glittering like black coals, fixed upon its prey. Stefan could feel the intensity of the heat radiating out from the fire-ravaged body as it advanced upon him, forcing him back. At each move, the creature seemed to anticipate him, driving Stefan slowly towards the far corner of the room. Finally, there was nowhere left to go. The creature's jaws gaped open, and its body arched back, ready to leap at Stefan one final time.

Stefan reached for the heaviest object he could find, a bronze figurine lying amongst the tumble of artefacts at his feet, and hurled it at the creature as it sprang through the air. Metal struck against bone, and the creature exploded, showering the room with sparks and shards of shattered bone.

Stefan heaved a long sigh of relief and mopped a hand over his brow. He stood watching the smoking debris until he was certain the creature had been destroyed. This business doesn't get any easier, he reflected.

He now had some decisions to make, and most of them revolved around himself getting out. He couldn't be sure that there weren't yet more deadly familiars lying in wait around the building, and, on balance, he didn't much want to find out. He retrieved the crystal and set it down carefully on the marbled floor in front of him. He took hold of the figurine in his other hand, and brought it down hard upon the stone. The figurine cracked in two, bronze splinters spraying out in all directions. The stone skipped away across the floor. To his dismay, Stefan found it was completely undamaged; not so much as a scratch upon its smooth, polished surface. Cursing, he wrapped the cloth back around the stone and replaced it hurriedly in his pocket.

As he ran from the chamber Stefan all but collided with a guard rushing in the opposite direction. Stefan pushed the may aside, then ducked away just quickly enough to avoid being decapitated by the sword of a second guard. He kicked the first man hard in the guts as the second man took aim again. The blade sliced through the cloth of Stefan's tunic, missing his flesh by a hair's breadth. Stefan swung his own sword two-handed and delivered a heavy blow to the man's head with the flat of his blade. The guard fell backwards down the staircase, his armour hammering noisily upon the stone steps.

Without waiting to see if he would rise again, Stefan sped down the stairs and made good his escape through the same window.

Outside, the grounds of the mansion were still deserted, but as Stefan sprinted towards the perimeter wall he could hear at least a dozen voices in pursuit behind him. With the shouts of the guards ringing loud in his ears, he cleared the wall and landed heavily upon the flint-strewn ground below. He picked himself up and ran back down the avenue, the only path out of the Furstlager mansion.

The twin moons had retreated behind the clouds, but in the darkness Stefan could nonetheless see that his escape had been cut off. A coach pulled by two black horses had appeared, positioned so as to block the neck of the avenue where it rejoined the main street. Heart hammering, Stefan drew out the pitted blade once more, and prepared to meet whatever further twist of fate now awaited him.

As he approached the unlit carriage, the door facing him swung open and a voice called out: 'Get in, Kumansky.'

Stefan hesitated, sword poised in mid-air. The voice had the air of urgency, but Stefan sensed no hostile intent. Behind him, the sound of footsteps hard in pursuit on the gravel road.

'Get in,' the voice repeated. 'We need to get away from here, fast.'

Stefan considered his alternatives. He might put what remained of Furstlager's guards to the sword, and he might evade the attentions of whoever was inside the coach. But his situation was precarious; he was in need of allies, wherever they might be found. He sheathed his sword and stepped up into the waiting coach. The vehicle jolted into life instantaneously. The pursuing guards came into view, then quickly receded into the distance once the carriage began to pick up speed.

Stefan settled himself upon the narrow bench, bracing himself against the rocking of the carriage as the coachman drove the horses on. A barrage of noise filled the carriage as the iron-clad wheels turned ever faster upon the road. Soon the shouts of the pursuing guards were drowned out, or faded away as the men gave up the chase.

A face peered at Stefan from the seat opposite, lit by the glow from a solitary lamp. It was a man of middle years, rounded but lean, with greying hair cropped close against his skull. A priest of some sort, perhaps, a man schooled in penitence and devotions. The man's eyes probed him intently, but not altogether unsympathetically. He seemed in no hurry to break the silence.

'Well,' Stefan said finally, raising his voice against the clamour of the wheels, 'everyone seems to know my name. Might I have the honour of knowing yours?'

The man opposite ignored the question. 'We've had our eye on you for quite some time now,' he said. 'And on your merchant friend, of course. I take it,' he went on, 'that Furstlager is dead?'

Stefan eyed his interrogator closely. He might look like a priest, but the man had the direct manner of a soldier, or one of the feared scourges who passed judgement upon the guilty wretches confined within the Palace of Retribution. For all that, something in his tone still suggested an ally rather than an enemy. 'I think Ernst Furstlager died a long time ago,' he replied. 'And the man I killed tonight was no friend of mine.'

His companion nodded, seemingly satisfied with Stefan's response. 'What of the crystal?' he asked. Stefan was momentarily taken aback, but there seemed little point in denying any knowledge of the gemstone. He touched his hand against his pocket, but kept the cloth-wrapped packaged concealed. 'It's secure,' he said.

'Excellent,' the other man replied, content again with Stefan's answer. 'You know,' he went on, 'whatever the truth of it, it wouldn't look good if, to all intents and purposes, a respected man like Ernst Furstlager is found dead by your hand. Wouldn't look good at all.'

Stefan braced himself, waiting to see where the conversation was going to lead.

'Luckily for you,' the other man continued, 'you didn't kill him. Ernst Furstlager died in the sudden and savage fire that will be sweeping through his home... about now' He waited a few moments longer, and pulled back the curtain fastened across the window of the carriage. Behind them, in the distance, Stefan could clearly see the first flickerings of flames lighting the sky above the Furstlager mansion.

The other man looked up at Stefan and smiled, knowingly. 'A tragic accident, I fear.'

So Stefan now had a benefactor. Why and who remained a mystery.

'On the whole, it has been a good night's work,' the man concluded. 'A good night's work indeed.'

Stefan pulled back the curtain over the window and peered out into the night. The carriage was still travelling fast, headed, it seemed, for the very heart of Altdorf.

Somehow, he had the feeling that the night was far from over yet.

CHAPTER TWO
The Map of Darkness

THE MAN'S NAME was Otto Brandauer, that much at least Stefan had learnt. And it seemed at first that the likeness to one of the dread scourges might not have been so wide of the mark. The carriage had taken them directly to the Palace of Retribution, the feared grey edifice that lay walled within the heart of Altdorf, a fortress within the city. This was not a place that Stefan would ever have chosen to visit. This was a palace of few splendours, and fewer comforts. This was where those accused of crimes were brought to be judged, and, for those judged guilty, where savage retribution was brought to bear. Many passed beneath its portals, transgressors bearing their sins like penitents to the shrine, but few who entered here ever returned. It was not a thought that Stefan found comforting.

As they entered the palace, Brandauer's demeanour changed. Far from gaining in stature, as would befit a man of high office, he seemed almost to diminish, to shrink. As he stepped down from the carriage, his head bowed, Brandauer would surely have been taken for a man of little consequence, a bearer or humble scourge's clerk at best. Stefan fell in step with his host, out of place and ill at ease in his new surroundings.

They skirted the edge of a broad courtyard, grey, featureless walls stretching to the sky on four sides. Stefan could only wonder at how many hundreds of condemned souls lay beyond those walls, their existence now limited to the windowless cells that confined them. He suppressed an involuntary shudder, and moved on, keeping close behind Otto Brandauer. Soon they came to a rusted iron door set into one of the walls which Brandauer unlocked. Beyond the door, a narrow stairway snaked its way down below ground. The stairway burrowed down beneath the palace to a passageway lit only by meagre tallow candles. The air was dank and stale. Stefan and his companion descended into a cold, silent world. The few people that they encountered acknowledged neither Stefan nor his companion. It was as though they had become invisible.

After a while walking in silence, they came to a second door and Brandauer paused. He turned and smiled at Stefan.

'Welcome to my domain.' He opened the door and bid Stefan enter ahead of him. 'We can talk here.'

Only once he had closed the door of the chamber behind them did Otto Brandauer regain his earlier air of self-assurance. Stefan sat down, taking in the austere surroundings. The chamber was cramped, with bare walls, a single desk and three upright wooden chairs. Two doors: the one they had entered by, and a second on the opposite side which remained shut. This was certainly not the office of a lord confessor.

Brandauer shed his cloak, and seemed to grow a few inches in stature. He turned the key in the lock of the outer door and seated himself.

'First things first,' he said. 'The gemstone, Stefan.'

Stefan hesitated. His intention, once he had recovered the stone from Furstlager, had been to find a way of destroying it. That was already proving more difficult than he had imagined. Now he had little option but to trust Brandauer. He unwrapped the cloth from around the crystal and placed the stone on the table in front of them. The polished gem flickered like sulphur fire in the lamplight, insidious and seductive.

'A thing of beauty,' Brandauer observed.

'Harmless, too, by Krenzler's account,' Stefan said. Otto Brandauer shook his head. 'Hardly,' he said, sadly. 'The crystal is formed from mithradur – an element once much prized by the dark elves. It would have been mined from the ancient quarries near Gratz. In your hands – or mine, perhaps – it might be harmless enough. Once in the possession of anyone versed in the dark arts, it could become very dangerous indeed.' He looked up at Stefan. 'I'm afraid we have no choice but to destroy it.'

'I tried,' Stefan replied. 'It seems indestructible.'

Otto Brandauer smiled, then opened a drawer in the desk. He reached inside and pulled out a small, silver grey hammer. Given Stefan's experiences with the heavy bronze figurine, this looked hopelessly inadequate for the task.

Brandauer balanced the tool carefully in his right hand. 'This hammer is forged from a flux of metals, mithradur principal amongst them,' he said. 'Take a good look at both it and the stone. I doubt you'll see the like of either again.' He sighed. 'Such a pity.'

Otto raised the hammer, and brought it down smartly upon the polished gem. The yellow stone shattered with a pop like an egg bursting open, scattering shards of crystal across the room. He swept the remnants into a small casket made from lead, which he fastened with a lock. He replaced the casket in the drawer of his desk.

'Now the gemstone is safe,' he said. 'The Gratz stone is a thing of the past. Now, we must talk of the future, and we must decide whether you and I have something to offer each other.'

Stefan drew out his sword, and set the blade down across the table between them. 'If it's a question of wielding this,' he said, 'then you'll find few better swordsmen in all Altdorf.'

Otto Brandauer nodded. 'Absolutely,' he agreed. 'In fact, I'd go as far as to say none better. Your prowess with the sword isn't in doubt.' He gazed at Stefan, and drummed lightly upon the wooden surface of the table. 'Nor, for that matter, is your bravery. No doubt of that at all.'

'Well then,' Stefan countered. 'What?'

'Let's talk about Stefan Kumansky for a moment,' Otto suggested. 'Talk about the path that has led you here.'

'What more is there to talk about?' Stefan demanded. 'You seem to know all there is already.'

'On the contrary. I know your history, the events of your life. The deeds and skills that distinguish a great swordsman from a dead one.' He took a sip of water from the cup at his side. 'But, for what I am to ask of you, I have to be sure of the strength that lies *within* as well.' He touched one finger against his forehead. 'I have to know what lies in here, and…' he lay his hand flat against his heart. 'In here. Because, I assure you, the task I have in mind will test every part of your being to its very limits.'

Brandauer paused for a moment, content to let his words sink in.

'So,' he continued at last. 'Let us review the life of Stefan Kumansky. Only eleven years old, your life is turned upside down when your village in Kislev is attacked by raiders from Norsca. Odensk is razed to the ground, your father is dead.'

'I live that memory every day of my life,' Stefan told him 'There's no need to revisit it now.'

Otto Brandauer looked up at Stefan, and raised one hand in a placating gesture. 'Together with your brother you come at last to Altdorf,' he continued. 'Two orphans, taken in by your uncle Gustav. One of your uncle's last acts before he dies is to secure you a position in the Altdorf civic guard.'

Stefan nodded. His tenure in the guard had been brief, and, from his point of view, unmemorable.

'After barely a year, and before your twenty-first birthday, you leave the service of the lord elector, and quit the guard to take up the life of a mercenary.' Otto Brandauer exchanged a glance with Stefan before going on.

'What makes a young man throw away a good career in the Guard for the uncertain life of a hired sword?'

'I don't know,' Stefan replied, a little defensive now. 'Perhaps it was boredom. Guarding the city from drunks and petty thieves pales after a while. Soldiering in the guard wasn't quite what I'd expected it to be.'

'Possibly not,' Otto agreed. 'Except that I doubt it was simply boredom that took you to the Grey Mountains. That endowed you with the skill and courage to single-handedly slay an orc chieftain. And it certainly wasn't boredom that stopped you from resting until you had tracked down the

Gratz stone and seen it destroyed.' He fixed Stefan with a stare that would have befitted the most feared of confessors. 'So,' he demanded. 'What was it?'

Stefan held himself firm against the intensity of the other man's gaze. It felt as though the grey eyes in front of him were staring into the depths of his very soul.

'I did it – all those things,' he said at last, 'because I had to.'

'Go on,' Brandauer said. His expression was no less severe, but there was an unmistakable note of encouragement in his voice now. 'Go on,' he urged. 'Say more.'

Stefan pondered the question. His heart knew the answer, but he struggled for the right words to convey the emotions that had become so familiar.

'I see a world,' he said at last. 'A world where there is much good, but also–'

He stopped, mid-sentence. Otto Brandauer nodded, encouraging him to go on. 'Also much that is evil,' he continued. 'It may not always be visible to us. But it is there, always with us.' He paused and wiped a hand across his face, taken aback by the feelings rising, unbidden, within him.

'Go on,' Brandauer repeated. 'Tell me more, Stefan. Tell me what lies inside.'

'I think, I – *feel*,' Stefan continued, 'almost as if there is a battle – a battle being waged all around us, even now, as we speak – between those forces. And I'm a part of that battle. Ever since my father died, ever since Odensk, I've been a part of it, whether I like it or not. And whilst the battle continues, there will be no rest.'

He stopped and looked at the man sitting opposite him. 'Don't ask me to explain why,' he said, 'because I can't. All I know is I don't have any choice.'

What was Brandauer thinking? Stefan felt strangely exposed, vulnerable. He had rarely expressed himself in this way to anyone, not even to his own brother. It was a part of himself he had learnt to keep well hidden. Doing otherwise had rarely earned him anything other than mockery or disdain. But there was no mockery in Otto Brandauer's eyes now.

'How will you know?' he asked Stefan. 'When the war is won?'

'I don't know,' Stefan replied. 'That's the thing. I can't be sure it will ever be won.'

Otto Brandauer nodded in silent agreement. 'I need you for your skill with the sword, Stefan,' he said. 'That was never really in doubt. But I also need what is in your heart.' He lay his hands upon the parchment scroll on the desk in front of him, began to open it and then paused.

'Is there anything that matters more to you than that battle, Stefan?'

Stefan considered the question for a moment. 'No,' he said eventually. 'I don't think that there is.'

'Good,' Brandauer said. He reached across the desk, and smoothed open the parchment scroll.

It was a map, but a map unlike any other that Stefan had seen before. Through his uncle, and at school in Altdorf, he had learned to study the plans of the city, and sometimes those rarer scrolls that plotted the span of the Emperor's realm.

This map went beyond even the boundaries of the Empire. There, laid out in the precise lines of the cartographer's hand, were the lands of Bretonnia, and Kislev too. Stefan knew enough of those distant places to recognise that the map accounted for a good part of what men knew as the Old World.

He gazed at Kislev, and traced a finger around the line marking the borders of his motherland. He followed the outline of the coast to the mouth of the River Lynsk. The map was dotted with names, both known and unknown, but no name was any longer marked upon the place where Odensk once stood. He sat for a moment, thinking about a place, a life, that had vanished.

'Take a good look at the map,' Otto instructed him. 'Take a good look, Stefan Kumansky, then tell me where in all this good land the blight of Chaos might be found.'

Stefan stared up at Otto, momentarily taken aback. It was not often he had heard the name of the Dark Powers spoken of so openly, or so candidly. He stared at Otto for a few moments then forced his gaze back to the map. 'I don't know,' he said, still discomfited by the question. He gestured with one hand towards the far edge of the map, towards where – he supposed – the northern lands of Norsca might lie.

Otto Brandauer leant forward towards Stefan, and spread his hands wide across the parchment scroll. 'The truth is,' he said quietly, 'the poison of Chaos can be found anywhere, within our borders as well as without. Anywhere at all.' He looked up and held Stefan in an unblinking gaze. 'Isn't that what your heart tells you, too, Stefan? Isn't that what you know?'

Stefan took a deep breath. He could feel the sweat prickling the skin on his face and hands. It was as though the whole of his being was laid bare.

'I think,' he said at last, 'that there is far more darkness in this world than men ever imagine.'

'You are right,' Brandauer told him, softly. 'The gods be my witness, I wish that you were not. But you are right.' He rolled the parchment slowly and placed it away out of sight. 'And you were right to say that you did not know when the struggle would end, Stefan. The truth it is, it will never end. It is eternal.'

He stood up and took a few steps across the narrow chamber. 'Nowhere is that struggle now more desperate now than in Kislev,' he said. 'Kislev is the mighty dam; the gatekeeper that stands between the darkness and the light. The forces of Chaos understand that only too well. They and their followers have been repulsed before, but they will always return. Now they are readying to lay siege once more. If the dam should ever be breached, then a tide of evil might sweep, unimpeded, across the world. The light would be extinguished, forever.'

He paused, lost in contemplation of his own words for a while. 'The question is,' he continued, 'are you ready to give your all to this struggle for Kislev? Ready, if necessary, to give your life?'

Stefan thought again of the map. In his mind it had become a map of darkness; a wash of black creeping across the face of mankind, slowly obliterating it. He shuddered, but it was a shudder born of anticipation as much as of unease. He had no doubt of what his answer must be.

'What is it that you need me to do?' he asked. By way of answer, Otto Brandauer opened the second of the two doors and spoke quietly to a servant waiting outside. A few minutes later the door opened again. A third figure stepped into the room, and without waiting for invitation or introduction, sat in the remaining empty chair by Otto's side. The newcomer pulled back the cowl of their long grey robe and turned to face Stefan.

'Stefan,' Otto said. 'Allow me to introduce you to Elena Yevschenko. Your companion on the journey to come.'

Stefan found himself looking at a young woman, no more than twenty years old, possibly less. Her hair was cut shorter than was customary for a noble, and though she wore the sculpted silk gown common amongst the women of the high court, she looked curiously ill at ease in her finery.

The young woman turned to appraise Stefan. A high forehead and deep-set blue eyes gave her features a severe, intense look. Striking, rather than beautiful, Stefan decided.

'An unwilling companion, actually,' she said, picking up on Otto's remark. Beneath the flawless Reikspiel, the slightest trace of accent still remained.

Elena maintained her gaze upon Stefan, looking him over rather as though she were weighing up a commodity she'd been invited to buy. Stefan discovered, to his surprise, that he'd taken an instant dislike to her. The sceptical, mildly disdainful expression on the girl's face told him the feeling was probably mutual. Not a good start.

Brandauer broke the tense silence that had followed Elena's opening words. 'Elena is yet to be convinced of the need for your services,' he explained. He eyed the young woman carefully before continuing. 'But I take a very different, and very firm view on that.'

'It would help if I knew what service it is I am asked to perform,' Stefan said, puzzled by the turn of events since the girl had stepped into the room.

Brandauer exchanged glances with Elena.

'I should explain a little of Elena's history,' he said. 'She has been living here in Altdorf, under the protection of the court. Originally, however, she is from–'

'From Erengrad,' Stefan said, voicing the connection he had made in his mind a few moments earlier. 'Or somewhere very close.'

Otto nodded, appreciatively. Elena merely glowered. 'Your accent,' Stefan added. 'Very faint, I grant you. I doubt anyone else would be able to tell. I was born not thirty leagues from the city walls,' Stefan said. 'I'm honoured to meet a kinsman.'

They exchanged a stiff, rather formal greeting, Elena responding to Stefan's bow with a rather perfunctory curtsey.

'Elena has been here in Altdorf for the last two years,' Brandauer explained. 'Now it's time for her to go home. That's where we need your help.'

'Where *you* need his help,' Elena countered, testily. She got up and began to pace the room, managing somehow to look both graceful and awkward. A proud but untamed animal, penned within a gilded cage.

'No offence, sir,' she said to Stefan. 'But I can look after myself.'

I'll bet you can, Stefan thought to himself. He looked from one to the other of them, seeking to piece this new puzzle together. 'You want me to take Elena home, back to Erengrad,' he said. 'And that's all? I understand what you've shown me, and it's clear the lands to the east are in peril. But with no offence to you–' he paused, and glanced over at Elena, 'how is one young woman going to help redeem Kislev?'

Brandauer smiled at the girl, and made the slightest of bows toward her. 'Elena, you may as well explain.'

Elena spoke slowly, making only occasional eye contact with Stefan. 'My family is one the oldest in the western territories of Kislev,' she said. 'I am – so they tell me – a distant cousin of the tsarina herself.'

'A noble, powerful family,' Otto underlined, quietly. Elena smiled sourly.

'For decades, our family has been locked in a bloody, pointless feud with another, the House of Kuragin. The feud has simmered across the generations, but the last three years have taken our noble kin to the brink of civil war. In that time, half of our respective families have murdered each other.' She raised her eyebrow a fraction, as if to emphasise the futility of her history. 'I was smuggled out of Erengrad, across the border to the Empire a month before my eighteenth birthday. I've never been back since.'

'And now?' Stefan asked

'Now,' Brandauer interjected, 'it is vital that Elena return home. The fabric of Erengrad and the whole of the western territories is collapsing. We can no longer afford the indulgence of an Erengrad that is torn apart at its heart. Chaos presses from all sides, and there are many who would abandon the ancient alliance between Kislev and the Empire, in favour of some treaty of servitude to the dark powers. If Erengrad should fall, then others will follow. Then it may only be a matter of time before–'

'Yes,' Stefan said, quietly. 'I understand. But how can Elena do anything to change all of this?'

'An opportunity exists,' Brandauer told him. 'It may not stay long, but, for the moment, it exists. A chance to forge a new bond between the Houses of Yevschenko and Kuragin. To unite the people of Erengrad once again, and form an alliance strong enough, perhaps, to turn the tide against Chaos.'

'So this alliance,' Stefan said, 'is going to be forged–'

'Through me,' Elena replied, crisply. 'I am to be married, to Petr Illyich, eldest son and heir to the House of Kuragin.' She reached inside the pocket of her blouse and pulled out a silver locket. She released the catch and held the locket open for Stefan's inspection. The painted image of a young, blond-haired man in his late twenties looked out at him from astride a horse on the field of battle.

'Be in no doubt, Stefan,' Otto told him, 'Elena is destined to play a vital part in the struggle between light and darkness.'

Stefan found himself momentarily dumbstruck by the thought that the future of Kislev – and, perhaps, much of the world beyond – could hinge upon the fate of this diminutive young woman. Elena looked at him and laughed.

'What's the matter, Kumansky?' she asked him. 'Haven't you always wanted to rescue a princess?'

'Elena must return to Erengrad without delay,' Brandauer went on. 'The alliance is fragile, and the pressures bearing upon it are many. This family feud has becoming a weeping sore at the very heart of Erengrad. It must be healed now. We cannot afford to wait any longer.'

'Of course,' Stefan agreed. 'It must – it must be hard,' he said. 'Being away for so long. This separation. It must have been painful for you both.'

'I wouldn't know,' Elena replied, acidly. 'The two of us have never met. At least, if we have, I don't remember it.'

She snapped the locket shut. 'I'm told he looks rather older now,' she added. 'Older, and fatter, as well.'

'Elena is a soldier,' Brandauer continued, gravely. 'She knows what sacrifices she must make, if true and righteous order is to prevail.'

'I still don't see where I fit into this,' Stefan insisted. 'If you're telling me that Elena has the protection of the court, then you surely don't need to hire swordsmen, however perilous the journey. You have hundreds of civic guard at your disposal.'

Elena laughed, but there was bitterness in her voice when she spoke. 'A fine notion,' she said. 'But I don't think the noble court of Altdorf places quite that value on my head.'

Stefan shook his head, still not satisfied. 'But if it's so important for the alliance that you are returned to Erengrad–'

'The politics of the Old World are delicately balanced,' Otto cut across. 'With the active support of the Emperor, we would doubtless be more secure. But Karl-Franz has been long from court.' He cast his eyes around the chamber. 'Too long, in fact. Without his assured patronage, we can neither be sure who will support us, and who will not.'

'They'd be happy enough to get an ignorant Kislevite out of their fine court,' Elena commented. 'But don't expect them to go to any trouble. I'm just a misfit here. Most of your gracious nobility couldn't care less if I lived or died.'

'It's more complicated than that,' Brandauer insisted. 'We could arrange an escort for Elena if we really needed to. But it's also a matter of who we can trust. These are dark times, Stefan. Times when it pays to trust as few people as possible.' He glanced across the chamber at the sound of footsteps approaching along the passageway outside. The footsteps seemed to slow to a halt by the door, and then move on. Otto waited until the sound had died away.

'If you accept this commission then you should be under no illusion,' he continued. 'There are people in Kislev, in the Empire, even here in Altdorf, who would very much want Elena dead if they knew who she was.' He paused. 'And they will kill you, too, if they have the chance.'

'Which is why,' Elena cut in, 'it's better if I travel *alone*.'

'Which is why you must be protected,' Otto countered, 'but discreetly.'

'How discreetly?' Stefan asked.

'A small party. Small enough to travel anonymously, to pass almost invisibly on their journey east. Nor can you expect to spend too much of your time on the beaten paths; they may be too dangerous.'

Stefan turned the proposition over in his mind. The idea of facing danger held no fear for him, and the answer he had given Otto was true. There was nothing in his heart more important than to take arms against the darkness. It was a path he had been destined to follow ever since that grey morning in Odensk.

'I'm a swordsman,' he said at length, 'not a scout. The forest trails east of Altdorf would be a match for all but the ablest woodsman. How do you propose we find our way, other than by staying close to the trade routes?'

'I have mapped the journey,' Otto replied. 'I may look as though I've spent my life safe behind city walls, supping with the elector counts. But it was not always so. I know more of the world than you might imagine.' He flicked a gaze between Stefan and Elena, and Stefan glimpsed the steel behind the features now softened by comfortable living. 'I will lead the mission,' Otto continued, 'at least as far as Middenheim. There you will find papers waiting for you; new identities, new lives. You will travel on as part of a merchant caravan, bound for the border with Kislev.

The story had the ring of truth, yet Stefan still sensed there was something missing, some component of the story not yet told. For all that Elena Yevschenko might be a formidable character, he couldn't believe that a single marriage could prevent the flood of evil from sweeping across the western plains of Kislev.

He looked long and hard at Otto Brandauer. 'Now tell me the rest,' he said at last. 'There must be more.'

Otto bowed his head ever so slightly, and exchanged a glance with Elena. The young woman shook her head, almost imperceptibly. Otto hesitated, then went on. 'There is,' he conceded. 'The marriage of Petr and Elena is vital. Their union will end the strife between the families. Without an end to their feud, there can be no lasting peace. But that alone will not be enough to mend the wounds of Erengrad.'

He glanced again at Elena. The young woman seemed to read his meaning, and bristled. 'Why am I supposed to trust this – this mercenary?' she demanded, her face flushing red. 'If his sword can be bought and sold for a pocket of silver, what's to say he won't sell me?'

Well, Stefan thought. At least we know where we stand. Otto stood up, and took a few paces around the room. For the first time his voice when he spoke to Elena betrayed a trace of irritation. 'You must trust Stefan because *I* trust Stefan,' he said. 'And, if you don't, then you may as well not trust me either.' He glared at Elena, waiting to see whether she was going to respond. When she didn't, he said: 'Now, if you please, show him.'

Elena Yevschenko hesitated, then, reluctantly, reached to her neck and lifted a silver chain over her head. For a moment she sat with an object locked within her fist upon the desk. Otto signalled his rising impatience; Elena opened her fist and let a metallic object fall free. She glared at Stefan, as though defying him to make sense of it. 'Well?' she demanded.

Stefan looked. The piece seemed to be fashioned from a dull silver or lead. It was moulded in the shape of a broad, flat arrowhead with a long, narrowing tail. He shrugged. 'It could be a spear,' he suggested. 'Or a bird in flight, perhaps – a dove?'

Otto nodded. 'Good guesses,' he said. 'The spear and the dove. Conflict and peace. Yes, it can be both of those things.' He slipped a sheet of white paper onto the desk. He handed a pen to Elena, and waited while she drew the outline of an identical shape onto the paper next to the pendant, then a second next to that. She looked up at Stefan, and, for the first time, she smiled.

'See?'

Stefan saw. Together the three shapes combined to form a six-pointed star.

'The Star of Erengrad,' Elena said, quietly.

'Individually, the three segments of the Star are all but worthless,' Otto told him. 'In union, they exert a mighty, binding force over Erengrad and its people. Remember, Stefan, magic can work for good as well as for evil. In the right hands, the Star can be a powerful force for good.'

'In the right hands,' Elena emphasised.

'Too powerful for one family alone to possess,' Otto added. 'But now Erengrad has need of the healing power of the Star.' He turned to Elena. 'And it has need of the peace that your union will bring to those who would rule it.'

Stefan gazed down at the new single shape made from the three. 'Where are the other two parts?' he asked.

Elena slipped the silver chain back around her neck. 'The second of the three parts of the Star is in Erengrad,' she said. 'It belongs to the man I am to marry, to Petr Illyich Kuragin.'

'And the third–'

'Is in Middenheim,' Otto said. 'The other, and principal, purpose for your journey to the City of the White Wolf. When the bloody feud engulfed Erengrad, the three parts of the star had to be separated. We permitted the Houses of Kuragin and Yevschenko to keep one part each. But, so that neither family might gain absolute power, we arranged for the third segment to be carried to the Empire, to Middenheim. There it rests in the safekeeping of one trusted man. A friend of Erengrad. A friend,' he added, 'of mine. He will be awaiting your arrival.'

Stefan turned the words over in his mind, carefully. 'And who,' he said at last, 'is "we"? More to the point, who exactly are *you*?'

Otto smiled, as if to signal that he had been awaiting this question. 'I am a loyal servant of the Empire,' he said. 'But I am also allied with a group of men who recognise the wider boundaries that border good and evil. Men who see the world painted stark in darkness and in light. Men, Stefan, much like you.'

'Do they have a name?' Stefan asked.

Otto considered for a moment. Stefan noticed Elena paying close attention, as if much of this were new to her, too.

'We are known as the Keepers of the Flame, though the name is rarely spoken,' he said. 'We tend the light that stands, eternal, against the forces of dark night. We are ever present. Ever vigilant.'

Stefan exhaled a long breath, taking stock of the unexpected journey that this particular night had brought him to. He tried to make eye contact again with Elena, but she had turned her back on him. The decision was his alone.

'How many men, then?' he asked. 'Aside from me?'

'Two,' Otto said, simply. 'No more than that. The choice of companions is yours, but...' he looked across at Stefan. 'I think you understand the qualities we need.'

Stefan nodded. Such men were rare, even in Altdorf, but he knew who they were.

'Well, thank you for further mapping out my life for me!' Elena declared, sardonically. She glared at both men, then seemed to accept something of the inevitability of the situation. 'Once these arrangements have been made, we must leave Altdorf as quickly as possible. Agreed?'

'Agreed,' said Brandauer. 'Without delay.' He opened the door to the chamber, allowing a little air to freshen the room.

'We'll need horses,' Stefan said. 'And provisions, of course.'

'Whatever you require will be provided,' Otto assured him. 'Else you will be given money to procure what you need.'

'What about during the journey?' Stefan asked. 'It's going to be a long ride.'

'Arrangements will be made for you to draw fresh supplies. You'll be told more of that in due course,' Otto said. 'Now, for the moment: is there anything else?'

Stefan considered. It seemed there should be a thousand questions to be answered, but, in another way, it seemed ridiculously simple. Simple, and dangerous.

'No,' he said finally. 'I don't think there is.'

'Then begin your preparations,' Otto said. He held the door open wide for Stefan to pass through. 'In the meantime, there's a carriage waiting to take you back to wherever it is you need to go.' He shook Stefan firmly by the hand. Elena now sat at her place by the table, gazing distractedly towards the window. Maybe time would be the best healer for their differences after all.

Just before Stefan left the room, Otto took him aside. 'Just remember, Stefan,' he said. 'Evil will not always confront you with a weapon raised. It will just as likely come to you as a comrade, or as a sweet beguiling friend. But do not ever doubt its purpose, or the determination of those serve their masters in Chaos. Beware their many guises, Stefan. Beware the poison that runs within the stream.'

* * *

IT SEEMED SURE that no one noticed Stefan Kumansky as he left
the Palace of Retribution to rejoin the outside world. Few
townsfolk were still on the streets at that hour, and those that
were took little interest in the drab, unlit carriage that clattered through the gates and then sped, without ceremony,
through the sleeping streets towards the edge of the city.

But far away, beyond Altdorf, in a place that was neither the
Empire nor even the Old World, he had indeed been noticed.
Deep within the cold, merciless nebula that spanned the dark
realm of Chaos, Kyros, Lord of Tzeentch, the God of Change,
sensed Stefan's presence in the mortal world.

For so long Kyros's focus had been fixed upon Kislev, upon
Erengrad. The prize his master had so long coveted was now
all but within their grasp. The subtle powers of change had
eaten away, almost unseen, at the fabric of the city, weaken-
ing its foundations of strength and unity. With the hand of
Tzeentch to guide him, Kyros had steadily tightened the dark
thread he had woven around and through its crumbling edifices. Soon, by stealth or by force, Erengrad would fall.

One by one, the obstacles along the path had steadily been
removed. All except... Kyros had cast his sightless eyes over
the face of humanity, across the numberless hordes of weak,
yet obdurate mortal men. Creatures to be pitied and despised
in equal measure.

His inner gaze had sifted through their masses, drawn suddenly back towards the west. He could neither see, hear nor
physically touch the young swordsman, for Kyros's corporeal
body had long since been rendered to dust. As yet, he did not
even know Stefan by his name. But he knew now of his existence, just as he had come to know of the daughter of Kislev.
He sensed them both, as a spider senses the first tremor in its
web. And he sensed a purpose that, if allowed to blossom,
would lay threat to his intricate design.

Kyros brooded upon his discovery, tracing out the myriad
consequences scattered upon the seas of chance. He unrav-
elled the paths of possibility, following them though to their
end. He must watch them: the mercenary, the Kislevite, the
scheming courtier. He must watch them all. He must
despatch his servants to walk amongst them. Unheard and
unseen, they must wait; wait for the moment to act.

It was time for the children of Tzeentch to awake.

CHAPTER THREE
Bruno

STEFAN HAD NOT been the only one troubled by his dreams. Since coming home to Altdorf, Bruno Hausmann had struggled to bury the past, but the past had refused to die. Memories had returned, time and time again, invading the night hours. At first, the nightmares had come only rarely; Bruno had believed he could live with that. But over the last few weeks he had been visited night after night by the same, terrifying dreams; dreams that filled him with a sense of foreboding that stretched on, long into the waking day. Now his health was in decline; a sick weariness was drenching his body, sapping his strength and reflexes. He was growing sluggish and careless. And, that morning, carelessness was about to cost him dear.

He didn't react to the sword until it was inches from his face. A rush of adrenaline spared him from the blade as he reeled back. Bruno was seized with the sudden impulse to run, flee in whatever direction would take him away from the conflict. Then he remembered where he was, and why. There would be no escape. The stocky man in his bright new armour had him cornered at the back of the narrow barn.

There would be no running from his sword. Bruno would have to stand, and give account of himself here.

A voice roared in his ears. 'Defend yourself, sir!' Again the sword sliced the air, just inches from his face. In front of him, a burly, barrel-chested man in bright, burnished armour stood, sword in hand, preparing to strike again.

Defend yourself. Fight back. Bruno raised the new-forged steel of his blade just in time to parry the next flurry of blows. His thickset opponent grinned, sensing that his adversary was at last to make a fight of it, and swung his weapon with a renewed vigour.

Bruno found his sword was light and fast. He parried the blows the knight was aiming at him with something approaching ease. Yet there was a sickness in his limbs and in his mind. The threads of his dreams wound themselves around him, dragging him down into a place of despair. In his mind, he had already lost the fight.

Sweating and swearing beneath his mail and breastplate, the figure in armour began to force Bruno steadily back towards the far wall of the barn. A stray stroke broke through Bruno's guard and nicked the side of his face. He tasted blood dribbling into his mouth, but felt no pain. A few seconds more, he imagined, and it would surely be over.

His opponent suddenly broke off his attack and stood back, resting on his sword. He scowled at Bruno.

'Come on man, fight me!' he shouted. 'Can't you do better than this?' He whipped the flank of his sword against Bruno's blade once again.

'Are you useless,' he chided, 'or simply a coward?'

The word stung Bruno more than a hundred cuts from a sword. A sudden rage coursed through him, filling him with a new, raw energy. His sword flashed in the air as he beat away his attacker's blade as though it carried no more weight than a feather. He struck forward with speed and a hungry aggression. Within a few seconds he had regained all the ground he had previously lost. The other man found himself defenceless against the speed and agility of the attack. Soon he was down on one knee, his sword held up to protect his face. In the next instant the blade had been swept out of his grasp, knocked clean away by Bruno's sword.

Bruno bore down upon his opponent, the tip of his sword poised above the man's throat.

'Think twice before you call me a coward,' he advised.

'Herr Hausmann!'

Bruno turned at the sound of his name being called. He looked round to find his employer, Oswald Schaffner, hurrying across the barn towards him, his face red with agitation. Behind Schaffner, a second figure looked on from the shadows of the main building.

'In Taal's name, Bruno!' Schaffner exclaimed. 'I pay you to entertain my customers, not to kill them!' He extended a solicitous hand to the prostrate figure of the knight, and helped the big man regain his feet.

'My deepest apologies, my Lord Augenrich. I trust you're not harmed?'

The burly man dusted down his battered armour and eyed Bruno and his sword for a few moments. A wide grin split his features.

'By all the gods, I ought to be,' he declared, beaming. 'Don't fuss about like an old woman, Schaffner. I insisted that your man here demonstrated the wares before I lined your pockets with gold.'

He took the sword gingerly from Bruno's grip. 'I'm thinking I'd best buy a gross of these beauties rather than a score!'

Herr Schaffner relaxed visibly. He, too, allowed himself a smile.

'Now tell me the truth,' Augenrich continued. 'Sigmarsfest may be the season of goodwill, but I won't be swindled here. Is this sword of yours really as good as it seems, or is this young man just an excellent swordsman?'

'The sword is truly without peer,' the armourer assured him. 'And' – he caught Bruno's eye – 'the young man can handle it very well indeed.'

Lord Augenrich threw an arm around Schaffner's shoulder. 'Then I reckon we have some business to conclude.'

Oswald Schaffner gave Bruno a look that said well done – but don't try it again.

'Oh, Bruno,' he said. 'You almost make me forget. There's someone waiting out in the yard to see you. You'd better see what it is they want. I can manage back here for a while.'

Bruno wiped the blood from around his mouth and made his way slowly but purposefully towards the front of the armourer's shop. He wasn't expecting company; he discouraged visitors at his work. A nagging unease in the pit of his stomach put him in mind of his dream, of a memory that cast deep shadows from the past.

His visitor was sitting on the far side of the yard, his back towards Bruno, a crimson cape hung loosely over his shoulders. From a distance it might have been anyone, but Bruno knew otherwise. Even before the tall, dark-haired young man stood to greet him, Bruno knew who was waiting for him.

The past had stepped from the shadow of his dreams, and returned to haunt him once again.

'Stefan,' he said, his voice faltering. 'It's been a long time.'

Stefan Kumansky smiled warmly, and held out his hand. 'I was hoping I'd still find you here. You're looking well.'

Bruno brushed his own hand across his brow, avoiding the offered greeting. The sight of his former comrade stirred a chill sense of dread within his heart. The unease that had gnawed at him since the lonely hours before dawn now took on solid shape.

FOR TWO DAYS, ever since he'd left Otto's chambers in the Palace of Retribution, Stefan had been thinking of how it would be when he finally faced Bruno again. The two men had not met or spoken since that day upon the mountain, although it had not been for want of trying on Stefan's part. But Bruno had made it plain that he wanted nothing further to do with Stefan, and, over time, Stefan had come to accept that their friendship was at an end. But if he had been able to take only one man with him on the journey east, then it would have been Bruno above all others. He knew that he must try to mend the rift between them.

From a distance, he had stood watching Bruno's combat with Augenrich. Even after a year, there was no mistaking his comrade. The swordsman's style and movement could belong only to one man. The edge that had made him one of the best fighters in Altdorf might have dulled a fraction, but Stefan knew that he would prove more than a match for the overweight nobleman in his expensive armour. He felt a surge of joy to see his friend again, and to find him apparently well and thriving.

Closer to him, Stefan now noticed the changes that the months had marked upon Bruno. A little thicker in the girth, for sure; maybe a sign of a more sedentary life. The thick, rust-coloured curls of his hair were a little shorter, and the beginnings of a beard emphasised a similar fattening of his face. But it was still Bruno; still the man that Stefan would trust above all others. Trust with his very life.

As he looked into Bruno's eyes, Stefan saw again the emptiness where the light had once shone bright and strong. It was a look that mirrored Stefan's last memory of his comrade, on the final day in Stahlbergen. If their adventure had ended with the orcs put to the sword, and the gemstone destroyed, then things might have been different. Victory would have been glorious, and untainted. Neither of them was to know that their mission was to have an unexpected and unwanted epilogue.

THE TWO MEN walked for a while without speaking, picking their way through the foundry and the smelting yards outside the armourer's shop. In the end it was Bruno who chose to break the silence. 'Before you say it, before you say anything. My answer is no.'

'You don't know what I'm going to say yet.'

'Stefan, I know what you're here for. The answer's no.'

They walked on, Stefan a pace or two behind his former comrade. It felt as though the short passage of time had worn a path of a thousand miles between them.

'You're doing all right for yourself here,' he said at last. 'Working for Schaffner. It seems to be going well for you.'

'He pays me a living wage,' Bruno said. 'Plenty enough for my purposes. And he respects my needs and skills. That's all I want.'

'Weren't those needs and skills always respected before?' Stefan asked.

Bruno turned away, unwilling or unable to face the question in Stefan's eyes.

'We've never talked about it properly,' Stefan continued. 'What happened in the mountains. I don't feel good about how things ended. It was hard for all of us.'

'I made my choices,' Bruno replied, 'and you made yours.' He started to walk away, so that Stefan had to pick up his pace to keep abreast of him. He tried to catch his comrade's eye as they fell in step.

'I was right about Krenzler,' he said at last. 'And right about the stone. Krenzler betrayed us all.'

Bruno pulled up short and turned to face Stefan. His eyes burned with a deep-buried anger. 'Did he? Well, I'm glad you're vindicated at last,' he said, walking on.

'I'm just trying to explain what happened,' Stefan told him. He hadn't expected Bruno to forgive him easily. But he had hoped he might come to understand.

'Look,' he said at last. 'You're right. I'm here to – I don't know. Ask you to reconsider. To "coax you from retirement" – whatever you want to call it. The thing is–' He caught Bruno by the sleeve, forcing him to stop and turn towards him.

'Bruno, you're a *soldier*, not an armourer's apprentice or whatever it is you do here. You were born to the sword. It's your life. I know it.'

Bruno tugged himself free and strode on. 'My sword arm gets plenty of exercise here,' he replied, tersely. 'As you see. I nearly spilled a man's guts back there. Spilled them for nothing.' There was a tremor in his voice as he spoke. 'Thanks for your concern, Stefan. But there's plenty enough here to satisfy the soldier in me.'

'Wait,' Stefan said. 'I'm not just here to sign you up like a hired hand. The cause–' he hesitated for a moment, wondering how much he should say.

'The cause that brings me here is just. An important cause, very important indeed. I need good men to ride with me, men I can trust to the very core of their soul. There's none I'd trust before you, Bruno.'

Bruno halted, and turned back to face Stefan. His face softened momentarily.

'Don't think your words mean nothing to me, Stefan,' he said. 'I haven't forgotten that life, not one moment of it. A day doesn't pass when I don't find myself there, right there as though it were yesterday.'

He hesitated, and the warmth faded from his features. 'But this is my life now,' he said. 'That other life – Stahlbergen, all of it – is over, forgotten. All things come to an end, and that's how it is with me. Don't try and change my mind. You'll be wasting your time.'

He started to walk briskly past Stefan back in the direction of the armourer's shop. 'Schaffner has a customer with him,' he said. 'I'd better get back.'

'Bruno,' Stefan called after him. Bruno paused, his head half turned towards Stefan.

'We never really talked about what happened at Stahlbergen,' Stefan said, quietly. 'You did your best for those people, and they still died. I had to leave you to deal with that on your own, and that means as much to me as it did to you. But there wasn't anything else I could have done. I had to try and find Krenzler, Bruno. I *had* to.'

'You don't know what it meant to me,' Bruno muttered. He stopped once more, and turned about. 'I'm going back now,' he said. 'There's nothing left to talk about.'

'Tell me at least you'll think it over,' Stefan shouted after him. 'In Taal's name, man, you at least owe me that.'

'I owe nothing to any man,' Bruno shot back. 'I owe nothing – to any living soul.'

Bruno quickened his pace. He finally stopped, a few paces short of the yard, and looked back at Stefan for a last time.

'Goodbye, Stefan,' he said. 'It was good to see you again.' He placed a hand upon the gates and pushed them open. 'But my life is here now, as you see. There's nothing more to be said. Nothing at all.'

BY LATE AFTERNOON, the Two Moons in the heart of Altdorf was nearly full. Most of the seats around the scattered tables of the ale house had been taken. A motley assortment of apprentices, potboys and dealers were making swift work of their quarts of ale, swapping tales before getting back to the business of the day. Only one table, in a corner, stood empty, occupied by a lone figure who seemed to take no interest in the proceedings around him.

The man might have been a cleric of some kind, a novitiate of the priesthood, perhaps. Small, lightly built, he cut an unassuming figure amidst the loud, sturdily built men around him. Unlike them, he seemed in no hurry to drink or to move on. An observer might have noticed that he had nursed the same half flagon for almost an hour. Unlike his fellow drinkers, he seemed only concerned with the traffic passing outside, his gaze focused upon the green door of a house on the far side of the street. Every so often, two or three of the labourers standing drinking by the bar would approach the table, intending to avail themselves of the free space. The solitary drinker would look up, his eyes meeting the newcomers. Without a word being spoken, they would turn about, leaving him alone.

If he had a name, it would be Varik. Over countless lifetimes he had been known by many different names, but this was the name by which he was beholden to his master. His lord had gifted him with immortality; the form he now inhabited was merely borrowed flesh, nothing more than a temporary vessel for the emissary of Kyros. For the moment, it was a vessel that suited his purpose very well.

Through the flawed lens of the window, Varik scanned the mortal forms that passed to and fro outside the tavern. Students hurrying along with their scrolls tucked under their arms; domestic servants carrying bundles of garments; market traders bowed under the weight of baskets of reeking fish. How many of them would number amongst his master's flock? He doubted that even he, Varik, knew the true number. Some would be willing followers, enthusiastic disciples of Chaos drawn like moths to the purging fire of transformation. Others – many more – would not even be aware of the destiny that lay hidden within their souls. They were the sleeping soldiers of Tzeentch; less willing servants, perhaps, but they would serve, nonetheless.

For the moment, those nameless, numberless others did not interest him. He was searching for one face amongst the crowd, and one only. At length, a figure passed by the window of the tavern and crossed the busy street towards the green door. Varik looked again to confirm the figure's identity, then stood up, carefully and without hurry. He stood, leaving his flagon of beer unfinished on the table, and turned to make his way through a gang of apprentices standing drinking by the tavern door.

The young guildsmen eyed Varik suspiciously as he eased his way past. The emissary met their accusing gazes with the same mild, blue eyes. *If I so wished,* he reflected, *I could snap your thick necks apart in the fingers of one hand.*

'Please,' Varik said. 'Take my table. I've finished my business here.'

THE GREEN DOOR had been fastened shut by the time Varik left the tavern and crossed the street. He raised his hand and laid it flat against the grain of the wood, and closed his eyes. He felt a tremor run through the heavy oak and heard the dull click as the oiled mechanism of the lock sprang open. Varik pushed gently and the door yielded to his touch, swinging open before him.

The emissary stepped inside, savouring the sights and smells of the building. He had never been in this place before, and yet it seemed almost as if he knew it. Varik realised he was already penetrating the waking thoughts and memories of his unwitting acolyte. This one, he knew instinctively, would not resist his will for long. Noises of movement percolated through the stillness of the house. He followed the sounds up a flight of stairs to an upper room. The door lay open. A figure stood inside, the hood of a thick cloak drawn up over its head. Whoever it was stood with their back to the emissary, staring out from the window into the street below. Perhaps, Varik thought, they realised they were being followed. If so, like so much knowledge, it had come too late.

He allowed a sound to escape his lips; the faintest of sighs, little more than a breath exhaled. It was enough. The watcher at the window spun around as though they had been stung, and stood staring, stupefied, at the emissary.

'Who are you? What do you want?'

Varik saw something glint in the light: an iron bar, perhaps a rod from the hearth, being raised. Varik smiled, and stepped forward into the full light of the room. He watched the iron lift into the air and then suddenly stop, the energy of the blow suspended. He smiled, and walked towards his acolyte. With one hand, he prised the iron from the frozen grip.

'You wonder what I am doing in your rooms,' he said, mildly. 'You wonder who I am.' He turned his head upon one side, a knowing expression settling upon his features.

'You truly don't know me?' he asked. 'No, of course you don't. Why should you?' Varik turned the iron bar through his hands, then tossed it upon the ground. 'But I know you,' he said softly. 'I have known you for almost all of your life.'

The figure on the other side of room stood like a statue before the hearth, eyes locked upon Varik in an unblinking stare, breath suspended. Varik drew a chair away from the single window and settled himself down upon it. Now that he had his prey, he was in no hurry.

'I shall tell you something you will never have heard before,' he said. 'When you were a child, you were gravely ill. Yes, you remember that. How could you forget? Your parents may have told you that you almost died, that only the blessed mercy of the goddess Shallya spared your life.'

He smiled, indulgently. 'But that was a lie.' He waited for a moment, holding the gaze of the other. 'You did die,' he said, softly. 'You died, and only the intervention of a far, far greater power could save you.' Varik got to his feet and went to the window. Down in the street below, a verminous flood of humanity continued to push and shove against one another in their futile struggle for survival, oblivious of the greater presence now amongst them.

'Your loving parents made a bargain with my master,' Varik continued. 'My master, who holds in his hand the keys of transformation. Transformation of light into darkness. Of movement–' He paused, and circled slowly around the other. 'Into absolute stillness. The gift that my master bequeathed you was life,' Varik explained. 'And the price of that gift was the pledge of your soul.'

He laid the palm of his hand upon the other's forehead, all the time holding the gaze in those frozen eyes. 'Now the time has come for that pledge to be redeemed,' he said. 'Now, I am *your* master, and you will serve me. You will be my ears, and–' he touched his fingers against cold, immobile lids – 'and you will be my eyes, on the long journey that lies ahead.'

He ran his fingers down the contours of the face in front of him. He could feel the muscles beneath the skin convulse and then harden, as if paralysed by a serpent's venom. Which, in a way, Varik reflected, was exactly as it was.

'Spare yourself any futile struggle,' he advised. 'Your struggle ended long long ago, at the moment your soul was offered in pledge. From now on,' Varik whispered, 'you have no further cares or concerns of your own. From now on, you shall know no other will but mine.'

CHAPTER FOUR
Warriors

A SENSE OF anticipation had infused the air since early evening, fuelling the intoxication of the crowds flowing through the streets. There was a smell that went with it, indescribable yet unmistakable: the smell of excitement, fear and hope all mingling into one. Tonight was the night of the festival games, the crowning point of Sigmarsfest, and it seemed that all of Altdorf had turned out to celebrate it.

Stefan reached the Imperial arena of Altdorf less than an hour before midnight. The games had been in progress for almost three hours: a procession of pageants and ritual battles re-enacting the heroic past of the Empire. The arena was all but full, close on ten thousand people packed together inside.

Stefan followed one of the tunnelled passageways that cut through into the interior of the vast stadium. He was surely anonymous amidst the countless spectators, yet, not for the first time that day, Stefan had the uncomfortable sense of being observed. He drew the hood of his cloak up over his head and hurried inside.

In view at the tunnel's end lay the great open space of the arena. High, curved walls stretched skywards on all four sides of the vast square, topped by seated galleries above the tiered rows of terraces. The steep banks were a sea of blurred faces, and the air resonated with the sound of ten thousand souls in full voice. Stefan stepped out from the shadow of the tunnel into a cauldron of heat and adrenaline.

He climbed the steps to the upper tier of the gallery and found a seat amongst a gaggle of traders swilling wine and noisily arguing the details of a wager. They had been betting on who would survive the night on the field, Stefan surmised, and who would not.

One of the traders, much the worse for drink, turned to Stefan as he took a seat, and acknowledged him with a nod of the head. 'You've missed the best of it, mate,' he slurred. 'The Araby crusades, Vampire Counts, the lot.' He offered Stefan a drink from his flask, and belched expansively. 'More dead than you could load on a barrow tonight.'

Stefan smiled, and declined the flask politely. He wasn't here to lose himself in drink, or to watch history being re-enacted for that matter. 'Don't worry,' he assured the man. 'I think the best is yet to come.'

The dense pall of smoke carpeting the base of the arena gradually cleared to reveal the field of combat, an expanse of bare white stone, unadorned save for iron grilles set at intervals across its face. Minutes before, the field would have been strewn with the bodies of the dead: adventurers wagering their lives or prisoners brought from the Palace of Retribution, hoping against hope to survive the night and win their freedom. The bare white stone had been cleansed of their blood, ready for the night's final act.

A distant clock struck twelve as the last debris from the Battle of Hel Fen was cleared from the field of combat. The noise from the crowd, which had been rising steadily, now dropped away until something approaching a total, eerie calm hung over the entire arena.

Now the night would reach its climax. The games would close with a battle selected for its special significance. A drum roll echoed across the night. Armed soldiers of the Imperial Guard took up position all around the borders of the arena, forming a human shield between the crowd and the battleground. The drum pounded on, a doom-laden sound.

A gate on the east wall was suddenly flung wide and an enormous figure sprang out under the lights. Dark, heavily muscled, and at least seven feet tall, the figure bore aloft a shield and broadsword that most men would struggle even to lift from the ground. Its huge head was encased inside a horned steel helmet, covering all of its face except for a single, narrow slit for the eyes.

The warrior-figure moved fast, with little grace, but with a commanding sense of violent purpose that drew an awed response from the watching crowd. Stefan recognised the monster for what it was immediately: an orc, and a giant amongst its kind at that; a warboss at the very least. Only a madman or a hero would step inside the ring with such a creature loose.

The soldiers guarding the rim of the arena drew their swords, bracing themselves in case the orc tried to break through the cordon. The towering beast moved its iron-clad head from one side of the field to the other, seeking out any possible point of weakness. Even with the odds at thirty to one, it was an intimidating spectacle.

Now a corresponding gate on the west side was raised, and another figure emerged. The second warrior was tall and powerfully built, but unmistakably a man. He wore light armour of the sort designed for fast combat. It might deflect a blow, but it would not save his life. Against the bulk and weight of the heavily armed orc, it looked very, very fragile.

The armour rendered the human warrior unrecognisable, but Stefan had no doubt of who it was. This was the moment he had been waiting for. This was the man he had come to watch. If Bruno Hausmann was the ally that he would value above all others, then this was the man he would fear most as an enemy. Only a madman or a hero, Stefan reflected again. Or a man that had something of both.

Emblazoned upon his breastplate the warrior wore the insignia of the white eagle carrying a wolf between its talons. It was the livery of Magnus the Pious, and the battle they were about to watch would depict his fateful struggle with the forces of darkness at the gates of Kislev. It seemed to Stefan to be an ironic and fateful choice.

The orc bellowed rage and hatred at his opponent as it prepared to avenge a long captivity. The man bearing the colours of Kislev's champion drew his sword, and stood firm upon his ground as the orc charged. Stefan knew that the soldiers had no role to intervene in the combat itself. The warrior would face the orc alone.

Man and beast met in the centre of the arena with a thunderous clash of steel. Fiery sparks showered the night sky as sword smashed against shield, blow following upon blow. Stefan remembered the orc chieftain he had fought and slain in the howling winds above Stahlbergen. Remembered how close he had come to losing his own life on that freezing day high in the Grey Mountains. This time the outcome would be no less uncertain.

The crowd in the arena screamed in unison as the orc launched its first savage attack. That his human opponent was brave was already beyond doubt, but it seemed far less certain that he could withstand the sheer power of the orc attack. It was as though the green-skinned beast was channelling all its ancient hatred of the human race into the thunderous blows it now rained down upon the one, lone figure. The man staggered back, desperately trying to remain on his feet. If he fell now, it would be over.

The man fell back, stabbing repeatedly at the orc's left flank with short thrusts of his sword. Several of the blows must have found their mark, yet the orc seemed oblivious to any wound inflicted. The rage boiling inside the beast had dulled what little pain it might otherwise have felt.

Suddenly the orc found clear space for an attack and swung its heavy steel blade in a rapid arc. The sword caught the champion beneath his breastplate. The armour sprung free, clattering to the ground. The man fell, knocked off balance, and only narrowly avoided a second crushing stroke of the sword falling upon his prostrate body.

The orc was slower than his human opponent, but it showed no sign of tiring. The knight had regained his feet and was wielding his sword skilfully, but to little noticeable effect. Blood from the creature's wounds ran in dark streams across the arena floor, but nothing seemed to hurt it or diminish the fury of its attack.

The orc seemed uninterested in defending itself, almost as if it was inviting the knight to attack, to burn up what little must be remaining of his strength. They may act stupidly,

Stefan reminded himself. But that's not the same as being stupid.

The champion stumbled, dropping down upon one knee. Exhaustion, as much as the orc's relentless attacks, seemed to be about to overpower him. The orc threw aside its heavy shield and unfurled a length of mesh fastened at its belt. A cruel net to snare its prey, fashioned from coarse, barbed steel. The creature cast the net one-handed but with awesome power. The man rolled sideways out of its path, but the crowd cried out as one as the champion's foot became entangled in the web. The orc bellowed a sound that was half triumph, half contempt for a defeated adversary. It started to haul the net back in, dragging its struggling foe across the floor of the arena like a captured animal.

The crowd fell silent, sensing the moment of horror approaching. For the first time, it struck home with Stefan that he may have come to watch a comrade's death. Then, somehow, the champion worked his leg free. He caught hold of the mesh in both hands and pulled back, tugging the huge orc off balance. The orc let go the net and lifted high its sword, preparing to run its opponent through with a single killing stroke.

As the orc loomed over him, the knight lifted a foot up into the middle of the creature's body. Not in a kick, Stefan suddenly realised, but as a lever. Digging deep into reserves of strength that Stefan could only marvel at, the man fastened a grip upon the creature's arms and heaved it bodily through the air. In the same movement he pulled himself back to his feet. Within a few brief seconds the position of the protagonists had been reversed.

The orc stared up at its opponent in dumb confusion. The change had been executed too quickly for it to comprehend how it was no longer the victor.

The warrior offered the orc no opportunity to reflect, stabbing his sword down two-handed into the creature's chest. As he pulled the weapon clear, the orc lifted its head, in agony or in final desperation. The warrior tugged hard upon the horned crest of the orc's helmet, exposing a thick expanse of green-leathered neck. Then he swung his blade, two-handed, and in a single, scything movement, hewed the creature's head clean from between its shoulders.

For a few unreal moments the head rolled, like a gore-spattered ball, across the floor of the silent arena. Then the sound of ten thousand voices exploded in celebration in the night air over Altdorf. The Feast of Sigmar had been brought to its conclusion.

Stefan's neighbour turned towards him, his puffy face bleached white from shock. 'Sweet mercy of Ulric,' he said, awe-struck. 'You don't see that every day.'

'Indeed,' Stefan replied. If he'd had any lingering doubts before, they had been dispelled. 'Indeed you don't.'

Now, he knew, this was the man who must ride with them.

STEFAN HADN'T WAITED for the closing ceremonies to begin. He had left his seat at once and fought his way through the scenes of revelry until he reached the quiet recesses of the arena, a world well away from the crowds and the glare of the lights, a place where the players upon the stage would prepare themselves, ready to meet whatever fate the gods had ordained. Doubtless there would be many in the vast crowd who would dearly wish to be where he was now, to be able to see, perhaps even touch the man who had relived Magnus's great victory over the greenskin hordes.

But it was business, not homage, that had brought Stefan here. The self-same business that had occupied his mind since his meeting with Otto and Elena.

After the maelstrom of the arena, the interior of the tent seemed very quiet, almost sombre. He pulled back the canvas flap and looked inside, waiting as his eyes attuned to the darkness. The tent was plain and unadorned, like that of a soldier. The only sign of the heroism that had gone before hung suspended on a chain beneath the wooden frame. It was the orc's horned helmet. Stefan stepped past it, noting that the contents of the trophy had been removed.

The tent had one occupant. A man with his back to Stefan sat before a small square of mirrored glass, dabbing at the cuts upon his face with a camphor-gauze. The champion's garb had been removed, leaving a simple cotton shift over tattered and bloody breeches. Without turning around, the man addressed Stefan.

'I hope you enjoyed the evening's entertainment.'

'I don't know if enjoy is the right word,' Stefan replied. 'But I was certainly impressed.'

The man turned about, moving out of the shadow. Light illuminated the clean-shaven, strong-boned face of a man in his late twenties. His complexion was dark, his eyes the deep colour of storm-tossed seas. He wore an expression that radiated confidence, complete assurance. The look of a man who knew what he wanted, and how to get it.

'Stefan Kumansky,' he said. 'It's been a while.'

When he stood, he bettered Stefan's six feet by all of half a head, his height and bulk making Stefan appear almost slight by comparison. He offered Stefan his hand in greeting. 'I take it this isn't a social call,' he said.

Stefan smiled. 'I'm looking for swordsmen,' he replied. 'Good ones – the best.' The other man lifted his weapon, the blade burnished bright once again after the night's battle.

'How many swordsmen?' he asked.

'No more than two,' Stefan replied.

His companion's deep, searching eyes registered no surprise. 'Two only? Who else do you have in mind?'

'I wanted Bruno Hausmann,' Stefan said. 'But I may as well be honest with you. He won't join us.'

The other man nodded, a smile playing at the corners of his mouth. 'I heard our brother-in-arms lost his appetite for adventure after our little escapade in the mountains.'

Stefan made no comment. Loyalty to Bruno outweighed any other thoughts he might have on his comrade's decision. 'Whether it's two of us or three, what's important is that I find the right men,' he said. 'Men I can trust. Men who fear no adversary.'

The other man lifted his sword towards the helm suspended from the roof of the tent, turning it under the light. He stood for a moment, as though distracted by its brutal beauty.

'Tell me about the mission,' he said at last.

'It's probably better I tell you nothing, not here,' Stefan said. 'But if you're interested to hear more, then I can take you now to meet a man who can tell you all you need to know.'

His companion prodded the helm with the point of his sword, setting it swaying like a pendulum. A shadow shaped like the head of some grotesque beast swooped across the

canvas of the tent. 'Tell me one thing, then,' he demanded.
'Will it be dangerous?'

Stefan reflected for a moment. 'Yes,' he replied. 'As far as I
can tell it will be very dangerous indeed.' The other man set
his sword down and fixed Stefan with a wide smile. 'In that
case,' he said, 'it's time that your friend was introduced to
Alexei Zucharov.'

THE BLACK CARRIAGE sat waiting for them on a road near the
approach to the arena. The door swung open at their
approach, and drove on as soon as Stefan and Zucharov were
aboard. They were heading up the hill, away from the centre
of Altdorf and the palace. Stefan shot a quizzical glance
towards Otto. 'Where are we headed?' he asked.

'A short ride only,' Otto replied. 'Somewhere out of the way.
Somewhere discreet.' He shook his head slowly and fanned
his face with the brim of his hat. He looked tired tonight,
tired and old. 'Where we're headed will be safest,' he added.
'Well, safer, at least. I don't know–' he looked around the carriage at his fellow passengers and smiled, almost
apologetically. 'Perhaps when you start seeing shadows even
in the Palace of Retribution it's about time to give it all up.'

Alexei Zucharov raised an eyebrow at mention of the dread
Halls of Justice, but said nothing. Stefan turned his head
towards the window of the carriage, trying to get a glimpse
through the narrow-slatted shutter. He thought again about
his sense of being watched, that evening, and earlier in the
day.

'Anyway,' Brandauer continued, addressing Zucharov now.
'I understand you enjoy taking risks, sir?'

Alexei fixed his gaze, steady and unblinking, upon Otto.
Stefan sensed that the question amused him slightly. 'I suppose that's true,' he replied.

'Is that always such a good idea?' Brandauer continued.

'Why not?' Alexei responded. 'I'm handsomely rewarded
for my risk-taking.'

'Perhaps,' Brandauer agreed. 'But somehow I doubt that
you measure your reward in silver or gold.'

Alexei Zucharov smiled. 'It's true I don't do what I do
because it earns me money,' he said. 'Though money I do
undoubtedly earn.'

'Your father is one of the richest silver merchants in Altdorf,' Brandauer stated. 'You've no need to earn your keep through swordplay, or by any other means, for that matter.'

Zucharov turned toward Stefan. 'You've briefed your patron well,' he said. 'He seems to have the very essence of me.' Stefan shrugged, obliquely. There had been nothing he could tell Otto about Zucharov that he did not know already.

'I know what I need to,' Otto replied. 'That's my job.'

Alexei released the smile again. He seemed in no hurry to tease out the details of the assignment he was about to be offered. The promise of danger seemed enticement enough.

'Very well,' he replied, after some thought. 'I live the way I live because I choose to do so; because I can. And if there are risks, well, then I choose those too. Anyway, is not all of life risk? None of us can say with certainty how the gods may play.'

Brandauer nodded, thoughtfully. He rapped lightly with his staff upon the glass partition separating them from the driver. The carriage slowed to a halt.

'I told you our journey would be brief,' he said. 'We can all step down now.'

Stefan emerged from the carriage to find himself outside the Blue Feather, a small inn in a quiet district of the city. It was a place he rarely had occasion to visit.

He started making for the door of the inn. A fair-sized crowd of drinkers were still inside, most of them, as far as Stefan could make out, noblemen or the wealthier breed of tradesman.

'Not that way,' Brandauer told him, 'in here.' He indicated a door off one side of the inn. He knocked once upon the panel and the door was opened. Brandauer led the way inside, past a maid dressed in a neat black and white smock, and up a short flight of carpeted stairs.

The upper floor of the inn was cramped, with a low ceiling that shelved towards one end. Stefan, and particularly Alexei, had to bow their heads to pass through. They entered a narrow corridor that led off from the room. As they walked down, one of the doors leading off opened and a young woman stepped out. The girl pulled a flimsy gown around her otherwise naked body and cast a cool, appraising eye over the three men as she snaked past them down the corridor. The girl arched one plucked and painted eyebrow as she registered Stefan.

There was a moment's silence as she swept past, then a roar of laughter from Alexei Zucharov. 'It's a bawd-house!' he exclaimed. 'A bordello!'

Still laughing, he clapped a hand upon Otto Brandauer's shoulder. 'What's the idea?' he asked. 'Some kind of prize or inducement? Thanks for the thought, old man,' he said. 'But I can find my own sport, and I don't need you or anyone else to pay for it.'

Otto Brandauer shrugged the hand off. He was in no mood for joking. 'Astute observation,' he muttered, a faint sarcasm in his voice. 'It is indeed a bordello. In other words, a place that looks after its clients without prying into their business.'

He opened a second door further down the corridor. 'In here,' he said.

Inside, a table had been set with three glasses and a flask containing only water. Candles placed upon the table had been freshly lit.

Stefan had half expected Elena to meet with them, as she had done on that first night, but there was nobody else in the room. Looking around, he felt a brief flicker of relief, mixed, perhaps, with just a little disappointment.

Otto read the question in his mind. 'She won't be coming,' he said. 'Until it's time, I'm keeping Elena out of the way as far as possible. In any case,' he added, 'it's probably better if we aren't seen together too much. People make connections.'

He bade the two of them sit. 'I wasn't at the games tonight,' he told Alexei. 'I'm not so much interested in what you can do with your sword. I know that Stefan can vouch for that.' The older man laid a finger against his forehead.

'What really interests me,' Brandauer continued, 'is what goes on in here.'

'So,' Alexei replied, a smile playing upon his lips. 'Now you're going to examine me, to make sure I'm absolutely sound, is that it?'

Otto smiled, too, but there was no humour in his words. 'There are no absolutes in this world, my friend,' he said. 'And there are no certainties.'

Alexei's face darkened, momentarily. He looked at Stefan and Otto in turn, then laughed. 'Well, anyway,' he said, 'You're rather assuming your offer will be to my liking.'

'Yes,' Brandauer agreed. 'I rather am.'

IT WAS PAST midnight before Brandauer left them, and when Stefan and Alexei made their way down to where the more routine business of the inn was still in full flow.

'By the gods!' Alexei declared. 'All this talk of adventuring has worked on my thirst. I'd ransom my soul for a draught of decent beer!' He moved towards the door leading into the bar of the tavern, but Stefan pulled him back.

'Not here,' Stefan said. 'I'm not so familiar with these parts. I'd be happier drinking somewhere where we know the lie of the land.' He turned in the direction of the back streets that led towards the hub of the city.

'Keeping company with a Kislevite noblewoman will be intriguing,' Alexei said. 'Something of a beauty, is she?'

Stefan thought of Elena's intense, questioning expression, her chiselled, almost severe features. 'Not a beauty, maybe,' he said. 'But she makes an impression right enough.'

'And what will you do about Bruno?' Alexei asked. Stefan shook his head.

'Nothing more,' he said. 'Bruno has made his decision. He says it's final.'

'Oh, I wouldn't be so sure about that,' Alexei commented. 'So few things in this life are ever final.'

Stefan was about to reply when he caught the sound of footsteps on the cobbled street behind them. He put a finger to his lips, signalling to Zucharov. The steps quickened as whoever was behind them broke into a run. A voice called out: 'Stefan! Stefan Kumansky!'

Stefan looked around to see a figure hard on their heels, a half-finished pot of beer still in one hand. It was a man probably ten years Stefan's senior, with a loping gait and fighter's physique that was now fast running to seed. The man pulled up just short of Stefan and Alexei, and scraped a plume of greasy hair back from his face.

Stefan recognised Tomas Murer at once. He'd ridden with him on several occasions in the past, and there'd once been a time when Tomas had held a sound reputation amongst the

swordsmen of Altdorf. That time, however, was long past. It
was clear Tomas had come from the bar of the Blue Feather,
and from the look and sound of him, it seemed likely he'd
been there for quite some time.

Murer raised an arm in greeting, spilling yet more of the
beer.

'Stefan!' he shouted again. 'Stefan, old friend!'

Stefan forced a smile, though he was far from delighted to
meet Tomas. This, at best, was bad luck.

Murer looked around at his new companions, beaming at
them. He fixed Alexei with a stare and stabbed a finger
towards him.

'Alexei Zucharov, am I right?'

'Absolutely right,' Alexei concurred. He shot Tomas a look
of ill-disguised disgust. Tomas continued to look pleased
with himself.

'By the gods, Stefan, I'm glad to find you here,' he said.

'Why have you been following us?' Stefan demanded.

'I haven't, Stefan, I swear.' He pointed back towards the
lights of the Blue Feather. 'I was drinking in the tavern with
some mates from the old days. Saw you come out. What luck!
I'd been hoping to run across you.'

Stefan regarded the newcomer in silence for a few
moments. Murer was amiable enough company when he was
sober, but that was all too rare of late. Stefan decided to get
shot of him as quickly as possible.

'We've business to discuss here, Tom,' he said. 'What is it
you want?'

Tomas spread his hands wide. 'Business!' he exclaimed.
'Exactly that. That's what I wanted to talk about too.
Business.' He drained what was left of his beer and slammed
the empty mug down to smash on the cobblestones.

'Won't beat about it, Stefan,' he said. 'Need some work, find
a gang to ride with.' He pulled a grimy-looking blade from
his pocket. 'Time to give the old girl some exercise again.
What do you say?'

Stefan exchanged glances with Alexei. 'I'd say, what makes
you think anyone is riding anywhere?' he replied.

Tomas turned from Stefan to Alexei and rolled his eyes in
a look of exaggerated incredulity.

'What do you take me for?'

'A drunk,' Alexei replied, sourly. Tomas either ignored or failed to hear the remark.

'Two of Altdorf's finest swords,' he said. 'What else do you do but ride? Swords for hire–' Tomas clutched at Stefan's hand, his watery eyes shining. 'Let me ride with you, Stefan. Today, tomorrow, next week. Whenever you go. You need a tracker, a scout, whatever. I've still got what it takes.'

Alexei Zucharov sighed, and turned Tomas about to face him. 'Show me that knife again,' he said.

Tomas shot him a quizzical look. 'Show it to me,' Zucharov demanded again.

'Steady, Alexei,' Stefan cautioned. He was conscious that Tomas had done them no harm, at least as far as they knew. Tomas hesitated. Reluctantly, he reached inside his jerkin and retrieved the knife. The weapon was battered, but lethal enough in its way. Alexei examined it, then handed it back.

'Very well,' he said. 'You reckon you've still got what it takes. So show me.' He stood back, arms at his side, leaving his body unprotected. Tomas looked around, unsure whether this was a joke.

'Come on,' Alexei instructed him. He pointed to his chest. 'Prove it.'

Stefan looked on in silence. He was worried about what Tomas, drunk, might try. And more worried what Alexei would do to him if he did.

Tomas took a step back. Suddenly he looked very sober. 'Look,' he said to both of them. 'We're friends, right?'

Zucharov hadn't moved a muscle. 'This isn't about friendship,' he said, coldly. Tomas glanced around nervously. He had realised he had left it too late to back out. He fumbled with the knife, trying to steady his shaking grip upon the blade.

'I've killed more men than I can remember,' Tomas shouted. 'Don't push me, Alexei.' He looked down at Zucharov's hands hanging, motionless, at his sides. They were nowhere near his sword. A ghost of a smile flitted across Tomas's face. For a second he made as though to put the knife back inside his pocket.

Then he attacked. Lamplight shone off the steel blade as he plunged it towards Alexei's body. The knife never reached its target. In an instant Zucharov had grabbed hold of Tomas's arm and twisted, slamming him down face first upon the ground. With his other hand he snatched the knife from Tomas's grip and brought the point of the blade against his throat. Tomas looked up at him, dazed.

'Tracker?' Alexei sneered. 'You couldn't track a three-legged dog in your state.' He let go of Tomas, and threw the knife down on the ground by his side. 'Go home and sleep it off.'

Tomas stared at up first at Alexei, then at Stefan, his face red with shame and anger. 'Go home, Tom,' Stefan counselled, softly. 'This is no place for you.'

Tomas glared back at him, then snatched up the knife. He clambered to his feet and stumbled away down the street without another word.

'There was no need for that, Alexei,' Stefan said at last. 'He was a fair soldier in his day, and a good scout, too.'

'His day is long over,' Zucharov snapped. 'Anyway, what was he doing lurking around back there? Maybe I should have finished the job – just killed him outright and be done with it.'

'You're over-reacting,' Stefan told him. 'Tom Murer props up the bar in half the taverns in Altdorf. It was just coincidence, that's all.'

'Coincidence?' Alexei muttered. 'There's no such thing.'

'I wouldn't have let you kill him, Alexei,' Stefan said. 'I wouldn't have let you do that.'

The two stood staring at each other in silence. The comforting warmth of the tavern seemed suddenly far behind them. Then Alexei's mood seemed to lift. He clapped Stefan upon the shoulder and grinned. 'Ah, you're probably right,' he laughed. 'He won't even remember where he's been in the morning. Now, let's find us that ale house.'

Stefan hesitated for a moment, his mind still mulling over the incident that had just passed. He decided to let it go. 'The Cutlass might be open,' he said at last. 'They've enough strong beer to blunt even a thirst like yours.'

Zucharov laughed again. 'I doubt that's possible,' he said. 'But I'm willing to give it a try.'

The two men walked on, seeking some warmth in the cold hours of early morning.

CHAPTER FIVE
Four Encounters

THE MORNING SUN shone a bright, unforgiving light on the scattered remains of the feasting day. Shattered glass sparkled like diamonds strewn across the city streets, and the gutters ran dark with a stinking brew of beer, wine and worse. A good number of the revellers could be found where they had dropped the night before, lying curled outside doorways or sprawled, senseless on street corners.

Of the few other townsfolk who were about, none seemed to pay much attention to the short, rotund figure stepping smartly through the Hauptmarktplatz towards the centre of Altdorf. For once, however, Otto Brandauer was taking no comfort from his apparent anonymity. Every few seconds he would check his pace and glance about him, scanning the faces of the work-bound clerks and merchants. He had taken Stefan's concerns about being watched seriously. Perhaps the young man's imagination had become over-active. Perhaps, and perhaps not. Either way, Otto found that now he, too, was watching his back.

The sense that he was being followed had been with him since he left his house shortly after dawn and had not diminished. Brandauer was not a suspicious man, but a lifetime spent amongst shadows had nurtured instincts he had learned to trust.

Perhaps he was letting his worrying get the better of him, but just lately there had been much to worry about. The darkness spreading like a disease, unseen but deadly, through the body of the Old World. The urgency of getting Elena Yevschenko back to Erengrad while there was still time to tip the scales of fortune back in their favour. Preparations were well advanced, but still, he feared, they were not moving fast enough.

Could it really be possible that even the Palace of Justice could no longer be considered secure? Months, even weeks ago, the very idea would have seemed ridiculous. Now he couldn't be so sure. Times grew less certain, almost, it seemed, by the day. This day had dawned bright, but night was coming. The shadows were drawing in around Altdorf.

Brandauer shivered, and tried to shake the morbid thoughts from his mind. He quickened his step along Vollenstrasse.

In a few minutes he had reached the gates of the Jaegerspark. The palace was visible in the distance, its gilded towers reflecting the morning sun. Brandauer stopped before the gates. Each day he would walk to the Palace of Retribution, taking the shortest route through the Jaegerspark. It had become habit, part of his routine. He took a step towards the open gates, then hesitated. Perhaps today was a day to break with routine.

Imagination, he told himself, too many shadows. Yet something prevented him from continuing on through the gates, following the course of his normal route. The lonely expanse of the Jaegerspark lay before him, beckoning. Five minutes' stride across the hard ground and he would have reached the marble towers of the palace. Five minutes only.

But not today. On impulse, Otto Brandauer turned suddenly sharp left, away from the Jaegerspark and into the warren of tiny interweaving streets that lay between Vollenstrasse and the docks. Even as he set off, he was chastising himself for being a superstitious fool.

You're getting too old, Brandauer, he told himself. You're seeing shadows everywhere now. Yet he quickened his pace rather than lessening it. He came to a point where the street divided. He took the right fork and immediately stepped within the recess of a doorway, from where he could take stock of the street behind.

For a few moments he truly believed he had gone mad. Without the sound of his own footfall upon the flagstones, the street was silent save for the distant whisper of traffic in the port. You idiot, Brandauer. How long are you going to hide here like a cowardly fool?

Just at the point when he'd convinced himself his imagination really had got the better of him, the silence in the street was broken. The sound of footsteps approaching, keeping up a brisk pace.

Just a clerk, late for work, or a student, clutching his books as he hastened towards the Ostfuhr College. Or could it be someone else? Someone searching, looking for him. The footsteps slowed as they neared the fork in the street.

Brandauer reached inside the lining of his cape, and drew out the slender rapier he kept concealed within. Whoever it was had stopped, close enough for Brandauer to hear the sound of breathing. He held his own breath, and waited. His heart was pounding inside his chest, so loud, he imagined, that it might give him away.

A shadow fell across the doorway in front of him as the figure crept forward. Otto Brandauer braced himself and, keeping firm hold of the rapier, stepped out into the street. The figure had passed the doorway where he had been hiding: took a few steps on, and then turned back. In that instant he felt a delicious fear pump through him. The delicate sword was cold and slippery in his hand. But as he looked into the face of the potential assassin, his grip on the rapier loosened and his body relaxed.

Otto Brandauer swapped sword for handkerchief, and wiped a line of sweat away from his brow.

Surprise mingled with relief in his voice. 'So!' he exclaimed. 'It's you.'

ALEXEI ZUCHAROV LIFTED the helmet down from the oak shelf and turned it between his hands. On his instructions it had been left as it was; the blood had not even been cleaned away. The smell of orc was still strong upon the tarnished metal.

Alexei set the helm back in its place amongst the other tro-
phies. It was a handsome piece, and would serve as a fair
memento of his night's sport, but it paled against some of his
finer prizes: a Tilean hunter's knife, inscribed with a chieftain's name; a bowed blade snatched from a pirate prince of
Araby; the skull of a skaven, pared nearly in two across its low
forehead; a breastplate ripped from the body of a monstrous
Chaos knight, inlaid with carvings paying homage to the
Blood God.

Alexei ran a hand across them all, savouring the feel of
metal and bone, and the sweet memory of conquest held
within each. The orc helm added yet one more jewel to his
collection, but he knew it would not be the last. Whilst he
lived and breathed a warrior, there would always be one
more battle to fight, one more trophy to be won.

He closed the doors to the cabinet and turned the key in
the lock. As he did so, he sensed the movement in the room
behind him, sensed it as clearly as he could smell the blood
of the slain orc. Before he could turn round, he felt the hands
go about his neck.

'You're getting careless,' the girl's voice said. 'Letting just
anyone creep up on you like that.'

'If you were just anyone,' Alexei responded, 'you'd be dead
by now.' He twisted his face to one side in time for his sister
Natalia to place a playful kiss upon his cheek. 'Anyway,' he
went on, laughing now. 'Shouldn't you be at your studies,
instead of creeping about the house?'

Natalia Zucharov frowned, then kissed her brother again.
'Even students of magic need rest,' she said. 'In any case, my
studies are going very well. You can ask anyone at the college
how good I am.'

'For which our father will be eternally grateful,' Alexei commented, 'having mortgaged his inheritance to pay your fees.'

His younger sister snorted derisively. '*I'm* the one who's
grateful,' Natalia said. 'Grateful to you for twisting the old
man's arm. He'd have me married off to some half-wit count
with a hundred acres in Ostmark by now, not studying at the
Imperial College of Magic.'

Alexei held his sister at arm's length and looked at her.
'Mind you repay our trust,' he said. 'Father's and mine. Don't
just be good. Be the best.'

'Like you?' Natalia asked, teasingly.

'Yes,' Alexei replied. 'Exactly like me. I'll want a full account of your new skills when I get back to Altdorf.'

'It's true then,' Natalia said quietly. 'You're leaving again?'

Alexei nodded. 'There's some travellers making a long journey out to the east,' he explained. 'The road can be dangerous. I'm needed as escort for their safe passage. It's as simple as that.'

'Simple?' Natalia said, her eyes widening. 'Dangerous doesn't sound quite the same as simple to me.'

'I can take care of myself, you know that.' He placed his arms protectively around his sister. 'We're alike, you and I. We weren't born to sit on our backsides in merchant houses, nor to wed half-wit counts.'

He kissed her forehead again. 'But I won't always be around to look after you, so you must take care as much as I.'

Natalia took her brother's arm as they walked side by side. 'You're wrong, you know. You will always be around. Here, in my heart, you'll be with me, always.'

She walked to the window and pulled back the long curtain. A figure on horseback was sitting waiting outside the gates of the house.

'We have a visitor,' she said excitedly. 'Who could that be? The mysterious Stefan Kumansky, perhaps? I've been looking forward to meeting him.'

Alexei joined her at the window and looked down onto the long driveway fronting the Zucharov house. 'No,' he said. 'Not him, I think.'

'Who is it, then?'

'Another comrade.'

'Another mystery man? Shall I go down and bid him come in?'

'No,' Alexei said, quietly. 'No need. I'll go down myself. I fancy we'll want to ride a little.'

ALEXEI ZUCHAROV EMERGED from the house and strolled across the courtyard towards the waiting rider. He reached up a hand in greeting to the man seated astride the grey mare. The rider took his hand and shook it formally, without enthusiasm.

'Your note said this was urgent,' Bruno said, stiffly. 'I thought it best to ride here directly.'

Alexei looked up at him, a grin playing on his face.

'What sort of greeting is that?' he demanded. 'I thought at the very least it would be "Good to see you, Alexei! It's been too long!"'

'It has been a long time,' the other man agreed, soberly. 'Your note said it was urgent, otherwise it might have been longer still!'

Alexei stepped back and appraised the rider. A look of concern passed over his features. 'You look pale,' he said. 'Have you been ill?'

'I've been sleeping badly, that's all,' said the other man. 'It will pass.'

Alexei nodded, and patted the flank of the mare. 'Well then,' he said. 'I thought we'd both enjoy a brisk ride out. If you wait here a moment I'll have my horse saddled.' He fixed a firm gaze upon the rider. 'You see, we ought to talk. I know something that I think you should hear.'

'If this is about Stefan, forget it.' Bruno told him, sharply. 'I've already said all that I have to say to him.'

'Quite so,' Alexei agreed. 'But you haven't heard all that *I* have to say,' he continued. 'And I really think it would be in your best interests if you did.'

Zucharov turned in the direction of the stable block, then paused. 'You know what, though,' he added, brightly. 'Shop keeping can't be all bad. I do declare, Bruno, you've put on weight!'

STEFAN KUMANSKY WALKED through the doors of the Helmsman just after noon. The usual corner table, he noted with satisfaction, was still empty. He wasn't in any sense a creature of habit, but in this one ritual there was perhaps an exception. He bought a large pitcher of beer and two mugs from the serving girl and sat down at the table. Today of all days it seemed right that sentiment prevailed, because he was here to bid a farewell. A farewell, gods willing, that would be only temporary.

He had to wait a few minutes before his drinking companion arrived, ruddy-faced and breathless from running, through the door of the tavern. The man was Stefan's junior by a couple of years, lightly built, with the straw-blond complexion typical of those born north of the Empire. Stefan pushed back a chair for his brother to sit down.

'Sorry I'm so late, Stefan,' Mikhal apologised. Stefan grinned up at him.

'Business or pleasure?' he asked.

'Business,' Mikhal said, emphatically. 'A trading ship's just in from Cathay – would you believe it? And she's laden down with enough fine silk to carpet the Hauptmarktplatz. As for the prices, well!' Mikhal paused, embarrassed. 'I'm sorry,' he said. 'You don't want to hear all of this nonsense. It's deadly boring to a fellow like you.'

Stefan pushed a mug of beer into his brother's hand. 'Not a bit of it,' he said, and meant it. Since they had arrived in Altdorf as orphans, the two brothers' lives had taken quite different paths. Stefan, the poor scholar and indifferent guardsman, who found his road as errand boy for the mercenaries who had lit his imagination with tales of heroism and adventure. Now those tales were about him. Mikhal had been the avid student of commerce, the apprentice who was a match for the shrewdest market trader at fifteen, and a merchant in his own right at twenty.

Each brother had found his own adventure, and Stefan was no less proud of Mikhal than he hoped his brother was of him. Proud, and glad that his brother had chosen a path that would keep him from harm's way.

'Here's to carpeting the Hauptmarktplatz,' Stefan said, toasting his brother. They drank, and talked for a while of everyday things. Then Mikhal set down his mug and looked at Stefan.

'So,' he said. 'You're off on your travels again?'

'Yes,' Stefan replied. 'Only this is different. I'm going back to Kislev. To Erengrad.'

Mikhal sat silent for a moment. 'I see,' he said at last. 'Erengrad, though. It can't be far from – I mean, how do you feel about going back there after all this time?'

'I don't know,' Stefan said. It was true. The last few days had passed so quickly he had found himself with little time to ponder what it would mean to be returning so close to the place of his childhood. A place that, in more ways than one, was now truly another country. But that morning, thinking about his meeting with Mikhal in the Helmsman, the memories of that other place had flooded back.

'I'm sorry,' he said to Mikhal, pulling himself back from his thoughts. 'I know those memories are painful for you too.'

Mikhal sipped at his beer, thoughtfully. 'If it wasn't for you,' he said, 'I doubt I'd still be here to have memories of any sort. The Norscan would have killed me, for sure. I'll never forget that.'

'Nor I,' Stefan replied. That was one memory that was seared upon his very soul, a permanent reminder of the past. Even as Mikhal spoke the words, Stefan was back in Odensk, watching the village burn. Darkness and torchlight. The smell of dead fires in the morning, clinging to the charred skeleton of the village. The dead eyes of their father, staring back up at him, and the other face too: the face of the Norscan raider bearing down upon Mikhal as he lay, paralysed by fear, by the road. Then the feel of the knife in his hand as he swung it, full force, into that cruel, milk-white face. Seeing the blade gouge deep into the man's eye, the blood spraying with astonishing force from the wound. And hearing, for the first time, the sound of an enemy screaming as his blade found its mark.

'I should have killed him,' Stefan said, quietly. 'Killed that murdering scum, just as his kind killed our father. The thought that he might still live haunts me to this day.'

'We were children, Stefan,' Mikhal reminded him. 'Just boys, that's all.'

'Aye,' Stefan agreed. 'But childhood ended that day.' He took a long draught of ale and sat for a moment, lost within his thoughts.

'So, you're going back,' Mikhal said at last, pulling his brother back. 'How many are you taking with you?'

'Not many,' Stefan said. 'We have to avoid drawing attention to ourselves.'

'So, then,' Mikhal went on. 'Is Bruno with you?'

Stefan shook his head. 'No,' he said. 'I wish that he were, but no. Something changed with Bruno last time up in the mountains. He won't talk about it; he's shut me out.' He finished his beer and refilled the pot. 'I don't know,' he said. 'We ran into some bad business. Innocent people died. Maybe he's just had enough. He's doing well for himself now. I don't blame him.'

Mikhal reflected for a while. 'You'll miss him,' he said. 'Who else do you have?'

'Alexei Zucharov,' Stefan said. 'You've heard of him?'

'Indeed,' Mikhal affirmed. 'Hero or hothead, depending on who you listen to.'

'A bit of both, perhaps,' Stefan said. 'But I tell you what – I'd rather he was for me than against.'

'Yes,' Mikhal concurred. 'I hear he's a good fighter – formidable, in fact. But surely there is someone else, someone who will ride with you in Bruno's stead?'

Stefan shrugged. 'Maybe. I don't know. It would have to be someone I could trust with my life.'

A silence fell between them, one that Mikhal was able to break only with some awkwardness. 'Look,' he said at last. 'I don't know whether you thought I should–'

Stefan looked puzzled for a moment before he caught his brother's meaning.

'No, no, no!' he said. 'That's not why I came here at all. Listen,' he went on, clasping his brother's hand. 'If I had half your brain for bargaining I'd probably be a merchant myself. But I haven't. This is how it's turned out for us. I'm a swordsman, and you're a trader, and an excellent one at that. Don't misunderstand me,' he said. 'There's no one I'd trust more than you. But you belong here, not on the road with one hand always resting on your sword.'

Mikhal tried his best to look a little disappointed, but his face was a picture of relief. 'If you need any money,' he offered. Stefan waved Mikhal's gesture away.

'We'll be well looked after in that respect,' he assured him. He reached inside his pocket, and pulled out a small object wrapped in oilskin. 'I wanted to give you this before I left.'

'What is it?' Mikhal asked, puzzled. Stefan unfolded the oilskin to reveal a silver disc the size of a large coin. Time had dulled its lustre and blurred the engraving a little, but Mikhal recognised the little icon of Shallya at once.

'This was our mother's,' he said.

'That's right. Father gave it to me the night that he died,' he told Mikhal. 'He made me promise in keeping it that I'd always look after my little brother.'

Mikhal took the icon and held it in his hand for a moment. 'Not so little, now,' he said eventually.

'No,' Stefan agreed. 'But you're still my brother. I want you to keep this until I return. That's my pledge to my family – to all of us. I'll go back to Kislev, but I will return.'

Mikhal took the icon and placed it carefully in his own pocket. 'How long do you think you'll be gone for?' he asked.

Stefan thought for a moment. It was a good question. 'I don't know,' he admitted. 'But – I tell you what–' He was suddenly seized with an idea.

'Let us fix a date, here and now,' he said, 'for us to meet again, at this very table of this very tavern, and then I shall know that I am meant to return!' He paused, trying to calculate the passage of time to match the journey to Kislev and back. He allowed a full six months; surely more than enough. 'What shall we say?' he continued. 'Upon the eve of Kaltzeit, at this very table?'

Mikhal took his brother's hand and held it firmly within his own. 'Done,' he said. 'I'll have your beer waiting, and woe betide you if you're late!'

'Done!' Stefan agreed. A clock in the square chimed the hour. 'Time rushes on,' he said, and hugged his brother a final time. 'Gods keep you, Mikhal.'

'And you,' Mikhal replied. 'Gods keep you from all harm.'

STEFAN EMERGED FROM the tavern into the afternoon sunshine. A fresh wind was blowing in off the water, and on impulse he decided to walk back along the quay, rather than take the shorter route through the heart of the city. The port was busy; a large crowd had gathered around one of the wharves. The Cathay merchantman was still in; most of her cargo had been offloaded now and she was sitting high in the water. From the dockside Stefan could clearly see the dragon's head carving upon her prow and the same motif emblazoned in bright scarlet upon the sails set billowing in the steady breeze. The ship looked like a traveller from another world.

One day, Stefan promised himself. One day.

But it was not the exotic trading-vessel that was attracting all the attention. The clamour and crowding was directed at something further down the quay, alongside the dock rather than in it. Most likely it was a quarrel of some sort – the deep-water port of old Altdorf was a melting pot of different creeds and races, and not always an altogether happy one.

Rarely a day went by without an altercation of some sort, and often blood would be spilled.

But, as he got closer to the crowd, Stefan knew this was something more serious. Several beefy-looking stevedores were pushing their way out from the back of the throng, and one at least had stopped to be sick into the dock.

He stopped a man as he pushed his way past. 'What is it?' he demanded. 'What's happened?'

The man met his eye and crossed his hand upon his chest, making a warding sign. 'Murder,' he said. 'Found some fellow tucked in amongst the bales back there on the wharf. Nasty business.'

Stefan forced his way through to the front of the crowd. The first thing that struck him was the amount of blood. Blood everywhere. With the bales of silk removed, the quay looked like a charnel house. A body was lying upon the ground, part covered by a tar-befouled sheet. What was left uncovered looked like the work of some berserk animal. The body was barely recognisable as human.

'Gods preserve us,' Stefan muttered. 'What manner of beast has done this?' He stepped forward, and gently lifted the blood spattered sheet draped across the dead man's face.

As he did so, he realised two things. The first was that this was no indiscriminate, frenzied attack. The body had been mutilated in a way that was entirely deliberate. The second thing Stefan realised was that the victim was not a stranger. As he lifted the sheet he recognised at once what remained of the man's face.

It was Otto Brandauer.

CHAPTER SIX
Leaving

VARIK STEPPED FORWARD tentatively, into the unyielding space that was the realm of Kyros. He stood within a void filled with a blackness more impenetrable than any night. It was like entering a world without dimensions. There was no contrast, no light; no beginning, and no end. It was said that the soul of the Lord Kyros was so wedded to the powers of darkness that daylight had become unendurable, that he could only suffer the withering sun vicariously, from within the host body of a disciple. Yet another story had it that the warping power of Chaos had wrought such terrible disfigurements upon his body that Kyros forbore any of his followers to look upon him without the covering cloak of darkness.

The emissary paid no attention to stories. Varik had survived, flourished – even, in the shadow of Kyros's insane majesty by keeping his thoughts to himself, until he was required to do otherwise. He stood, penitent and head bowed, waiting upon his master's pleasure. He had learned never to try and anticipate the will of Kyros.

The silence stretched on until the emissary became aware of something stirring, some denser form moving amidst the darkness. Varik did not move forward, but fell upon his knees, and waited. He could feel the might of Kyros bearing down upon him like an iron bar upon his back.

'Magnificence,' he intoned. 'Your emissary attends your command.'

Varik heard, or rather felt, the Chaos Lord's reply like a thunder echoing within his skull. The voice of his master flooded into him, filling him with a dark, divine energy.

'You have not recovered the icon.'

Varik clasped his hands together, and pressed his forehead to the cold ground; supine and subservient. 'Master,' he said, slowly. 'It is true the pieces of the Star remain scattered across the blighted realm of man. But we will retrieve them them. Every day brings us nearer that goal.' He raised his head, fractionally. 'The Kislevite herself shall lead us to our prize.'

Silence. He sensed Kyros measuring his words, probing them for deceit, weighing their worth in the balance.

'What of the old meddler?' the Dark Lord demanded at last. 'If he was not the custodian of the Star, then he would have had knowledge of it.'

Varik took a deep breath. He was aware of his entire body shaking. 'Our servant could glean nothing from the old man,' he said. 'They searched his quarters afterwards, and could find no trace of it.'

'Afterwards?'

'The old man is dead, lordship. He will stand against us no further.'

There was a pause. When the voice of Kyros spoke again, it was in more measured tones. 'Much will depend upon this one servant. You are sure that they will not fail us?'

'Their human will has been completely subdued,' Varik assured his master. 'Their soul has been suspended between the world of the living and that of the dead. It is yours to command.'

Varik felt the pressure bearing down on him lift a fraction. The pain encircling his head like a vice began to ease. His body felt suddenly lighter, blessed with a divine forbearance. Varik knelt quietly in the darkness, savouring his master's indulgence.

* * *

STEFAN KNEW THAT if Otto's death signified one thing, it meant that they must now move quickly. His immediate task had been to send word to Elena Yevschenko. Normally he would have gone to her chambers at the Palace of Retribution, but after what had just happened, he was no longer sure that even the palace was safe.

He kept the note brief, only telling Elena that she must come to his rooms in the Altquartier, alone and without delay.

After what seemed like an age there was a knock at the door, and Elena stood before him, her head and body covered by a heavy cloak she wore wrapped around her.

'This better be good,' she told him, curtly. 'Otto must have told you I'm not supposed to go wandering the streets of Altdorf without good cause.'

'I needed to speak to you alone, somewhere where I could be sure we wouldn't be overheard,' Stefan explained. 'Look,' he said, his tone more gentle now, 'you'd better sit down. I'm afraid Otto's not going to be helping us any more.'

Elena reacted to the news in near silence at first, sitting quietly, wringing her hands. Finally, the words came as the tears began to flow.

'He often talked of his own death,' she said. 'He would tell me that he would greet the end of each day as a victory, as death postponed. But he knew all the same that he would confront it, eventually.'

'He met a cruel end,' Stefan said. 'I'm sorry.' And saddened, he might have added. He had barely had time to know Otto, yet he had the certain feeling that, finally, he might have found a kindred spirit. Someone, at last, who understood. With Otto dead, Stefan knew that he stood alone once more.

'How long was he – was the body lying there long before it was found?' Elena asked.

'Not long, I think,' Stefan said.

'Then it had not been well concealed?'

Stefan hesitated. He knew this was going to be the most difficult part of all.

'I don't think there was any intention to conceal his body,' he said, quietly. 'I think that whoever did this meant him to be found, and quickly.'

Elena stared back at Stefan. She knew there was more to come. 'Tell me,' she said. 'Don't keep the truth from me.' Grief leant a sudden harshness to her tone. 'What else did you see?'

Stefan took a deep breath. Recalling the scene at the wharf was hard enough, describing it to Elena was going to be far worse. 'It looked at first as though Otto had been torn apart by some kind of wild beast,' he said. 'Cut apart, into pieces.'

Elena blinked. A tear fell across one cheek. 'Go on,' she said. 'I need to know.'

'But then,' Stefan continued, 'when I – looked again, I saw that this – terrible carnage – had been deliberate. And careful, in its way. Otto had been cut, his body butchered to fit a deliberate pattern.'

Elena paled. She touched a shaking hand to her lips. 'Pattern?' she said, weakly. 'Pattern of what?'

'Insignia,' Stefan said, continuing to force the words out. 'I've seen most of them before, though there was a time when I would never have thought to see them here, in Altdorf. Nor displayed in such a terrible way.'

'What kind,' Elena demanded, her voice steadied now, 'what kind of insignia?'

'The stigmata of evil,' Stefan continued. 'Runes and spell-charms. Daubings paying foul homage to a dark god – the god of transfiguration.'

'The Changer of the Ways,' Elena said slowly, aghast.

'Yes,' Stefan affirmed. 'There was quite a crowd gathered by the time I got there. I don't think many of them knew what they were looking at.'

'But you did,' Elena said.

'Except for this,' Stefan replied. He reached into his pocket and drew out a folded slip of paper. He opened it out and flattened it upon the table. 'I found this mark near where Otto lay.' he said. 'Someone had daubed it – in his blood. I copied it down.'

Elena took the paper from Stefan's hand and looked at the likeness he had drawn. He knew at once that she recognised it. Elena threw the paper down and pushed it away as though she could not bear to have it near her.

'What does it mean?' Stefan asked.

Elena was shaking now. Fear had replaced the grief in her eyes.

'Are you sure?' she asked. 'Are you sure this is right?'

'Quite sure,' Stefan told her. 'What does it mean?'

Elena did not answer directly, but Stefan caught the whispered word that she spoke, before turning away: *Scarandar*. He took hold of her arm, and drew her back towards him. 'Elena,' Stefan said, gently but firmly. 'This is important. Scarandar? Who or what is that? Why would it be here, in Altdorf?'

'I'd never thought to that see that mark outside of Kislev,' Elena said, horrified. 'In fact, not even outside Erengrad.' She buried her face in her hands. 'Oh, Goddess Shallya protect us!'

'Elena,' Stefan persisted. 'Please.'

She looked up out of her hands at him, her eyes reddened. 'The Scarandar are the servants of evil,' she began, struggling to control the trembling in her voice. 'They are human – at least, I think they are – but they have set their face against mankind and all its works. They worship a daemon, a terrible master pledged to deliver first Erengrad, then all Kislev to the Lord of Change.'

'How will he do that?' Stefan asked, gravely. 'What do the stories say?'

Elena held down a deep breath, fighting to keep her composure.

'That he will bring down the walls of Erengrad from without and from within,' she said. 'From without, by bringing a mighty conflagration of fire and blood. From within, by sowing the seeds of unrest and hatred which will divide the people against themselves.'

Stefan sat down, and rested his head in his hands. 'Unless, of course,' he said, 'something or someone is able to unite the people, and deliver them to another destiny?'

Both of them sat in silence, the significance of their words suddenly weighing down upon them. Stefan had understood the seriousness of things when Otto had first shown him the map. But somehow, now, this had become personal. It was about Elena. And it was about him.

He felt Elena's hand upon his own. Her nails gripped into the flesh of his wrist. When he looked up he saw the tears flowing freely down her face.

'But why now?' she sobbed. 'Why choose to seek Otto out and murder him now?'

'I don't know,' Stefan replied. 'Maybe they – if it is the Scarandar – were looking for something they thought he had. Maybe they want the Star.'

Both were silent for a moment as the implications of Stefan's words sank in.

'I think Otto's death was meant as a message,' he went on, quietly. 'A message for us. I think they meant to show that they know who you are.'

'But then why give us warning?' Elena demanded.

'Yes,' Stefan agreed. 'Why indeed?' He folded the paper carefully and put it away. 'One thing is clear,' he said. 'We can't afford to delay our departure any longer. I've sent a message to Alexei Zucharov. He should be here at any moment.'

'Then we're leaving,' Elena said.

'Yes,' Stefan replied 'Without delay. Tonight.'

Elena glanced at Stefan then looked away. 'Very well,' she said. 'We'll be ready.'

It took a moment for the word to register with Stefan. 'We?' he asked, slowly. 'Who do you mean by "we"?'

Elena got up, and turned away from Stefan. 'My maid, Lisette, and I, that's who,' she said, curtly. 'Surely you don't expect me to travel half way across the Empire with just two strangers for company?'

Stefan wasn't sure any more what he expected. All he knew was that, in the midst of his grief for a dead comrade, Elena had suddenly thrown a totally unknown factor into the equation.

'Why didn't you tell me about this before?' he demanded. He didn't know what he felt about Elena's maid riding with them. What he knew was that he had been wrong-footed, intentionally or otherwise, and it didn't agree with him one bit.

Elena rounded on him, eyes flashing angry fire. 'Why in the name of Taal should you have been?' she demanded. 'You don't own me, Stefan Kumansky. It's my decision if I choose to take a whole troop of servants. Surely you don't begrudge my having my maid ride with me?'

'What I begrudge,' Stefan continued, pushing back his own anger, 'is that you make arrangements without telling me.'

'Well, I'm telling you now,' Elena snapped. 'Lisette is more than a maid. She's a companion, and an outsider, just like me.

She's the only person who knows what it's like, always to be the stranger in a strange land.' She brushed a tear away from her face. 'That's why I chose her to attend me, rather than those sneering madams they sent me at court.' She stared up at Stefan, her defiance undimmed. 'I'll be damned if I'll give her up now, and Otto would tell you himself it was my right.'

'Otto's dead,' Stefan said, quietly. 'He can't tell us anything any more.'

The sound of footsteps outside cut short the quarrel. Stefan turned away from Elena and opened the door. Expecting just Alexei Zucharov, Stefan was at first alarmed to see two figures, their faces hidden beneath heavy woollen capes. The second figure pulled the hood clear of his face and looked up, expressionless, at Stefan. 'I assume it's not too late to change my mind?' he said.

'Bruno!' The dark cloud pressing down upon Stefan lifted at the unexpected sight of his friend. Bruno shook Stefan's hand and smiled, briefly. Behind the smile there was still something, some distance that Stefan could not fathom. He let the question go.

'It's good to see you,' he said, warmly.

'You're still looking for someone to ride with you?'

'If that someone is you, then yes,' Stefan affirmed.

Bruno exchanged glances with Alexei. Stefan thought he saw something in Bruno's look, discomfort or unease. Again, he let the question go.

'Bruno's thought things over,' Alexei said. 'Come to think better of his decision.'

'Just promise me one thing,' Bruno said to Stefan. 'Accept that my decision now is to ride with you. Don't question me about why. Things have changed, that's all.'

'Things have changed indeed,' Stefan agreed. He turned to Zucharov. 'Otto Brandauer's been murdered,' he told him. 'It looks like someone knows about the mission.'

'Then we need to make a move,' Zucharov said.

'Yes,' Stefan confirmed. 'We must be on our way by moon-rise. But there's another problem to resolve, now.'

'Which is?'

'Otto was going to lead the mission, at least as far as Middenheim where we meet up with the merchants travelling east. Otto was to have been our pathfinder through the forest.'

'There are maps here,' Elena said. 'It can't be that difficult.'

'Let's take our chances,' Alexei agreed.

'Not good enough,' Stefan said, firmly. 'I've known men who've set off into those forests armed with the best maps in the Empire. Those who didn't lose their lives usually lost their minds trying to find their way out of the Drakwald. At very best we'd lose time: days, weeks, probably.' He shook his head, firmly. 'We couldn't afford that. We need a guide. Someone who knows the ways of the woods.'

'Philip Alben,' Alexei offered. 'He was born and raised in the Drak. Knows his way about the forest as well as any man.'

'Then it's a pity he didn't know his way around a bar room brawl,' Bruno said, breaking his long silence. 'Alben was found floating in the dock with a knife in his back over a week ago.'

'Well,' Stefan demanded, 'Any other ideas?' He looked around at the three others in the room, waiting for an answer. 'In that case,' he said at last, 'I have just one. Not the man I would choose willingly. But the choices seem to have just run out.'

HE HAD FEW problems finding the address. Plenty of people knew the name, and had stories they could offer as well. None of them made Stefan feel any better about this. But, as he kept reminding himself, there wasn't a lot of choice.

After about half an hour's walk he found the house buried deep within a rundown part of the city. The street was strewn with refuse and rotting food, rats outnumbering the people going about their business. This, Stefan said to himself, is the last stop on the way down. A place where you come to die. Steeling himself against the stench wafting from the interior of the house, Stefan climbed the staircase towards the single room on the top floor of the tottering building. The door of the room lay half-open, and a stale reek of cheap liquor hung on the air.

Stefan's call met with no response, but it didn't take him long to find what he was looking for. The room was sparsely furnished – little more besides a table stacked with empty bottles, and a single, bare bed, grey with human grime. A man lay splayed across the bed, still fully clothed. Only the faint, laboured sound of breathing betrayed the fact that he wasn't dead.

Stefan fought back a wave of revulsion that almost had him turning straight back. No choice, he reminded himself yet again. He looked about the room and found what he was looking for, a pitcher half full with water. The water had a greasy scum covering its surface, with at least a dozen dead flies glued upon it. But it was cold, and would serve Stefan's purpose. He levelled the pitcher towards the bed, and slung the contents over the sleeper's face.

The man groaned, cursing an imaginary foe, and gradually came to sitting. A fit of coughing seized his body as his eyes opened and focused upon Stefan standing before him.

'Get up,' Stefan commanded, throwing a cloth in the direction of Tomas Murer. 'Everyone gets a last chance in this life,' he told him. 'This is yours.'

THEY MET AT Wilhelm's Gate, by the old toll road that skirted edge of the city. Bruno, hardly speaking, lost within a place known only to him. Tomas Murer, sober now, was shivering in the cold. Alexei Zucharov, eyeing the newcomer with obvious mistrust. And Stefan Kumansky, watching them all. These would be his comrades in the coming months, his companions through whatever adversity the fates chose to cast at them. Somehow, together, they had to see this through.

It was now an hour past sunset. Mannslieb and Morrslieb had taken their places in the sky above Altdorf, dappling its spires and turrets in a pale silver light. The night was clear and cold after the rain that had been falling over the city.

Horse-hooves clattered upon the cobblestones, approaching the abandoned tollgate. Elena Yevshenko emerged out of the darkness, a second rider on horseback following a few paces behind. Elena drew up next to Stefan, and nodded a brief acknowledgement.

'This is Lisette,' she announced, motioning the maid forward. The second rider threw back the hood of her gown, revealing delicate, almost elvish features. The girl had the olive-dark complexion of western Bretonnia, with dark curled hair and deep hazel eyes. It struck Stefan immediately how slightly built she was; small enough almost to be taken for a halfling. Lisette seemed to read Stefan's thoughts, and drew herself up in the saddle as if to accentuate her height.

Stefan found himself staring at the girl, not so much in curiosity, or even admiration – though she was undeniably pretty. What caused him to stare was a feeling uncomfortably close to recognition. He cast his mind back over the events of the last day, the faces glimpsed in crowds or upon the street.

'We've met before, I think,' he said. The girl's face flushed a sudden red. Lisette turned her head to one side, avoiding Stefan's inquisitive gaze. 'You're mistaken, sir,' she mumbled.

'I think not,' Stefan insisted. 'You were at the festival games last night, sitting not far from me. Earlier that day you were in the Altquartier, and then later in Hergeldstrasse, following the same path as me. It's either a remarkable coincidence, which I doubt, or else you were purposely following me. Why?'

The Bretonnian girl hesitated, caught between denial and a plausible explanation. The tense silence was broken by Elena. 'Because I told her to,' she snapped. 'Why not? For the last few weeks I've been a virtual prisoner in the palace. Why shouldn't I gain my own account of you and your comrades, from someone I can trust?' She glared at Stefan and the others, growing angrier as she became more defensive, then muttered a few words of reassurance to the girl in Bretonnian. The girl's face flushed, with embarrassment or relief. Sitting up next to her mistress she seemed an unlikely spy, and as docile in nature as Elena was fiery.

The explanation might have been innocent enough, but Stefan was furious that, again, Elena seemed to have gone out of her way to cross him. If she hadn't made it clear before that she was a reluctant companion, there was no mistaking her view now. For a relationship that would inevitably be close over the coming months and miles, this had been an ill-favoured start.

Alexei Zucharov pointed to the sky. 'The light's good,' he said. 'We should make full use of it while it lasts.'

'Agreed,' Stefan said. He looked back at Elena. 'We have a job to do, you and I,' he said. 'Let's put this behind us and get on with it.'

'Agreed,' Elena replied, somewhat stiffly. For a moment their eyes met. Stefan found himself wondering if their apparent differences didn't mask the fact that, on some level, they were very alike. Time alone would reveal the truth. 'Let's go,' he shouted to the others. Stefan took up the reins and spurred his horse onward, out of Altdorf, on the road that led to the east.

THEY RODE IN silence until the lights of Altdorf were a distant glimmering on the horizon behind them. By then the well-paved road had given way to one of loose stone, little more than a rough track beneath the horses' hooves. They had steered away from the road favoured by the traders, the highway that ran between Altdorf and Talabheim, and instead skirted east of the Talabec river on the rutted tracks winding north-east from the city.

Stefan was relieved to be on the road at last. For sure, danger lay ahead, but he was glad nonetheless to be putting Altdorf behind them. The years had seen him grow accustomed to the face of death, but Otto's murder had unsettled him, and left him feeling hollow inside.

Rarely had slaughter seemed so premeditated, so deliberate in its manner. He wondered at the meaning of it. That it was the work of cultists he was in no doubt, and the bloody insignia left at the scene seemed to signal it clearly as the work of the Scarandar. At first Stefan had reasoned that the murder was meant to serve as a warning, but, if so, to what end? If the idea had been to frighten Elena into abandoning her plan, then the ploy had failed. Indeed, Otto's death had hastened the urgency of their departure from Altdorf by several days.

And that was what was troubling him still. The forces that opposed them were not simple, nor stupid. Otto Brandauer's murder had been calculated; it had a purpose. And Stefan could not be sure that they were not even now fulfilling that purpose as they rode away from the city.

He marvelled at how empty the world had suddenly become, how desolate. He had rarely travelled this way from Altdorf, and never before by night. The darkness accentuated the sense of solitude enveloping them. Once clear of the city walls, the crowded, human bustle of Altdorf quickly became a distant memory. Here and there they passed clusters of houses, hamlets or small villages, but for the most part they were derelict and deserted. It was not what he had been expecting.

As the hours passed, however, he noticed that they were drawing closer to what looked like some kind of barrier lining the horizon ahead of them. Whatever it was gradually expanded until it filled their entire line of sight, like a wall wrapping itself around the world. No light seemed to escape from within it; it seemed darker even than the surrounding night. Gradually the conversation amongst the travellers died away as, each in turn, they became transfixed by the towering darkness rearing up in front of them.

'Gods watch over us,' Lisette whispered. 'We are riding into the very heart of it.'

'What is it?' Elena demanded. 'It looks so vast.'

Tomas kept his eyes trained on the dark expanse, like a hunter suddenly re-united with an ancient foe. 'It is the forest,' he said softly. 'The Drakwald.'

As one, the riders drew up their horses and sat, staring, at the unending vista unravelling ahead. Now, truly, the enormity of their journey began to hit home.

'Well,' Alexei said, breaking the silence at last. 'Welcome to the world beyond.'

The waxy light from the moons had ebbed over the last hour until, suddenly, it was gone. Now the darkness enveloping them was all but total.

Stefan contemplated the forest. It looked all but impenetrable, difficult even by daylight. Perhaps for now they should push their luck no further. 'This is as far as we go tonight,' he said. 'We won't tackle the Drakwald until dawn. That's still some five hours distant. We'll find somewhere to lay up for the night, get some rest.'

Lisette had already climbed down from her horse and was at the reins of Elena's, waiting to help her mistress dismount. Elena looked around at the bare moorland, the dark shoulder of the forest towering over them. She shivered.

'It's so dark,' she said. 'And I'd forgotten I could feel so cold!'

Alexei laughed. 'You've been too long from Kislev,' he observed.

'Anyway,' Stefan said, getting down from his own horse. 'We best all get used to it. There'll be plenty of nights like this.'

They tethered the horses near the river, and set about making camp beneath the shelter of some nearby trees. Once they'd done, Alexei produced a flask of Bretonnian gin. He offered it around, but got no takers. Finally he turned towards Tomas Murer, sitting apart from the rest of the group at the water's edge. Alexei held out the flask. 'You can't function without this stuff, can you?'

Tomas looked from Alexei to the leather flask being held in front of him. A look, part fear and part hunger passed over his features. He extended one hand, tentatively, then stopped, and shook his head. Stefan got up and snatched the flask away from Alexei.

'That's enough game playing,' he snapped. 'It's been a long day. And a difficult one,' he added, catching Elena's eye. 'We'd better all get some sleep whilst we can.'

'Maybe,' Alexei said. He reached out to retrieve the flask from Stefan's side. 'But I think I'll sit out and keep this gin company a while yet. I'll take first watch.'

Stefan gave him a searching look. 'Everything all right?' he asked, quietly.

Alexei grunted, non-committally. Stefan didn't mistake his tone for indifference. Zucharov might be strong-willed, and he was certainly unpredictable, but Stefan had learnt to respect his nose for trouble.

'It's probably all right,' Alexei said. He unfastened the stopper from the gin and took a slow swig. Stefan looked around, and listened. The only noise he could hear was the swirling water of the river nearby, a vaguely comforting sound.

'I think so too,' he said. 'I don't think anyone has followed us. In fact I don't think there's anyone but us for miles about.' He looked over at Tomas. 'What about you, Tom?' he asked. 'What do you reckon?'

'I think you're right,' Murer replied. He kept his eyes averted from Zucharov as he spoke, staring all the while down into the water. 'I think we'll be safe enough here for the moment.'

Alexei pulled the stopper from the flask. 'Well,' he said, contemptuously, 'that's all the reassurance we need, then.' He took another mouthful of gin.

'Let's get some sleep,' Stefan said again, firmly. 'Wake me in an hour,' he told Alexei.

Elena and Lisette were already bedding down upon the blanket, their cloaks wrapped tight around them against the cold. Bruno was standing at the edge of the camp, some way apart from the others. Stefan walked over to join him.

'How are you?' he asked.

'I'm fine,' Bruno said. 'Tired, that's all.'

'Then sleep,' Stefan advised. 'We'll need to be riding again as soon as the sun is up.'

'Of course,' Bruno said. As he turned away, Stefan caught his arm.

'Every man has the right to keep his own counsel,' he said. 'I respect that. But we have a long journey together, and a perilous one. Some time along that road we will need to talk of what's in our hearts.'

Bruno returned Stefan's gaze, his body stiff and uncomfortable. Then he smiled, briefly but warmly, rekindling a brief memory of the friendship that had sustained them on so many travels in the past. Stefan lay a hand upon his comrade's shoulder. 'Good night, old friend,' he said. 'Rest well.'

BRUNO WAITED UNTIL Stefan had joined the others already bedded down. Before long Stefan's breath had fallen into the slow steady rhythm of sleep. But sleep did not come so readily to Bruno. For what seemed to him like ages he lay awake, his eyes wide open, staring into the dark, empty night. It did not worry him unduly. Lately he had spent many nights awake until near the dawn, turning his thoughts over in his mind, unwilling to surrender himself to the mercies of sleep.

Bruno wrapped the blanket around him and turned his face towards the churning waters beyond the bank. He lay for what seemed an eternity, listening to the unending song of the river. Gradually his eyes fell closed.

Within moments his eyes were open again. Light – a bright, steel grey light – was dazzling him, reflecting off a sheer precipice that towered above. Confused, Bruno climbed to his feet and looked around him. Stefan and the others were nowhere to be seen. He could no longer hear the river. In fact the camp and the riverbank had disappeared completely. He was no longer on the road to Kislev, but somewhere else entirely.

He took a few hesitant steps forward, aware now of the massive white peaks filling the skies around him. Then he remembered where he was. He had returned to that place once again. His breath started coming in sharp, rapid gulps. Somehow the icy mountain air never seemed to fill his lungs. He needed more and more of it. He should stop and rest, but he knew he had to go on, knew he had to hurry. Bruno looked down and saw his sword fastened at his side, a short knife tucked inside the belt round his waist.

He started walking forward, towards the opening to the cave that sat like a black mouth on the white face of the mountain. He could hear voices, voices calling out in distress.

Bruno pulled the knife from his belt and hurried forward. Something was scaring him. He had been here before. He should turn away, go back. But he could not turn away. The voices calling needed his help. He could not abandon them.

'Hold on,' he heard himself say. 'Hold on. I'm coming.'

CHAPTER SEVEN
Betrayal

'EISENHOF,' ELENA SAID, turning her tongue slowly around the word, as if trying to get a sense of the place. 'Where in the name of Shallya is that?' It was, Stefan conceded, a fair question. A question to which he might have added, 'when will we get there?' or even, 'how do we know we are on course?' They had been travelling through the forest for nearly a month, a journey through a relentless maze of trees, living and dead. Now, as they sat resting for the first time that day, they could have been within a brief ride of their destination, or they could have been back at the point where they first entered the Drakwald. The landscape around them never changed, never varied other than in the dense pattern of the trees woven around them. It seemed to go on forever.

It could not be said that Stefan had underestimated the Drakwald. He had come to the forest with no prior assumptions for good or for ill. It had been a stranger to him, an alien land that must be traversed on a journey back to where his life had begun. For all that, the Drakwald had surprised, even shocked him. Few of his adventures, even upon the wooded foothills of the Grey Mountains, had prepared him

for a habitat like this. The forest was a place of perpetual twilight, where all life was locked inside an unending struggle
just to survive. Over the four weeks that they had travelled
into the forest, his ears had grown accustomed to the incessant sound of water dripping from the gnarled, light-starved
trees, just as his eyes had learnt to cope without the blessing
of light. Now and again, sunlight from above the canopy of
trees would break through, dappling the forest floor in a
spray of gold. When it did, it was a rare and unexpected gift
from the gods. Most of the time they journeyed through a
grey gloom, steering a wide path around the few fortified set-
tlements that would emerge suddenly from within clearings
in the trees. Roots and creepers tugged at the horses' feet;
paths beckoned wide and smooth ahead only to turn back
upon themselves or peter out into nothing. Progress had
been slow.

'I don't know exactly where Eisenhof is,' Stefan said,
answering Elena's question at last. 'But judging from the
chart that Otto left us, and–' he glanced at Murer – 'if our
navigation has stayed true, then it should be no more than a
day or two's ride north of where we are now. So long as we
can keep making steady progress.'

'Steady?' Elena asked, incredulous. 'You call the last four
weeks steady progress? I call it coming within a knife's blade
of being murdered – more than once. Not to mention the
horse we've already lost, the countless wrong roads, false
roads, blocked pathways and the eternal, stinking damp of
this place!' She stopped short, as though taken aback by her
own sudden outpouring of rage. 'I mean to say,' she went on,
'it's hardly been a steady journey, so far, has it?'

Stefan hesitated. His first instinct was to hit back at Elena.
He had long since come to tire of her carping and complaints. But it wasn't just her. It was all of them, himself
included. Tempers frayed easily out here in the forest, and
patience was quickly tested to its limit. So far, the attempts
upon their lives had been the least of their worries. They had
been attacked – three times in all – but it had been nothing
that they hadn't been able to handle. Bandits, grown used to
the rich pickings offered by the few merchants bold enough
to venture through, had assumed that Stefan and his company would be similarly easy meat. They had paid for that

mistake with their lives; at least a dozen had been put to the sword without the travellers coming to any serious harm.

It had been unnerving, perhaps, but Stefan knew he would have found it more unnerving if they had encountered no trouble at all. The forest-dwelling bandits had made an unpleasant spectacle – murderous men who placed little value upon human life. But none had borne any obvious taint of mutation, or betrayed any sign of being in thrall to a greater, darker power.

These had been the more predictable foes; the forest itself was proving to be a more testing enemy. It seemed to be possessed of an innate cunning of its own, luring the travellers down promising byways, paths that cut through the shortest route across the forest, only for those paths to lead nowhere, or, worse, arc backwards in a subtle, bewildering curve that left the traveller further back than when he had first set out. On top of that, the laming of their one spare horse, and the poisonous, milk-white mould that overnight had laid waste to a portion of their provisions, had been two further burdens that they could have done without. Nevertheless, they had been making progress. They were still on schedule for Eisenhof, near enough.

'We're doing fine,' he told Elena. 'We knew it was going to be hard when we set out.'

'We've had some bad luck, that's all,' Bruno commented, shivering from the morning chill. Zucharov shot him a questioning glance at the mention of luck, and his face briefly darkened. 'Luck?' he said at last. 'Wherever Eisenhof lies, it won't be Krankendorf. Warm beds, and plenty of beer. We could have been there more than a week ago. Now that would have been luck.'

'We could,' Stefan confirmed, sharply. 'But we were never going to go that way. Plenty of beer, plenty of prying eyes too. Otto warned us to stay well away from the trading road. We'd have been drawing too much attention to ourselves travelling through a place as big as Krankendorf. Otto will have arranged provisions for us at Eisenhof. We've got enough to see us there as long as we're careful.'

They had each found their own path as the journey had progressed, their own way of surviving the forest. Elena had mostly taken refuge in the company of her maid. Lisette had

proved the perfect foil for her intemperate mistress, always
there to soothe or calm. Much of their conversation was in
Bretonnian, further isolating them from the rest of the group.
But, if it was what Elena needed to get through, then Stefan
had no quarrel with that in the end.

Bruno's isolation was of another sort. He had worked at
least as hard as any of them, taken on more than his share of
late night watches, and, when the occasion demanded,
fought with his customary steel and skill. In that sense, his
contribution had been faultless. But that was just the outer
man: a shell. The Bruno inside the shell seemed to have disappeared, drifted away into a world every bit as cold and
lonely as the desolate forest itself. Stefan saw it in the
haunted look in his eyes, heard it in the tormented murmur-
ings of his sleep. Bruno had done everything that had been
asked of him. But, for all that, Stefan had asked himself if his
insistence on having Bruno with them wouldn't yet prove to
be his first mistake.

As for the others, Alexei clearly couldn't wait to be rid of
the suffocating Drakwald. At every resting point he would
prowl the forest like a caged bear, searching for a way clear of
the forest where none existed, urging his comrades to hurry
on with the journey. He was not, he had told them more than
once, a man for confined spaces. None of that affected the
way he wielded his sword; Alexei alone had accounted for six
of the dozen bandits slain.

Tomas Murer had done his job, so far at least. He had made
mistakes, sometimes leading them back towards the west,
rather than east, sometimes around in a complete circle. But,
by and large, the trickery of the forest itself bore most of the
blame for that. Tomas had done his best in difficult circum-
stances, and, so far as Stefan could tell, he had done it sober.
Certainly, since that first night he had continued to resist any
temptation that Alexei Zucharov put in his way, and Stefan
had never seen him take so much as a sip of anything
stronger than water.

Certainly, there had been times when Tomas had wandered
off alone, away into the enveloping woods. If asked for a reason, it would always be so that he could get his bearings for
the onward journey. He was rarely gone more than a few
minutes, and, if he was falling back into drinking while he

was away from the others, then it wasn't showing. Not yet, at least.

In any case, there were times when each of them craved time alone, even if only for a few moments. Even Lisette, who most of the time could not be prised from Elena's side, could be seen wandering apart from her mistress, immersed in thoughts of her own. It was a need that Stefan understood as well as anyone.

He stretched and climbed to his feet, working his limbs back into life. The dank air of the forest had a way of creeping into his bones so that he started to ache in almost every joint if he sat for more than a few minutes. Alexei was right; it was time they got underway once more. Time was now a luxury after the various setbacks of the last few weeks. They must waste no more of it. He walked over to where Elena was sitting, Lisette at her side. The little Bretonnian girl was busy working a comb through her mistress's hair, doing her best to ignore Elena's curses when the comb tugged against a knot. Elena snatched the comb away from her as Stefan approached, then gave Lisette a brief, forgiving kiss upon the cheek.

'The others are saddling up,' Stefan informed her. 'We need to be ready to leave in a few minutes.'

'That's fine,' Elena replied, her sarcasm only thinly veiled. 'I'm getting used to being ordered around.'

Stefan shrugged, turned to depart, and then stopped. He crouched down upon his knees so that he was face to face with Elena. 'Look,' he began, firmly. 'We've got a long way to go. A long time on the road together, you and I. I don't know exactly what it is that you've got against me, but, for both of our sakes, I think we'd better have it out now.'

Elena stared at him for a moment. It was clear that Stefan wasn't going to move until he had her response. She took a deep breath. 'Lisette,' she said. 'Go and make sure all our things are stowed ready to ride.' She exchanged glances with her maid. 'Don't rush.' Lisette made muttered excuses and got up, gathering her skirts beneath her.

Stefan sat down upon the mossy soil next to Elena, the two of them remaining a few feet apart. 'What is it, then?' he asked. 'You think I'm just a mercenary, in this for the money?'

Elena threw him an accusing glance. 'Well,' she said. 'Don't try and deny you're not being well paid for your services. I know the sums Otto had set aside for you.'

'I live by the sword, as all men must live by some means,' Stefan agreed. 'But I'll tell you what,' he said, with conviction, 'there are easier ways of earning money than this, with the sword or without.'

The briefest of smiles flickered over Elena's features. Her face softened just a little. 'Look,' she said, 'don't take it personally. It's not about you, not really.' She paused. 'It's just, well, I've always wanted to stand on my own two feet. I don't take very well to having my life ordered for me.'

'I can identify with that,' Stefan said.

'I'm sick of being preached at the whole time. My father was always excelling at that.'

'Was? Is he–'

'Dead? I've no idea,' she said, quietly. 'The last I heard of him, he was alive and well, living in Couronne, or some such place.' Underneath the off-hand tone, there was something bruised, very fragile in her voice. 'You see,' she said, 'he was one of the ones they don't tell heroes' tales about. When things started to get bad in Erengrad he had a choice: stay and stand his ground, fight for what he believed in, or get out. My father discovered he wasn't cut out to be such a hero after all. So he chose to get out. I haven't seen or heard from him since.'

'I'm sorry,' Stefan replied. He looked towards Elena, but she kept her face turned away from him.

'What about you?' she said at last. 'Your family, I mean.'

'I have a brother, Mikhal, back in Altdorf.' Stefan said. 'My parents are buried in Kislev. My father made the other choice, I suppose. He defended his home, fought for his village to the last. It cost him his life.'

'What's its name?' Elena asked. 'The village you came from?'

'It doesn't have a name any more,' Stefan said, shaking his head. 'It's a place that no longer exists.' They sat side by side for a while, not moving or talking. The anger had been washed away, replaced by a shared sense of loss.

'We must look to the future now,' Stefan continued at last. 'Think of what lies ahead for us. This priest, in Middenheim, for example. What of him? Do you know him?'

'I only know his name – Father Andreas. And Otto forbade me to mention even that to anyone but you. I know too that he is one of the very few men who could be entrusted with the third part of the Star.'

'Then Andreas must also be one of the Keepers of the Flame,' Stefan surmised. 'Let's hope that the Scarandar don't find him before we do.' He stood up. 'We'd best make ready to strike camp,' he said, quietly. 'We really do need to–'

'To move on,' Elena said. 'Yes, I know. You are absolutely right.'

Both turned at the sound of footsteps approaching through the damp undergrowth. Stefan looked around, expecting to see Lisette returning, but it was Bruno, with Tomas Murer following close behind.

From the expressions on their faces, Stefan could see at once that something was wrong.

'What is it?' he demanded, getting to his feet at once. Bruno shook his head, perplexed. 'It's the provisions,' he said. 'The water, I mean.'

'What's the matter with the water?'

'Four of the dozen remaining skins have split,' Tomas mumbled. Stefan stared at him in momentary disbelief. 'What do you mean, split?'

'Split or cut open,' Bruno clarified. 'I found it just now.'

'How much water has been lost?' Stefan demanded. This was the one commodity they could not do without.

'All of it,' Bruno said. 'Every drop. All we have is what's left in the last eight skins.'

All of them, Alexei included, were gathered around by now. Stefan looked around the group, facing each of them in turn. 'Who knows anything about this?' he said. 'Who was last near the horses?'

None of the others replied, but Alexei fixed Tomas with a murderous stare. He'd gladly put a noose about his neck, Stefan realised. But there's no more evidence against him than there is against me, or Alexei himself, for that matter.

'Could this be an accident?' he said to Bruno. 'Could this be anything other than deliberate?'

Bruno shrugged. 'I don't know. It's a clean tear through each of the skins. But they were all full. Maybe the pressure inside–'

'It's no accident,' Alexei said, sourly. 'No more than half the other troubles that have befallen us.' He turned, and glared at Tomas once again. 'No accident,' he repeated.

Of one thing Stefan was sure. He wasn't going to be pushed into making any hasty judgements, and now wasn't the time for an inquest. More pressingly, they would need water. Their supplies had been measured to get them as far as Eisenhof, and no further. Now they would need to replenish along the way.

'We'll get to the truth of this in due course,' he said, gravely. 'For the moment we need a new supply of water. Any ideas?'

'I wouldn't take any of the water from here about,' Bruno said. 'Too much of a risk.'

'What about the river?' Lisette suggested. 'The water there must be as fresh as we will find.'

'Yes,' Elena said, picking up on the idea. 'the Talabec will be our salvation. It skirts the forest, doesn't it?'

Stefan turned to Tomas Murer. 'Well?' he asked, 'What about it?'

Tomas looked doubtful. 'No,' he said at last, 'it's too far. The river lies right on the far side of the forest. Probably a week's journey in itself.'

'Then what do you suggest?' Elena said, petulantly. 'We just go without?'

Tomas looked around. Stefan noticed the faintest of tremors in both his hands as he stood before them. 'There are places, in the forest,' he replied. 'Hidden wells, that draw their water from the underground streams that flow beneath the Drakwald. Hunters use them, those that know where to look. If we're where I think we are, then there's one no more than half a day's ride from here.'

Stefan looked at Bruno. 'What do you think?'

'I'd say we have little alternative,' Bruno said. 'The river is too far, and we'll never make Eisenhof with what we've got left.'

'Very well then.' Stefan said. 'That's decided. We'll find this well and then hope we can make up time to Eisenhof. Let's get on with it.'

Alexei waited until Stefan and Bruno had turned to follow the two women back to the horses. He caught hold of Tomas Murer, and pulled him back.

'You might fool the others with your poor-drunk-on-the-mend act,' he said, quietly. 'But you don't fool me.' Tomas paled, and started to protest. Alexei pressed the palm of his hand hard against his face.

'Just listen to me,' he said. 'I don't believe in coincidences, I don't believe in chance. I didn't believe it that night back in Altdorf, and I haven't believed it since.' He pulled his knife from his belt, and brandished it in front of Murer's face. 'I'll be watching you,' he promised Tomas. 'Watching you like a hawk. Don't believe for a moment I won't slit your throat as clean as those waterskins, if you give me the slightest excuse.' He put the knife back and shoved Tomas forward, pushing him on towards the waiting horses.

'We're coming,' he called out to the others. 'Just having a friendly word before we get underway.'

IF THE PACE along the road was slow before, it now fell slower still as the travellers set off in search of the well buried deep within the forest. In places the path beneath the horses' hooves disappeared altogether, as the riders navigated their mounts through a blanket of matted creeper that rose to the height of their feet in the stirrups. Tomas had them frequently stop so that he could check or replot their direction.

'How can he tell one path from the other in this infernal tangle of weeds?' Bruno asked, incredulous. Stefan pointed up towards where the sun was struggling to break through the canopy of leaves overhead. 'He's navigating by the sun,' he told Bruno. 'What remains of it. Taal help us if we don't find this well by the time it starts to set.'

Tomas's estimate had been three hours. They had passed that point a full hour previously, with still no sign of the well in sight. Then, just as the forest seemed to be drawing in even more tightly around them, the horses broke through into what looked like a small clearing in the trees. Tomas dismounted smartly and walked to the centre of the clearing where branches had been cut and laid down across the floor of the forest. He bent down upon his knees then turned back towards the others.

'This is it,' he told them. 'Help me, please.'

Bruno jumped down from his horse and began helping Tomas lift the branches clear. Stefan dismounted more slowly, taking a long and careful look at the surroundings as he climbed from the saddle. 'Stay mounted,' he told Alexei. 'It looks all right, but looks are often deceptive out here.' Alexei nodded, drew out his sword, and laid it resting beneath his hand on the saddle in front of him.

It took a few minutes for the two men to clear away the covering of branches. If they had been deliberately placed, then they proved an effective camouflage. At last they had cleared away the last of it, and Stefan saw Tomas reach down into what looked like a small pit in the forest floor, and grip hold of something buried there. He struggled for a few moments, cursing as he worked. Then, suddenly, he fell back, pulling a silt-encrusted iron plate with him. He clambered back on to his feet and held the rusted object up like a trophy for the others to see.

Bruno peered down into the pit and signalled back to Stefan and Alexei.

'He was right,' he shouted back. 'There's water here, about ten feet down. Smells clean, and fresh too.'

'What luck,' Alexei commented, quietly. 'Let's not tarry here too long,' he counselled.

'All right,' Stefan said, motioning to the two women. 'We'll drink what we need while we're here then gather enough to refill all the remaining water skins. I agree with Alexei. We don't want to be hanging around here any longer than we need to.'

He approached the edge of the well, ready to test the first cupful that Tomas drew out. As he knelt down, he was aware of something moving directly above him, something dropping down on top of him from one of the trees overhead. Pure reflex made Stefan roll to one side, out of the path of the falling object.

At first he took it to be part of the tree itself falling, so alike in shape and colour did it seem to be. But in the split second that the object dropped through the air it changed, so that by the time it hit the floor of the forest, still upright, it had taken on the shape of a man.

In that same fractured moment, as Stefan reached for his sword, he saw more figures dropping out of the trees on every side. The forest was suddenly filled with the screams of creatures that sounded barely human, and the air was a blur of rainbow colours as dull browns and greens burst into new lurid colours all around them.

The creature made a lunge at Stefan, determined not to miss its target a second time. Stefan still hadn't decided whether the garish creature bearing down on him was man or beast, but he knew it meant to kill him. It raked at Stefan's face with claw-like hands, but in its haste to attack got too close. Stefan swerved away from the blow and jabbed at the creature's body with his sword. Barely had the first attacker fallen when a second was upon him. This one was more clearly a man, yet its limbs were almost twice their natural length. This attacker brandished a knife in one gnarled hand, and he was no less reckless in pursuing Stefan than his predecessor had been. Yet again, Stefan exploited his attacker's animal aggression to his own advantage, dodging the thrusts from the knife until he could land a single, telling blow with his sword. The blade caught the painted man just below the neck and sliced open his chest. A gout of crimson blood spouted from the wound as the man fell forwards, screaming, into the undergrowth.

At last Stefan had a moment to look around. Their attackers had outnumbered them by at least two to one at the outset, but those odds were being rapidly narrowed. Three more of the vivid-hued monsters lay dead upon the ground, slain, Stefan supposed, by Bruno and Tomas. Alexei was setting about a further two of the creatures in a fury, and Elena, too, seemed intent on making her mark. As Stefan watched, she ran one of the attackers through with her sword, killing the creature with a single stroke.

Two of the remaining creatures moved in on Elena, feathered chameleons that shimmered in rainbow colours as they attacked. Stefan pushed his way between the mutants, scything through the torso of one with his sword before turning to face the other. Before he had time to aim a second blow the creature toppled face-first in front of him, felled by a thunderous blow to the neck from Alexei Zucharov.

The attack ended as unexpectedly as it had begun. Suddenly, as if on a signal, the creatures pulled away and retreated back into the cover of the forest. The bright reds and yellows daubed upon their bodies faded back to dull grey and ochre, quickly making them invisible. Even those that lay slain upon the ground began to disappear, their bodies seeming to rot away where they lay, melting into the loamy soil until they literally became one with the forest.

The travellers took stock of their wounds. Most had collected scratches or grazes where the creatures had managed to connect with talons or knives, but none was seriously wounded.

Alexei Zucharov had acquired a cut that ran the length of his left forearm, but he shrugged the wound off as nothing more than an irritation. He seemed more concerned that the creatures had managed to retreat before he could kill more of them. Stefan, too, was unhappy that at least half of the attackers had got away, but he was relieved they themselves had survived intact.

'Who in Sigmar's name were they?' Bruno asked. 'Who, or maybe what?'

'What indeed?' Stefan echoed. This, for sure, had been no simple bandit raid. Whatever the creatures were, their motive had been to kill, not to rob.

'Changelings, chameleons, whatever you want to call them,' Bruno went on. 'Those were mutants.'

Stefan nodded. There was little doubt of that. 'Mutants,' he agreed. 'Creatures of Tzeentch.'

Elena stepped forward. Her dress was torn and bloodied, but she seemed to have survived the encounter without a cut. Lisette was similarly unscathed, but she looked utterly petrified by her experience, and she clung to Elena as a child might clutch at its doll.

'Do you think they were guarding the well?' Elena asked, voicing the question in Stefan's mind. 'Do you think they were just lying in wait in those trees, ready to attack whoever came to drink from it?'

'I suppose it's possible,' Bruno said. 'Possible that it's just–'

'Another coincidence?' Alexei interrupted. He looked fired with rage: still pumped full of energy after the battle. And there seemed little doubt where he was going to direct his energy next. 'No,' he said. 'We've had far too many "coincidences" already. We were led into a trap.'

Tomas took one look at Zucharov, and quickly read his intention. He turned to flee, but there was never any chance that he was going to outrun the younger, bigger man.

Zucharov brought him to the ground, pinned him there, and held a balled fist above Tom Murer's terrified face.

'Give me one reason why I shouldn't finish you off now, you bastard,' he spat. He raised the fist ready to strike.

'I'll give you a reason,' Stefan said. He stepped in and caught hold of Alexei's arm. It was like trying to hold back a mighty hammer, but he managed to keep Alexei from smashing the blow down into Tomas Murer's face. Alexei turned towards Stefan, his eyes burning with anger. 'Come on!' he shouted at Stefan. 'We'd be better off rid of him. What murderous trap is he going to lead us into next?'

'It doesn't look good, Tom,' Stefan said. 'You led us here, and they were waiting for us. What's your explanation for that?'

Tomas looked from Stefan to Alexei, in clear fear of his life. 'I don't have an explanation, Stefan. I just did my best to find the well for us, that's all, I swear it.'

'Well, someone told them where we were going to be,' Alexei said, his voice quieter now, but no less venomous. 'And right now, you're the obvious choice.' He turned to Stefan again. 'We can't take the risk of letting him go,' he said. 'We have to kill him.'

Stefan knew there was truth in what he said. Until now, he had been prepared to give Tomas the benefit of the doubt. But Alexei was right: this was one misfortune too many, and Tomas Murer was the most likely culprit. It was rarely in his heart to kill a man on no more than a suspicion, but he wondered now if they had any choice.

He looked up at Elena, who seemed at once to read what was going through his mind. 'You're not going to kill him?' she asked, incredulous. 'On what evidence? Just a suspicion? By the gods, you're no better than the so-called evil we've set ourselves against.'

'Well,' Stefan said, 'have you a better idea?'

Elena thought for a moment. Tomas fixed her with a pleading stare, realising that this might be his only hope. 'Yes,' Elena said at last. 'I do have a better idea. Let him still ride with us. We can keep him under guard if you like – we should be capable of that much between us. Let him ride – we still need a guide for the forest. Let us take him with us to Middenheim, and there the priest can judge his soul. Then if he's found wanting…' She let the words tail off, but there was no mistaking the meaning.

Stefan turned to Bruno. 'What do you think?'

Bruno shrugged: 'There's justice in that, one way or another.' He lifted a cup to his lips, and took a small sip of the water drawn from the well. 'There's no trickery with this,' he said. 'The water's pure.'

Stefan nodded. His heart felt lighter. 'What about you, Alexei?'

'I say kill him and be done,' Alexei said. 'It's a risk to do otherwise.'

'All life is risk,' Stefan countered. 'And Elena is right; if we kill without justice we start to become that which we would destroy. Over time, we destroy ourselves.'

Alexei grunted, with little satisfaction, but released his grip on the other man. 'Consider your judgement postponed,' he said to Tomas. 'But not indefinitely.'

Stefan looked for Elena again, but she had already begun walking back towards the horses. Something there at the edge of the clearing had drawn her attention. Stefan watched her move amongst the tethered animals, then give a sharp cry that sounded like anguish or despair.

As one, Stefan and Bruno ran towards her. It quickly became obvious what was wrong. The saddlebags had been stripped from the horses' backs. Most of their provisions were gone; what little remained lay strewn over the ground, trodden into the sodden earth. They had been carrying enough food for another week's journey. Now they would be lucky if they had enough left to see them through until dawn.

For a moment the travellers could only stand, staring at what might prove to be the utter destruction of their hopes. Finally Elena bent down, and, with Lisette's help, began gathering together what remained of the bread, fruits and pouches of salted meat.

'Maybe it'll be all right,' she said, quietly. 'Maybe we can survive living off the land.'

'Forget that,' Alexei said, sourly. 'If you were lucky enough to find anything to eat out here it'd as like as not poison you.'

'Is that right?' Stefan demanded of Tomas Murer. 'Is there no chance of surviving off what we can find in the forest?'

'It's true,' Tomas said. 'There's hardly a thing that lives or grows in the Drakwald that a man could eat.' His voice sounded hoarse, weak. 'Stefan, I swear, I had no idea this was going to happen.'

First the water, now the food. Stefan was finding it harder by the moment to resist the thought that they were being conspired against.

'Well, somebody did,' he muttered. He gathered up the reins of his horse, and pulled himself up in the saddle. 'One thing's for sure, now,' he told the others, tersely. 'We can forget about reaching Eisenhof. We need to find food and water, and we need to find it soon.' He pulled his horse around, hoping the gods would grant him direction. 'We're going to have to take our chances now.'

CHAPTER EIGHT
Enemy Within

PETR ILLYICH KURAGIN gazed down upon the map of the Old World spread before him, and sighed. The map was recent; two or three years old at most. As was customary, the map had the land of Kislev set at its centre, its borders drawn in strong black lines, solid and secure. The names of the great cities – Kislev, mighty Praag and Erengrad itself, stood out in rich, tooled script, proud and impregnable. He found himself wondering how much longer that the Kislev of the map would exist.

It would survive at least as a memory, as a place in his mind, so long as he survived, he supposed. How long would that be for? The Kuragin mansion, set high upon the hill overlooking the heart of Erengrad, was fortified and well guarded. For now, it seemed he was secure enough. Erengrad itself was another matter.

He stood up, and gazed for a moment at his reflection in the mirror. What he saw did not greatly comfort him. The face staring back at him had grown fat with good living over the years. Now deprivation was leeching it thin. His skin had begun to droop down in folds around his face, leaving it like a crumpled, empty sack. He grimaced, scraping his thinning hair back from his face. In a few weeks he'd have taken on the look of a cadaver.

'You're getting old,' he said to himself, quietly. 'Old and tired. Tired of this miserable struggle.'

Wearily, he returned to the map and located the foreign city that lay far to the west of Kislev. He stared at the name: Altdorf. He tried to visualise the place, struggled to fill the city of his imagining with colour and life. No images came. It hardly mattered. He doubted he would ever go there. Perhaps he would never set foot beyond Erengrad again, not in this life.

He placed a battered locket on the map next to the point where Altdorf was marked. He opened the locket, as he had done often in the last few weeks. The face of a young girl stared confidently out at him. What would she look like now? Try as he might, he could make no connection between the portrait and the living, breathing woman he had pledged union with.

Apparently they had been introduced once – he a young knight, Elena Yevschenko barely more than a child. Had he been able to see into the future, might he have said to her at that first meeting, 'One day we shall be wed'? She probably wouldn't have believed it then. He wasn't sure he believed it now. Altdorf was a lifetime away. Who knew if the first daughter of the House of Yevschenko was really on her way back to Erengrad? And, even if she was, what difference would it make? He feared that Erengrad was dying, that their efforts to save it would prove too little, too late. The alliance between their two once-great families – and the restoration of the city – had rarely seemed less probable.

'One day we shall be wed, and Erengrad will be saved.' He laughed, but with bitterness, as he spoke the words out loud. Now that time was running short, it seemed like clutching at a last desperate straw. A straw that had nonetheless come to stand for Erengrad's last hope.

He walked out upon the walled ramparts of the Kuragin mansion and looked down upon the city. Like a nobleman brought low by ill luck, Erengrad retained its grandeur, but the scars of strife were unmistakable.

From high upon the battlements, Petr Illyich Kuragin could look out beyond the tall granite walls that encircled the city. Those walls still held firm. The forces of darkness had learned how difficult it was to break a city from without. Not even the might and sorcery of Chaos had been enough to breach the fortress at Praag. The dark ones knew that force alone would not suffice. They had suffered the wounds of Praag, and learned from them.

This time, it had been different. Instead of battering against its walls, Chaos had curled itself around the very heart of Erengrad, tightening around it like an invisible serpent. A blight had taken hold of the city, within and without. Crops had failed; food had rotted and decayed where it lay in store. Strife and discord had displaced unity and peace. While the rulers of Erengrad set against each other in their petty squabble, the people had begun to sicken, and to die.

Petr Kuragin looked down into the sprawling mass of city streets below. Dotted here and there, he saw several grey bundles of rags that had not been there the night before. The sight was becoming so commonplace that it was an effort to remember that these were once people, men and women with homes and families, lives cut short by famine, sickness or bitter feud. This was where the real battle of Erengrad was being fought. The people were starving for food and starved of leadership, pitted against each other like dogs as, day by day, the life of the city leaked away. All the time the serpent lay in wait, tightening its coiled grip, whispering lies into the ears of the weak and the needy, words that would turn brother against brother, family against family. This was a hidden war of attrition, and it was a war that his city was losing.

He tugged the chain around his neck free of his tunic and gazed at the dull silver icon. At times like this it seemed laughable to believe that this – this and some giggling schoolgirl he could barely remember – could possibly turn the tide of darkness threatening to engulf his city, his land. But he had to hope, and he had to believe, for without that belief, there would be nothing left. He bent his head and placed a kiss upon the Star in a moment of silent prayer.

He felt a touch, light upon his shoulder. He turned to find his manservant standing before him. He shook himself out of his reverie.

'I'm sorry, Dimitri, have you been there long?'

The old man bowed his head in deference. 'I didn't want to disturb your thoughts, highness, but there's someone here to see you.'

'Someone?' Petr felt his heart take an absurd leap of hope for a few moments before he realised, from the look upon Dimitri's face, that this visitor was not the bearer of good tidings.

'A visitor,' he said, more soberly. Dimitri inclined his head. 'It is Count Vladimir Rosporov,' he went on, without emotion. 'He begs that you might spare him a few minutes for an audience.'

Count Rosporov. Kuragin had no doubt that he had come bearing the fruits of temptation as his offering. If that was so, then he would get the same short answer he had received on each of his previous visits. Petr Illyich would gladly have thrown Rosporov bodily from the ramparts and let the wild dogs feed on his carcass. Such was the parlous state of politics in Erengrad now, however, that he knew he had little choice but to receive him.

'Show him in,' he said, curtly. Dimitri nodded and turned to go.

'Oh, and Dimitri–' the old man paused in mid-step, waiting. 'I was just noticing–' Petr Illyich went on. 'You're looking so thin these days. Are you still managing to get enough to eat? Surely we have enough food in store?'

Dimitri smiled, sadly, at his master. 'I wasn't going to mention it, sir,' he said. 'But you've grown more than a little thin yourself these past few weeks.'

His master nodded. 'It'll do none of us any harm,' he said. 'No doubt we've all been allowing ourselves to grow too fat in the good years, eh?'

'No doubt, highness,' Dimitri replied. The old man looked kindly upon his master, but the same sad look still burned in his eyes. 'Shall I show the gentleman in now?'

Petr Illyich Kuragin swallowed hard upon his pride and his hope. 'Yes,' he said. 'Show him in.'

DEEP WITHIN THE cold, dead realm of Kyros, Varik bowed his head in the familiar posture of submission.

At length, his master chose to address him.

'Erengrad has still not fallen. The Star is still not in our possession. What news do you bring me that offers better tidings?'

The emissary took a deep breath. Familiarity with his position had not lessened the terror he still felt each time he submitted to the mercy of the Dark Lord. Kyros was known for many things, but pity was not one of them. On a whim he could inflict pain upon a disciple every bit as cruel and excruciating as the punishment meted out to his enemies. Pain that, though it lasted but a few seconds, would be experienced by the sufferer as an eternity of torture. The emissary prayed that his master was not in one such mood this day.

'We do not have the Star, yet,' he conceded, weighting his words carefully. 'But each day draws us closer to the place where it may be found.'

The blackness enfolding him deepened. The temperature in the chamber crept down further. The emissary shivered involuntarily as he sensed the presence of Kyros move closer. 'The Kislevite woman continues to travel east,' he said, 'towards the cursed citadel of Middenheim. There a priest waits for her. He is the second guardian of the Star. But my servant will ensure that the icon is delivered to us.'

'Is this your strategy, then?' the Chaos lord asked. 'To let this woman and her followers roam freely until a time of your choosing?'

Varik paused. He knew the importance of the answer his master sought of him. 'I do not presume to make such choices,' he replied. 'My strategy is to honour the divine majesty of the greater god. As for freedom, that is only illusion. The Kislevite and her people are mere puppets. Puppets that may dance only so long as your pleasure allows. They may be crushed at your will, like insects.'

'That is as it should be,' Kyros affirmed. 'Almighty Tzeentch shall decree when the icon shall be given over. Until then you must be certain that the Kislevite and her mercenaries have no knowledge of the identity of your servant amongst them.'

'They are masked from the eyes of the Kislevite,' Varik said. 'Not even our minion itself fully glimpses what lies within its soul.'

He hesitated. 'However, all things are transitory. We may not be able to rely upon them for much longer.'

'Once the segment is secure that will not matter,' Kyros replied. 'Once we have the two parts of the Star your servant may be destroyed. We will have no further use of him, nor of the Kislevite and her familiars.'

The emissary bowed lower. 'It will be done, magnificence,' he promised.

Kyros's voice took on a harsher tone. 'This in itself is not the end,' he reminded Varik. 'Until we have all three parts in our possession the Star is worthless metal. What of the third and final part?' he demanded.

'It still rests with the Warlord of Erengrad,' the Emissary assured him. 'Petr Illyich Kuragin is a proud, stubborn man. But he is only mortal. He has neither the strength nor the will to resist us indefinitely. Soon, either by persuasion or by force, he will capitulate.'

The emissary looked up, cautiously. He hoped his words had found favour. He could still see nothing of Kyros in the darkness, but the cold prickling running the length of his spine told him that the presence of the Dark Lord was very close indeed.

'Varik,' Kyros said. The emissary sat bolt upright in shock, so rare was it for his lord to address him directly by that name.

'Magnificence?' he asked, unable to suppress the tremor in his voice.

'Winning Erengrad is all to me,' Kyros told him. 'If you are the instrument of that conquest you shall be richly rewarded.'

The emissary bowed until his forehead touched the cold ground. 'You are all-bountiful, magnificence,' he whispered. He tried to move his head and found it weighed down by an irresistible force, as though a shield carved from lead had been laid across it.

'But fail me in this,' Kyros continued, 'and you will beg Morr in vain to free your soul from torment.'

The force bearing down on him intensified until, suddenly, it was gone. The emissary raised his head, and a pale light infused the surroundings of the chamber.

The emissary clambered to his feet, and retreated, backwards, from the room. 'I devote my soul to your service,' he muttered, humbly. 'I shall never fail you.'

* * *

THEY HAD TRAVELLED on, deep into the dark interior of the Drakwald, hope and despair riding with them as equal companions. Since leaving the site of the well there had been no further sign of the mutants; they had been able to progress unhindered by anything other than the now-familiar obstacles of the forest. But, as what daylight remained began to give way to dusk, Stefan began to question whether they would ever come across the settlement hidden within the woods.

Otto's map referred to it only as 'Jaegersfort' – a small, well-fortified encampment where hunters could take refuge from the perils of the forest. A hand-written note confirmed the position of the settlement upon the map was no more than approximate – it was a place that featured on no known trading route, one that few outside the forest would ever visit. There was no way of telling for sure what kind of reception they would find at Jaegersfort, or whether there would be food and water there. More to the point, there was no way of telling whether they were going to locate their destination before night fell. In fact, there was nothing to tell Stefan whether it truly existed at all.

As the hours had worn on through the day, spirits amongst the travellers had begun to ebb. Surviving the ambush would count for little if they were now to perish from cold and hunger in the unforgiving, dark heart of the forest.

Now, suddenly, where before there had only been the steadily deepening hues of the dying day, there were lights. No more than half a dozen in number, barely enough to penetrate through the gloom, but it was undoubtedly the glow of lanterns that they could see.

'Jaegersfort?' Bruno asked.

'I don't see what else it could be,' Stefan replied. 'Let's get a bit closer. Take it steady.'

The travellers dismounted and walked their horses toward the source of the light, careful to keep sound of their approach to a minimum. The settlement was indeed small – little bigger than a trading post – and bounded on all sides by a stockade built from the trunks of trees. As far as they could see, there was just a single point of entry – a door cut into the timber wall, with a narrow slit through which to observe the outside world. A wide trench had been dug around the outer edge of the wall, presumably to deter intruders. And, atop of the wall, mounted on iron spikes driven into the wood, a further reminder for those still inclined to try their luck.

Alexei stared up at the line of severed heads, most of them rotted beyond all recognition, and smiled.

'Fond of their privacy, I reckon,' he murmured.

'So would you be, if you had to survive out here,' Stefan replied.

'Either way,' Bruno said, 'It doesn't look as if they'll be extending much of a welcome to the likes of us.'

Alexei turned to Stefan. 'What do you think?' he asked. He drew out his sword. 'Shall we talk our way in with this?'

'I doubt that's going to work,' Stefan said, appraising the size of the task facing them. 'The place is built to keep worse than us out. We'll need to try and convince them we mean no ill.' He looked around at the faces grouped behind him. All of them looked tired, hungry – and desperate.

'There's no guarantee that they won't try and cut us down as soon as we get within range,' he said. 'Any volunteers?'

The reply, when it came, was softly voiced, and from the least likely quarter.

'Yes,' Lisette said, quietly, 'I'll go.'

PETR KURAGIN HEARD the door to the room open. A face appeared, reflected in the mirror in front of him. Kuragin slowly turned to confront his visitor.

Count Vladimir Rosporov held out a hand in greeting, exposing his right arm, withered and leeched pale by past disease. Rosporov smiled. It was a smile equally without warmth or malice, but it spoke of the confidence of one who knows his victory is close at hand.

'My dear Kuragin,' Rosporov began. 'I do declare you've been starving yourself. A man in your position really should set a better example to his people.'

'The city's starving,' Kuragin replied. 'The crops have all failed. What's left in the storerooms is blighted or rotting. Or perhaps you hadn't noticed.'

Rosporov bowed deferentially. 'You should have said before,' he murmured. 'If I'd known you were in difficulties I would have arranged for provisions to be sent over.' He flexed the smile again. 'You know, even in these times of hardship, little luxuries can be found.'

'Don't bother,' Kuragin replied, curtly. 'I'd rather we just got to the nub of your business, if it's all the same to you.'

'Please,' the count insisted. 'Let us call it *our* business.' He indicated a chair. 'May I?'

Count Vladimir Rosporov took a seat and settled himself upon it. He was dressed carefully, as befitted a champion of the people. His clothes were clean and tolerably well cut, but drab in colour and shorn of frills. He wore his hair cropped short and his beard neatly trimmed. His appearance suggested a modest man possessed of a sober soul. A man who had shrugged off his noble birth to take up the common cause. It was, Petr Illyich had to admit, a good disguise. Good enough for the people to have started following the self-styled 'Preacher of Reconciliation' in ever-growing numbers. Good enough for the head of the House of Kuragin to be obliged to grant him audience, however distasteful that felt. Good enough for Petr Illyich Kuragin to have grown increasingly fearful for the future of his city.

'Tell me, Petr Illyich, what is it you hope for the people of Erengrad?'

'I hope that they may yet prosper and prevail,' Kuragin replied, his voice unwavering. 'And that they find common cause against the pestilence that afflicts us all.'

Rosporov smiled, as though amused by Kuragin's response. 'Quite so,' he said. 'But what if the common cause turns out not to be that which you champion?' he asked. 'What if the plague you speak of is, in fact, none other than the crippling alliance with an Empire which has leeched Kislev dry for generations?'

Petr Illyich laughed, sardonically. 'Don't waste your seditious speeches on me, Rosporov. Your words may play well with the confused, with the weak. With those brought so low that they begin to lose their reason. But not here, not now, not ever!'

Rosporov rose from his chair and went to the window. The streets were quiet for the moment, the loudest noise from below the howling of the wild dogs, a sound that had become almost incessant over the past days. 'Do you know,' he said, 'I heard it said the other day that people in Erengrad will soon be dying faster than they can be buried. Do you think that can possibly be right?'

'And whose fault would that be?' Kuragin demanded. Politics or not, he would have this wretch thrown out.

'You live in the past,' Rosporov snapped, his mask of civility slipping momentarily. 'You and your family, wedded to your wealth and your cosy alliance with your parasitic "protector".' He glared at Kuragin. 'You talk of those weak of mind. You talk of the goodness of the alliance, and the "evil" of Chaos.' The count paused, and took a breath. His voice regained its measured, reasoning tone.

'Do you know how some speak of Chaos, my friend? They say that, far from being evil, Chaos is the eternal, the life-force of the universe. It is the force of change and renewal, the hub upon which the wheel of all existence turns. Resisting it is like the twig in the river resisting the force of the tides.'

'You could be burned alive for that heresy!' Kuragin thundered.

Count Rosporov resumed his seat and smiled deferentially towards his host. 'These are not my words,' he countered, mildly. 'I only report what I hear. I presume to represent no one but the good people of Erengrad,' he said, humbly. 'And I ask only that you consider the whole picture, without prejudice, before you condemn them to a continuation of this slow death.'

Kuragin swore under his breath. How far had the serpent spread its honeyed venom through the city? How many good men, brought low by hunger and fatigue, had had their minds turned against the truth? And how would the tide be turned?

'You didn't come here to talk politics,' he snapped. 'And you're wasting your time if you have. What do you want?'

'I come to make you an offer,' the count said simply. 'Or rather, to repeat an offer already made. You have something I am interested in acquiring.'

'The Star of Erengrad is not for sale,' Kuragin told him. 'Even if it were, do you think I'd be insane enough to sell it to you?'

'Why not?' the count replied, sanguinely. 'After all, the single piece you own is worthless in its own right.'

'And equally worthless to you,' Kuragin retorted, angrily. 'So why the continued interest?'

'I have friends,' Rosporov continued. 'Connoisseurs, if you like: collectors. They are confident of acquiring the first and second segments. They will need only your single piece for the Star to be complete.'

'Get out,' Kuragin spat, his patience finally exhausted.

The count stood, and gathered his cloak around him. 'I am able to offer you enough gold to make you a very rich man,' he said matter-of-factly. 'With it you could escape the city and make for yourself whatever life you wanted in the world beyond Erengrad.' He paused and stared coldly at Kuragin. 'Or you can choose to sit here and wait until the walls of the Kuragin mansion are reduced to rubble, and your miserable icon is plundered from your rotting corpse. I thought you were a man capable of making an intelligent choice. Perhaps I was wrong.'

Petr Kuragin drew his sword. 'I granted you free entry to this house,' he declared. 'That invitation has just expired. Get out, and don't return on pain of your life. You will never have the Star of Erengrad, neither whole nor in part.'

Count Rosporov bowed in mock servility and walked towards the door. 'A shame,' he said. 'You'll probably not live to see yourself proved wrong.'

He paused in the doorway and turned to face Kuragin a last time. 'My friends are already sure of the first two pieces of the Star,' he said.

'And, I promise you, they will not be kept waiting for the third.'

It was only with the greatest difficulty that Elena Yevschenko could be persuaded to let Lisette venture on her own towards the fortified stronghold that was Jaegersfort. As for Stefan, it was a duty that he had been prepared to take on alone, but in the end he, too, was persuaded. If anyone could appear to offer no threat to the people within the stockade, then it was surely Lisette.

The tiny Bretonnian maid looked very small indeed as she walked towards Jaegersfort. As Lisette reached the edge of the ditch that encircled the fort, Stefan felt Elena's hand in his own, her nails biting into his flesh. She turned, her face flushed and met Stefan's gaze. 'She's precious to me,' Elena said, by way of explanation.

'It'll be all right,' Stefan told her, realising at once that he had no idea if it would. After what seemed like an age, the door in the wall opened. Still no one emerged, but a battered length of wood was pushed out across the ditch, forming a bridge. After only a moment's hesitation, Lisette stepped across it and disappeared behind the door.

What must have been another eternity for Elena passed before Lisette re-emerged, smiling and beckoning towards her companions.

'Praise the goddess,' Elena said, expelling a sigh of relief. 'We're safe.'

They led their horses inside the walls of the stockade, towards a bare, sparsely lit space with a cluster of low buildings at its centre and what looked like sheds or stables nestling around the sides.

A single figure dressed in a tattered green shift beckoned them forward, towards the nearest of the three structures in front of them.

'We come in seek of food and shelter,' Stefan began to explain. 'Once we have those–'

The man gestured towards the building with one hand and pulled open the single door with the other. 'In there,' he muttered. 'You can tether the horses outside.'

Stefan stepped across the threshold of the wooden building, and into another world. His senses were immediately assailed by the babble of what sounded like dozens of voices raised in conversation, and through the thick, smoky haze that permeated the room, an equal number of faces. The place was full to bursting with men eating, drinking, smoking, and talking.

For a moment Stefan might have been in one of the cosier taverns back in Altdorf, although, on closer inspection, there was little that was very cosy about those gathered around the tables here. There must have been twenty, or even thirty of them crammed inside the tiny tavern, and all looked practically identical. All had the barrel-chested, almost dwarfish build typical of the forest dweller, and looked as hairy and unkempt as the beasts of the forest themselves. The newcomers stood out in stark contrast, and Stefan was anticipating the hush that would suddenly fall upon the room as they were spied for the first time.

But the foresters kept drinking, seemingly oblivious to their presence, even as Stefan led the way through the crowd towards the bench at one end of the room that served as a bar. A short, heavily bearded man who might be the brother of any of the others greeted Stefan with a crack-toothed smile and handed him a pot of what looked like beer.

'Not exactly Altdorf's finest,' he said to Stefan. 'But not bad, considering.'

Stefan looked at the contents of the pot and then at the innkeeper standing before him. 'Who said anything about Altdorf?' he asked.

'Obvious, isn't it?' the man replied, still grinning. 'Altdorf or Middenheim, you got to be on your way from one to the other.'

Stefan raised the mug to his lips. It certainly wasn't Altdorf's finest, but, right then, just about anything would have tasted just fine. The others took his lead, drinking eagerly from the clay pots that the innkeeper had filled for them.

'What's he done?' said the innkeeper, indicating Tomas Murer, standing like a forlorn captive at the edge of the group. Stefan nodded to Bruno. 'Untie his hands,' he said. 'Let the man have a drink at least.'

'Where were you headed for, anyway?' It was a voice from somewhere amongst the gaggle of drinkers behind them. Stefan put his beer down on the counter and turned around. One or two of the faces now regarded him with what looked like a vague curiosity; most were still absorbed in their own chatter.

'Eisenhof,' Stefan said. It could do little harm now; they would have to forget about their scheduled rendezvous. He was about to return to his beer when another voice, colder and more sober said: 'Lucky, then.'

Stefan scanned the faces, looking for the one who had spoken, but none of the woodsmen were looking in their direction now.

'What did he mean, "lucky"?' Stefan asked, turning back to the innkeeper. The thickset man shrugged, jovially, but his tone was contrastingly serious.

'Lucky that you didn't continue on as far as Eisenhof,' he said.

'Why is that?' Elena demanded, coming to stand at Stefan's side. The innkeeper paused, and glanced around the room before going on. 'Couple of the fellows came past that way, couple of days back,' he said. 'Place had been pretty well razed to the ground, by all accounts. Not many folk left alive.' He leant across the bar and whispered towards Stefan 'Those who did it,' he said, 'were creatures of darkness…'

Stefan set his beer down, his thirst suddenly diminished. 'We need to buy provisions from you,' he said. 'Water, bread, meat or vegetables if you have them. We'll pay you a good price. And we need a place we can rest, for a few hours at most. Then we need to be on our way.'

The innkeeper poured Stefan another beer and set it down in front of him. 'No hurry, friend,' he said. 'Drink your fill and get some sleep, first. We'll sort you out once you're done.'

'Good idea,' Alexei agreed, already holding out his pot to be replenished. Stefan put his hand across the pot before the innkeeper could reach for it. He didn't like the sound of what had happened at Eisenhof at all.

His heart told him to buy the supplies they needed and get back on the road without further delay. But his head told they must also rest, if only for a few hours, before they travelled further.

'No,' he said. 'Thanks. We'll get the food and water sorted out now, and then get some sleep, if that's all right with you.'

'Very well,' the man agreed. 'You'll find comfortable beds upstairs.'

'Thanks,' Stefan replied. 'But we'll be happy to bed down in the barn with the horses and the rest of the provisions. We've had some bad luck upon the road just lately. Best we keep everything together.'

The innkeeper fixed Stefan with a look that was noticeably less friendly than before, then shrugged again. 'Suit yourself,' he said.

BRUNO HAD BEEN first to volunteer to keep a watch, whilst the others slept. He had told Stefan he wasn't tired; but the truth was he didn't want to sleep. Too much of what he feared lay in the place of his dreams. Better to stay awake, in control. He could not stay awake the rest of his life, but this night, he vowed, he would not sleep. He settled himself at the door of the barn, in a place where he could keep a close watch on any activity outside.

For an hour or so he watched the foresters passing in and out of the alehouse, out mostly to relieve themselves against the walls of the stockade, back in to fill up on what seemed to be an inexhaustible supply of ale. There was no sign that the drinking would stop much before daybreak. A steady commotion of voices rumbled on, a sound Bruno found familiar and comforting in its way. After a few minutes, and despite the bitter cold, he began to feel drowsy. Maybe the beer that he'd drunk had been a mistake. He leant back against the door, trying to find a more comfortable position. As he did so, his eyelids drooped and his head fell towards his chest.

A sudden cry from the direction of the alehouse made him sit bolt upright. It had sounded like a woman's voice, calling out in distress. Bruno got to his feet, and peered out into the night. He rubbed his eyes, unable to comprehend what he was seeing. There, by the side of the alehouse, where there should have been only the solid wooden wall of the stockade, was a dark, shadowed hole like the mouth of a cavern.

He stared at it in frank disbelief, but the apparition refused to vanish. Bruno drew his sword and walked slowly towards the gaping void. It was as though a passageway, invisible before, had suddenly opened up in front of him. He kept walking, past the noisy alehouse, into the shadows, towards a faint flickering of light that shone from deep within the darkness.

The passage was long, much longer than Bruno thought could have been possible. He had no clear idea of the internal dimensions of the tiny fort, but he surely should have reached the outer wall by now.

But he hadn't. He kept walking, and the dull amber glow grew stronger. As he closed upon the source of the light, Bruno could hear voices again, coming from somewhere ahead of him. The sounds were faint, but gradually growing more distinct. A woman's voice rose above the blurring sounds, calling out for help. Calling out – Bruno suddenly realised – for him.

He abandoned caution and ran. He knew he had to run, run as fast as he could, or he would be too late. A sudden panic took hold of him. The woman was screaming now, call-ing his name over and over again. Just when it seemed as though the path would stretch out forever, he rounded a cor-ner and came upon the scene.

He felt the sword – no, it was a dagger now – balanced in his hand. He saw the woman now, just a few feet away, plead-ing for help. And he saw the green-skinned monster that had its pitiless grip upon her, crushing the life from her body. 'Help me,' the woman implored him, 'help me, please.'

Bruno felt the muscles in his arm flex and stretch, the grip upon the dagger in his hand shift. Too late, he remembered where he was. Remembered that the outcome would be the same, would always be the same. Too late, he swung his arm and watched again the dagger take its fateful flight.

'STEFAN! STEFAN, WAKE up!'

Stefan roused himself from what felt like the depths of a long sleep. He pulled himself upright with difficulty, to see Bruno in front of him, his face drained of colour and his eyes stretched wide.

'Sigmar's breath, Bruno! You look as if you've been to the gates of Morr and back!'

Bruno shook his head, furiously. 'I'm sorry, Stefan. I fell asleep. I don't know how long for – I'm sure it was only for a matter of minutes but–'

Stefan held up a hand to stem the flow of words. He was still struggling to shake the weariness from his body. It was as though he had succumbed to some potion that had sent him to sleep for days rather than just an hour or so. 'It's all right,' he assured Bruno. 'Everything's still quiet.'

'That's exactly it,' Bruno went on. 'It's completely quiet. You'd better come and look at this.'

Stefan followed behind Bruno as he led them on a tour of the handful of cramped wooden buildings that was Jaegersfort. Each and every one of them was now empty. Jaegersfort was completely deserted.

'When did this happen?' Stefan asked, puzzled. 'Where did they all go?'

'I don't know,' Bruno admitted, his face flushing red. 'I was asleep for just a moment or two. When I came to, I found the place like this.'

Stefan looked at Bruno for a few moments. He could feel the heaviness in his own eyes and limbs. The warm straw of the barn seemed impossibly inviting. It would be so easy just to forget about this; to curl up in the warm embrace of sleep. He rubbed his eyes, vigorously, forcing them to stay open.

'This is more than weariness,' he said. 'I suspect the landlord's brew had more of a punch to it than any of us bargained for.'

They went back inside the alehouse. The room that had been full to bursting only a while before was now empty save for the insects swarming around the greasy plates of half-eaten food, and the pots of beer, unfinished upon the tables. The woodsmen had totally vanished.

Stefan stood in the centre of the room, listening to the silence. There was nothing but the sound of the wind, sighing in the trees, and the faint groan of the timbers around the stockade.

'Looks like we've been left alone,' Stefan said. Somehow, his instincts told him, they wouldn't remain alone for long.

'I've got a bad feeling about this,' Bruno said, quietly. 'Is it another trick, another trap?'

'Rouse the others,' Stefan commanded. 'We're not going to stay around to find out.'

THE GATEHOUSE AT the entrance to the fort had been abandoned, its occupants melted away to leave the fort unguarded. Stefan hurried the riders along, across a makeshift bridge and out into the forest. They threaded their way back into the heart of the Drakwald under a black, moonless sky. About fifty yards clear of the fort, Stefan pulled his horse up and looked round. At first there he saw nothing except impenetrable night, but he had not long to wait. Like stars rising above the horizon, a prickling of lights appeared out of the darkness to the north and east of Jaegersfort, heading in their direction.

'Men on horseback,' Bruno muttered, 'bearing torches to light their path.'

'Men?' Stefan asked. 'Or mutants?'

As they watched, the lights multiplied until they numbered twenty or thirty, spreading out as they approached, a cordon encircling Jaegersfort.

'What new game is this?' Alexei muttered.

'One that we are not going to get caught within,' Stefan said. 'Time to go,' he told them, briskly. 'Let's get out of this while we still can.'

CHAPTER NINE
Soldiers of Tzeentch

MONTHS HAD NOW passed since Andreas had last received word from Otto Brandauer. The priest was accustomed to long gaps in correspondence with his old friend, but this was different. The last letter he had received had not contained the usual mixture of news and speculation. It had come under seal, and had been written in an elaborate code known only to the few sworn to the Keepers of the Flame. It had taken the priest the better part of a day to decipher the elaborate pattern of the runes encrypting the letter. His efforts were rewarded with the news he had been waiting nearly four years to hear. The burden was soon to be lifted from his shoulders. The Star of Erengrad was returning home; the fragments were to be made whole once more. The wounds of a generation were to be healed.

In his letter Otto had described the arrangements being finalised for the journey from Altdorf to Middenheim and then on to Kislev. He described Elena and her companions, and the detailed plans for their meeting in Middenheim. Otto had promised to write again on the day that they rode from Altdorf, but that second letter had never come. The priest feared in his heart that the light of their brotherhood had been extinguished in this life. Otto Brandauer was dead.

But the girl, Father Andreas told himself, the girl is still alive. And she is coming, coming to Middenheim. In the still of each night since that last letter the priest had lain in his bed, waiting, listening. He had never met Elena Yevschenko, yet he sensed her soul was very close now. He had been preparing for her coming for four years, and now the time was nigh.

For the past week Father Andreas had set a watch upon the appointed meeting place. Night had followed empty night, and the due time for their rendezvous had now passed. But this night, his heart told him, they would surely come. Throughout the daylight hours Andreas attended dutifully to his sacraments in the tiny chapel of Morr. It had been a good day, by recent standards. Fewer than fifteen deaths all told in that quarter of the city. Fewer than the day before. Fewer by far, if the stories were true, than the mounting toll of death to the east.

The priest neither abhorred nor shunned death – his life's work was devoted to smoothing the passage of souls through the gates of Morr – but he grieved for every one torn early from the path of their natural life. He greatly feared that Otto was one such soul.

His ministrations complete, Andreas locked all the doors within the chapel, and knelt in solitary prayer. Silence settled upon the cold marble facades of the chapel. Andreas closed his eyes and bowed his head, and pledged devotion to his god.

The priest repeated his litany of prayer until the exterior world faded away and the Gates of Morr opened before him. In his mind he gazed through portals into the lands of the dead, towards an eternity without horizon, a final resting place for the children of Morr. Andreas listened to their voices; the ceaseless song of tormented souls brought finally to peace. He searched the endless plains, trying to find Otto, a lone soul amongst the multitude. In his heart he hoped that, if Otto were truly dead, then he would find him there. But there were too many voices. Not hundreds, not thousands, not any number that mortal man could reckon. All life fell to dust; the souls that survived were gathered here. Since

time began, all the children of the great god Morr had been
scattered upon these, his fields of rest. Now they numbered
more than the grains of sand upon the shore.

He would meet again with Otto, but not until he himself
had walked that final path. Andreas's breathing deepened
and grew slower. His soul slipped further within the kingdom
of Morr. 'Great god of eternal peace,' he intoned. 'Show me
your children on both sides of the great divide. Grant me
sight of the living as well as the dead.'

Gradually the swell of voices broadened and filled. Now
Andreas sensed the presence of those yet to be called beyond
the gates of Morr. Sadness welled within him as he listened
to the anguished cries of those about to be consumed by the
fires of death: the sick and the dying, the wounded lying
upon the field of battle. Souls struggled within their mortal
frames as the swell of fate carried them, inexorably, along
their last journey.

Andreas concentrated, filtering the wider pandemonium
from his thoughts. He focused his mind upon the nearer
shores, upon the flickering energies emanating from the souls
of those within the city walls themselves. Middenheim now
revealed itself to him as a tableau, a shifting pattern of light
and sound. The clamour of living souls grew in intensity
inside Andreas's head, some further, some nearer to their
final destination. Few if any knew the true duration of their
remaining span of life, but to the priest, immersed deep in
prayer, all was laid bare.

He focussed his mind, sifting the lives that flashed before
him. Humanity was there in all shades of virtue and sin, but
Andreas was searching for one amongst the sea. An image
sparked; a picture of a young woman on horseback. Near,
very near now to Middenheim itself. A jolt passed through
the priest's body as he recognised the shape of the Star concealed upon her, a pulse of bright energy in the darkness.

The woman was flanked on either side by riders; their spirit
lights shone strong and clear. These were the escorts Otto had
written of. His sorrow deepened with the certain knowledge
that his beloved comrade was not in their midst. Andreas set
aside his grief and forced himself to concentrate, probing
these other souls. They were growing closer by the moment,
close enough now to almost touch–

Andreas sat bolt upright, shaken by some unbidden force out of his pious reverie. His body was shaking, and for a moment it felt as though an icy claw had taken a grip upon his heart. He scrambled to his feet and drew his robe around him, struggling to regain warmth. Without knowing quite why, Andreas was suddenly filled with fear. He had touched the spirit of the young woman. She would reach Middenheim safely, and all was well. And yet – for a moment he had sensed something else, something so close by as to be almost indivisible from the riders. Its form in that instant had seemed human, yet Andreas had sensed within it terrible evil.

He shuddered. The shadow faded from his consciousness but he knew that danger was close at hand. Andreas set about his preparations. As he did so, he muttered a final prayer to the gods, a prayer that it might not already be too late.

THE EMISSARY FLED the old man's body an instant before he died. As the stooped figure of the shopkeeper crumpled lifeless upon the ground, the emissary's spirit flew free, fixing itself again in the new host body standing waiting before him.

Through new eyes, he looked down at the body without pity. The old man's dim brain and blinkered spirit had served as host for the emissary, a vessel with which to pass beyond the spell-guarded gates. Having served that purpose, it was just a husk; refuse to be scraped like excrement into the gutter.

Varik reflected how no two of Lord Kyros's disciples were ever the same, their souls as diverse as their earthly bodies. Some willingly embraced the black host, cleaved to its song as though they had longed for it all of their lives. Others struggled against the inner voice as they might struggle against a canker eating away at their flesh – with equal desperation, and with equal futility. Others still, only dimly aware of their own existence, had virtually no sense or knowledge of the power that could possess them at will. Men such as this shrivelled old man could be easily controlled, but had limited potential. But it had been enough. The warding spells that the elders of Middenheim had set about the city had been weak; no match for the disciple of Tzeentch. Very soon now he would show them what true magic could achieve.

The emissary stretched his newly acquired limbs and drew down a deep breath. It felt good to possess a strong, powerful body once again. He rubbed his eyes hard and refocused, taking a moment to adjust to clear his vision after the rheumy half-sight of the old shopkeeper. Haarland Krug, the Middenheim miller whose body now played host to Varik's soul, was a very different proposition, a willing and enthusiastic acolyte of the dark power.

The emissary allowed Krug a few moments of shared consciousness before sublimating his soul. Now, there were urgent tasks to attend to, and there must be no more distractions. The sleeping soldiers of Tzeentch, spread like dormant seeds across the city, must be woken and made ready. Varik allowed himself a moment to savour the hour drawing near. Thus far, he had no doubt, the Kislevite would have believed she led a charmed life. Now she would discover how quickly, how fatefully the winds of chance could change.

THE HOURS SINCE they had escaped the ambush at Jaegersfort became days, and there were no more attacks. But by now it was clear to Stefan that their most tenacious, resilient enemy was the forest itself. The Drakwald was the enemy that never tired, never gave up. Night and day it was with them, sapping away their strength and their will to carry on. And then, almost a week after Jaegersfort, and just when their endurance was all but exhausted, the travellers emerged at last from the forest's dark embrace.

The Drakwald released them as suddenly as it had swallowed them up, the thick folds of trees giving way without warning to a path that led steeply up a sparsely wooded slope. It seemed as though they had travelled for half an eternity since Jaegersfort, but now, at last, they found themselves within sight of their destination. As the sky opened out above and ahead of them, Stefan halted upon the path to gaze at last upon the city that had once seemed so distant as to be no more than a dream.

Night had fallen, and the lights of Middenheim beckoned like a thousand jewels shining in the night sky high above the forest. 'Shallya be praised,' Elena murmured. 'There were times back there when I wondered if I'd ever live to see this sight.'

Stefan smiled. 'I think we've kept Middenheim waiting for long enough,' he said. 'Come on.'

As night gave way to day, the great city began to reveal itself to the travellers. In the first glimmerings of dawn it looked improbably huge and imposing, a mighty citadel perched upon a great fist of rock that seemed to grow far above the forest floor. With its high granite walls the city dominated the landscape, an oasis of humankind amongst the wilderness of endless forest. To the traveller's eye it looked very solid, very secure. Stefan had never travelled there before, yet now, after the hardships of the Drakwald, it felt like coming home.

'The City of the White Wolf,' Stefan murmured. 'Named after Ulric himself; god of the wolves.' He spurred his horse on, seeking the road that would lead them to the gates of the city.

STEFAN KEPT CLOSE by Elena's side as they tracked through the rain-spattered streets of Middenheim. He shook away the tiredness weighing down upon him. Now above all he had to remain vigilant.

Up to a point, he shared Elena's relief at being within city walls once more. The vivid life and pungent smells assailing him from all sides seemed reassuring and familiar. But who amongst the thousands of faces streaming through the narrow might be their ally, and who their enemy? The forces of darkness would have their acolytes here in Middenheim, of that he had no doubt. And once they had the second part of the Star it would surely not be long before they stepped out from the shadows.

The riders skirted the heart of the city, seeking the wide metalled road that led to the Morrspark. The grey-granite streets of Middenheim with their dark-timbered buildings seemed improbably crowded after the desolation of the forest. Although the hour was growing late, people still flocked about their business, moving between taverns, pushing hand-carts laden with wares from market stalls. The horses were forced to slow to a walking pace.

Finally the street ahead narrowed and there was no way through. The passage was blocked by a knot of townspeople arguing over something; a disputed purchase, or a debt. The argument was growing heated, drawing onlookers into its midst. Stefan drew his horse to a halt in front of the crowd and called down from the saddle.

'Hey there,' he shouted, cordially but firmly. 'Can't you take your quarrel somewhere else? We need to pass through.'

Those towards the back of the crowd either didn't hear Stefan, or chose to ignore him. Alexei swore, impatiently, and started to climb down off his horse. 'We'll need a little more persuasion to clear this lot,' he commented.

'Wait a minute,' Stefan said. 'We don't want to get caught up in this if we can help it.'

He nudged his horse forward until he was right at the edge of the throng. 'Hey you,' he shouted, focusing his attention on a large man standing with his back to them. After a momentary pause the man broke away from the brewing fight and turned to face the riders.

Stefan saluted the man amicably. 'Can you help move these people along?' he asked. 'We need to reach the Morrspark before last bell.'

The man stared glassy-eyed at Stefan for a moment. Just at the point when Stefan was beginning to think he must have chosen badly, a flicker of animation crossed the man's face, and he sprang into action. Turning back into the crowd, the burly figure began clearing people aside unceremoniously. A path opened amidst the squabble, and Stefan and the others were able to pass.

Stefan nodded towards the burly giant as he eased his horse through the gap in the crowd. 'Thanks for your help, friend,' he said.

Haarland Krug gazed up at Stefan without blinking, and nodded back.

DISTANT BELLS WERE chiming the last of the day as they approached the Morrspark. In a few minutes the gates to the fields of rest would be locked shut, and the rendezvous would have passed for another night. That was a delay they could not afford. As they drew closer to their destination, the traffic upon the road became almost all one-way; grey figures departing slowly from the direction of the Morrspark, mourners returning from their lonely vigils amongst the dead.

A mist had started to settle over Middenheim by the time they reached the fields of Morr, a sulphurous blanket of grey that masked both sight and sound. Even so, there was no mistaking the scale of the place.

'It's big,' Bruno commented.

'Aye,' Stefan concurred. 'Let's hope we don't have to search to find our priest.' He brought his horse to a halt, and sat, scanning the outer wall of the Morrspark. The wall ran as far as he could see in either direction before disappearing into the mist. There seemed to be only one entrance, some way down on their left, a pair of sturdy iron gates flanked on either side by what could be guardhouses. A light still burned in the lower window of one of the buildings, but the gates themselves appeared shut. Nothing stirred, living or dead.

Stefan turned to Elena. 'Any other way in, as far as you know?'

Elena shook her head. 'Otto described the park as a great circle, walled around in its entirety. His instruction was that there is only one principal entrance, approached on the road from the Nordgarten.' She looked to the gates in front of them. 'This must be it.'

Stefan lifted the reins and turned back towards Alexei, riding at the rear, a watchful eye upon their captive. 'Any sign of anyone unwelcome?' he asked. The swordsman shook his head. 'None that I've been able to pick up on,' he said. 'But the dark ones will be cleverer, this time,' he added, glancing at Tomas. 'I'd take no comfort from this quiet place.'

'Don't worry,' Stefan assured him. 'I won't.' He looked round for Bruno. 'Keep him here for the moment,' he said to him, indicating Tomas. 'But keep him safe.'

Bruno nodded his assent, casting a brief glance in the direction of Alexei Zucharov. 'He'll be safe enough with me,' he confirmed.

'Well then,' Stefan said to Elena. 'Are you ready for this?'

'I've been ready for four years,' Elena replied.

'Then let's not waste any more time,' Stefan said. 'We'll ride together to the gatehouse.'

Lisette picked up the reins, preparing to follow her mistress towards the Morrspark. Elena caught Stefan's eye, then shook her head ever so slightly. Lisette looked from Stefan back to her mistress in confusion.

'Madam, I'm pledged to ride by your side,' she protested. 'If there is danger–'

'It's best you wait here with the others,' Elena said, somewhat uncertainly.

'This is for the safety of all of us,' Stefan confirmed. 'Wait here with Alexei and Bruno. As soon as we know all's well, you can join us.'

Lisette hesitated, part of her still intent on staying by Elena's side. But a glance at her mistress told her that her mind was made up. Reluctantly the Bretonnian girl turned her horse and trotted back to where the others stood waiting. Elena and Stefan rode on towards the Morrspark.

The gates were locked, and the park itself looked deserted. The last of the mourners had long departed into the mist.

'The appointed time was between eleventh bell and midnight each evening,' Elena murmured. 'Perhaps we're too late.'

'I'd advise we wait a while,' Stefan said. 'But don't dismount just yet. We may need to leave in a hurry.'

Minutes passed. The fog blanketing the city streets thickened, and the sky grew dark as clouds gathered above, obscuring the moons. After what seemed a long time a door at the side of the gatehouse opened, and a figure emerged carrying a lantern. Stefan looked down at a squat figure of indeterminate sex and age, dressed in the drab, dun-coloured robes of the priests of Morr. The man stood before them, holding the lantern above his head to cast a light upon the riders.

'Good evening, father,' Stefan began. 'We have business at the garden of rest. I trust we're not come too late?'

The priest tilted the lantern slightly in Stefan's direction. 'What business would that be?' he asked.

'We come to mourn a brother lost,' Elena said, speaking her words with a careful precision. 'For only in devotion to the dead can the souls of the living be re-born.'

The man moved the lantern towards Elena. 'Then you hope to find virtue here?'

'If we are found worthy,' Elena responded. 'Then we pray the gods may choose to bestow the gift of virtue upon us.'

The priest nodded abruptly, and turned to unlock the gates.

'Father Andreas?' Elena asked, a tremor in her voice now.

'Follow me,' the priest said, ignoring her question. Elena looked to Stefan.

'Do we go alone?'

Stefan thought for a moment. There was still the matter of Tomas Murer to be resolved. 'Father,' he asked. 'There are others who ride with us. May I take your lantern to signal to them?'

The priest paused for a moment, then handed Stefan the lantern. As the priest unlocked the gates to the Morrspark, Stefan held the lantern aloft to signal to Bruno and Alexei waiting further along the road. The riders passed in single file into the Morrspark. The priest pulled the gates to behind them, and fastened them securely.

WERNER SCHLAGFURST HAD been sick for most of that week. The headaches had begun as a persistent throbbing in his head a few days ago, and had grown in intensity until, for much of the time, it felt as though someone were pounding against the outside of his skull, trying to break in. The headaches came and went throughout the day, but each day they were getting worse. It seemed to make no difference whether he drank nothing, or whether he drank a lot, which he did most days. Together the pain in his skull and the rotgut brandy combined to compound his already evil temper, until his own wife and children shunned him for fear of the violence he might do. That day Werner had not gone to work. The hammering inside his head had begun at first light and continued unabated throughout the day. The foundry could go to Morr, and take their filthy stinking job with it. Werner didn't care. More than that; for all the throbbing ache battering his skull, he knew that there was something, something much more important, that was about to happen to him. Images – dark, violent images – swam into his mind then darted away from him like eels at the last moment. If only they would lie still for just a minute. If only this cursed hammering in his head would stop.

He had lain, cursing and sweating, wrapped within the sheets of his filthy bed since morning, rising only to add to the stinking slops swilling in the pot at the foot of the bed. Let Marta empty it. He'd be cursed to Morr if he'd do any work that day.

On the table by his bedside a flask of the brandy that had been his constant companion most of his working life.

Several times during the day Werner had reached out for it, but he never took the stopper from the bottle, and he never drank. He didn't know why. It was something to do with the pounding in his head. Something to do with the sense of importance that was growing in intensity with the throbbing pain. Curse those slippery eels. Curse them to Morr.

Finally, Werner slept. His sleep was filled with the sort of dreams that most men would call nightmares. Horned serpents slithered out of the darkness to slink in and out of his body, darting tongues seeding him with an insidious poison. In the dreams Werner felt both weak and powerful as if, like a serpent, he was sloughing off one skin and growing new scales of armour. All the time the hammer inside him beat against the anvil of his soul, tolling incessantly like a bell.

Something cold and wet hit him in the face and Werner sat bolt upright in bed. His wife Marta stood over him, candle in one hand. Somewhere in the distant night, a bell was indeed chiming.

His wife was holding something in her other hand. A stump of wood, or something like that. Dimly, Werner remembered it as being part of a chair he had smashed apart last evening. Marta, he noticed, had a bruise like a ripe fruit below one eye, and she was trembling as though in dread of what he might do to her for having woken him.

He gazed, fascinated, at his wife. It was as though, somehow, he could read in her all manner of things that were invisible to the mortal eye. Read them – if only Werner had been able to read – like the recipe for some mage's potion. In Marta's trembling face he read uncertainty and confusion, and he read fear. Fear that something was happening to her husband, that a change was coming upon him that could never be undone. Werner drank in her fear, and realised that he enjoyed the feeling it gave him.

'What is it?' he demanded of her, sourly. 'You'd better have good reason for waking me when I'm sick.'

'There is a man waiting below,' his wife said, hesitantly. 'I've never seen him before. But he says – he says that you must go with him now.'

Werner cursed and spat effusively upon the wooden floor, but, to his own surprise as much as his wife's, found himself pulling back the sheets and rising from the bed. Marta bit

upon her lip. 'Werner!' she pleaded. 'This man – I don't
know, he looks bad – please don't go with him.'

Werner Schlagfurst stumbled from the bed, pushing his
wife aside roughly to get to the door. He lurched unsteadily,
cursing as his foot connected with the slop-bucket, spilling its
stinking contents across the floor.

The door at the foot of the stairs was wide open. Cold air
blew around the interior of the house. Werner staggered
down the steps and came face to face with the figure waiting
for him in the doorway. Marta had been right about one
thing; he'd never met this man before, he was sure. Yet, as his
gaze locked upon the stranger's black, unblinking eyes,
Werner knew that the same incessant drum was beating
inside his head.

The stranger looked at Werner without any smile of welcome or recognition. Werner found himself stepping aside to
let the man enter the house.

'Arm yourself,' the stranger told him. 'The time has come.'

By the time Werner emerged from the crumbling house, his
limbs had filled with a new energy. White-hot air pumped
through his lungs, feeding his blood, raising it to boiling
point. An old crossbow, rusted with disuse but now newly
oiled, was slung across his back. He saw a woman, a bruised
and miserable figure, standing in the doorway behind him,
calling to him in confusion and desperation. But he neither
acknowledged nor remembered Marta now. In fact, Werner
Schlagfurst barely remembered himself. His mind was
focused on the road ahead, his stride matched to the steady
hammer beat inside his head. The serpent's skin, glittering
and new, moulded itself to his soul.

THE FIGURE IN priest's robes led them through the Morrspark.
Soon the sounds of the outer world, already muffled by the
fog, had faded away entirely. It seemed like they were completely alone in the murky darkness. Alone, save for the
thousand dead lying at rest all around, waiting their call unto
the next life.

But they were not completely alone, and it was not completely dark. As they neared the centre of the Morrspark a
light became visible through the mist, a feeble glow-worm
phosphor filtering through the gloom. Stefan saw a figure

standing hunched beneath the light of a tallow lamp, a griz-
zled creature with an unkempt grey beard. The man was hard
at work, attacking the cold earth with a pick.

The workman paused in his labours at the sound of footsteps approaching. He set the pick to one side, but did not
put it down. Instinctively, Stefan's hand closed over the hilt
of his sword.

As they came closer, the priest raised his hand. The workman returned the greeting, and turned his gaze upon the
newcomers. He seemed particularly fascinated by Elena and
Lisette, his gaze barely leaving them as they approached.

Soon all eight were gathered around the grave the old man
had been digging out. Elena turned to the priest, unsure of
what was expected of her. 'What now, father?' she asked. 'Is
there something else you require of us?'

The priest slipped back his cowl, revealing a clean-shaven
young man with dark, receding hair. For the first time, he
favoured Elena with a brief smile.

'I'm flattered to be called father,' he said. 'But it's a little pre-
mature.'

The gravedigger laughed and rested upon his pick. 'For me,
on the other hand, this meeting is long overdue.' He held out
a soil-crusted hand. 'And very welcome,' he added. 'I am
Father Andreas.'

Elena hesitated, still confused. Stefan seized the offered
hand. 'A good disguise, father,' he said. 'We had not expected
to find you still at work so late in the evening.'

Father Andreas laughed again. 'Oh, this?' he said, indicating the pick. 'That was just my insurance.'

'Insurance?'

'In case you were visitors of the unwelcome kind, and I had
cause to crack open your skulls.' His eyes for a moment were
hard steel grey. Stefan saw that he was not joking. Suddenly
the priest looked much younger, not to mention much
stronger, than the decrepit gravedigger of a few moments ago.
Father Andreas turned towards the man in priest's robes who
had led them through the Morrspark. 'Good work, Johann,'
he said. 'You can leave us now.'

The younger man looked uncertain. 'Are you sure?' he
asked. 'I sense a heavy foreboding come upon this place
tonight, father.'

'All the more reason for you to go now,' Andreas told him. 'I'll brook no argument, Johann. Go. And go safely.'

Father Andreas watched the younger man retreat into the night. 'He'll make a fine priest of Morr before too long,' he commented. He turned his attention to Elena, his stare lingering upon her, weighing her up.

'You carry a great burden upon your young shoulders, my lady.'

'Then it's a burden I carry willingly,' Elena replied. 'And I'm resolved to carry it to the end.'

The priest nodded. 'I know that you are,' he said. 'I was told as much by–' he hesitated, and his sharp eyes seemed to grow dull. 'Otto is dead, isn't he?' he said, his voice quiet.

It was Bruno who spoke first. 'I fear your guess is right. He is dead.'

'Murdered,' Stefan added. 'I'm sorry – he was a friend of yours?'

Father Andreas bowed his head and drew a hand across his eyes. He stood there for a few moments in silent contemplation. A sound, like a small cry or a muffled sob, escaped his lips. Then he pulled himself upright, and drew down a deep breath.

'Come,' the priest continued. 'Let's waste no more time on welcomes.' He looked around the group. 'No one followed you here, as far as you could tell?'

Alexei Zucharov shook his head. 'But I suggest we don't read too much into that.'

'Agreed,' Father Andreas replied. 'We should not presume that we're safe yet.' The priest's eyes fell upon Tomas Murer, a forlorn figure with his hands secured tightly behind his back. 'What story attends this sorry fellow?' he asked. Tomas spoke up before any of the others could reply. 'Sir, I have been much maligned, and the victim of misunderstanding,' he insisted. 'As the great god of death shall judge me, I stand before you a good man and true.'

'We shall see the truth of that,' Stefan responded. 'That's a matter we seek your judgement upon, father, once our principal business is done.'

Andreas looked Tomas up and down. 'So, you beg the judgement of Morr?' he said, gravely. 'Say your prayers if he should find you wanting.'

The priest paused, deep in thought. 'Well. We've waited four years. Let's wait no longer.' He produced a rusted iron key from inside his robe, and walked towards the vaulted tomb standing behind them. With a knife, he worked free one of the stones set into the marble façade, exposing a lock. He placed the key in the lock and turned. The façade became a door, swinging outwards to reveal a narrow stone staircase leading down below the earth.

He beckoned, and Elena stepped forward, with Lisette at her side.

'Wait!' Andreas commanded. 'The bearer of the Star only. The others must wait, and keep watch over the vault.'

'But Lisette is my handmaid,' Elena said. 'She only wishes to attend me, as is her duty. Surely there can be no harm–' The priest held his hand aloft, stifling her protest. 'Wait, though,' he said, reflecting for a moment. 'Which of you is Stefan Kumansky?'

Stefan stepped forward. The priest looked him over carefully. 'Yes,' he said at last, as though Stefan's appearance tallied with a description. 'You should also step below. The others, wait here.'

Stefan followed the priest and Elena down into the musty gloom. Below ground the temperature plummeted. The air frosting their breath had the still, cloying sweetness of death itself. The stairs led down to a single cell, a narrow chamber lit by the light of candles affixed to each of the walls. Once the door had been secured behind them, the priest turned to Stefan and Elena, his expression grave.

'Otto's death is a source of mighty grief to me,' he said.

'We feel that loss every bit as keenly,' Stefan assured him.

'There is more bad news,' Andreas went on. 'News that will concern your onward journey.'

'Has there been a change to the plan?' Elena asked.

'Not a change as such. But the merchant convoy you were to travel with left Middenheim two days ago. The main trade routes between the Empire and Kislev were about to be sealed. They would delay their departure no longer.'

Stefan considered the priest's words. This was a major blow to their plans. 'Then the border itself has been closed?'

The priest nodded confirmation. 'If you are to reach Kislev then there are only two routes now open to you – through the Forest of Shadows, or through the Middle Mountains. Both are perilous, but the mountain paths are now ruled by bandit gangs. Stay away from them.'

He sat himself on one side of the table and stretched out his arms. 'But more of that anon,' he said. 'For now, give me your left hands.'

Stefan and Elena extended their hands and the priest took each of them in his own. He closed his eyes, and lowered his head. Stefan assumed for a moment that they were about to join in prayer. Then he felt something, like the jolting sting of a river eel, surge through his body. Once the shock had receded he realised that he was not being attacked. It was rather as though the energy was coming direct through the body of the priest, searching him out, delving into the depths of his soul.

When, a few moments later, the priest released his grip upon their hands, he was smiling. 'Now,' he said, 'let me see the Star.'

Elena unfastened the top of her robe and pulled the chain from around her neck. She hesitated for a moment before handing the icon to the waiting priest.

'I'm not used to letting this out of my possession,' she explained.

'Well,' the priest replied. 'There has to be a first time for everything.' He lay the segment down, then pulled a drawer out of the table in front of him. It appeared empty. Then Andreas lifted the silver leaf lining the bottom of the draw to reveal another compartment. Inside lay the icon's companion piece, the second segment of the Star of Erengrad.

The second piece seemed at first to be an identical copy of the first, but when Andreas lay the two together, the segments matched exactly so that barely a line could be seen dividing them.

Elena gasped, seeing the two pieces together. 'I've long dreamed of this moment,' she declared.

'So have I,' Andreas said. Stefan realised he had been expecting something more spectacular; thunder or lightning, perhaps, some token from the gods at this momentous event. But it remained very still, and very cold, in the chamber.

'What now?' he asked.

'Now?' the priest looked bemused for a moment. 'Now you take the two parts of the Star, with my blessing. And may all the gods take you safe to find the third.'

Elena looked down upon the icons lying joined upon the table. 'How should I carry them?' she asked.

'Ah.' Andreas lifted the Star, and separated it once more. He gave the original piece back to Elena, and slid the second across the table towards Stefan.

'This must be your burden now, until our quest is fulfilled,' he told him.

Stefan reached out, tentatively, and closed his hand upon the icon. The piece felt cold to his touch, yet, as he placed the silver chain around his neck, he felt a surge of warmth radiate out from it, suffusing his body. He looked across at Elena. From the look of astonishment on her face, he guessed she must be experiencing the same thing.

'The separate parts are inert, dead metal,' the priest said. 'But, bring them close together and you will begin to feel the power of the Star.'

'And these are just two of the three segments!' Elena exclaimed.

Andreas nodded. 'Now you begin to truly understand its worth, and why it must not fall to the wrong hands.'

Stefan sat for a moment, lost in wonder at the strange, elemental force. Then he remembered they had other business that must be attended to before they bid farewell to the priest. 'One final thing,' he said. 'We must know the truth of Tomas Murer,' he said. 'And then deal him the justice he deserves.'

WERNER HAD BEEN taken to an abandoned building on the edge of the city, a foul crumbling place that reeked of dye and decaying fat. He remembered the building from somewhere. It was the old tannery. He had collected some leather there once for his master. Or the man whom once he had called his master.

Dimly, Werner realised that he had a new master now. Things were going to be different.

The tannery was long abandoned, but tonight it was not empty. Faces loomed out of the darkness, soldiers waiting for the call to arms. Some Werner recognised, some he did not, but, for the first time in an otherwise worthless life, Werner Schlagfurst knew he was not alone.

Before long, they were on the move, walking alone or in groups of two or three. At their head Werner saw a man – if man it was – wearing a helm of black steel that gave his head the appearance of bearing wings or horns. The face of the helm had been moulded in the likeness of a snake striking at its prey. Werner knew this man from somewhere – or had known him, in the other wretched life that was rapidly fading away. He struggled momentarily for the miller's name. It no longer mattered. All that mattered was here, now. The helmed head moved from side to side, the snake eyes reaching out, penetrating deep inside the head of each and every man amongst them.

Werner gazed around, almost sick with a giddy excitement as more and more figures emerged from the mists around him. Their numbers were growing with every moment, and yet they seemed to pass silently along the darkened streets. It was as though the fog shrouding the pathways was swallowing any sound. They had become ghosts.

Even before they reached the Morrspark, Werner knew where they were headed. And he knew why. Knew that there would be fresh blood spilt upon the fields of the dead that night. As he neared the portals of Morr, Werner saw the helmed figure raise his arms towards the sky, and an arc of light flash across the air, setting the mist aflame. For a moment, Werner was blinded. When his sight returned he saw that the fog had parted, clearing a passageway for his brothers into the Morrspark. As Werner and his comrades passed through, the mists closed in like waves falling back upon the shore, sealing off the outer world. Without understanding what had happened, Werner understood that this was the work of powerful magic, magic that served the same master as he.

A drum was pounding. Werner could no longer tell if it was beating inside or outside his head. Nor could he fix upon the words that the snake man was offering up, but, nonetheless, he understood. Understood that he had waited a lifetime for this moment to come. At last, he knew his purpose.

* * *

FATHER ANDREAS LAID his hands upon Tomas's forehead, and let them rest there whilst he stood, eyes closed, listening to the inner voice of his soul.

Eventually he lifted his hands, and opened his eyes once again.

'Well?' Stefan asked, his throat dry. Andreas looked down at Tomas Murer, and bid him rise to his feet.

'This is a life that has known much sin,' he said at last. 'Sins of weakness, and the follies born of excess. But I also see a sound heart, honest and strong in its way.' He looked towards Stefan. 'I find no taint of darkness in him.'

Tomas expelled a mighty sigh of relief. For his part, Stefan felt a weight lift off his shoulders. 'That's good news,' he said.

The priest's brow furrowed. 'Not entirely,' he said. 'I say I find no darkness in Tomas's soul, that much is good. But evil is close, very close. I sensed it just now, even as we talked up above.'

Elena shot Stefan an anxious glance. 'What are you saying?' she asked the priest.

'I'm saying that darkness attends you, lady,' he replied. 'Not in yourself, of course,' he assured her. 'But close at hand. I sensed it earlier today when I was immersed deep in prayer. And, since your party has come to me, I sense it even more strongly. There can be only one explanation. One amongst you carries the dark seed.'

Stefan felt a sickness growing in the pit of his stomach as he listened to the priest's words. 'We must find who it is,' he said without hesitation. 'We can go no further until we have.'

He turned to begin climbing back towards the top of the vault, but was met almost immediately by Bruno, rushing down the steps as fast as his legs could carry him.

Bruno gazed round at them, his eyes wide, almost crazed. 'You'd better get up here fast,' he said to Stefan. 'We've got company, and plenty of it.'

CHAPTER TEN
The White Wolf Bleeds

THE DARK FIELDS of the dead were suddenly alight, countless figures bearing torches pouring through the breach in the wall where the gates had stood. Stefan put the odds against them at something like ten to one. Maybe worse. He could count only what he could see, and he feared that many more lurked in the shadows beyond the torchlight. Certainly, the insane chant rising from the mob had the sound of an army about to bear down upon them.

Father Andreas stood by Stefan's side, mouthing the words of a prayer. Stefan found himself momentarily shocked, unable to fathom how so many armed enemies could be upon them so suddenly. 'Where can they have come from?' he demanded of the priest. 'How could they have entered the city?'

'They had no need to gain entry to the city,' Father Andreas replied, his voice steady but sombre. 'They've been amongst us all along, waiting. Waiting for this moment.'

Stefan's mind suddenly filled with the image of Otto, standing over the Map of Darkness. *Who knows where the serpent might rise next*, Otto had said.

Now they knew.

'As for how they found us so quickly,' the priest continued, 'I fear that one among us has led the dark powers here. Drawn them to us like a beacon.'

Stefan swallowed hard upon the uncomfortable truth. To face battle on this scale was bad enough. To do it knowing that someone close at hand was a traitor – someone, perhaps, he might have trusted with his life – was almost unbearable.

He looked at Andreas. Part of him desperately wanted the priest to be mistaken, but his heart told him it was not so. 'We must find them,' he said, firmly. 'Find them, and eliminate them.'

'No time now,' Andreas replied. 'More pressing demands are upon us. Besides–' he looked around. 'I suspect our traitor will soon betray himself.'

There was a hammering of hooves upon the ground, and the horse bearing Alexei Zucharov appeared through the gloom. Alexei's face was flushed and animated.

'They'll soon be all around us,' he declared. 'They'll have the Morrspark completely surrounded. There's no escaping them.' He paused, fighting for breath. 'We live or die by the deeds of our swords.'

'So be it,' Stefan said. 'But how many swords do we have?'

'Every stroke of mine will exact a heavy cost,' Alexei promised him.

'Mine, too.' They both turned at once. Elena stood before them, with Lisette at her side. The young noblewoman's eyes burned with a fierce defiance. 'I haven't come this far to surrender our prize and our lives to some filthy mob,' she declared. 'What's the matter?' she demanded angrily. 'Didn't anyone tell you a Kislevite woman can fight as well as sew?'

Stefan turned on Elena, his head still spinning with thoughts of a traitor amongst them. 'There's no point in fighting at all if we don't manage to keep you alive,' he insisted. 'Like it or not, that's the whole reason for us being here. We have to keep you out of harm's way for as long as possible.'

'Then it's just you and I,' Alexei said. 'And Bruno. Just like old times.'

'Just like old times,' Bruno responded. His voice sounded distant, detached. Stefan stared at his old comrade. Please the gods, no, let it not be Bruno. He pushed the thought out of his head, and his gaze fell upon Bruno's captive. The priest had found Tomas true of soul. Maybe now wasn't the best time to put that to the test, on the other hand, maybe there wouldn't be another time.

'Bruno,' he called, sharply. Bruno turned with a jolt, as if coming out of a daydream.

'Untie Tomas's hands,' Stefan commanded. 'Give him back his sword.' Alexei stared at Stefan, his expression somewhere between bemusement and dismay.

'You're arming this wretch to fight alongside us?' he said to Stefan. 'Are you sure?'

'No,' Stefan snapped back. 'Are you? All I know is, every sword we muster shifts the odds back in our favour. And, as the gods are my witness, we need all the favour we can find right now.'

Tomas wasted no time in buckling his harness back around his waist.

'Thank you Stefan,' he said. 'You won't regret this.'

'Don't be so sure that you won't regret it,' Stefan replied. 'This is no game we're about to face.'

He noticed the priest standing at the edge of the group. 'Father,' Stefan said. 'You've fulfilled your part in our story. If you can find some refuge–'

Father Andreas shook his head. 'I have no fear of entering upon the garden of Morr.' He drew a short, bevel-headed sword out from under his robe. 'If that is my path, then I would rather tread it with honour. I fear I won't add much weight to your odds,' he added. 'But if I'm to die tonight, it'll be with this sword in my hand.' He tucked the weapon back inside his belt. 'Let us pray Johann has got beyond their reach,' he said. 'Pray he may have raised the alarm.'

THE EMISSARY GAZED at the men around him, machines made of muscle and of flesh pushing through the gaping fissure in the walls. Now the Morrspark, and all within, would be his. There was not a soul in Middenheim that would stand against him. The spell of entrapment he had cast around the outer walls would hold until dawn, sealing the Morrspark like one vast, single tomb. Cloaked by the shimmering deceit of the spell, his followers had set about the gates at will, unseen and unheard by the outside world. The heavy iron might have looked impregnable, but it had been built to contain the dead, not resist the living. Within a matter of minutes, they were through.

Varik had at first despaired of ever being able to lead such a rabble, but now, he realised, there was almost no leading to be done. The wretched creatures were like starving dogs. It was blood they hungered for; he had put the whiff of it under their nostrils. Now they would stop at nothing until they had tasted more.

Had he cared to, the emissary could have counted amongst them students, tradesmen, clerks and publicans. Some even wore the livery of the civic guard. All of them might have passed unnoticed through the streets of Middenheim. And all of them were now his: flesh vessels, emptied of all thoughts save his commands. The rage of Kyros flowed in the veins of each and every one.

He was pleased enough with the host he had chosen for himself. The miller Krug had been a dull-witted man in his own life, but he was young, and he was strong. This was a body that could stand and fight until the light of dawn, if necessary. But it would be ended much, much sooner than that. Long before the guarding spell had waned, it would all be over.

So far they had encountered only one adversary. The figure decked in priest's robes had rushed at them, dagger held in outstretched hand. Varik had taken him himself, repelling the cleric's feeble assault with ease. One almost lazy sweep of his sword had sliced the head from the man's shoulders.

For a moment the emissary had allowed himself the hope that this might be the very priest they had been searching for, the bearer of the Star. He rolled the severed head under Krug's hefty boot and turned it face up. No. This one was too young. The emissary looked down upon Johann Eichler's bloodied features and experienced a momentary twinge of disappointment. But if the other lives were to be extinguished as easily as this, then his master would surely have his prize long before the sun had risen.

Varik kicked the head aside contemptuously. His servants were funnelling into the Morrspark like termites filling a nest. The same expression was etched on the features of each and every one. No reason, no sanity. No other thought or purpose but to fight until their given foe had been driven to death. Varik regarded them with satisfaction. This mindless infantry would show no mercy to the Kislevite and her mercenary scum. He would let them gorge themselves, slaughter the mortals as they wished.

Except for one. The emissary remembered the proud young man on horseback who had shouted at him to give way in the streets near the Morrspark. There had been more to him than just the usual arrogance and bravado of the hired sword. Varik had sensed a disturbing power, a steely determination implacably opposed to the forces of the Chaos lords. Here was danger. Here was one man, above all, who must not be allowed to leave the Morrspark alive. Varik would take a particular pleasure from killing that one himself.

He faced the swelling mob gathering behind him. 'Spread out!' he commanded. 'Cover every inch of this cursed ground. No living soul must escape. Find me the Star and you can do what you will with whoever carries it.'

First he must have the Star. Then the baying mob could slake its thirst for blood. They could drink until the well was dry.

STEFAN WATCHED THE lights closing in as their pursuers tightened the ring around the Morrspark. The animal cries of the hunters rang in his ears, and the reek of smoke from the torches filled his nostrils. For a moment, he was swept back to his childhood. Back to that other night of smoke and fire, the night that the invaders had come to his village. In his mind he pictured his father's face as it had been on that night, before he strode from the house to meet the evil tide with his sword. The last time he had seen his father in this life.

His father's sword had not turned the tide that dark night, and Stefan's belly tightened at the thought that tonight he, too, might fail. The forces of darkness, he now knew, were everywhere within the world.

There was no refuge from the poisoned stream, no more than from the air that men breathed. It ran through all life. What if it were as all-powerful as it was omnipresent? What if Stefan's sword, righteous and mighty though it might be, was not enough?

For a fraction of a second Stefan felt something akin to fear, but, almost instantaneously he had banished it. He thought again of that grey dawn long ago over Odensk; the dead eyes of his father staring to the heavens. That was not cause for fear. That was the reason he was here, the reason he would wield his sword against the black tide as his father had done before him. And he would not yield whilst there remained a flicker of life in his body. If he was to die tonight, then he would give his enemies cause to remember his name for eternity.

Elena was another matter. For all the adrenaline racing in his veins, Stefan knew his head must stay clear. In this battle there was one objective that must remain above all others. Elena must live to reach Erengrad, and fulfil the destiny of the Star.

'Is there any other way out of the Morrspark?' he asked. 'Tunnels, passageways below the earth?' Father Andreas shook his head. 'Below ground is the domain of the dead alone,' he replied. 'Aside from the main gate, there's only a single passage leading out on the east side.'

'Very well,' Stefan said, his mind racing to work through the possibilities still open to them. 'That's the only chance we have. We'll have to hope we can break through. Stay close together.'

'But that's folly,' Elena retorted. 'If we stay in one group we make ourselves an easy target. If we split up, at least one or two of us may have a chance to make it through.'

'No!' Stefan was conscious of precious time slipping away. 'Do that and they'll pick us off like carrion,' he said. 'It may take them longer, but they won't worry about that. If we keep close and join swords, we may have a chance.' He looked round at his comrades. 'Agreed?'

Bruno nodded. 'It makes sense. It's the only way we have a chance.'

Alexei Zucharov merely shrugged; he seemed distracted, as if his mind were already engaged with the conflict to come. 'All roads lead to battle,' he said, finally.

'What about you?' Stefan asked Tomas. 'Perhaps this is more than you bargained for?'

Tomas fixed Stefan with a determined grin. If the fear was starting to eat into him, then, to his credit, he wasn't letting it show. 'I'm with you,' he said. 'You only die once.'

'If you're lucky,' Alexei added, coolly.

'Very well then,' Stefan concluded. 'Mount up, stay close together, and ride hard'. He extended a hand to the priest. 'Father, you should ride with me. Be our pathfinder.' He extended his hand, and helped the priest climb up into the saddle behind him.

They set off in close formation, Stefan and the other swordsmen grouped around the women in a protective ring. Swords aloft, they rode hard for the east wall, threading a route through the narrow paths that ran between the silent graves. Soon they were bearing down upon a jagged line of flaming torches, that was moving in upon them from the north-eastern edge of the grounds. As the distance between the two groups narrowed, Stefan saw the lights ahead bunch together to block the path ahead. Any faint hopes that their adversaries could be cowed into stepping away from the line of flight died there. Stefan knew then that this was to be a conflict which only death itself could end.

He exchanged last glances with the men around him as the collision approached. Alexei Zucharov looked as he always did as battle neared: energised, totally focused, his face red with the flush of blood in his veins. Tomas looked pale and drawn, but there was no fear showing in his face. It was the vacant, staring eyes of Bruno that worried Stefan most. It was as though his body was keeping pace with the pack, but his mind was elsewhere.

Stefan dwelled upon his worries for the briefest of instants and cast the thought away. They would prevail. They had to prevail. There was no one else to call upon.

'Stay together and we may yet break through,' Stefan yelled. 'Use your swords to clear a path, but don't break formation to carry on the fight. Once we're clear, keep riding!' He spurred his horse forward, wringing every last ounce of pace from his mount. Stefan could hear the enemy ahead of them, their animal chant rolling across the cold fields of Morr. If they craved death, then Stefan would see to it they had satisfaction of that, at least. As the moment of reckoning approached, he drew his sword across his body in front of him, and braced himself.

'All glory to the noble Alliance!' he shouted, 'and death to the spawn of Chaos!'

A moment later and they were amongst their enemies. Stefan's horse whinnied and bucked as they struck the advancing line of Scarandar, and Stefan struggled to keep the animal from throwing him and his companion from the saddle. The horse reared up and twisted, then dropped to earth again. Stefan went with the motion, the momentum adding weight to the arc of his sword as it sliced into the knot of faces below. Stefan looked down at them. Expecting to find monsters, what he saw shocked and dismayed him. These were the faces of ordinary men, the simple people of every-day life. For an instant a terrible possibility invaded his thoughts. That these were no spawn of Chaos. That he had fatally misjudged the situation; launched a murderous attack upon innocent men.

Then the voice of one of his comrades – Alexei, perhaps, or Bruno – rang out a warning at his side. Stefan remembered the map, remembered the shadow spreading, unstoppable, across the face of that very ordinary world.

He drew back his blade, already running red with blood, and struck and struck again.

FOR THE MAN who had been Werner Schlagfurst, it was like an unseen light guiding him towards his destiny. Or a bell, call-ing him to temple perhaps. Not that Werner had ever made devotions at temple, even in his other life. Perhaps he might have gone if the call had been as clear, as beguiling, as this.

He had crossed the Morrspark with a clutch of brothers towards the south wall, away from the main attack. For a few minutes they had wandered aimlessly, their torches casting light on nothing besides grey memorials to the worm-eaten dead. He was burning with a thirst to add fresh meat to their number, but their search had revealed noth-ing.

Then the light had sparked inside his head, and he had turned, following in step with his unknown comrades. This way, the light promised, your burning thirst shall be slaked in full. Or perhaps, he realised, it was neither a light nor a bell, but a voice, sweet and soft like a whore's caress. It beckoned him on, and Werner had no mind to resist. Whatever it was, it called irresistibly, a signature marking time to the hammer beat inside his skull.

Werner marched, his body forming a segment of the snaking line working its way into the heart of the Morrspark. Not a word was exchanged. Each man was locked inside a private world, yet each, Werner dimly understood, marched to the same incessant beat. Their quest was single and pure; the pure red of fresh blood washing across the grey tombs of Morr.

Now, directly ahead, the first signs of the feasting to come. Riders on horseback were trying to get across the open ground in front of them. The riders were pushing their mounts hard, but their pace was being slowed by a steadily thickening knot of figures, converging remorselessly upon them. Like vermin, Werner realised: vermin trapped by a pack of starving dogs.

The outermost riders were wreaking a havoc of their own with the flashing steel of their blades. So many of his brothers fell beneath their swords that Werner lost count, yet this was no cause for dismay. For every man that fell, two more would take his place. The hunger would be sated.

Werner and the men around him broke spontaneously into a run, hungry to join with the pack. They would have their share of the feast.

'Death!' Werner screamed. Though his body appeared unchanged, his voice was now barely recognisable as human.

'Death! Death! Death!'

STEFAN LOOKED ABOUT him in growing desperation. Ten or more of their foes now lay dead upon the ground. All four swordsmen were bruised and bloodied, but there had been no real casualties. And yet Stefan knew it would not be enough. The children of Chaos still flocked around them like moths about a lamp. Their progress had slowed to a crawl. He swung his sword yet again and hacked through the body of another attacker, a crazed mannequin in the uniform of the Civic Guard. The guard toppled back, lifeless, sending two or three others sprawling in his wake. Bruno and Alexei were harvesting a bloody crop between them, and Tomas was at least holding his own. They were surviving, but for how much longer?

Stefan backed off from the melee and turned to face the priest. Father Andreas had claimed the life of at least one attacker, cutting the man down with his inlaid silver sword. His face still bore the look of steely determination, but Stefan knew at once that he shared the same fear.

'We're not going to make it,' Stefan shouted over the din of clashing steel. 'There's just too many of them.'

'I know,' Andreas responded. 'What are we going to do?'

'We must change plan,' Stefan said. 'Find refuge if we can. Is there any where in the Morrspark where we could hope to hold them off, at least until dawn?'

'There may be one,' Andreas replied. Doubt clouded his features. 'But you should know–'

'No,' Stefan interrupted him. 'If it's a chance, then it's our only chance. Which way?'

Andreas pointed diagonally across the Morrspark. 'Break off!' Stefan shouted to the others. 'Hold fast, father,' he urged. He twisted the reins and dragged the horse about, ploughing through a smaller group of attackers gathering on his left flank. He kicked in his spurs and pushed on, keeping close by the priest. Marshalled by the Scarandar, the attackers checked their relentless march and turned to follow. They moved slowly, methodically. They're in no hurry now, Stefan thought. They think they have us trapped inside the Morrspark.

He just had to hope they weren't right.

THE CHANGE OF course back into the interior of the park had bought them some breathing space. Before long they might be overrun again, but for now Stefan and the others had managed to break clear of their attackers.

Father Andreas guided them along a path that led between vaulted marble tombs to a dark recess ringed by low-hanging trees. Stefan and the priest dismounted, and, by the light of Andreas's single lantern, picked their way through the thicket until they reached a single black iron door set directly into the ground.

Stefan looked to the priest.

'You have the key that unlocks this door?' The priest nodded.

Stefan took stock of the door, then walked back towards his horse. He reached up and stripped a bag from the saddle, then gave the horse a heavy slap upon its flank. The animal whinnied, and took a few steps forward. Stefan delivered a second slap and the horse began to trot, quickly disappearing into the dark.

'What in the name of all that's holy are you doing?' asked Elena, incredulous. 'You'll have lost that horse for good.'

'Maybe,' Stefan agreed. 'But I'd rather give them a chance than leave them up here to be butchered.'

Tomas now dismounted and followed Stefan's lead, stripping what provisions he could carry from his horse. 'You never know,' he said, 'They might even set our friends running after them for a while.'

'It's a slim chance,' Elena commented.

'Better than none at all,' Stefan replied, firmly. He stood, waiting until the rest of them had climbed from the saddle and despatched the horses. Then he turned again to Father Andreas.

'Let's get going,' he said.

'This will lead us to some kind of refuge below ground?' Elena continued, 'a place where they can't reach us?'

Andreas looked at both of them in turn. His face betrayed no sign of relief. 'Understand that this is not a shelter,' he said 'nor a refuge of any sort that I would choose.'

'What is it then?' Bruno asked, uneasily.

'A tomb,' Andreas replied. 'Of sorts.'

'Time enough for explanations later,' Stefan said. 'Whatever it was, or is, we're going in.' He nodded to the priest. 'We're ready, father.'

It was then that Stefan noticed that one of the party was missing. 'In Taal's name!' he exclaimed, 'where's Zucharov?'

'He was with us when we broke away from the mob,' Tomas offered.

'I didn't see him fall,' Bruno added. 'He was riding right behind me.'

'Well, he's not behind you now,' Stefan said. He swore under his breath. He could ill afford to lose any one single man, let alone one with the strength and skill of Alexei Zucharov. That Alexei had been slain barely bore thinking about, yet the alternative – that it was he who was the traitor in their midst – was far worse.

The lights of the torches suddenly sprang up at the edge of the thicket. Their pursuers were close at hand.

'There's no time left,' Stefan declared. There was no choice. If Alexei was still alive he would have to fend for himself. 'Unfasten the door, Father Andreas, as quickly as you can.' He helped the priest haul upon the heavy iron door, lifting it clear of the moss-covered earth. 'Hurry,' he said to Elena, 'The two of you first.'

Elena's face was lined with anxiety. She steadied herself upon the first step and took a deep breath. Stagnant air, pungent with the sweet scent of decay, wafted up from the subterranean chambers. 'Come on,' she said to Lisette. 'We won't let each other out of our sight. With the gods' blessing we'll come through this unscathed.' She gazed quizzically at the Bretonnian girl. Lisette was struggling to find her footing behind her, as though she were dazed or carrying a wound.

'It's all right,' Elena assured her. 'It's the living we must fear, not the dead.'

Lisette looked unconvinced, but finally managed to move her foot down upon the smooth stone step. Her face in the thin light of the lantern was leeched pale.

'Lisette!' Elena called again. 'Are you all right?'

'I think so,' she called down to Elena. 'I'll be fine.' She steadied herself upon the stairway and took another step down. 'Gods protect me,' she whispered. 'Gods protect us all.'

The steps led down below ground and grew rapidly steep, becoming more like a ladder than a stair. The space inside was so narrow that they were forced to descend one at a time, as though climbing down a shaft into the belly of a mine. The smell of damp earth filled their nostrils, and it quickly became cold enough for them to see their breath frosting in the air around them.

Father Andreas waited at the top of the steps until Stefan, last in line, had reached the bottom. Then he drew down the heavy door above them, and fastened the locks in place. Now the darkness was total. They had left the domain of the living behind them, and had crossed into the realm of the dead. There could be no retreat.

The priest climbed down and re-lit his lamp, casting light into a narrow corridor at the foot of the steps. 'This way,' he said. 'I can promise you no comforts, but at least we will not lack for room.'

'You're sure there's no other way out?' Stefan asked, looking around him. 'Or in?' The priest shook his head with a rueful smile. 'These tombs were built for one purpose only,' he said. 'Those who enter here make but one single journey, without return. Neither might nor magic will breach the door above us.'

Stefan gazed into the darkness ahead of him. There was no movement, not the faintest stirring of the air, but he sensed no tranquillity. 'What is the history of this place?' he asked. The priest drew a sceptre from beneath his cloak, and clasped his hands tightly around it.

'The passageway before us leads to the Tombs of Baldrac,' he said, 'most dread of all the Halls of Morr.'

Stefan shook his head. The name meant nothing to him.

'Long ago,' the priest continued, 'long before any now living were even born, Malthus Baldrac brought an army to the gates of Middenheim to attack the city.'

'But he failed,' Bruno said. 'His army was defeated?'

'At length the army was indeed driven back,' Andreas confirmed, 'but not before Baldrac and a squadron of his most terrible warriors had managed to enter the city.' He paused, and took a breath. 'It took a long and bloody battle before they were at last destroyed. Their remains were brought here for burial.'

Stefan had the distinct feeling the worst was yet to come. He waited for the priest to continue.

'The tomb below is carved from the thickest stone. Bar this door there is no other way in, or out. You see,' the priest explained, 'Baldrac was a necromancer. This was the only tomb deemed safe enough to contain those who might yet rise again to wreak their havoc upon the living.'

Andreas looked at the sombre faces gathered around. 'It's not so much a tomb as a prison,' he said. 'A prison for the unquiet dead. Not a place I would willingly spend the night hours.'

A quiet descended upon the group as Andreas's words sank in.

'Nevertheless,' Stefan said, finally breaking the silence. 'Choice is a luxury we don't have. I'll take the unquiet dead over the insane living.' He looked around the others. No one was offering any disagreement.

'How long are we going to have to spend down here?' Elena asked. She could find little humour in being entombed below ground with only the desiccated corpses of the undead for company.

'As long as it takes,' Stefan replied. 'But my guess is they won't risk continuing the attack beyond dawn.'

'And how will we know when that will be?' Elena demanded, edgily. 'It's eternal night down here.'

'We'll worry about that later,' Stefan retorted. 'The important thing is that we are secure.' He looked at the priest, his question hanging unspoken.

'The door was built to withstand the most murderous of assaults,' Andreas assured him. 'And the stone walls encasing the vault are as thick as any in the Temple of Morr itself. No one will reach us – not from the outside, at least.'

Elena took Lisette's hand in hers and gripped it tightly. 'Come,' she said, forcing some cheer into her tone. 'Let us not fear the dark.'

'It is not the dark I fear, only what it brings,' Lisette said. She turned her face away from her mistress, her eyes wide with fear.

'I can hear them,' she whispered. 'And they can hear me.'

CHAPTER ELEVEN
Awakening

THEY DESCENDED, SINGLE file, into the belly of the cold earth. The noise of the assault hammering the ground above their heads grew steadily fainter until they had only silence for company. For all that it was quiet, Stefan sensed none of the peace of final rest in these chill Halls of the Dead.

'It makes my flesh crawl,' Elena commented. 'Like something cold running the length of my spine.'

'It is an ill-favoured place,' Andreas agreed, sombrely. 'Many troubled souls are here laid to earth. Their mortal lives have ended, but I doubt that their spirits have found repose.'

Bruno exhaled and watched his breath extend like slow coiling smoke in front of him. 'Seems calm enough,' he said, not entirely convincingly. 'And safe enough for you to have visited these tombs before, evidently.'

Andreas laughed. 'As few times as possible,' he said. 'I must bless this joyless place as I bless all the Houses of Morr. Do not think that I outstay my welcome, though.'

Stefan found himself shivering. It must be colder than he had realised. 'How much further?' he asked.

'Just here,' the priest said. 'The roof drops steeply and then we enter the great hall.'

Stefan followed the priest, stooping below the low ceiling. Further ahead the space around them opened out, and he was able to stand upright in a wide, open chamber. The place they were standing in, he now saw, was in fact a hub off which other corridors radiated like spokes from a wheel. Although there seemed to be no source of ventilation, Stefan could feel a faint breeze rippling around his face. The same musty, slightly sweet, smell wafted upon the air.

'This is where the dead are entombed,' Andreas explained. 'Each of the six passages leads to a chamber containing their remains.'

'But the chambers are sealed?' Elena asked, anxiously.

'Oh yes,' the priest assured her. 'Sealed with stone and mortar. There are rooms here that even I do not enter.'

'And this space?' Stefan asked.

'This is the great hall of the dead itself,' the priest replied.

Stefan gazed around, taking in his surroundings. The great hall was a circular chamber thirty or forty feet in diameter, with a domed ceiling rising to about twice the height of a man. Runes paying homage to the god of death were carved upon the walls, giving the place the look of a simple chapel. Set in the very centre of the chamber was a low platform or table hewn from the same grey stone. Placed at intervals across its surface were six unlit candles.

'This is the place where their spirits come to give worship to the great god Morr.' He smiled, gently, at the group around him. 'Of course, that's just a story.'

'Well,' said Elena at last. 'At least we'll be safe enough from those monsters up above.'

Stefan took the priest to one side. 'What of the monsters below?' he asked, quietly. 'The monster who may be among us even as we speak?'

Andreas looked around, and shook his head. 'I'm sorry, Stefan,' he said. 'Dark spirits abound everywhere in this place. It would be like looking for a single shadow amidst a forest.'

'Very well,' Stefan replied. He turned back to face the others. 'We must set a watch, if we're to be here the night. Who will be first?'

Tomas stepped forward without hesitation. 'Let it be me,' he said, firmly.

Stefan looked at him, doubtfully. 'What's the matter?' Tomas demanded. 'Still don't trust me?'

Stefan thought about it. It was Tomas alone who had been examined by the priest and found to be true of soul. Ironically, he could be trusted above any of them.

'All right,' he said at last. 'You'll keep watch the first hour. Then wake me, and I'll take over.' Tomas nodded briskly, clearly pleased that his value had been recognised at last. 'Don't worry, Stefan,' he said. 'I won't–'

'I know,' Stefan said, anticipating him. 'You won't let me down.'

THE WORDS STAYED uppermost in Tomas Murer's mind over the next half hour of his vigil. He wasn't going to forget that this mission, and this watch, was a last chance. A last chance given him after a lifetime of wasted chances and lost opportunities. He would not throw it away now. He had no idea how much Stefan and the others really trusted him. Not much, in all probability. Zucharov, he knew, would as soon run him through with his sword. But Zucharov wasn't here to threaten and bully him. Now he could be judged by his deeds.

Above all, he had to keep himself from falling asleep. His whole body seemed to cry out from lack of rest, and from the cuts and bruises he had sustained above ground. Too many hard years had taken a heavy toll on Tomas Murer, he knew that. His body no longer forgave him so easily. Soon, he would rest, but not yet, not yet.

He at least had an ally in that respect. It was bitingly cold in the chamber, so cold that his hands and feet soon began to throb with an incessant, numb ache. Tomas stood up and stamped his feet a few times. When this had no effect he took a few steps around the chamber, cautiously at first. He felt the blood start to pump around his body again, and took a few steps more, circling the huddle of sleepers on the floor of the chamber. He found he had no fear of the tombs of Morr, nor of the priest's tales of the undead army of Baldrac. There had been too many times when death would have been a welcome release for him to be afraid of it now.

In fact, there was little inside the tomb to occupy him at all. It was cold, quiet, and almost totally dark once he had stepped from under the weak pool of light cast by the lantern. Almost, but not quite. Tomas stopped in his tracks, his eye suddenly caught by something glinting upon the floor of the chamber.

Tomas rubbed his eyes and bent down low. He knew what he appeared to be seeing, but couldn't quite believe it. It was a bottle, or rather a flask made of a polished, silvery metal. He took a few steps closer. The apparition failed to vanish.

Tomas Murer stood over the flask, then, after a moment's hesitation, bent down and picked it up. The familiar scent of Bretonnian gin filled his nostrils as he lifted the flask to his face. Tomas cradled the flask, turning it in his hands. Then he pinched his fingers around the cork stopper and gently pulled it free. There could be no harm in that. The perfume seeping from the flask blossomed out, filling the chamber. Tomas now forgot all sense of cold, or his own weariness. All he had in his mind was the warming, sweet smell of the liquid gently swilling inside the flask. It was like turning a corner, and suddenly chancing upon an old friend.

Tomas had not greeted this particular friend for many months, not since that day that Stefan had woken him in his lodgings. He had struggled since then to live without this, his particular daemon. And hadn't he succeeded in that, over the weeks of hardship that he had endured? But now, here in the freezing silence of the tombs, he suddenly felt in need of his friend once more. He had endured much: too much, most men would say. To have suffered the perils of the Drakwald was one thing. To have come within an inch of losing his life to the men he had believed his comrades was another. He deserved some respite. Surely no one could begrudge him that.

He lifted the flask towards him and tilted it. The smell of the gin brought the memories back in a flood. Memories of good times, and of bad. Memories of what he had once been – and of what he had become. Tomas tilted the flask towards his lips, and then kept turning, tipping it until it was upside down and the precious liquor was draining away before his eyes.

As Tomas watched it seep away, he felt the loss stabbing through him. He shook the flask, vigorously, fighting against himself. And, as the loss began to subside he felt something besides, something he could not remember experiencing in a long while. It might be fleeting, or even yet prove to be an illusion. But it was a feeling Tomas remembered as being whole once more. A feeling of self-belief.

He stood up, taller and stronger. Half of him felt as though he had gone mad, but he was smiling nonetheless.

He was still smiling as he turned back towards the light, and something hit him, hard, full in the face. Tomas Murer fell back, senseless, his head cracking against the stone floor of the tomb.

LISETTE STOOD OVER Tom Murer's prone body, momentarily unable to remember where she was or how she had got there. She did not remember being asleep; she did not remember waking up. But, after a few confused moments she recognised Tomas, and saw at once that he had been wounded. A stone statue, a carved icon of Morr, lay upon the ground by his side. The statue was smeared with the same blood that now ran from a gash across Tomas's brow.

Lisette's first instinct was to do what she could to help him. She was no healer, but she liked to think that Shallya sometimes blessed her with those powers in times of need. But, before she could bend down to tend to the stricken Tomas, Lisette was overpowered by an altogether more powerful instinct.

Where before there had been only silence, something now stirred deep in the belly of the tombs. A sound like sleepers waking from their long dream, struggling to break free of an unnatural confinement. The sound terrified Lisette, yet she found that she was drawn, irresistibly, towards it. She got to her feet, Tomas completely forgotten, and walked slowly towards the largest of the tunnels leading from the chamber. Though she was moving closer to the source of the sound, it did not grow any louder. She realised that the sounds of frenzied scraping were actually inside her own head, rising above the throbbing pain that still pounded at her skull.

They hear me, Lisette remembered. *And I hear them.*

Inside the tunnel it was pitch black, yet she found herself walking ever faster, as though led on by invisible hands. Where she was going, there would be no need of light.

She came at last to the end of the tunnel, a smaller chamber framed by thick, stone walls. A dank, lifeless chill hung upon the air, beading Lisette's face with moisture. Unbidden, her arm lifted up, and reached out into the darkness. Her fingers found the outline of carvings upon the face of the wall. This, she understood, was where the unquiet dead had been lain to face eternity. The clawing sounds inside her head doubled in intensity as if something lying trapped behind the stone wall now sensed her presence.

Her hands continued to move over the stone, tracing the pattern of the carvings overlaying the face of the tomb. These were the holy seals, the chiselled runes that held the dead confined. These spells could not be overcome from within the tombs. Only from without.

As if on a given signal, the sounds and the pounding pain inside her head both ceased. Lisette experienced a moment's blissful peace, and then the spell entered her mind, an incessant, flowing mantra repeating the words in an ancient tongue.

Lisette's lips parted and she spoke, giving the words life.

THE SOUND WAS like a low, animal moan, and it sent a tremor through the walls, as if the tombs themselves were calling out in anguish or pain. Stefan rubbed his eyes hard to make sure he really was awake. He looked round, momentarily disorientated. The first thing he saw was Tomas, face down upon the floor, a pool of blood spreading out beneath him. Stefan shook Bruno awake. 'For Taal's sake,' he said. 'We're under attack.'

The two men lifted Tomas and lay him upon his back. Elena appeared by their side, and lay one hand upon Tomas's chest.

'He's still breathing,' she said. 'It's not as bad as it looks.'

'I assure you, it's very bad indeed.'

Andreas was listening intently to the sounds coming from all around them, his expression betraying the gravity of what he knew.

'It's the Scarandar,' Bruno said. 'They've found a way to break into the tombs.'

Father Andreas shook his head. 'No,' he said. 'Those sounds aren't coming from outside.'

Lisette emerged from the shadows, her face deathly pale. She clutched her hands together in desperate prayer. 'Our presence has disturbed the fragile sleep of the unquiet dead,' she said, slowly. 'Great Morr forgive us.'

'This is not Morr's doing,' the priest muttered. 'These cursed souls have been called back to this world by a darker power. The dead are rising from their graves.'

Elena's attempt at a laugh choked in her throat. 'But the dead can't do us any harm, can they – I mean it's not as if they'll be–'

'Armed?' The priest hesitated as though burdened with some very bad news indeed. Stefan spared him the need to answer Elena's question.

'If I understand it correctly, it would be the custom to bury with the dead along with the tools of their wrongdoing,' he said. 'In which case…'

'Armed,' Bruno affirmed.

A sound like a great door being broken apart filled the chamber. Stefan turned back to Father Andreas. 'Is there anything you can do?' he asked. 'Any prayer, or incantation that might reverse this?'

'The prayer of transfiguration,' Andreas replied. 'Offered by the graveside to speed the soul on its journey to the kingdom of Morr. But I don't know whether– '

'In the name of the gods, do what you can,' Stefan exhorted, drawing his blade. 'The power of prayer may prove as mighty a weapon as the sword now.'

The sounds around them were growing louder by the moment. 'It looks as though we'll soon have the chance to put those weapons to the test,' Bruno commented, grimly. 'How are you supposed to kill a man who's already dead?'

A good question, Stefan admitted. 'We'll find out,' he told him. He held his sword steady and stood his ground. Wherever Alexei Zucharov was, right at that moment Stefan was cursing him.

The first warning of the attack came as a gust of air expelled from each of the six passageways surrounding them. But this was no cooling breath of life, but the very stench of death itself, foul and corrupt.

A bitter bile rose in Stefan's throat as the putrid draught invaded his lungs.

'Stand your ground!' he shouted. 'Mortal or not, they'll still yield to our blades.'

Now that the moment was finally upon them, any fear inside Stefan dissipated. The sword in his hand became an extension of his body. He knew he would wield it to savage and merciless effect. He forced down a deep breath, and, as he did so, the first opponent emerged from the mouth of the passage ahead of him.

It was a being that had rested long in the embrace of the dread Lord of Decay. The bleached ivory bones protruding from the tattered remnants of clothing marked the figure as once human, but no longer. The flesh upon the corpse's face and arms had been replaced by the same blood-red worms that had feasted upon it. Its jaws hung slack open, and a foul yellow pus dripped from the remnants of its mouth.

The creature plunged at Stefan, one maggot-arm fastened around a sword encrusted with the filth of the grave. Stefan met the sword stroke with an upward thrust from his own. He pushed the attack away, then swung the full weight of his blade down, slicing the creature's body in half across the waist. A sea of writhing worms spilled across the marbled floor of the tomb as the creature disintegrated before him.

Stefan had barely a moment to savour his victory before two more of the undead were upon him. He found himself under attack by what, once, would have been a young man. The cadaver's face was bleached to a green-tinged white, but its skin was still smooth and unbroken. In its face, Stefan saw the vestiges of the kind of a man with whom he might have shared ale and stories around a tavern table. He did not let such thoughts deflect the purpose of his sword. His parrying stroke slipped through the creature's guard and slit open its head from throat to forehead. Like his ghastly comrade, the cadaver crumbled upon the ground.

Stefan had destroyed two of the undead in quick succession, but it did not lessen the resolve of the others still pouring from out of the tombs. It seemed that they who had no life could have no fear of death. A third assailant was upon Stefan now, forcing him to retreat from the sheer ferocity of the attack. Stefan stared into the face of the dead man. The eyes bulged, bright and clear, in the creature's otherwise decaying face. But they did not seem to see Stefan, or even to be aware of his existence. Some malign force was turning the carcasses to its will, animating the rotting bodies like grim marionettes.

Marionettes or not, the creatures could still wield a sword to deadly effect. Stefan lost his balance momentarily and had to roll sideways across the floor of the tomb to avoid the chasing sword of the undead. As he looked up, he saw Elena despatch the creature with a double-handed stroke. She was covered in all manner of filth from the battle, but she drove on with her blade as though possessed with an avenging energy more than equal to that of her opponents.

The moment's respite gave Stefan a chance to take stock of the turmoil raging around him. Father Andreas was upon his knees before the table, the sceptre of Morr held out before him. His eyes were fastened and his lips were moving, endlessly repeating the words of a prayer. Stefan's other comrades were holding fast in the thick of battle; no one yet had fallen. But Elena now had a clutch of attackers upon her. Lisette was huddled at Elena's feet, her body drawn up in a ball. She held her hands tight over her ears, as though trying to block out a deafening noise. The undead creatures appeared to take no notice of her, but were drawn like flies towards their pursuit of Elena.

Stefan rushed forward but found his way blocked by at least three more of the creatures. He caught sight of Bruno on the far side of the chamber and shouted his name, trying to alert him to Elena's plight. After a split second that seemed like an eternity, Bruno broke away from the combat, saw Stefan, then turned toward Elena.

Hurry, man, Stefan implored, beneath his breath. They'll cut her to pieces. Bruno beat a path through with his sword until he stood but a few paces short of Elena and her attackers. Blood was trickling down her face from a cut across her forehead. She was fighting with the courage of a warrior, but the strength and number of her adversaries would inevitably overpower her.

As Stefan regained his feet he saw Bruno lunge forward as if to thrust his sword into the midst of the cadavers bearing down on Elena. And then, for no apparent reason, he stopped. Bruno was standing fixed to the spot, as though his body had suddenly been cast in ice.

Stefan screamed out his comrade's name again, but this time to no effect. The sword was knocked from Elena's grasp. As the creatures closed upon her, Stefan saw Tomas clamber to his feet and lurch unsteadily towards the ring of attackers. He was barely conscious, but his clumsy sword bought some precious respite.

Stefan now wielded his blade in a fury, despatching each successive cadaver that moved in to block his path. Butchered limbs still writhed and twisted upon the ground where they had fallen, and eyes rolled in the sockets of severed heads, but they would do no more harm. A gore-spattered apparition staggered in front of Stefan, a sabre rammed into the bloodied stump of one flailing arm. Stefan thrust his sword to the cadaver's gut, releasing a cloud of winged insects that glittered in the lamplight before falling to earth. Stefan kicked the tottering corpse aside and reached Elena, drawing her in behind the protection of his sword.

'Thanks,' she said. Her body was shaking. 'Thank you, both of you,' she said to Stefan and the still dazed Tomas. Stefan looked around for Bruno. Like a clock that had been rewound, he was fighting again as though nothing had happened, beating back more of the undead.

Father Andreas had not moved. He still knelt before the stone table, holding the sceptre of Morr aloft.

'Our lord of all souls,' he intoned. 'Grant these your children their eternal rest'. He intoned the phrase over and over, the words gaining intensity with each repetition.

A shadow fell across the priest where he knelt as something emerged from the mouth of the passage in front of him. Stefan gazed at the creature in disbelief. He doubted whether it could have ever have been human. It stood head and shoulders above the tallest man, and was so broad that it completely blocked out the passage from which it had emerged. A gangrenous pus leaked from the weeping sores upon its body, and horns of blackened bone could be clearly seen budding on top of its swollen head.

'Our Lord of Souls,' Andreas repeated. 'Grant these your children–'

Suddenly, the giant cadaver seemed to falter, swaying as though overcome by some mightier power. As the monster fell back, it lashed out at Andreas, raking his face and body with yellowing claws. The priest dropped face down upon the ground, and did not move again.

Several things now seemed to happen at once. Stefan and Elena rushed forward as one, Elena to tend to the fallen Andreas, Stefan to press home the attack upon the monster which had fallen back upon its haunches at the mouth of the passage. As the huge creature sank to the ground, so the parody of life that had been animating the cadaver army seemed to ebb away. Bones splintered and cracked, flesh peeled away from bones. Heads drooped and hung slack as the light retreated from dead eyes.

Lisette had spent the last minutes cocooned in a ball upon the ground. Now she suddenly leapt to her feet, and raced ahead of Elena towards Andreas as though her very life depended upon it.

For a moment the two women were jostling for space over the priest's prostrate body. 'Please, I beg you, mistress,' Lisette entreated. 'I have the power of healing. I may be able to help him.'

Andreas seemed to hear, and opened his eyes momentarily. 'I am beyond help now,' he mumbled, pain blurring his words.

Elena looked at Lisette for a moment then stood back. 'All right,' she said. 'Do what you can.' Lisette bent low over the priest, and lay her hands upon his body.

'The prayer,' Andreas whispered, 'did it work?'

'It worked,' Stefan affirmed. 'Hold on. You're going to live.'

The priest smiled briefly. 'No,' he said, his voice now growing weak distant. 'But fear not for me. Soon I shall journey to meet an old friend.'

Lisette continued to work desperately, as if unwilling to accept that her healing could not prevail. At the last Andreas opened his eyes and found Elena.

'May all the gods bless your journey,' he whispered. As his head slid to one side his gaze fell upon Lisette. As the priest looked upon the girl his eyes widened. A final urgency suddenly seemed to grip the priest. He started to raise his head, and his mouth opened and closed, desperately trying to form around the words.

'Peace!' Lisette implored, her hands pressing the sick man down. 'Peace!'

'He's trying to tell us something!' Elena shouted. She pulled Lisette back. 'Andreas, what is it?'

A convulsion shook the priest's body, then his head dropped back against the ground. Elena stared for a moment at the priest's body. Lisette was still crouched over the dead man. She seemed either not to have heard or heeded Elena's words.

'In the name of Taal, get away from him!' Elena commanded. Lisette turned a baleful stare upon her mistress and, finally, backed away. Stefan took hold of Elena, and pulled her gently away from the priest. 'It's too late,' he said. 'We've lost him.' He turned towards Bruno. 'What happened back there?'

'What do you mean?' Bruno responded.

'You froze,' Stefan said. 'Elena nearly died.' He stood staring at Bruno, waiting for some kind of explanation. Bruno shook his head. He looked confused, uncertain.

'I don't know,' he said. 'Everything went blank. I don't remember any more.'

'You'd better start pulling things together,' Stefan said, his anger cooling. 'You're not going to survive for long like that.' He looked round at Tomas, leaning upon Elena for support. 'For your part, well done,' he said.

Tomas's face was a mask of blood, and a heavy bruise was starting to swell above one eye. 'It was nothing,' he said.

Stefan fixed the wounded man with a stare and then smiled. 'No,' he said. 'It wasn't. It wasn't nothing by a long way.'

CHAPTER TWELVE
Reckoning

VARIK SURVEYED THE carnage of battle through the unblinking eyes of Haarland Krug. He gazed upon the dead with equanimity. He had not chosen to count the number fallen, but knew that it was many. It mattered not. It was of no consequence to him whether he had lost ten of his men or a hundred, so long as he had resources left to finish the job.

And he had. A dozen or more of the Scarandar, the youngest and sturdiest of the crop, were gathered round him at the entrance to the tombs. They had borne their share of wounds inflicted by the Kislevite and her mercenaries, but their lust for blood was undiminished. They would not have long to wait.

On the open field their quarry had proved elusive; fast on horseback and – Varik was forced to concede – skilful with the sword. But now, in seeking refuge below ground in the tombs they had allowed themselves to be trapped. There was, he knew, just a single way in – or out – of the tombs. The iron door was still secure, but not for much longer.

He would gain entrance to the tombs by the simplest of means.

The emissary sank down upon one knee and squeezed shut his eyes. His mind floated free of the shackles of its human form. He had not far to reach out; it took but a moment to touch the tortured soul sitting alone amongst the exhausted mortals below ground. It took but a moment to utter the command. And this time the command was straightforward: *Open the door.*

The emissary rose to his feet, and waited, his ears attuned to the slightest of stirrings below ground. There were footsteps upon a stone stairway, deep beneath him still but growing ever closer.

Varik shouted a command and had three of the men around him ready to haul upon the iron doorway set into the ground at their feet. The footsteps grew louder until they had all but reached surface level. The emissary listened to the sound of a key turning inside a heavy lock, and smiled as the lock sprang open.

The Scarandar seized the door and freed it from the earth. Varik stepped forward and stared down into the vault. The expression on the face looking back up at him was both terrified and expectant.

Emissary Varik moved down onto the first step, a chosen dozen of his men close behind.

'Yes,' he affirmed, in answer to the unspoken question. 'You have done well.'

DEEP BELOW GROUND, Elena sprang round in sudden alarm. 'Fathers of Kislev,' she cried, 'What was that?'

'The door,' Stefan shouted. 'They've breached the door above us.'

He looked around desperately for some means of barring the passageway leading to the great hall, but knew it was almost certainly already too late. The chamber echoed with the sound of the Scarandar descending from above. They would pour into the tombs like water through a breach in a dam.

'We'll have to stand and fight them here,' Stefan declared. 'I'll kill the first that dares to show himself. And we'll take it from there.' It wasn't much of a plan. But, right then, it was the only plan he had. He braced himself at the sound of footfalls upon the steps.

The sounds from above had reached the bottom of the shaft. Now their pursuers were in the short tunnel that led to the great hall. If they are to take us, Stefan vowed, then it will be at a handsome price. As he raised his sword to deliver the first blow, two figures emerged out of the gloom of the tunnel.

'No!' Elena shouted. 'Wait!'

Stefan's blade hung poised in mid-air. In front of him stood a huge, bear-like man with a pock-marked face like a battleground. Somewhere, Stefan knew, he had seen him before. But it was the figure being held captive by the giant that really caught Stefan's attention. Lisette's face was white with fear, her trembling frame dwarfed by that of her captor. The man looked directly at Stefan and spoke in a voice that seemed somehow not to be his own.

'Behold,' he said. The man's face was immobile, yet the voice was full of mocking laughter. 'Your faithful thief is returned to you.'

Elena stretched out a hand towards her maidservant, then hesitated, confused. 'What is he talking about?' she demanded, of Lisette, of anyone.

'Lisette took the key from the priest as he lay dying,' Stefan said. 'She's our traitor. The one that Andreas tried to warn us of.'

'It can't be true,' Elena cried. But they could both see, from the look in Lisette's eyes, that it was. For a moment, Stefan actually experienced relief. The dark, almost unbearable suspicions about Alexei, even about Bruno, were suddenly washed away. Then he found himself facing the Bretonnian girl again, and his question echoed that voiced out loud by Elena.

'Why?' She gazed at Lisette in stunned disbelief. 'Why have you betrayed me?'

Tears were streaming down Lisette's face. 'I'm powerless against them,' she sobbed. 'It's like there's someone inside my body, someone evil. And the voice – the voice inside my head. I can't get rid of it. It tells me what to do. I have no choice but to obey it, mistress, *I have no choice.*'

The man shoved Lisette forward, roughly. Light glinted off the blade of a knife that he had pressed close to the girl's throat. As they moved into the chamber, more of the Scarandar followed in behind them.

'We are here for the Star,' the man said, speaking again with that strange, disembodied voice. 'We have no other interest in any of you. Surrender the two parts that you have, and it's over. Otherwise–' He traced a gentle line along Lisette's throat with point of his blade. 'Otherwise we start here.'

'Give them the Star and they'll let us live,' Lisette said, desperately. 'I'm sorry mistress, with all my heart, I'm sorry.'

Elena struggled with the emotions warring inside her, anger battling with pity. 'I can't let him kill her in cold blood,' she said finally to Stefan. 'Whatever she's done, I can't let that happen.'

'They're going to kill us all anyway,' Stefan said, quietly. 'They just want us to surrender the Star before the butchery begins.'

'The Star will be of no use to you,' Elena told the man wielding the knife. 'Killing Lisette or the rest of us will bring you no closer to its power.'

'I'm waiting,' the man said, the voice cold and emotionless. 'Surrender the Star and we'll leave you alone.'

'Mistress, I beseech you, ' Lisette begged. 'The Star is all they want.'

Stefan weighed their chances of survival. In the confined spaces of the tombs they would doubtless despatch a good many of the Scarandar. But this was no phantom army of cadavers waiting to be cut down. These flesh and blood men were well armed, and would fight until the last. Their minds might be enslaved but their bodies looked anything but feeble.

Stefan rated the chances of success as slim at best.

'All right,' he called out. 'Let the girl come over here and I'll give you what you want.'

'The Star,' the pock-faced man repeated. 'First the Star, then you can have the girl.'

'Tomas,' Stefan said. 'Give our friend here what he asks for.' Tomas looked momentarily blank, then, after a few seconds' hesitation made a show of fumbling in the pockets of his breeches and shirt. 'Here somewhere,' he said. 'Sure it's here somewhere.'

Stefan was directing his focus on the leader. If he could get close enough before the guards on either flank moved against him, he might be able to get one clean strike. They might not win the day, but their deaths would not be without a price.

VARIK'S PATIENCE WAS reaching an end. It would have been easier to retrieve the Star of Erengrad before they put the woman and her escort to the sword, but if they had to tear the tombs apart to find it, so be it. The Star would be his, before or after the Kislevite and her friends met their doom. He would not tolerate being made a fool of by this callow mercenary and his followers. The emissary tightened the grip upon the knife in Haarland Krug's leathery hand. The girl was as good as useless to him now. He may as well start the work of slaughter there.

Lisette writhed and whimpered in his arms, begging for her life to be spared.

'You promised me,' she screamed at Varik. 'You promised you would set me free.'

'So I did,' the emissary concurred. 'Never let it be said I failed to honour a promise.'

In a single motion he drew the blade of the knife back across the exposed flesh of the girl's throat. Lisette's dying scream echoed through the chamber as her body crumpled upon the ground.

Varik had already forgotten the girl. He was fixing his attention upon the swordsman they called Stefan. Here, he knew, the real threat lay. The emissary focused all of his energy like a single beam of light into the mind of Haarland Krug. The miller's normally feeble brain was racing at a speed that would have defeated all but the quickest-witted of men. Stefan moved fast, but for Varik it was like watching events unfold in slow motion. He drew his own sword, relishing the combat to come. He was going to enjoy this.

In the moment before their swords met, a sudden commotion somewhere in the passage behind distracted him. Simultaneously, Varik registered irritation, panic and alarm. One of his men emerged from the darkness, clutching at his side.

The emissary had just enough time to see the crossbow bolt protruding from the man's flank. Just enough time to notice the second figure, further down the corridor in the gloom, levelling the weapon at him.

Steel rang upon steel as Stefan Kumansky's sword drove against his own with a force that Varik would scarcely have believed possible. In the fractured second that his host body toppled backwards, the emissary saw his second assailant level the bow and curl one finger around its trigger. Time enough for him to remember that this should not be happening. That they had trapped all their enemies below ground, and set a watch above. Time enough to realise that the bolt now spinning in the air between them had been launched with unerring aim.

The view of the crossbow bolt racing in was the final image ever to pass through the mind of Haarland Krug.

WERNER SCHLAGFURST LAY face down in the filth of blood and soiled earth. He was cold, wet, and confused beyond all comprehension. A few futile attempts to stand or even move his prostrate body along the ground told him that he was badly wounded, though shock was numbing most of the pain. Even as he tried to ask questions of his own memory, the answers relating to events of only minutes ago seemed to flee from him. He no longer even remembered who he was, or had been.

Images crowded into crumbling thoughts like soldiers marching in and out of a fog. He remembered himself as a warrior of some kind, a killer of men. Remembered how good that had felt. Remembered a leader that he had followed, and an image of himself in a bar brawl flitted through his thoughts. He remembered waiting, being told to wait with the others, somewhere near where he found himself now. That had been frustrating, hadn't it? Waiting, not killing? But the leader had commanded it. Werner was to be a guard now.

Most clearly of all Werner remembered the daemon who had come, the daemon in the shape of a man. The daemon had fallen upon them like a remorseless machine, its only purpose to kill or be killed. Werner had enjoyed that at first, until he realised that the man-daemon was more than a match for all of them.

He watched them die, those strangers who were also his comrades, falling one after another beneath the red-dripping blade of this merciless enemy. And then it had been his turn.

He was the only one left to guard – to guard – Werner struggled and failed to remember what it was he had been
guarding. He had fought hard; he had no other thought but
to fight. But it was never going to be enough.

A face swam into view in Werner's fading memory. The face
of the man who had struck him down. He had bent low over
Werner to claim the crossbow that he had been carrying.
Snatch it away from him as though he were a baby.

The face that held nothing but contempt for him, and the
dark eyes that shone with a lust for battle that easily out-
shone his own.

Werner had no idea who the man had been, or why they
had been attacked. A few minutes after the daemon had
left him lying in the mud, something else had happened to
Werner. It was as if a light had suddenly been snuffed out,
and all reason and purpose channelling his being vanished.

Of one thing, at least, Werner Schlagfurst could be fairly
sure. Soon he was going to die.

VARIK WAS DYING, too. It was not an experience he had ever
expected to become familiar with. Over the course of lifetimes in the service of his lord he had perfected the art of
evading death, fleeing from the failing body of one human
host into another at the moment of dissolution. Many times
he had mocked the heralds of Morr, turning back from their
dread portals at the moment of final reckoning. He had come
to consider himself immortal.

But, this time, he had left it too late. Long before Haarland
Krug's clumsy frame had crashed finally upon the hard
ground, he should have fled, sought sanctuary in one or
other of his servants gathered round him. But the attack had
come too quickly. Varik had focused his whole being upon
the destruction of Stefan Kumansky. He had not considered
for a moment that another, equal threat might lurk behind
him. Filtered through the consciousness of Krug, his mind
had a fleeting instant to register the mocking smile on the
face of his second assailant. Then Kumansky's sword had
crashed down upon him like a mighty hammer and, as he
turned his surrogate face away, the crossbow bolt had struck,
piercing him through the heart.

Varik lay upon the cold floor of the tombs, blood pouring
in a red tide from the wound. The light was fading; it was as
though he was drifting away into the mouth of a dark tunnel.

With what remained of his mortal sight, Varik stared up at
the two men standing above him. The cursed Kumansky,
leaning arrogantly upon his sword, and the smiling assassin
with the crossbow.

'This one's dead,' Varik heard him say to Kumansky.

Dead. The word reverberated through Varik's disintegrating
thoughts like the taunting laughter of the gods.

Dead.

It could not be. This couldn't happen. With what strength
yet remained to him, Varik channelled every ounce of his
being into breaking free of his host. He would be revenged
upon them, he would be revenged.

But the physical limitations of Haarland Krug's dying body
were lying heavy upon him now, weighing him down like
chains. The gateway to the outer world was closing. He was
barely capable of thinking any longer.

Lord Kyros, he beseeched. *Do not desert your servant now.*

STEFAN LOOKED ROUND at the scene inside the tombs with a
mixture of bewilderment and relief. With their leader fallen,
the rest of the Scarandar had lost all interest in the fight.
Some slumped to the floor, seemingly stripped of all energy.
Others wandered around as though unable to remember why
they were there. Or even who they were.

Looking down upon the figure lying on the ground, Stefan
suddenly felt very tired. He raised his sword once more then
lowered it to the ground and rested the weight of his body
upon it. For a while he simply stood there, watching.

'This one's dead,' a voice next to him said. 'The rest of them
will be easy meat now.'

Stefan turned to look into the glittering eyes of Alexei
Zucharov. In contrast, his appetite for battle seemed barely
whetted. Then again, Stefan noted with some bitterness, he
hadn't already had to fight off the army of the undead.

'Leave them,' Stefan said at last. 'They're no threat to us like
this. We won't waste any more time on them.'

'They're the scum of Chaos,' Alexei retorted. 'Impotent or
not, they should be cleansed from the face of the world.'

'Not now,' Stefan told him. 'We have to get out.' Weariness was pouring over him. He doubted he had the strength to fight on. 'What happened to you?' he demanded of Zucharov. 'We could have done with you down here.'

'I wasn't of a mind to run and hide,' Alexei replied. 'I decided to stay above ground where I had room to swing my sword. Anyway–' he grabbed the hair on the dead man's head and twisted the body round, exposing the bloodied stock of the crossbow bolt still embedded in the chest of Haarland Krug. 'I reckon I've played my part down here, don't you?'

'I'm not arguing with you,' Stefan persisted. 'But if we're going to come through this then we have to work together, not follow our own whims.' He saw Zucharov's face darken, and realised that exhaustion was drawing him into a quarrel that he neither needed nor wanted. Suddenly another voice cut across them.

'Both of you,' Elena shouted. 'Shut up.' Her face was drawn and stained with tears, but there was a hard edge to her voice that made both men step back and listen.

'There are good times to have arguments,' she said, 'and there are bad times. This is a bad time. A very bad time.' She moved towards Alexei and, to his obvious surprise, put her arms around him and kissed him once. 'We're glad you found us,' she said. 'Very glad. And, now that we have, we need to get out. We need to leave, and leave now.'

'I'll second that,' Tomas said.

'It makes sense to go while we have the chance,' Bruno concurred. Stefan looked around at the four of them. He paused at Alexei, waiting for any word of dissent he might have to offer. Zucharov shrugged in a way that suggested the argument was set aside, but not necessarily forgotten. He slung the crossbow back over one arm.

'We're agreed then,' Stefan said. 'There's still a few good hours in the night yet. Let's put as much distance as possible between Middenheim and us before the sun lights the new day.'

CHAPTER THIRTEEN
Holding On

FROM AMIDST THE endless wastes of grey eternity, Lord Kyros looked down upon the narrow span of light that marked the mortal world. A part of Kyros, too, had once been mortal; one human life fused in the myriad soul of the mighty being that Tzeentch had created as his champion.

Kyros had no feeling for humankind. No feeling for those, like the Scarandar, who served his purpose, nor for those who would oppose it. All of them were but pawns, flesh figurines on the chequered board upon which the struggle between light and dark raged, a war without end.

Kyros had no doubt that victory would finally be his. But, for now, he tasted disappointment. Varik had disappointed him; his promise to destroy the Kislevite and secure the icons had proved hollow. While the Star remained outside his grasp, Erengrad might yet hold out. Kyros savoured the stirring of anger for an instant, then cast it from him, a disposable and unnecessary weakness.

He had watched Varik through the throes of his death, an unexpected transformation for the servant who had believed himself as immortal as his master.

Death would be a just reward for his emissary's failure. Kyros could let him die, or he could yet free his spirit to serve him anew. The seconds of Varik's death agonies spanned hours or days in Kyros's universe. All in good time, he would decide upon his disciple's fate.

Like a blind man, the Chaos Lord sensed rather than saw the events unfolding in the corporeal universe; smelt the ebb and flow of the energies as the struggle turned first one way and then the other. He knew that the girl had escaped him for the moment. Varik had underestimated the Kislevite. Underestimated, too, the pack of mercenaries, and the proud defiance of their leader.

Kyros peered deep into the fabric of the mortal void, trying to pluck a face or name from the clamour below. Somewhere, the paths of their destinies had crossed before. An image swam into focus: a village in flames, a boy fighting with unexpected savagery. Kislev, the sea crashing against its coast-line. And a name: Odensk.

Odensk. Memory flowered inside the being that was Kyros. With it came a cruel pleasure. So the Kislevite was on her way to Erengrad in the company of the boy from Odensk. That would be the right place for them to die. As for the others that rode with them – Kyros savoured a deepening sense of plea-sure, and knew that his god was smiling upon him. Yes, for the others, many futures lay in wait. And, upon one of them at least, the Lord of Change would bestow a special gift. A special gift indeed.

PETR ILLYICH KURAGIN had walked until his body and soul had wearied of walking. All morning he had traversed the streets and alleyways of Erengrad, surveying the great edifices and monuments of a city rich with glorious memories. Those memories only mocked him now. The walls of Erengrad, like the hopes he still clung to, were crumbling. Its foundations were rotting away. And its people – sick, hungry and divided in despair – were dying.

Kuragin recalled the day, so many years ago, when he had toured the grand avenues of the city in an open carriage, flanked by his brothers in their finery. Three brothers, barely more than boys, fearless guardians of a dynasty that would last forever. He could still hear the cheering of the crowds

that lined the streets, smell the sweet perfume in the blooms
strewn along their path.

Now his brothers would lie forever beneath the cold fields
of Praag, and he skulked amongst thieves and starving waifs,
anonymous in his dung-coloured robes. He hid his face away
behind a heavy cowl, avoiding their gaze like a fugitive. The
people would not cheer for him now.

At Praag the dark ones had launched attack after murderous attack upon the unyielding walls until the dead were
piled high both sides of the divide, and the Lynsk was gorged
with blood. Petr Kuragin remembered the time only as a
shadow, indelible, upon his childhood. His brothers, Yuri
and Alexander, had been barely more than children themselves. But they had been old enough to fight, and old
enough to die. The forces of Chaos had paid their price there,
too, but they had learnt the lessons of Praag.

In Erengrad the assault had taken a different form. Chaos
had laid its siege not with arms, but by sowing the seeds of
malevolent change across the city, slowly choking off its
lifeblood until its heart would surely fail.

Beyond the city walls to the south, the fields of wheat and
barley stretched out to the horizon. Summer would soon
approach its peak; the fields, the bountiful larders of western
Kislev, should have been brim-full. Instead they had been
laid bare, filled only with blight and pestilence. The few crops
that had survived lay rotting in the ground.

Inside the walls, the extent of the blight was scarcely less
devastating. With a bitterness that bordered on self-disgust,
Kuragin acknowledged the guilt that he and his kinsmen
must bear. For it was not only the meddlings of Chaos that
had brought the city to this forsaken pass. His own family
had contributed to the fall. Pride, greed, and simple vanity
had brought them down – that and a simmering feud with a
family with a shared but opposing thirst for the trappings of
power. His family had learnt their humility, just as the
Yevschenkos had learnt theirs. But, like all lessons, it had
come at a cost. And this time the cost had fallen on the head
of every soul within the city.

Every day that passed brought fresh rumours that Erengrad
would be saved. Wheresoever Chaos blighted the land, so
there came those who would oppose it. Stories were rife of

convoys travelling from Praag and Kislev, of wagons groaning beneath the weight of food they carried west. But Praag and Kislev were still weak from the ravages of war, and any promise of help from the Empire seemed distant and weak. The O ld Alliance, Kuragin feared, was at risk of falling apart. And even if they came, there was no guarantee that Erengrad would be able to hold together for long enough.

Even time, perhaps, was now on the side of Chaos. How often had it been said that Father Winter would come to Kislev's aid in times of peril? No creature, it was said, not even the foulest incarnation of the Dark Lords themselves, could survive that bitter season. But, this time, it was different. The people might survive the months of summer, only for cruel winter to finally destroy them. Sick and malnourished, they would die in their thousands.

Could there really still be a chance that the wounds of Erengrad could be healed? Walking the stinking streets of the lower city, listening to the weeping of the people, Kuragin found it hard to believe. Harder still to believe in the healing power of three broken pieces of beaten silver, and a girl who might even now be lying dead, far away from the borders of Kislev.

In the last week alone, more than a dozen city militia had perished protecting the city from rioters. It was a sign that the enemy within was becoming as much a force to be reckoned with as any that might threaten from without. Or perhaps, he reflected darkly, those enemies were now one and the same.

Kuragin moved on, trying to lift his sombre spirits. A crowd had gathered around some spectacle or other at the foot of the hill. Petr Illyich Kuragin quickened his pace, resolved to determine what it might be.

STEFAN EXTENDED THE spyglass and scanned the length of the tree-lined valley they had recently crossed. Elena watched him in silence for a few moments, then reached for the spyglass and pulled it away.

'You've been checking the path behind us every day since we left Middenheim,' she said, not unkindly. 'And in all that time you haven't seen another soul – man nor beast. Perhaps there really is no one following us.'

They sat side by side on the hilltop. The high path they had been following for the last few days had brought them temporary relief from the endless span of forest. From up here they could see for miles: to the granite-toothed peaks of the Middle Mountains, the dark green expanse of the Forest of Shadows, and beyond, towards the borders of Kislev itself. The land was a patchwork of undulating greens and browns, lit by the gentle hues of the rising sun. From afar the Old World looked very much at peace. Stefan knew it was not so, but, for a few moments at least, he allowed himself to take refuge within that comforting illusion.

He sat back, savouring for a moment the warmth of the sun against his body. The season was changing; the fresh chill of spring had ebbed, and summer would soon be in full bloom. Time was passing: weeks now since they had left Erengrad, and close on two months since their journey had begun, a lifetime away in Altdorf.

How much time had they left to complete that journey? Stefan had no way of knowing. All he knew was that their own resources were growing thin. They had survived the battles, and had endured the deprivations that the gods had cast in their path. But they were tired, and had little money remaining. The purchase of new horses had not left them with much money for fresh provisions.

He retrieved the glass and raised it to his eye a second time. 'They won't need to follow us,' he said at last. 'There'll be plenty more of their kind to pick up where the others left off. Remember Otto's map?' he asked her. 'The map of darkness? Evil is everywhere. Behind us, ahead of us, all around. It knows no borders.'

'You make it sound as though all we are doing is clinging to faint hope,' Elena said. 'Clinging to the rock of hope against the black tide. Holding on until we are all swept away.'

'Maybe so,' Stefan replied. 'But I know there is as much light in this world as there is darkness. That tide can still be turned. But we have to believe it. Believe it with all of our hearts.'

Elena stretched out her legs on the grass in front of her, turning her bare ankles in the warming sun. 'What do you think Bruno believes?' she asked, suddenly.

Stefan turned to look at the figure of his comrade, sitting in solitary contemplation on the hilltop fifty paces away. 'I don't know what he thinks,' he said, and realised he was admitting to himself a truth that he had been trying to deny. A year ago, before Stahlbergen, he and Bruno had been as close as brothers. Together they had carried their swords in battle wherever the gods had decreed. They owed each other several lives; they had shared the joys and sorrows of the soldier's life on the road.

Now, Stefan realised, Bruno had become a stranger. The man who had come back from the Grey Mountains had filled his comrade's frame, but was his comrade no longer. In battle, since joining the expedition, Bruno had plied his sword when needed with the indifference of a hardened mercenary. There was no joy in their travels now, but Stefan sensed plenty of sorrow. And something worse.

'Back in the tombs,' he said to Elena, 'when those creatures were upon you. I saw what happened. I don't know why it happened. But I saw it, right enough.'

'You mean with Bruno?' Elena asked. She shrugged. 'It's in the past now.'

'Not for me,' Stefan said. 'You could have died because of Bruno. It was as though he had become paralysed by – what? Fear? I don't know. But the friend I used to know wouldn't have let that happen.'

'Are you saying he's become a coward?'

'I don't know what he's become,' Stefan replied. 'But he's not the same man I once knew, I'm certain of that.'

'You should talk to him,' Elena said. 'Find out what's changed.'

'I've tried,' Stefan said. 'He treats me like a stranger. Whatever it is that happened to him, he's built a wall around himself to keep the world out. But I will know what this is about,' he declared. 'And before we quit the borders of this land.'

'Perhaps all he needs is more time,' Elena commented.

Stefan sat for a while, watching the man who had been his friend. 'You know,' he said at last. 'There was a moment back there, in the tombs, when I thought it was him. Thought it was Bruno who had somehow betrayed us to the Scarandar. And I started thinking of what it would be like to have to hunt Bruno down with my own sword. What it would be like to kill him.'

'But it wasn't him,' Elena replied. 'It was Lisette.' In that moment the veil of sadness passed from Stefan to the young woman at his side. Elena's voice became heavy; her head dropped. For a few minutes they sat in silence, watching Tomas practise his sword-strokes with the enthusiasm of a schoolboy.

'Your judgement was right there, at least,' Stefan observed.

'It was your judgement, too,' Elena reminded him.

They watched as Tomas finished his practice and went to sit by Bruno. To their left, Alexei Zucharov prowled the hilltop like a caged bear. Of all them, he seemed the most anxious to be underway once more.

'What about him?' Stefan asked her.

'What about him?' Elena said. 'What do you mean?'

'I mean,' Stefan said, 'you seemed mighty pleased to see Alexei when he showed up in the tombs.'

Elena turned and stared at Stefan, a puzzled expression on her face. 'Of course I was pleased to see him,' she said. 'Weren't you?'

'Yes,' Stefan replied. 'In a way. But I didn't feel the need to kiss him.'

'I was trying to put an end to your stupid fight,' she retorted, irritably. 'That seemed to be the most direct way to break it up.' She paused, head on one side, looking at Stefan. A slow, knowing smile crept over her face. 'Wait a minute,' she said. 'Are you jealous?'

'Don't be stupid,' Stefan snapped. To his dismay he felt his face reddening under her stare. 'I just wondered whether you feel something deeper for him, that's all. I need to know about these things,' he added, regaining some composure.

Elena smiled at him kindly this time, then turned away to gaze towards the land beyond the mountains. Sitting on the hilltop, her arms hugging her knees, she reminded Stefan of a child at a carnival, eagerly waiting.

'Do you know,' she said at last, 'this is the first time I've really thought about going home.'

Home. The word sounded in Stefan's ears. Home. Was that where he was going, too?

'What part of Kislev did you say you were from?' she asked him. Stefan hesitated. 'I didn't,' he eventually replied. 'It was called Odensk. At the mouth of the Lynsk.'

Elena looked blank. 'What happened?'

'Our village was destroyed,' Stefan said. 'It was Norscans, men and mutants amongst them. They might have been headed for Erengrad, I suppose. But they found us first. They slaughtered every living thing they could find. Even the animals in the fields.' He paused, deep in recollection. 'That was my first taste of Chaos,' he said. 'I suppose you could say my life began anew there.'

He looked up, into her eyes. 'What about you?' he asked. 'The rest of your family, I mean?'

Elena laughed, but with little warmth or humour. 'My family? Let's not start on that again now.' She closed her eyes. 'Let's just enjoy the sun while we can.'

She let her head fall back until it came to rest, gently, upon Stefan's shoulder. Stefan felt himself stiffen instinctively and then relax, aware of the softness of Elena's hair against the cotton of his shirt. Aware, too, of a softening inside him, for a moment at least. It was not a feeling he had allowed himself very often on the long ride from childhood through to his life in Altdorf. A journey he was perhaps now retracing.

He looked up as a shadow fell across them where they sat. The tall figure of Alexei Zucharov loomed over them, blocking off the sun. 'Sorry to break up this tender scene,' he said, 'but I think we need to get moving now.'

HE WAS CLEVER, Kuragin had to give him that. He was working the crowd gathered in Katarina Square with the practiced skill of the street-trader and the piety of the priest. The clothes had changed – just a little shabbier and down at heel than when they had last met. And even the voice had changed; he had somehow managed to make it sound both humbler and yet more strident. And yet there was no mistaking who it was up on the platform, whipping the huddled mass into something approaching a pious frenzy. It had taken Kuragin only a few moments to recognise the sinewy figure of Count Vladimir Rosporov.

The carefully crafted transformation from wealthy noble to man of the people was all but complete. Certainly none amongst the crowd of starving wretches surrounding Kuragin seemed to think for a moment that Rosporov was anything

other than one of their own. Petr Kuragin tugged the hood of
his garment a little further over his face and pushed his way
towards the front of the crowd until he was little more than
an arm's length from his enemy. Then he stood to listen, careful not to get so close that Rosporov might spot him amongst
the throng. He suspected that this would be a bad time for
his true identity to be made known.

'Brothers!' Rosporov extolled them. 'Are we hungry? Are
we sickening, are we weak?' At each question the crowd
offered up an answering roar that belied the apparent frailty
of many of the men and women standing beside Kuragin.
Whatever their state of body and mind, he realised, they
were angry.

Rosporov raised his hands to the crowd to quieten them.
He prolonged the gesture, letting the sunlight play upon the
shrivelled, pock-marked flesh of his right arm.

He parades his infirmity before them like a badge, Kuragin
thought. A badge that says, 'I too have known pain. I too am
a child of suffering.' Clever indeed.

'Truly, we are dying of hunger,' Rosporov went on. 'But who
should we blame for the empty ache in our children's bellies?'

Most of the assembled crowd were silent. Rosporov let the
question hang in the air, playing his audience with a show-
man's guile.

'Could it be,' he continued, 'that the *real* enemy of Erengrad
lies not with some imaginary power lurking out there, but
here, right within the city?' A murmur rumbled through the
square, gaining momentum as the idea found favour with the
crowd.

'Where are our leaders?' Rosporov demanded 'What have
they done for us? Who are our leaders supposed to be? Two
crumbling dynasties, too bloated on the fat of our land to
give a thought to the needs of their starving people?' A cheer
went up now, ragged but heartfelt, and edged with a thirst for
vengeance. Kuragin shuddered.

'Two ancient families, too busy squabbling amongst themselves to care a fig for the city whose honest citizens have
sweated blood to earn them their wealth?'

The cheering doubled in intensity. An urge rose up in Petr
Kuragin to speak out, whatever the consequences in the

midst of the volatile mob. To announce himself to his people; to deny the heresy that Rosporov spun so smoothly. To his shame, he found himself unable to speak, his tongue seemingly locked tight in his mouth. But others – a few – did raise their voices against the tide. One man in particular strode to the front and stood before the platform with his back to the count and his men. Kuragin recognised him. It was Martin Lensky, an ostler from the north quarter, a coarse but steadfastly honest man who would have no truck with double dealing or duplicity. Kuragin was pained to see that he had looked as though he'd lost almost half his weight, and his voice, once lusty, now sounded reedy and thin.

'It's the meddling of Chaos that's brought us to this!' Lensky called out, struggling against the barrage of voices rising up around him. At the word Chaos, much of the sound seemed to die down, and a more sober mood fell across the crowd.

'Believe me, friends,' Lensky shouted at them, 'if we let Chaos gain a foothold in Erengrad, then before long the living amongst us will envy the dead.'

For a moment there was almost total silence. All eyes, Kuragin's included, fell upon Count Rosporov, awaiting his response. Again he held the silence until the tension seemed near breaking point.

'Then you have encountered Chaos?' he asked of Martin Lensky, mildly. The ostler shook his head, understandably nonplussed by such a question. The count arched his finely drawn brows, feigning surprise at Lensky's response. A low muttering spread across the ranks of people in the square.

'But you seem to have such deep knowledge of the so-called Dark Powers,' Rosporov continued. 'Or could it just be your empty belly giving you hallucinations?'

He raised one arm to cut off the ripple of laughter that, incongruously, greeted his reply. 'Who amongst you has encountered them?' Rosporov demanded of the crowd. 'Who can speak the truth of it?'

'I can.'

All eyes now swivelled towards a figure standing towards the middle of the crowd. Kuragin, too, found himself completely drawn to the spectacle. His searching gaze found a small, wiry man dressed in dung covered artisan's robes. He stood uneasily amidst the crowd, as if waiting an allotted turn to speak. Rosporov, like a kindly teacher, encouraged the man to continue. 'Tell us,' he urged, 'in your own words.'

The man spoke quickly, glancing around him as he delivered his words. 'I was starving hungry,' he said. 'I couldn't stand it no more. One night I sneaked out over the east wall, where the ramparts is lowest, just at the time when the guard was changing. I didn't know just what I might find, nor what I hoped for. Only knew I couldn't stand the hunger any longer.'

'And?' Rosporov prompted. The silence in the crowd was absolute now.

'I was feverish, mad from hunger,' the wiry man continued. 'I don't know how far I strayed, or what would have become of me, if they hadn't have found me.'

'*They*?' the count enquired.

'A body of men. Travellers, I was reckoning. But there were tall swordsmen in black amongst 'em. Men with armour, shields covered in strange runes and the like. I'm an ignorant man, your worship, but I knew what those runes signified, all right.'

'Go on,' Rosporov urged him, softly.

'They had the mark of the Changer upon them,' the man said. Gasps of astonishment broke out around him. 'But they didn't do me no harm.' The man looked around, nervously. 'Fed me a meal, then sent me on my way, so they did. First hot food I'd eaten in a week!'

A confusion of voices broke out, some raised in disbelief, some in hope. Petr Kuragin felt a sick chill running through him. Surely they could see that Rosporov had contrived all of this? Surely they could not believe a single word?

But that was just it, the chill told him. We have fallen that low. They want to believe.

Vaguely, he heard Rosporov's voice running on, teasing out the sham that he was passing off as interrogation, and then the wiry man replying:

'They knew we was starving,' he went on. 'Told me they would come to the aid of the city, but the guardians of Erengrad wouldn't allow it.' Shouts of outrage from the mass. Some voices – Lensky and others – were raised against them, but they were drowned out.

'And, these so-called "monsters" – have they launched great assaults against our walls?' Count Rosporov demanded. His eyes were ablaze now, and white spittle flecked his dark beard. 'No! I ask you again – who are our enemies here?'

Kuragin turned and pushed his way back through the crowd. Once clear, it was all he could do to stop himself from running. He had stood and listened to it all – every lie and manufactured word of it – and had not spoken a single word in response. Guilt burnt in his chest, but his lips were fastened shut.

As THE SUN began to set, the path started to track down, along the side of the valley, back below the tree-line. Stefan and Elena rode at the rear, Tomas ahead of them trying to converse with Bruno. Alexei Zucharov had taken the lead, impatient to make progress. His thirst for conflict was rarely slaked for long, Stefan reflected. After another hour or so they had reached the point where the road forked. To their right, the clearer, beaten track led away towards the highway linking the Empire with its eastern border. To the left, a lesser trail marked the way up towards the cloud-wrapped peaks of the Middle Mountains.

This was the point the priest had spoken of. Their way lay between these two, a path so overgrown as to be barely visible. This was the way that would lead them to the Forest of Shadows, and beyond, to Kislev.

Alexei, out front, checked his horse momentarily at the fork and then turned briskly onto the road for the mountains. Stefan caught sight of what he was doing and pulled up short. 'Wait – stay back with the others,' he instructed Elena. 'He's taken the wrong road.' He tightened his grip upon the reins and spurred his horse into a gallop. Riding at full pace he overhauled Alexei, pulling ahead of his horse then waving the other man down.

'What's the matter?' Alexei demanded, irritably.

'I wanted to stop you before you went too far,' Stefan told him. 'You're on the wrong road.'

Alexei looked back towards the crossroads he had just passed. 'But the other way leads to the border road,' he said. 'We agreed that even if the border was still open, the road through would be too conspicuous for us.'

'So we did,' Stefan concurred. 'We also agreed that we would avoid the mountains, and take the path through the forest. This is the mountain road.'

By this time Elena and the others had caught up. 'What's wrong?' she asked them.

'Nothing,' Stefan said. 'Just a misunderstanding.' Now he was the one anxious to be getting on. He turned his horse around.

'Just a minute,' Alexei said, shaking his head. 'There's no misunderstanding. Or maybe I misunderstood you when you spun us that fool's yarn about creeping through the Forest of Shadows.'

'That's exactly what we're going to do,' Stefan said, his hackles now rising. Alexei pulled a face that was half-derision, half-disbelief. 'Gods' breath!' he exclaimed 'Haven't you had enough yet of this infernal tangle of trees?'

Stefan took a deep breath. He would keep his temper under control. 'Andreas gave us clear advice,' he said. 'He was no fool, no more than Otto. I'm going to stand by his judgement.'

'Oh, come on!' Alexei looked to the others, seeking support for his cause. 'Through the mountains we can save two, three days' travel – maybe more. Who knows how long it would take us to pick our way through yet another vast, impenetrable wood!'

Stefan looked away, his eyes kept fastened upon the path to the east. Bruno and Tomas hung back, but Elena started to move towards Alexei.

'Maybe Stefan's right,' she told him. 'The priest must have had good reason.'

'I know the mountains,' Alexei countered. 'Know them as well as any. What's the problem, anyway?' he asked of Stefan. 'Afraid of a few bandits?'

'I'm afraid of no man,' Stefan replied, evenly.

'Have it as you will then,' Alexei said, contemptuously. He gathered up his reins. 'You can do what you want. I'm headed for the mountains.'

'No,' Stefan said quietly but firmly, his tolerance exhausted. 'No, you're not.'

As Alexei turned and headed on, Stefan spurred his horse to the gallop, pulling round in front of Zucharov and blocking his path. The adrenalin was pumping through him, his heart hammering in his chest. He was not going to take this.

'I made a decision,' he told Alexei. 'If it proves the wrong one, then that's my responsibility. But it's my decision and I'm staying with it.'

'Suit yourself,' Alexei replied, his lip curling in a half-sneer. 'I'll see you at the gates of Erengrad. If you ever make it.'

'Turn your horse about,' Stefan ordered. 'We ride together, through the forest.'

Alexei seemed to beckon with his hand, a gesture that might have signalled either compliance or disregard. Stefan drew his horse in closer. As he came within arm's length of the other man, Alexei struck him, hard, on the side of the face.

The blow knocked Stefan clean from the saddle and sent him sprawling upon the flint-strewn ground. He lay there dazed for a moment, blood running from his mouth. As he looked up he saw Alexei upon his horse, towering, imperious, above him.

'I made a few decisions, too,' Alexei said. 'One of them was not to put up with any more half-baked nonsense from anyone, including you. You call yourself a leader, and you think that gives you the right to treat me like some errand boy, running at your beck and call.'

Without waiting for any reply, Zucharov tugged back on the reins and turned his horse about. As Stefan regained his feet, Alexei was already pulling away from him, heading for the mountain road. In a few seconds he would be out of reach. Stefan launched himself forward and caught hold of a buckle trailing loose from the saddle. The horse bucked but did not slow as Alexei Zucharov kicked in with his spurs, urging the animal on.

Stefan gripped hold of the leather strap with both hands but it was going to be impossible to hold the powerful hunter. For a second time he was on the ground, now being dragged along behind the horse. Somewhere in the background he could see Elena running towards them, but it was too late. The horse was gathering speed.

The stony ground was punishing Stefan, bruising him and cutting into his flesh. He wouldn't be able to hold on for much longer. He put all his energy into one final lunge,

taking one hand from the harness and grabbing a hold on
Alexei's booted foot. Alexei turned and looked down, and
pulled his foot free of the stirrup to kick himself free of
Stefan, much as he might shoo off a chasing dog. For a
moment he was off balance in the saddle; Stefan gripped
his flailing leg with both arms and bore down with all his
weight. Alexei Zucharov rocked sideways, then toppled out
of the saddle and onto the ground beside Stefan.

Now it was Stefan's turn to make a point with his fists. As
Zucharov got up, Stefan punched him hard upon the jaw, the
blow connecting with a satisfying crack. Alexei flinched
under the unexpected force of the blow, but managed to stay
on his feet. Stefan hit him again, knocking him back, but by
the time he'd closed in on his opponent, Alexei had recovered. Stefan felt a heavy blow to his stomach, then more
blows raining down on his face and shoulders. Within
moments Zucharov had worked himself into a fighting
frenzy, not far removed from the killing machine that had
destroyed the orc in the arena.

Stefan knew his greater speed was his best weapon, and he
had to use it. He darted around Alexei, dodging and parrying
the other man's assaults so that at least half his punches met
only empty air.

At last the opportunity came. Frustrated, Alexei lashed out
carelessly, leaving his guard open. Stefan avoided the blow
easily and kicked out at Alexei, knocking his legs from under
him. As he fell, Stefan was on top of him. Running on pure
instinct, he pulled the short knife from his belt as he dropped
to the ground.

Alexei's stare widened as he saw the knife. Time missed a
heartbeat as the blade flashed in the air, then bit into the
hard ground inches from Alexei Zucharov's face.

Someone pulled him back. Elena pushed her way between
the two men.

'Enough!' she shouted. 'In Taal's name, end this now!'

Stefan stood for a moment, his breath coming fast and
short. 'It's all right,' he said at last. 'It's all right.'

Alexei looked from the knife to Stefan, standing over him,
sweat pouring off his face.

'You make your point well, Stefan Kumansky,' he said, smiling now. His rage seemed entirely spent, forgotten. Alexei

clambered to his feet, taking hold of his opponent's arm for support. He gave Stefan a wry smile.

'You win, this time,' he said.

Stefan was in no mood to make a joke of what had happened. 'Nurgle's breath!' he spat, half at Zucharov and half at himself. 'I could have killed you.'

Alexei gazed at Stefan and grinned, slowly. 'No,' he said, confidently. 'You'd never do that.'

CHAPTER FOURTEEN
Into the Darkness

IT WAS THE cold that Stefan noticed first. The day had begun much the same as many that preceded it: close, and humid as the sun burned away the morning mists. But less than an hour into their morning journey they had passed across the western edge of the great forest that bounded the realms of the Empire and of Kislev. As they entered the Forest of Shadows the temperature had dropped, and kept on dropping. Eventually they had been forced to stop and put on extra layers of clothing, and still nothing seemed to keep out the cold. Even the tombs of Morr had not chilled like this.

Few travelled here. The stories told of the forest were not those of seasoned travellers passing through its midst, but of lost wayfarers or the survivors of foolhardy errands. It was a dark, secret place, where the powers of the old gods were said to dwarf those of mortal man, or even his enemies. Those who travelled its tangled paths and returned counted themselves lucky to have done so with their lives and sanity intact.

These were the stories Stefan had in mind as they began their voyage into the dark interior. For all that, the Forest of Shadows was not, at first, what Stefan had expected. For a start, although nothing that could be called a road ran beyond the very fringe of the trees, the way into the woods was surprisingly open. The horses were able to find a path with ease, and, at times, it was possible to ride two or even three abreast.

Stefan looked around as the forest closed in behind them. Up above, the sun still burned, a bright disc in a now cloudless sky. Beams of dust-flecked gold played amongst the shadows and the towering pines. He had no exact idea how broad the forest was, but, with three or four hours of good daylight left to them, they would at this rate be well into their journey before night fell. The only sounds were the muffled clutter of the hooves in the soft, loamy soil, and the occasional conversation that passed between them. Stefan began to feel the forest lulling him into a cold but not unpleasant reverie, as he nudged his mount forward at a gentle pace.

It was just after they had stopped to gather extra clothes that Tomas commented on something strange. 'I must have lost account of time,' he said, puzzled. 'Is it near nightfall already?'

Stefan looked around him. Over the course of time his eyes had adjusted to the diminishing light. But now that he looked he found that the surrounding forest was slowly melting into a dimming twilight, something he would not have expected for another two or three hours.

Bruno turned his gaze skywards. The sun was still clearly visible overhead, barely below the highest point in the sky. 'By the mark of the sun I'd say it was close on four,' he said, 'But certainly no more.'

Elena rode huddled in her winter cloak. 'Yet down here it's all but night,' she said. 'This is not a welcoming place!'

'True,' Stefan acknowledged. 'But we knew well enough that this wasn't going to be easy.' He looked back up at the roof of the forest, struggling to reconcile the clear, sunlit sky with the gathering gloom around them. That the sun was penetrating into the forest was beyond dispute; the thick, oil-dark shadows that sprang from the trees and gave the forest its name bore testament to that. It was as though the forest was working some alchemy upon the sun's rays, leeching away the light and warmth, turning day into night. At this rate of decay it would be effectively dark within the hour.

'We'll keep on,' Stefan concluded. 'At least while we can. We may have to go more slowly, and stop once the forest has drawn night down.'

Alexei Zucharov emerged through the screen of grey, pulling his horse close alongside Stefan's. 'If we light torches we can still ride on, dark or no dark,' he said. 'This place is vast. We have a great distance to cover.'

'I know that,' Stefan replied. 'But we could lame a horse or worse in this. It's not worth the risk.'

He held Alexei's stare and scrutinised it, looking for any hint of their recent quarrel. Somewhat to his surprise, Alexei simply shrugged and turned away. 'Wouldn't want to lose one of the horses,' was all he said.

The paths were narrowing now. Almost without their noticing, the forest had taken on a breathtaking intensity; the woods far darker and denser than anything they had experienced in the Drakwald. The trees crowded in around them, and the ground had become overgrown with a tangle of roots and fallen branches.

They rode one by one, a tense, single file. In the fast vanishing light their progress had slowed to less than walking pace. Still the sun burned mockingly up above, but, down in the forest, its force was spent. Soon Stefan would have to admit defeat. His instincts told him to treat the mighty forest with respect, and to learn to live within the boundaries it imposed. That way, they might all yet feel the sun on their backs once again.

With what remained of the poor light he found a clearing amongst the trees. It was tight, barely large enough to accommodate their camp. He drew his horse up, bringing the other riders to a halt.

'This is it,' he called back to them. 'As far as we go this night, if night is what we can call it.'

Together they dismounted and set about pitching their camp with the quiet ease that comes with practice. When they had done, Bruno kindled a fire in the centre of the clearing, and Stefan and the others gathered round, trying to draw what warmth they could. By now the sun had vanished below the tree-line, and all above was dark as below, save for the feeble light from the twin moons like dull coins set in the early night sky.

The flames licked the night air as the fire caught quickly on the dry wood, but what heat or light escaped seemed to be drawn quickly into the forest's sombre embrace.

For all that, they took heart from the fire. It was good to be resting after the day's riding. Before long they were making lively conversation. Stefan joined with them, but kept a good part of his senses trained upon the alien world that had enveloped them.

They might be safe, for now, but this was not a safe place. Every so often the curtain of darkness encircling the camp was pierced by a momentary flicker of light, or low prowling eyes that glinted before disappearing as suddenly as they had come. Stefan supposed the forest was home to all manner of animal life, some harmless, some otherwise. For the moment, the curious amongst them were keeping their distance.

Alexei produced a flask and passed it round. Tomas took the flask at arm's length and passed it deliberately to his left. Stefan accepted it gladly; it was too cold and too soon to think of sleep, and any way of warding off the cold was welcome. The talk around the fire became more animated as the liquor warmed bodies and minds alike.

Amongst the competing voices around him, Stefan now heard something else; distant, but distinct. He strained to listen more closely, over the babble of conversation.

'Hold up a moment!' he urged. He rose swiftly, and, with two fast sweeps of his feet, extinguished the remains of the fire.

'What are you doing?' Bruno demanded, slightly drunk and very annoyed. 'I didn't build that for fun, you know!' The others stared at Stefan, waiting for an explanation.

'Shut up a moment,' Stefan told them. 'Stay quiet and just listen.'

The flames expired with a few last gasps and crackling of twigs. Now all they had for company was the eerie sound of the wind caressing the trees above. Almost, but not quite. As the fire died, another sound carried towards them from somewhere in the depths of the forest. All were silent now, barely able to make each other out in the darkness, each alone with the wind and the strange, distant sound. A sound like…

'Like shouting,' Elena said at last, a hushed voice across the clearing. Stefan assented, silently. It sounded like shouting to him too, but not from the throats of men.

'Can anyone make out what it is?' Tomas whispered.

'Could be animals of some sort,' Bruno suggested. He was known for his keen hearing, and his tone was chastened and sober now. 'But I don't like the sound of it.'

'Neither do I,' Stefan agreed. 'We'll assume it's not friendly, until proved otherwise.'

'The question is,' Alexei said quietly, 'what do we do about it?'

Stefan thought for a moment. He doubted whether they would be able to track the sounds through the wood in the pitch black. By the same token he hoped that whoever – or whatever – else was camped in the forest would be similarly unable to track them.

'We do nothing, for now,' he said at last. 'But as soon as whatever passes here for dawn has broken, we're going to find out.'

'Do you think they know we're here?' Elena asked, struggling to keep the note of anxiety from her voice.

'I doubt it,' Stefan said. 'They'd be keeping quiet if they had.'

This time the cold saw to it that no one fell asleep on watch. Stefan saw out the last duty, taking over from an exhausted Tomas, who immediately curled himself into a ball inside his cloak upon the forest floor. The night passed, slow but uninterrupted. Stefan was almost glad to abandon the pretense of sleep. It felt as though the cold had penetrated the very marrow of his bones, a deep chill that no amount of massaging of his tired limbs would relieve.

From time to time he heard again the sound of men or beasts, twisted upon the wind. But finally that, too, had ceased. Stefan kept his vigil with only the broken whistle of the wind, high in the trees, for company. Eventually the sky lifted to a dull metalled grey, and a new day struggled through the thick canopy of trees into the forest.

Stefan roused his comrades from their fitful rest, and the five of them ate a quick, cheerless breakfast of salted meat.

'Nothing further in the night?' Alexei asked, addressing the question to Stefan.

'Not a sound for two hours or more,' Stefan told him.

'What do you think they're doing?' Tomas asked. Bruno spat a knot of gristle onto the hard frosted earth in front of him. 'The same as us, I expect,' he said. 'Sitting out the night under cover, trying to keep body and soul alive in this infernal cold.'

Elena gave up on the leathery wafer, tossing the remnant into the trees. 'More to the point,' she said, 'who or what do we think they might be?'

Stefan stood up and brushed himself down. 'That,' he said, 'I intend to find out.'

Tomas guided them deeper into the forest, the position of the sound etched clear in his scout's memory. It soon became apparent the sounds they had heard had come from somewhere almost exactly upon the line they had plotted to take them through the forest. It seemed, one way or another, that the paths of the two parties were destined to cross.

After a short while the sun came up, a rose-pink orb shrouded in the fog that clung to the treetops. The feeble light gained a little strength until they were at last able to pick out a path through the woods ahead of them. If it got warmer at all, it was only relative to the dead chill of night.

'Make the most of it,' Stefan advised. 'I have a feeling that this is as good as it gets.' They trekked further into the forest, the trees growing leaner and more tightly clustered, almost forcing each other aside in the struggle for what little air and light remained. Before long, Tomas had dismounted and was leading his mare by the bridle. One by one, the others followed his example.

They continued in this way for almost an hour, until, emerging through a tangle of briar standing almost head-high, they found the way ahead blocked.

'Taal's breath!' Bruno exclaimed. 'That was a mighty tree before it fell.' He made to lead his horse off the path, seeking a way round the obstacle.

'Wait a moment.' Stefan stepped past him and joined Alexei at the point where the huge creeper-covered object lay blocking the path. 'I don't know,' he said slowly. 'I'm not so sure this was a tree at all.' He drew out his knife and hacked away at the outer layer of leafy vines clinging to the cylindrical shape in front of him. After a minute or so of cutting back, his blade struck against something hard, and sprang free with an almost metallic ring.

'If it is a tree,' he said, 'it's the first tree I've ever found that's not made of wood!'

Tomas rushed forward now, his face flushed with a sudden eagerness. He helped Stefan cut away at the mass of tangled vegetation. 'I know what it is,' he said. 'You're right, it's not a tree. It's the remains of a column, cut from stone.' He scraped back a last fibrous strand and stood back, triumphant. Where the creeper had been cut away, a length of moss-speckled stone was clearly exposed, its surface curved and undoubtedly the work of some craftsman.

'A column?' Elena said, incredulous.

'I think it's part of a larger structure that's long since disintegrated,' Stefan said, running one hand over the pitted surface of the stone. 'A monument, perhaps. Or the base of a tower.'

Elena was far from satisfied. 'A tower? And who would want to build such a thing, way out here?' she asked.

Stefan ran a hand thoughtfully along the mottled stone. 'The same race who once built towers all over the Old World,' he said at last. Tomas nodded enthusiastically, encouraged that Stefan had picked up on his line of thought.

'Elves!' he said, excitedly. 'It's the remains of an elvish settlement!'

'Rubbish,' Alexei scoffed, 'The elves never came this far.'

Stefan wasn't so sure. 'I don't know,' he said. 'Who knows what they may have achieved before the time of our reckoning.'

'Well, tower or tree, we have to get round it,' Alexei concluded. He climbed back into the saddle and nudged his horse forward, using his sword as a scythe to cut a fresh path around the obstacle. They pressed on, cautiously. Tomas continued to scan for any evidence of the ancient race, and before long he called them to a halt again.

'Look at this,' he insisted. All of them, even Alexei, gathered round. Tomas worked quickly with his knife, attacking the vegetation covering a low object to the side of the path. Eventually he stood back, clearly pleased with himself. 'What do you make of that?' he asked, indicating with his hand.

Stefan squatted down to inspect what might have been the low wall of a building or house, the upper portion long since broken or rotted away. Underneath the carpet of moss the stone was smooth. For all that it was old and crumbling, the stonework was unusually fine, and in places it was sculpted with the faint imprint of runes, the likes of which he'd never seen before.

'Well?' Tomas demanded, totally absorbed now in this new mystery. 'What do you think?'

Stefan was still considering his reply when they heard the noise. It came from the direction of the sounds from the night before, and sounded like a muffled explosion, followed by harsh voices raised in dispute. He got up, quickly.

'We don't know who or what that might be up ahead of us,' he said, lowering his voice now to almost a whisper. 'And until we do, we're going to be careful. Come on,' he said. 'And not a sound now.'

They moved on, slowing the pace of the horses to make as little sound as possible. As the clamour of voices grew louder, further evidence of a settlement right there in the forest began to emerge. Now that they knew what they were looking for, the foundations of houses, walls and even the remains of what might have been a small temple became visible through the gloom. The forest had long since reclaimed them as its own, muffling the shapes in layers of choking green, but the mark made by the ancient architects was clear.

Stefan found his imagination starting to run away with him. The shapes were unusual, beautiful in their way, but alien. What if it had been the elves? What if they had returned now to their ancient dwellings in the forest? What sort of encounter would lie ahead of them? He tried to visualise the tall, noble warriors of legend for a few moments, then reality and instinct pulled him back. Up ahead, jumbled sounds of many voices raised against each other in anger or confrontation. Elves? Almost certainly not. But they might not be men, either.

Smoke was visible now, a spiralling wisp of grey winding through the branches of trees no more than half a league ahead. Stefan reckoned it to be the remains of a breakfast fire, kindling wood set alight by their fellow explorers, oblivious or indifferent to the tell-tale marker left behind.

'Now I have them,' Tomas muttered. 'Strike a path due north and we'll be on them in a matter of minutes.'

'Steady,' Stefan cautioned. 'It looks at the moment that we know about them but they don't know about us. Let's keep it that way until we know what we're dealing with.'

They pushed on in silence, treading as softly as they could upon the brush-strewn floor of the forest. Soon they were close enough to smell the smoke and an acrid stench of burning meat. The voices were louder now. The words remained indistinct, but sounded foul-tempered and arrogant, and still engaged in the running feud that Tomas had been tracking them by for the past half hour.

Stefan raised his hand. 'Wait,' he commanded. 'Alexei and I are going in to take a closer look. Bruno, Tomas, stay back here with Elena.'

He nodded briefly to Alexei, and the two men advanced on foot into the undergrowth, using their swords to cut back the tall rushes and low-hanging branches. 'Quietly, though,' Stefan urged. 'Let's keep the element of surprise while we can.'

The path through the woods led up a gentle slope until they found themselves atop of a wide, circular valley. The two men stood amongst the ring of trees around its edge, and looked down towards the base. There beneath them, seven or eight large figures, masked by the trees, sat or stood clustered around the still smoking fire. Stefan edged forward to listen to the argument that seemed still to be simmering between them.

'I can't make out a word,' Alexei whispered.

'Nor I,' Stefan said. 'It's not Reikspiel, that's for sure.'

Alexei leant forward as far as he dared over the lip of the crater. As he did so, one of the circle stood up and turned about so as to face Stefan and Alexei square on. The figure reached up to its full height and slowly turned its large, horned head before propelling a gobbet of phlegm onto the ground with a sullen grunt.

Stefan and Alexei exchanged glances and pulled back, simultaneously.

'That's settled, then,' Stefan said quietly. 'Let's get back to the others.'

* * *

'BEASTMEN,' TOMAS REPEATED, uneasily. 'That's bad news, isn't it?'

'Very bad news,' Stefan confirmed. 'The good news is they don't know we're here. Yet.'

'What would they be doing out here?' Elena asked.

'The depths of the forest is where they'll often be found,' Tomas offered. 'It may be no more than that. Just–'

'I know.' Alexei interjected. 'Just bad luck?' He looked at Tomas, and raised one eyebrow.

'No,' Stefan replied. 'Definitely not bad luck. I don't think they're here by chance. From what we saw, I'd say there was some kind of tribal gathering about to take place.'

'Something of the sort,' Tomas agreed. 'Or a council of war.'

Elena shivered. 'I don't much like the sound of that,' she said.

'More to the point,' Bruno said. 'What do we do now?'

'Well,' Stefan replied. 'They're right in our path. So we either go round them, or we go through them. If we go round them, there's no guarantee they won't start tracking us. So the alternative is, we take them straight on.'

'Which means we fight,' Alexei added, in case anyone had missed the point.

'Which means we fight,' Stefan concurred. 'We only saw seven or eight of them. There's probably more, but at least we'll be fighting on our terms, and we have an element of surprise. It's our best chance.'

Alexei guided them back towards the ridge cresting the crater. By now they were trying desperately to silence every footfall, but, as they closed on the beastman camp, it became clear that the sound coming from inside the hollow would easily block out any sound of their approach.

Stefan raised his head cautiously above the lip of the hollow. The scene below had changed. Most of the beastmen had pulled back into a circle at the base. Two that remained at the centre were squaring up to each other over the embers of the fire. Whatever their dispute was about, it looked to be reaching its critical point.

'Let's take them now,' Alexei whispered beside Stefan. 'They're so caught up in their own quarrel, they won't even know we're here until we're amongst them with our blades.'

Stefan shook his head, slowly. 'Not just yet,' he breathed. 'I want to find out what they're doing here first.'

The bigger of the two beastmen was a figure some seven feet in height, a thick, muscled torso topped with a head grown in the likeness of a bull. The creature seemed to be haranguing the second, much smaller beastman, a half-man creature rearing up upon the hindquarters of a goat. The second beastman was shaking its head from side to side in apparent disagreement with the first. As it turned its head, the tall, curling horns growing from its skull darkened to a blood red, and a flush of rainbow colours ran the length of the creature's body.

The second beastman began speaking in a coarse, guttural voice. The other replied with a snorted contempt, spraying knots of dark mucus over the forest floor. It goaded the goat-like creature, jabbing it in the chest with a crude staff fashioned from firewood.

'Not a friendly chat by the fire,' Stefan murmured.

'They're using the dark tongue,' Tomas replied.

A momentary look of suspicion flickered over Stefan's face.

'I learnt a few words, knowledge passed on from other woodsmen,' Tomas explained. 'In the forest, it pays to understand your enemy as well as you can.'

Stefan nodded. 'All right then,' he said. 'Tell us what you understand of this.'

'I can make out a little of what they're saying. They're arguing – something about a battle plan.'

The second beastman regarded the first with pure loathing, but retreated a step or two back beyond the fire. The goat-man's eyes flicked around the rest of the beastman group, weighing up what support he could count upon. More than half of the horned beasts roared their support, and a daemonic, bestial wail filled the forest.

Emboldened, the second beastman turned back to face the bull-creature and let loose what sounded like a string of insults.

'What's happening?' Stefan demanded of Tomas. 'What is he saying?'

Tomas's brow furrowed as he struggled to make sense of the ancient tongue. 'He's invoking a name,' he whispered. 'Sounds like Kyra, or something similar. Kysos, perhaps.' He paused. 'There's something else, too – I'm fairly sure they're arguing about Erengrad.'

The bigger beastman jabbed again with his staff, but the caprigor's speech seemed to have had a sobering effect on him. He took a few steps back, circling the smaller creature cautiously. The goat-creature looked round, taking confidence from the sullen nodding of the other beastmen, and snarled a further insult.

The bovigor let fly a bellow of rage and charged towards the smaller creature, ready to lock horns with his opponent. The surrounding circle of beastmen broke up in confusion, supporters of each camp squaring up against the other.

On top of the crater, Alexei turned calmly towards Stefan. 'Now might be a good time,' he suggested.

'There won't be better,' Stefan agreed. He drew his sword and turned to Elena. 'Sorry, you've got to stay here.' He intercepted her protest with a hand across her mouth. 'No arguments,' he said. 'These are monsters, not men nor even animals. There'll be plenty of other times for bravery.'

He nodded once towards Bruno and Tomas, then vaulted into the bowl of the crater.

He focussed on the two leaders, locked in combat at the centre of the clearing. He was closing on them fast. The big, ox-headed creature was still oblivious to Stefan behind him; his focus was still upon exacting revenge from the smaller caprigor. At the last moment, the second beastman saw Stefan and the others piling down upon them. His warning to his comrades was cut short by the ox-head cracking open his skull with the heavy staff. One down, thought Stefan.

A moment later and he piled into the back of his target, with enough force to knock the heavy beastman forwards off his feet. The others knew they were there now. The moment of surprise had gone, but the advantage it had bought might yet prove precious.

The bovigor rolled on the ground, crushing his former opponent. The beastman was bellowing curses in the dark tongue, unable to fathom where the counter-attack had come from. Stefan soon let him know. As the massive creature clambered upright, Stefan drove his sword down, cleaving the beastman's shoulder from the bone. The beastman gazed at him with a look of dull shock.

'Don't worry about Erengrad,' Stefan told him. 'We'll save you the journey.' Clasping his sword two-handed, he swung the blade a second time and sliced deep into the bulbous neck of his opponent. The beastman staggered and fell, his thick cloven hands still groping for his weapon.

'Look out!' Stefan registered the voice in his ears and ducked instinctively, just in time to see a blade flash over his head. Stefan spun round, and was sprayed with a stinking gore as Alexei's sword laid low his attacker.

Three down, Stefan reckoned. How many did that leave? The forest seemed to be alight with the rainbow-hued hides of their enemies. Bruno was under attack from two beastmen at once; his tattered shirt was already flecked with red where blades had found their mark.

Stefan battled his way in amongst them, drawing one of the attackers off. To his left, Tomas was in single combat, under pressure but managing to hold his own. And Alexei, he knew, was in his element. All of them could better the beast-men for speed; Alexei alone could match most for bulk and brawn as well.

Yes, my mutant friends, Stefan vowed, we'll make you pay a heavy price for your adventures. He bellowed a battle-cry to match anything the beastmen could muster and set about his new opponent with a blaze of sword-strokes. Though almost a runt by beastman standards, the caprigor still stood shoul-der to shoulder with Stefan, and probably weighed half as much again. That gave Stefan an edge in speed which the beastman couldn't match; he danced around his opponent, dodging the flailing blows the beastman aimed at him with his axe.

Finally the goat-creature threw caution to the winds, and swung the axe wildly at Stefan's head. It missed him by an inch, scything a lock from his hair as it passed, and buried itself in the trunk of a sapling. Before the beastman could wrest the blade free, Stefan had struck back, his sword slicing through the mutant creature's forearm above its claw. For a moment the beastman stood staring at the severed claw, still fastened to the axe embedded in the tree. Then Stefan drove his sword deep into the creature's gut, running the beastman through. A foul stench filled the air as the beast fell back-wards, clutching at its ruptured belly.

Four down, or was it five? Stefan drew breath and tried to take stock of the scene. Bruno and Tomas had accounted for three beastmen between them, but both looked very, very tired, and Bruno in particular seemed to have borne a heavy brunt of battle.

In all, six beastmen now lay dead or dying upon the ground. On the far side of the crater, Alexei was trying to take on two that remained. He had lost hold of his sword somewhere along the way and was locked in a desperate struggle, wrestling empty-handed with a half-human apparition clad in a gore-spattered jerkin of leather. The last of the beastmen was circling round the combatants, waiting for the moment to stab Zucharov in the back.

'Alexei!' Stefan shouted, in alarm. In Taal's name – the man wasn't immortal. Alexei didn't respond, but Tomas looked round and pulled himself upright, suddenly seeming to find new energy. Before Stefan could move he was charging towards the beastmen. The creature with the dagger drew back his arm to strike at Alexei. Before the blow could fall Tomas crashed against him, burying his sword in the beast-man's thick body until only the hilt was visible.

Too late, the last beastman realised he was outnumbered and tried to break free. Alexei pulled the creature back towards him and smashed a fist twice into its bovine face. 'Dagger!' he yelled at Tomas. Tomas wrested the knife from the body at his feet and threw it to Alexei. With his opponent still stunned, Alexei whipped the knife sideways, ripping it across the leathery throat.

The beastman's dying gasps gave way to a heavy silence that seemed to fill the forest. Stefan and his companions slumped to the ground, succumbing at last to exhaustion and their wounds.

A sudden scuffling at the edge of the crater. Stefan looked around, and was astonished to see the first caprigor back upon its feet, running fast up the slope out of the crater. Alexei saw him too, and hurled the dagger through the air at the escaping creature. The dagger missed, bouncing harmlessly away off a tree. Just as it seemed that the last of their enemies would escape them, Elena appeared at the top of the slope.

'Saved one for me after all?' she called down. The beastman reached for his weapon, but Elena was faster. She parried a blow, then jabbed her sword into the caprigor's chest. 'Keep your filthy mutant claws off my country,' she snarled. The caprigor grunted, then fell backwards, somersaulting back down the length of the slope. He did not rise again.

'Bravely fought,' Stefan said, once he had his breath again. He caught Elena's eye. 'Each and every one.'

'We should be thankful to Elena in particular,' Alexei emphasised. 'I'll warrant there's more of these scum holed up not far away. If that one had got clear we could have had real trouble on our hands.'

'We still might,' Stefan cautioned. 'I suggest we don't hang around here too long.' His body called for rest, but they would all have to banish such thoughts for now. 'Who knows,' he said. 'We must get as far as we can before darkness calls another halt.' He sheathed his sword and had begun climbing the slope when he noticed Bruno standing off to one side, his head bowed as though he were studying something lying upon the ground. Bruno's right hand was stuffed inside his shirt. The grey cotton was soaked through with the lurid red of fresh blood.

'Ulric's toil!' Stefan exclaimed, running over. 'Let me look at that.'

Bruno looked up, attempting a smile. 'I'm supposed to say it's just a scratch,' he said, his voice weak.

'Some scratch,' Stefan commented. He peeled back the tattered and bloodied shirt to reveal a deep wound running the length of Bruno's forearm.

By now Elena had joined them. She turned Bruno's arm gently between her hands, inspecting the jagged fissure in his flesh. 'That will need to be properly bound,' she said emphatically, 'But it will need cleansing, too. Otherwise you risk losing your arm.' She scanned the forest floor around her. 'I've seen hempwort growing here. We must find some – it'll purify the wound.'

'You said we needed to get on,' Bruno protested, gritting his teeth. 'This is going to delay us. It can wait till we set camp.'

Stefan exchanged glances with Elena. 'No, it can't,' he said. 'Some things are worth the delay.' He put an arm about Bruno's shoulder, and drew him towards him. He felt his comrade's exhausted body begin to sag against his own.

'Bravely fought, old friend,' he said, quietly. 'Bravely fought.'

CHAPTER FIFTEEN
The Light Among the Shadows

HE HAD NO memory of how long he had dwelled within that forsaken place. Even now he could not remember whether it had been a place of light, a place of sounds, or of solid shapes. But he knew that the name of the place was death, and he knew that it had claimed his soul.

Varik curled a smile from lips which he still barely knew as his own. Once more, he had cheated death at the very last, and had returned to the world to walk again with the immortals. He still did not know who he now was. His body felt powerful, yet not young. Somewhere in the recesses of his mind, he glimpsed a memory of himself as a warrior, born of the Norscan lands, cunning and cruel. A body that had won many battles, and earned many scars. At that moment, his new identity was of no matter to him. What mattered, above all else, was that he had been redeemed. As the light of his soul faded in the Tombs of Morr, his Lord Kyros had not forsaken him. He had intervened, as Varik knew he would, to restore life everlasting unto his faithful servant.

He bowed his head in supplication. He stood in a place of silent darkness but he knew that the mighty Kyros was near.

'My noble lord and redeemer,' he said. 'Your humble servant pledges his soul anew in your eternal service.' The words felt strange and clumsy on his tongue. But there would be time enough now to mould this living flesh to serve the master's will as he had moulded that of countless others.

Yet something was different this time. It was as though another voice was speaking inside his head; the shadow, perhaps, of the soul that had been expelled when this flesh had become his.

The other voice inside his head now spoke, slurred and slow, but still powerful.

Not yours, it said. *Ours.*

The emissary shook the thought away. 'My lord,' he said again. 'Mighty Lord of Transfiguration. I am here to meet your will.' His words echoed inside the dark and boundless space before the Dark Lord replied.

'You have disappointed me.'

Varik forced his new body down upon its knees, a chill of fear electrifying his spine. 'Merciful master,' he stammered. 'I shall double and redouble my toil in your service until that debt of shame is expunged.'

'You shall,' Kyros concurred, 'else the worms will feast upon your body and death will chain your soul.'

Varik bowed still lower until his head was resting upon a floor of marbled ice.

Unbidden, inside him, the second voice spoke again. *Who are we?*

Varik slammed a fist into the ground, anger momentarily obliterating fear.

'Who am *I*?' he shouted, furiously. 'Who am I?'

'You are no longer sole keeper of your destiny,' Kyros told him. 'For I have joined you with another. This single body shall host two souls. Two souls to serve me in dual purpose.'

Varik raised his head from the ground. He could now clearly sense the presence of the other. Something was stirring inside him, feelings and sensations that were not his. A yearning; an evil, cradling hunger that threatened to consume his being. The feeling both thrilled and appalled him.

'Tell me what your first purpose shall be,' he said, quietly.

'My plans for taking the city are still thwarted,' Kyros glowered. 'My enemies still snap like dogs at my heels.'

'Erengrad will surely still be yours,' Varik muttered, humbly. A crack like breaking thunder shook the chamber in response.

'Promises are no longer enough!' Kyros roared. 'I will see the fruit of these labours, or I will not bear the price alone.'

Varik cowered until the storm began to subside. He clasped his hands together and raised his head once more towards the brooding presence of his master.

'We must marry certainty to our mastery of the laws of chance,' Kyros continued. 'If strategy and subterfuge does not achieve my purpose, then we shall crush the Kislevite cur with strength alone. I shall raise an army to march upon the walls of Erengrad. There, the doors of the city will be thrown open to us, else we shall trample them beneath our feet. You shall lead that army.'

'We shall serve in any way you command,' Varik said, 'but–'

'You are a creature of loathsome cunning, Varik.' The sonorous voice of the Chaos Lord cut across him. 'For all that you have failed me, I still have need of your guile. But, for the purpose of war I have melded your soul to that of a warrior, a remorseless bringer of death. Together, as one, you will deliver Erengrad.'

Varik felt a strange, adrenalin rush of animal lust. He could almost taste the blood in his mouth. For a moment he felt a delicious drowning as his head filled with images and thoughts that were not his own.

Our second purpose? the other voice demanded. He heard himself repeat the words out loud.

'Ah,' the Chaos Lord murmured. 'For here is your reward. Your second purpose is the common thread that binds your two souls to their quest.' He paused. 'The quest for revenge.'

A new image floated into Varik's mind. An image from the final moments of his last life. An image of a young man coming at him, blood-smeared sword held in both hands. The blade falling, cutting the air before his eyes. And the light of life ebbing away upon a sea of pain.

A name came into his mind. Kumansky. Stefan Kumansky. Suddenly Varik realised that the pain and the anger he felt were no longer just his own. They had fused with the furious rage of another; a murderous hatred which would not abate until Kumansky was dead. Varik had never felt such strength inside him driven by the lust to kill. In the dark, he ran unfamiliar hands across the contours of an unfamiliar face. There was something strange about this face, something that linked it to the hatred that still boiled within him.

'Who are we?' he asked. Out of the darkness, a gleaming panel of mirrored light opened up. Varik walked towards it, approaching his own reflection. He stared at the profile of the man who would conquer Erengrad, flexing his face experimentally. It was a face growing towards age; nearly forty summers, he would guess. But beneath the skin grown slack and lined with age and the thinning crop of corn-blond hair, there was still the strength. The strength of single-minded purpose. To kill and keep on killing.

All the time, the name kept echoing through his mind. Kumansky, Kumansky, Kumansky. Now the cursed swordsman had been given name, he could not keep it from his thoughts. The image in his mind darkened and melted. Something else was replacing it now. He saw the storm-lashed coast of Kislev drawing closer as his people hauled their boats towards the shore. The village yielding before them, the houses in flames. And he saw the small boy, kneeling amidst the ruins of Odensk, cowering but defiant. The knife in the boy's hand had been concealed; too late he now saw the blade that plunged toward his face.

Varik turned this new face the other way, exposing the left side to the mirroring light. For a moment all was inexplicable darkness again. Slowly, he lifted one hand to his face and touched the socket where his left eye should have been. Finally he turned and faced the light head-on, and stared at the blackened, pitted flesh where the eye had been gouged away. Now he truly knew who he was. And how sweet revenge would taste.

BRUNO HAD BEEN right. Tending to his wounds had set them back. Not for long, perhaps, but the hour spent was a cost in time they could barely afford. Even allowing for the speed with which unnatural night fell upon the forest, Stefan was still taken aback by the suddenness with which the day was extinguished. As they moved towards the centre of the dark woods the span of daylight seemed to be growing ever briefer. Far above their heads the sky spread out in a pane of pure azure blue, but below the high branches of the trees, no light now penetrated.

Reluctantly, Stefan turned his horse to straddle the path, signalling a halt to the other riders roped in line behind him. By his calculations, they were close to the very heart of the mighty forest.

All five of them had grown so familiar by now with the process of pitching camp that they could have done it blindfolded. That was as well, because, even with all five storm lanterns lit, only the feeblest of glows lit the air to help them at their work.

Each laboured alone, save for Bruno, whose arm was heavily strapped. Stefan worked with him, helping to lash the canvas awning against the overhanging branches of the closest trees. Both men worked in silence, but Stefan sensed that some fragile part of the bridge between them had been restored. The time for talk was perhaps close at hand. For the moment, he would wait and let Bruno find a time of his choosing.

TOMAS SAT FOR a while by Elena while they ate, but he found he had little appetite. He told himself it was boredom with the plain diet they were obliged to survive upon, but in his heart he knew it was more than that. Feeling restless, he got up and walked, holding his lamp low by his feet to find a path through the tangle of roots and fallen branches. To his surprise, he saw he was approaching a second lamp, invisible in the impenetrable dark only a few moments before. He found himself standing over Alexei Zucharov, head bowed down close by the side of the storm lantern, writing upon a sheet of paper.

'Oh!' Tomas said, taken aback. 'I didn't realise you were there.'

'Well,' Alexei replied, without looking up, 'I am.'

'I'm sorry,' Tomas added. 'You're busy. I'll leave you in peace.'

Alexei turned his head in Tomas's direction. Tomas, barely feet away, saw his face as a blur of grey, tinged orange by the light struggling from the lantern. 'No,' Alexei said, his tone warmer, more conciliatory now. 'Sit down here a while. I've nearly done with this.'

Tomas hesitated, aware of the nervousness the big man still inspired in him. Then he fumbled his way forward in the darkness and set his own lantern down upon the ground near to Alexei's. He climbed down next to it, and sat down next to Alexei while he continued to write.

'So,' Tomas began, tentatively. 'What is it you're writing?'

'A letter,' Alexei replied, simply.

'A letter?' The idea seemed odd in the extreme. 'A letter to who?'

'To my sister, Natalia,' Alexei said. He laughed. 'She worries over her big brother.'

Tomas sat for a while, pondering the improbability of getting a letter back from the Forest of Shadows – or anywhere else they were headed – to Altdorf.

'How do you – how do you know it's going to reach her?' he asked, finally.

'I don't,' Alexei said. 'In fact, I doubt that it ever will. But that's not the point.' Alexei put the letter away and held the lantern up close by Tomas so that he could see his face.

'I owe you an apology,' he said.

'No you don't,' Tomas replied, uncomfortably.

'Yes,' Alexei persisted. 'I do. You've every right to hate me, yet you don't seem to bear even the slightest of grudges. Tell me something – do you really think I'd have had you put to death back on the road to Middenheim?'

'Of course not,' Tomas replied, denying his doubts. He waited for some kind of affirmation from Zucharov, but none came.

'The truth is,' Alexei said at last. 'You've acquitted yourself well, not once but twice now. I was wrong about you. Doubly wrong.'

Despite the cold, Tomas flushed. He felt stupidly proud, and was glad of the cloaking darkness around them. But after a while the warmth faded, and the worm which had been gnawing at his stomach returned. He hesitated, unsure of how his words were going to sound, then said, 'Shall I tell you something about myself?'

'What's that?'

Tomas swallowed hard. 'You called me a drunk,' he said. 'And the truth of that is, you were right. I was a drunk. A stumbling, good-for-nothing, washed up wreck of a drunk.'

There was no judgement in Alexei's voice. 'You're not a drunk now,' he replied, evenly.

'No,' Tomas agreed. 'I'm not. But I'll tell you what. Without the drink, I can't hide from what I am, any more. It's like someone's taken away my shield, left me without any defence. Whatever's left underneath, that's all there is of me.'

'Which is?'

Tomas hesitated, and drew down a deep breath, struggling with the words. 'A coward,' he said at last. 'Fear. That's all I can feel, inside of me. I'm afraid, Alexei.' He stopped, waiting for Alexei's reaction, scorn or disdain. All he could see in the half-light from the lantern was the outline of his face in profile, and his breath like ice-clouds on the freezing night air.

'So are we all,' Alexei said at last. Tomas snorted in disbelieving derision.

'You? Afraid? Yes, you and Stefan both, I'll wager!'

'I'll wager it too,' Alexei replied. 'It's part of what tells us we're alive. Without knowing fear, we can never know courage. Fear is the shadow to the light of our bravest deeds. The drink may have numbed you to fear, but it did you no service.'

Alexei paused, and laughed, acknowledging the deeper truth. 'The time to start worrying,' he said, 'is when you stop feeling afraid.' He pulled closer with the lantern until the two men were only inches apart.

'Shall I tell you why you're here?' he asked.

Tomas nodded. He was still trying to work out if Zucharov was simply trying to make him feel better, and why he should want to do that anyway.

'Treasure,' Alexei said simply. 'That's why you're here.'

'Treasure?'

Zucharov nodded. 'Treasure. Riches and reward. Believe me, wherever there is conflict there is a prize to be won. This time will be no different.' He set the lantern down. 'The prize at the end will be different for every man. But, trust me, somewhere out there on the field of battle, your treasure awaits. Yours, and mine too.'

Tomas felt his heart beating faster in his chest. 'So what will your treasure be this time?' he asked.

'That's the thing,' Alexei told him. 'I don't know. Yet.'

Tomas sat quiet for a while, trying to find in his imagination what shape his prize might take. Alexei reached inside his pocket for his flask. Almost automatically, he offered the flask towards Tomas, then hastily pulled back.

'I'm sorry,' he apologised, 'That was stupid of me.' The bigger man stood up, and stretched his limbs. 'Time for sleep,' he counselled. 'Our treasure will wait that long at least.'

As soon as his eyes had flickered open, Bruno knew that something was wrong. He was enveloped in darkness; there was no sign of anyone, or anything, surrounding him. He assumed he had succumbed, finally, to sleep and then reawakened. It must have been the middle of the night, yet Bruno felt no sense of the crippling chill. On the contrary, he felt as though he was on fire, his entire skin, his whole body, burning with a fever. Fumbling blindly in the dark, he climbed unsteadily to his feet. He was dimly aware of his wounded arm, a dull throbbing pain at his side. That must be it. The wound had started to poison him, set a fever raging inside his body. For all he knew, he was dying. He reached to his neck, and touched the silver icon of Shallya that he wore there.

'Sweet goddess of redeeming light,' he whispered, gasping for cool air to soothe his lungs. 'Spare your follower this night.'

He knew he must find somebody. Find Elena, before his flesh burned away.

Head pounding, he took a few steps, stretching a hand out in front of him. Even the trees had vanished from view now. It was as though every last glimmering of light had been swallowed whole. Darkness was total.

Wait a minute, Bruno told himself. I've been here before. This is more than fever. This is the dream. It's happening again. He pulled the short knife from his belt and, bracing himself, touched the point of the blade against his wrist just below the bandage. The stab of pain told Bruno he was very much awake.

He called out to the others, but there was no response. The silence was as all-embracing as the darkness. He waited for his eyes to adjust, give some faint, groping semblance of vision. But nothing altered. The blackness remained absolute, and Bruno began to realise that he was marooned upon an island, with neither sight nor sound to guide him.

It can't stay this dark forever, he told himself. He would find his lantern somewhere upon the ground and relight it. Then he would find the others. He got down upon his knees, groping blindly for the lantern that he assumed must have toppled and failed. All he could feel between his fingers was damp earth and the prickling of thorny roots. It's here, he told himself. It has to be here. Everything must still be here, somewhere.

Suddenly, from out of the black heart of the forest, a stream of brightness spooled outwards like a cloud of fireflies, settling upon the ground ahead of him, a corridor of light winding through the darkness. Bruno stared at the light in disbelief, expecting the darkness to reassert itself at any moment. But the light remained, threading a golden path through the dark folds of the forest. Gradually the realisation came to Bruno that it was waiting. Waiting for him.

He hesitated for a just a few moments longer, then took a first few tentative steps along its length. With each step taken the snaking path pushed out further ahead, simultaneously fading into nothing in his wake. Bruno found himself having to walk ever faster to keep pace until he was running in pursuit of the light, not caring where it led so long as it took him out of the darkness. Wherever it was taking him, Bruno realised there would be no way back.

He ran on, anxious to reach whatever it was that lay ahead, the raging fever now forgotten. Then he heard the sounds. Faint, at first, like the distant cry of a child, but so, so familiar. Then Bruno remembered; remembered the sound and what would happen next. He stopped running. His heart was hammering inside him, and his face was running with sweat.

'No!' he cried out loud. 'Please the gods, no. I can't go through this again.'

And yet he knew that, this time, he would have no choice. As he stepped forward, Bruno released the breath pent up deep in his lungs. As he exhaled, he felt himself break free of his body and float apart from it. He gazed down at himself, running as though his life depended upon it, knife clenched in one hand, all trace of his wounds vanished.

Looking down, Bruno knew where this would end. And he knew how it would end. He saw himself enter the mouth of the cave. Saw the woman, her long gown torn and tangled upon the rocks. Saw the raw fear in her eyes, and the murderous expression of the orc that held her in its grip. And he saw his other self draw back the knife and take aim. The long moment was about to unfold again.

Bruno saw the knife turning as it corkscrewed through the air. Almost a thing of beauty. Time had slowed down; the churning blade seemed to hang almost motionless, fixed upon the air. No, Bruno prayed. Not this time. Not again.

A sound filled his ears. A sound of screaming, then deadening silence. Bruno felt himself falling back towards his own body, becoming whole once again. A juddering blow shook through his body as he fell upon the forest floor.

He got up, slowly, the pain throbbing once more through his arm. There was no cave now, no shimmering path of light. A hand touched lightly upon his shoulder, and he turned.

The fear had gone from her eyes, but Bruno recognised her instantly.

'Do you know me?' she asked him, gently.

'You're dead,' Bruno said. His voice sounded thick, distant. 'I killed you.'

The woman nodded. Her face was transformed; tranquil, at peace. She took Bruno's hand. 'I know,' she said. 'That's why we are here with you now.'

Bruno pinched himself again, but the dream refused to end. 'What is this about?' he whispered. 'What do you mean, *we*?'

The woman said nothing, but reached out her hand. Her fingers brushed against the icon hanging at Bruno's neck, and in a moment all pain, all trace of fever vanished from his body. She gazed upon him once more and smiled.

'You understand now,' she said, softly. 'The Goddess Shallya speaks to you through my soul. She is here to tell you that it is time to bury the past.'

She held out her hand. 'Come.' Tentatively, Bruno took hold of her hand. It was suffused with a gentle warmth that flowed into his body, replacing the storm that had gone before.

'It's time to forgive,' she said, smiling upon him. 'To forgive yourself.'

Bruno shook his head. 'No,' he said. 'I killed you. It's my fault you died. I can't forgive myself that.'

The woman looked away from him. For a moment a wistful sadness filled her eyes. 'My life ended the moment the creature trapped me in the cave,' she said. 'Nothing you could have done would have saved me. It was already too late. But you did all that you could. And no one could ask more of you than that.'

Bruno stood at her side, transfixed. She was surely some kind of spirit, or trick of his imagination, yet the flesh clasping his own hand felt so real, so – human.

He felt a weight, like a heavy stone, stir and lift away inside of him.

'What I ask of you is this,' the woman continued, 'honour my memory by your deeds in life.'

'You wish me to atone?'

'No,' the voice said. 'To celebrate. Celebrate each new day as a victory over darkness, and never abandon the struggle. Do that much, and my death will not have been in vain.'

WHEN BRUNO FINALLY awoke, it was from a sleep that seemed to have lasted for half his mortal life. Gradually, he came to, lying face down upon the floor of the forest. As consciousness returned he struggled to remember where he was, and how he had got there. All he could remember at first was that he had been asleep, deep within a world of dreams that was now locked away. He moved his hands and legs, gradually stretching his muscles, working the life back into a body that felt as though it had been drugged by some potion. But he was alive, for sure. That was the least of it.

Gingerly, he flexed his forearm where the wound had been bandaged. His arm felt stiff and heavy, but free of all pain.

Bruno turned his head and lifted it, and felt a glowing warmth upon his face. He opened his eyes, slowly, and immediately screwed them closed again. The light was too much, blinding after what seemed like an age inside the gloom of the forest. Shading his eyes with his hand, he opened them a second time. As he did so, memory began to return. He was lying in the same clearing in the forest that they had set camp in the night before. The ashes of the fire, long burnt out, were just a stone's throw in front of him.

Elena, Stefan, Tomas and Alexei – all of them were there, all sleeping or stirring from their own dreams.

Tired and confused, and in no mind for puzzles, Bruno tilted his head back and drank in the greatest wonder of all: the morning sun in all its magnificence, flooding down into the forest from the skies above.

CHAPTER SIXTEEN
The Gathering Storm

FAR BEYOND THE eastern rim of the forest, across the barren marshlands that stretched on into Kislev, Petr Illyich Kuragin was sunk deep within dreams of his own. He found himself standing by the gates of Erengrad, shivering in the bitter wind blowing in from the steppe. Tears froze against his face as he ran his gaze across a blighted land. Everywhere the dark was closing in. Erengrad was crumbling; soon her motherland, Kislev, would crumble with it.

From the horizon a rider on horseback approached the gates, a giant warrior mounted atop a giant steed. Petr Kuragin knew that the rider was Death, knew that he must stop Death from entering the city. He strained against the pitted wheel that would push back the open gates, but his arms and hands were frozen solid. The cold had set hard ice inside his limbs, locking his bones so tight that he could barely move. Every lost opportunity, every squandered moment from a lifetime of chances was running through his mind, mocking his frenzied efforts. With every second that passed, the dark rider raced closer. Kuragin screamed an oath to the gods and laid his shoulder against the gate-wheel. An icy

sweat glossed his brow. Gradually, inch by tortured inch, the
gates began to close.

But it will be too late, a voice inside his head told him. All
your efforts will be in vain. He shut the words out of his
mind, trying to push aside the poisonous doubt that sapped
his strength. The pounding of the hooves was like a thunder
in his ears. He looked up into the face of Death, eyes glowing
like red coals behind a dark mask. Death was riding through
the gates to claim Erengrad for his dominion.

Not while I live! Kuragin vowed, pushing every last ounce of
strength from his body in a desperate effort to force the gates
together.

The hammering of the horse's hooves became the beat of
his own heart. Death's horseman loomed large and terrible in
the too slowly narrowing gap. Petr Kuragin prepared to meet
his daemons.

He woke with a start, his body drenched from sweat.
Already the intensity of the nightmare was evaporating, vanishing from memory like a thief. But the sense of danger,
close at hand, lingered in the chill air of his chamber.

As his eyes grew accustomed to the gloom of the single
lantern, he saw that he was not alone. His manservant,
Dimitri, stood in the open doorway. Behind him stood
another man that Kuragin did not at first recognise.

'What's the matter?' he called out. 'What is the news?'

Dimitri bowed his head, apologetic. 'I'm sorry, master. This
man demanded to see you.'

'That is becoming all too commonplace,' Kuragin
remarked, sourly. He peered at the somehow familiar figure
standing behind Dimitri in the darkness.

'He said that you would be angered if he were turned away,'
Dimitri explained.

'Did he indeed? Let him come forward,' Kuragin ordered,
vexed that his sleep should be disturbed, yet equally
relieved to be set free of his dreams. He climbed from the
bed, wrapping a robe around him. 'This had better be good,'
he observed.

The man stepped forward, into the halo of light shed by
Dimitri's lantern. Kuragin saw at once that it was Martin
Lensky, the sole voice to have spoken out against Rosporov in
Katarina Square. The ostler looked out of breath, as though

he had been running for his life, and his face and shirt were streaked with blood.

'Forgive the intrusion, your lordship,' Lensky began. 'I wouldn't be here if it wasn't desperate.'

'It's all right,' Kuragin replied, mildly. He remembered the ostler's courage in the square, and a pang of guilt stabbed through him. He would minister to this man's needs if he could. 'What is it you want?' he asked.

Lensky staggered, and would have fallen had Dimitri not been at his side to support him. He rested his weight against the back of an oak chair, and stood breathing heavily for a few moments. 'It's begun,' he said at last. 'Evil has risen, and staked its claim to the city. Erengrad is at war.'

The image of the dark horseman flashed into Petr Kuragin's mind. Death. Death was loose upon the city. Dimitri started to speak, but Kuragin brushed him aside. He strode to the bookcase on the wall of his study and located a map of the city, which he spread open upon the desk. 'Show me,' he said to Martin Lensky. 'Show me where the trouble has begun.'

The ostler stared at the parchment drawing for a few moments, struggling to make sense of the cartographer's work. 'This is our commune,' he said at last, pointing to a place at the northern end of the city. 'In the district they call White Barrow.' He turned to look at Kuragin. 'We that live and work in the Barrow are good men all,' he said. 'And loyal to the true cause of Erengrad.'

He placed a second finger upon the map and traced a line encircling the warren of streets that formed the district. 'They are all around us,' he said. 'Too many of them to number. They're setting flame to our homes. Those of us who don't burn they put to the sword. The women, and our children, too.'

Kuragin stared down, horror and rage starting to boil within him. Rage that his people were dying, unprotected. Horror because he knew that their murderers had not come from outside the city walls, but from within.

'We beg your protection, lordship, for the city militia are nowhere to be seen. My kinsmen lack no courage, but courage alone is no match for axes and swords.'

The sergeant of the Household Troop appeared in the doorway, summoned from below by the sound of commotion in his master's chambers. Kuragin waved the man in. 'How many men-at-arms can we muster?' he demanded.

'How many men? Apart from those on guard around the walls?' the sergeant asked.

'No, damn you!' Kuragin shot back. 'How many men in total?'

'Near thirty in total, lordship. But that would leave the Kuragin House undefended.'

Thirty men. It seemed a pitiful number to pitch against the marauding mob that Rosporov had set upon the streets. Yet somehow it would have to do.

'Tell your men to gather their arms,' Kuragin declared. 'Tell them I shall lead them myself.'

'My lord, this is a dangerous course,' Dimitri counselled. 'A dozen men left behind would at least secure the house.'

Kuragin looked from Dimitri to Martin Lensky. 'We don't need thirty men to save White Barrow.' He said. 'We need fifty or more. But we will take every man that we have. I will not sit safe behind these walls and watch my countrymen die.'

Not any longer, he swore. Not for one day longer.

Count Vladimir Rosporov had sat, watching and waiting, until the first rays of the rising sun began flooding the city with orange light. It was a sign, he told himself, a portent of the time soon to come when purging fire would range the length and breadth of Erengrad.

He had taken no sleep that night; he had chosen instead to sit and await the news of events as they unfolded through the hours of darkness. And the news was good. The waking servants of Chaos had risen up and become the catalysts of destruction that night. The Scarandar had sown the seeds of insurrection; weariness and despair of a broken people had done the rest. His time was close at hand, he could sense it. He wanted to be alert to savour its every moment.

The count had a visitor, an ambassador from beyond the city. They served the same master, his visitor and he, but Rosporov formed his allegiances with prudence, wary of trusting any man. He greeted the newcomer with a stiff, formal bow.

The visitor was a northerner, a Norscan probably, broad and thickly muscled as well as tall. The mark of the Changer was clear upon him. What struck Rosporov immediately was his eyes – or, rather, his right eye, for the left was entirely covered by a leather patch. It stared out at Rosporov, deep and piercing. Somehow it seemed not to belong to the man's body. It was like another being enclosed within him, looking out with that cold and pitiless stare.

The big man looked around the cramped furnishings of the room with evident suspicion. 'Not much by way of chambers for a count, is it?' he commented, sourly.

'You forget,' Rosporov replied. 'I am a man of the people now. A champion of the common man. Trappings of wealth do not sit well with protestations of humility.'

The Norscan grunted, unimpressed. 'Anyway,' Rosporov continued, eyeing the ungainly bulk of the man with growing distaste. 'If we are to judge by appearances, you make a poor case for an emissary.'

The Norscan swore angrily and aimed one meaty fist towards Rosporov's face. The count grasped the fist in his own right hand, and for a moment, the two men stood locked in a trial of strength. Rosporov's puny limb looked like it would surely snap in two, yet, somehow, he was managing to hold the Norscan back.

My resistance surprises him, Rosporov noted. I have hidden strength. I have the body of the cripple, and the strength of a madman. He smiled, and slackened his grip.

'Things are not always what they seem, my friend.'

The Norscan cursed him, but backed off. He may have the look and manner of a murderous oaf, Rosporov mused, but the eye tells a different tale. He knows exactly what I am worth.

'We'll waste no more time,' the visitor said. 'I've come a long way, and taken a great risk to be here.'

'Of course,' Rosporov concurred, 'for is not risk but brother to change? Our Lord Tzeentch loves both his children equally.'

'Don't try mocking me with clever words,' the Norscan warned him. 'I am the first servant and emissary of Kyros. Fail to satisfy me, and you will answer to him.'

'Kyros would not find my answers wanting,' the count snapped back. 'I am close to delivering my part of the bargain. Closer, I'll wager, than you are to yours.'

The single eye turned and fixed, cold and unblinking, upon the count. 'Tell me what you have achieved.'

'The uprising has begun,' Rosporov said. 'The north of the city has already fallen.'

'Do you have the Star?'

'No,' Rosporov conceded. 'Not yet. Kuragin clings to his charm like a child to its doll. But it is only a matter of time before he is taken, and with him the icon.'

The big blond man slammed his fist upon the table. 'Time is what we do not have!' he thundered. Rosporov granted him a tight-lipped smile. How was it the servants of Change seemed so rarely able to grasp its subtle mechanisms?

'The city is in a state of flux,' he continued. 'The seeds of insurrection have been sown. All we need do now is wait for the harvest. Parts of the city are already ours – parts, even, of the city militia.'

'Not the parts that I encountered,' the Norscan growled. 'I had to pay my way in blood and guile to penetrate within the walls.'

'You haven't come here to impress me with your bravery,' Rosporov countered, coldly. 'What message does Lord Kyros's emissary bring?'

'He comes to tell you this,' the Norscan said. 'Comes to tell you that in two days, three at the most, he will return to Erengrad at the head of an army. And icon or no icon, insurrection or no insurrection, the city will yield to its might.'

'I savour the coming of that moment,' Rosporov told him. 'Indeed, I shall be there in person, to greet you at the open gates.'

The tall warrior got to his feet, drained the wine from his cup, and pulled his cape around his shoulders. 'And I tell you this,' he said, his hand upon the door. 'If you yet fail our cause, you may count yourself amongst our enemies once the final reckoning starts.'

THEY HAD SPOKEN of many things during the days that followed, but talked little of the events of that night in the forest. But Stefan had read and gauged the look upon his comrade's face, and realised that in Bruno something had changed. The wound he had suffered in combat had all but healed overnight; that was wonder enough. But there was an even more wondrous change to be observed in Bruno's spirit. It was as though a great, crushing weight had suddenly been lifted from him. Now, when their eyes met, Bruno would nod, clearly and affirmatively, as if to signal that the time to put differences aside was close at hand.

All of them seemed happier that morning. The warming sun which seemed to grow stronger with each passing day was helping to lift their spirits. It beat down upon them, casting warming light into the crooks and corners of the forest where only days before they had been icy dark. Periodically Stefan threw back his head just to bathe in its rays. The sun not only warmed, it also helped speed them on their way. With light dappling the forest paths ahead, they could ride probably twice as fast as they had managed in earlier days.

The Forest of Shadows had held them in its chill grip for the better part of two long weeks. Now, surely, it was ready to let them go. Nothing was said, but it was as though all of them could sense a turning point had been reached. They would be out of the forest before long.

The subject of the beastmen had never been far from the riders' thoughts, and they returned to it again that morning. Not for a moment did Stefan imagine that they had seen the last of them. The handful that they had come upon were probably nothing more than the vanguard, harbingers of the hordes that, somewhere, were even now converging.

'The closer we get to Kislev the more I think about it,' Elena said.

'"Converging on Erengrad" – I didn't like the sound of that. What could it mean?'

'I'm not sure, not yet,' Stefan replied. 'But if there is to be an attack, I'd wager it was coming soon.'

'One thing you can be sure of,' Alexei said. 'What's left of them won't be headed for Erengrad bearing gifts.'

True enough, Stefan reflected. It all added to the urgency of their journey. 'Pick up the pace,' he shouted back to the others. 'We'll be out of the woods soon enough.'

By the end of the day the paths they were on began to broaden. Wide gaps appeared between the trees as the forest started to thin out.

'Praise the gods,' Stefan murmured. They would escape the shadows at last. Minutes later they forded a stream, the cold waters splashing up high around the horses' flanks. 'This must be it!' Elena cried. 'The eastern edge of the forest. The boundary between the Empire and Kislev!'

They climbed the high bank on the far side of the stream and stopped. Elena drew her horse up beside Stefan's. She looked at him, head on one side, a faint smile on her face. There was something intoxicating, exhilarating, about the sense of light and space opening up around them.

Elena took a deep breath. The smile stayed with her, but began to fade on her lips. 'It's just starting to hit me, what lies ahead for us, beyond the border,' she said. 'All this time, travelling, the thought of Kislev's been like a dream, something not really happening. But now – I don't know. Perhaps it's beginning to dawn on me what I've taken on.'

'You've fared pretty well so far,' Stefan assured her. 'You can take pride in what we've achieved. We all can.' He looked up, along the slope of a hill towards the ring of trees perhaps a hundred yards distant. The end of the forest. 'Come on,' he said, spurring his horse. 'Let's make that dream real.'

They broke through, out of the forest, five abreast at a canter. 'You're right!' Elena shouted back to Stefan. 'We should be celebrating!'

Just as they crested the hill, an arrow, or a brace of arrows, skimmed the air a hair's breadth from Stefan's face.

'The celebrations can wait,' a voice called out. The arrows struck home against the trunk of a tree to his right, the shafts quivering in the sunlight.

By the time Stefan had drawn his sword they were surrounded. To their left, to their right and dead ahead of them, armed men on horseback barred the way. A dozen longbows were trained upon them, drawstrings taut and ready to fly. One of the riders, the same one who had just addressed them, now pulled ahead of the line.

'Drop your weapons,' the man commanded. 'Drop them now.'

Alexei looked from one end of the line of riders to the other. Thirty men or more, at a guess. 'We're not going to fight our way out of this one,' he said quietly.

Stefan looked at him, then at the riders sitting in wait ahead. When Alexei Zucharov said the odds were too great it was time to rethink strategy. Instinct told him these were no friends of Chaos. But, right now, they showed little sign of friendship towards them, either.

He pulled his sword up to saddle height, held it out, and let it drop upon the ground. 'Do what he says,' he instructed the others.

Stefan took the man issuing the orders to be the leader of the group. He sat tall in the saddle, with a weather-tanned face framed with ash blond hair that fell to shoulder length. Like the rest of his men, he was dressed for war, with a breast-plate buckled over a shirt of light mail. With his faint, clipped accent he could have been a Kislevite, or from the eastern fringes of the Empire or even Bretonnia. Stefan put his age at less than thirty, but he had the confident manner of a man well used to command. He waited until the weapons had been relinquished, then said:

'All right. Now ride out here, slowly, where we can get a good look at you.'

'Won't you at least tell us who you are?' Stefan asked.

'We'll know that of you first,' he replied. 'That and more. We've been tracking your party for a little while. Thought we'd flush you out before too long.'

'Doesn't look like they were with the goatheads,' one of the others commented. It was then Stefan noticed two of the group were carrying spears decorated with the severed heads of beastmen. He rode forward until he and the blond-haired rider were face to face. All the while he was weighing his possible opponent up, looking for anything that might become a weakness. The other man, he knew, would be doing exactly the same thing. Stefan guessed they would be well matched in open combat. But Alexei was certainly right; the five of them would have little chance against these odds. They must try somehow to talk their way clear. He seized upon mention of the beastmen, hoping this might be a good place to start.

'We came upon a group of them in the forest,' Stefan began. 'We killed at least half a dozen.'

'Good for you,' the man commented, the mildest hint of sarcasm in his lilting voice. Stefan felt a twinge of anger stirring in response, and forced himself to ignore it.

'We have a common enemy and no just cause for quarrel,' he said, trying his best to sound reasonable. 'All we ask is to be given free passage to go on our way.'

The soldier who had first mentioned beastmen, a beefy-faced man carrying a broadsword, now rode up beside his captain and continued talking as though Stefan was out of earshot. 'Maybe they're mutants?' he offered, by way of a suggestion.

'Maybe,' the blond man concurred. Stefan had the infuriating impression that he was enjoying every moment of this encounter. 'Do you think they look like mutants?' he asked his sergeant.

The beefy-faced man hesitated for a moment, running an eye over Stefan and his companions. 'Not really,' he concluded.

'Neither do I,' his captain agreed. 'But then, that's no proof of anything. Chaos is capable of many deceptions.'

'We have proof,' Elena broke in. 'If you're truly stupid enough to think we side with Chaos, then we can prove–'

'We can prove ourselves in any way you choose to name,' Stefan said, hurriedly, cutting Elena off. 'We mean you no ill. All we ask is that you allow us free passage.'

'Into Kislev?' the captain raised an eyebrow. 'I don't think so. Anyway,' he added, 'why should your journey bring you through the forest? No ordinary travellers would come that way.'

'We have travelled from Middenheim,' Stefan said. 'The trading road east from the city has been sealed, and the mountain passes are thick with bandit gangs. We were forced to cross the forest.' Alexei and Bruno were at his side now. Stefan felt the tension rising. If they weren't careful, this could end badly.

'We'll have to tell them our true business,' Elena whispered to him. The blond captain regarded them quizzically, then conferred quietly with his lieutenants.

'The border between the Empire and Kislev was closed for good reason,' he said finally. 'You may go free, but you'll have to head back the way that you've come.'

Elena, by his side, let out a gasp of disbelief. Bruno now pushed forward to join the two of them. His face bore an expression of steely determination that Stefan had not seen in a long time.

'You'll have to kill us first!' he told the captain. A dozen or so archers refocused their aim.

'So be it, if necessary,' the captain replied, coolly. 'I'm offering you free passage. Your choice whether you accept.'

'Listen,' Elena said, 'You must let us ride on. We have to reach Erengrad.'

The captain looked at Elena as though she were mad. 'Erengrad?' he repeated. 'Haven't you heard? There's a war storm brewing, and Erengrad is at its heart. Even if I were to let you pass, there's not a chance of you reaching the city on your own.'

'Then let us ride with you and your men,' Stefan said. 'If you are truly the enemies of Chaos, then we are allies, and you will have need of us.'

'And what exactly do you have that we would have such need of?'

'Give me my sword back,' Stefan said, evenly, 'and I'll show you.' For a moment the two men faced each other, each holding the other's unblinking gaze. The captain nodded, almost imperceptibly. 'I imagine that you would,' he said, quietly. 'But the fact remains, I have my orders – to seal the border, put any beastmen or other scum that emerged from the forest to the sword, and turn all travellers back.'

'Maybe this will convince you, then.' All eyes turned towards Elena. She had removed the chain from around her neck and was holding the segment of the Star aloft. Sunlight flashed off the silver metal. Most of the soldiers simply looked bemused, but Stefan could see from the shocked expression on the face of their leader that he understood all too well its significance. Immediately, he began to engage his lieutenants in conference. Every so often he looked round towards Elena and the Star. Finally he turned back to her and said:

'Where are the other pieces?'

Stefan and Elena exchanged glances. 'We have to trust them,' Elena said. 'If they are to trust us, then it's the only way.' Stefan hesitated, then took a deep breath.

'I have the second part,' he said. 'The third is still in Erengrad. If what you say is true, then it is in greater peril than we had imagined.'

'And your journey is of greater urgency than I had imagined,' the captain conceded. He rode forward and went to each of them in turn, and now shook them by the hand.

'I am Franz Schiller,' he told them. 'The men you see around you owe allegiance to many lands, but they are united here by a single cause.'

'The Old World is in peril,' Stefan said.

Schiller nodded. 'If Erengrad should fall, then the shadow of Chaos will surely blight us all,' he said. 'You must ride with us, of course. But understand,' he said to Elena, 'we don't know what we may meet once we approach the city. Great forces are converging upon Erengrad; forces for evil as well as for good. Only Sigmar knows who shall prevail.'

'I understand,' Elena said, 'but without the Star intact, all may be lost.'

'Then let us make haste,' Schiller urged. 'There are many hundreds more of us, camped to the south of Erengrad, at Mirov. We rest there tonight, and ride for the city at dawn.'

CHAPTER SEVENTEEN
On the Precipice

KURAGIN AND HIS men had ridden through the streets under skies streaked with the first glimmerings of the new day. But the sky was still dark enough for them to clearly see the fires burning in the north of Erengrad, tongues of yellow fire flecked with blue licking against the clouds hanging low over the city. They rode like the wind, sweeping aside any so foolish as to try and block their path through the twisting lanes that led from the merchants' quarter towards the district of White Barrow.

They encountered no opposition along their way at first, but neither did they gather allies to swell their numbers. Martin Lensky had been right: the militia had melted away, vanished in totality from the streets of the city. Safe back in their barracks, thought Kuragin bitterly, waiting to see which way the wind would blow.

He saw soon enough that the wind was blowing ill. Long before they reached the heart of the cluster of homes, shops and taverns that formed White Barrow they found its citizens fleeing from their homes, what was left of their lives tied up in bundles beneath their arms. Some raised their eyes toward

Kuragin and his men, and seemed to look right through them. It was as though hope was no longer even a possibility. The thirty men ploughed on, against the human tide.

Soon the air was thick with the sounds of carnage and plunder. Now the rage of the fires could be felt, as well as seen. A broiling heat was turning the streets into a furnace. At its epicentre, the merchants' hall; a tall wooden structure in the heart of the district. Smoke billowed through the windows and gaping holes in the timbers as fire took a grip on the upper storey. Men were running from the hall through the doors at either end, many of them bearing all the stolen wares they could carry. Most looked indistinguishable from the peasants and tradesmen that had been fleeing the flames, but their faces bore expressions of blank-eyed madness.

Kuragin saw figures dressed in black moving amongst the crowd, directing them with shouted commands and blows from their staves, as though they were herding cattle. Of Rosporov there was no sign, but Kuragin had no doubt that these were his acolytes. He turned to face his men riding three abreast behind him.

'Spare the townsfolk if you can,' he commanded.

'Sire, there are looters amongst them,' his sergeant reminded him.

'They are possessed by some madness,' Lensky said.

'They no longer know their own minds. The ones in black are our target,' Kuragin yelled. 'Destroy them and the mob will be ours.' He drew his sword, and stepped into the inferno.

THE EMISSARY HAD quit Erengrad much as he had entered it; with the magician's art and the assassin's knife. When next he returned, it would be as conqueror. All would bow to him then, Rosporov included. For a short while the count might well have the run of the city. Varik pictured the Kislevite as a scurrying rat, king of his festering sewer. Let him enjoy his triumph while he might. When Erengrad finally fell, there would be but one champion to lay tribute at Kyros's throne. He, Varik, would see to that.

Until then the verminous little nobleman was more use to him alive than dead. Even Varik had to concede that Rosporov was carrying out his task with a poisonous efficiency. Erengrad was tearing itself asunder. Like a ripe – rotten – fruit it was hanging, ready to fall. Whether it would fall before he returned to the city gates was another matter. If Rosporov's rebellion had won control, so much the better. Victory would be swift and easy. If not, then more blood would flow. But what did that matter, set against the great tide of blood soon to break across the plains of western Kislev?

He looked down from his vantage point upon the hilltop and surveyed the army of Kyros massing below. Already they were too many to number: hundreds, thousands of them massing beneath the black flags that were blooming like dark flowers across the fields, obliterating the blighted land of Kislev. Their numbers were swelling with each hour that passed; every day more ships were arriving on the northern coasts, spilling their murderous cargo upon the shore. Men and beasts, ready for the march on Erengrad, ready for war. The very air rang with the clamour of coming battle.

The emissary looked down upon these, his creatures, and felt a surge of power run though his body as countless eyes turned upon him, waiting upon his word. These were violent men who lived to feast off terror and destruction. And he knew them, knew them all. They were his to command, and he was one with them. He gazed down at the scarred, leathery hands that had fought so many battles, ended so many lives. How many souls had this human form despatched to Morr? And how many more would he, Varik, now savour, melded as he was with this new warrior self? Many, many more. He would see to that, too.

The beastmen had failed him. That did not surprise him much. He had been promised a full company, an alliance of tribes ready to march on Erengrad. None had arrived at the muster point. He imagined the loathsome half-breeds tearing each other apart over some petty squabble, or abandoning their pledge for some other, worthless trophy. Their evil brutality would be missed, but their low, animal minds were notoriously difficult to mould and shape. Ultimately he would only have had to destroy them.

There were others, too, drawn towards this dark army of conquest. Men and mutants, mercenaries and fortune seekers. The bitter misfits of the Old World seeking riches and revenge, swelling the ranks of the Norscan horde come to reclaim what was theirs by ancient right. The mark of Chaos was strong in the blood of many, but not all. Kislev had more enemies than it knew.

He stood, drawing himself up to his full height, and the warriors below saluted him. A mass of voices chanted his other name: Nargrun, destroyer of cities. His greatest, most powerful incarnation yet. The army massing below were ready to die for him, and they were ready to kill for him. He would let them kill, but there was one death that belonged to him alone. He touched his fingers against the leather patch stretched across the empty socket of his left eye. Two memories, two private shames met, burning in a single flame of hatred. Soon, he promised, we shall gain our retribution.

PETR ILLYICH KURAGIN sat amongst the smoking ruins of what had previously been an inn, and wept without shame. His tears were born of exhaustion, relief, and bitter sorrow. White Barrow had been held. The rebels would doubtless come again, but for now had been pushed back. The defenders had won a few hours of respite, maybe a day or so.

But that respite had only been won at a cost. Around him, scattered upon the ground or buried beneath the cracked and charred timbers of the fallen houses, nearly twenty of his men lay dead or dying. Amongst them was Dimitri, his loyal servant since boyhood, cut down by a rebel arrow in the first assault. Kuragin wept for him, and for all the other sons of Erengrad who had died that day, and for those who were yet to die. For this was a battle that had barely begun. That much he now understood.

Today he had reaped a harvest of death with his sword, scything the fields of flesh until the blade ran red. He had tried to single out the ringleaders, the black-clad engineers of anarchy whose name, he had learnt, was the Scarandar. He had despatched several of them to Morr, but the killing had not ended there. His mind ran back again to the moment when he had killed the first of his townsfolk. The man had charged at him along the street, a shard of jagged glass in place of a sword in one hand, screaming like a madman. Kuragin had looked deep into this man's eyes, and realised with a jolt that he knew him. He was a craftsman, a tailor or milliner. His name had vanished from memory, but Petr remembered his face from another, better time. Remembered, too, a wife and a son. Kuragin had helped their family buy an apprenticeship for the boy at the military academy.

As the man had rushed forward to kill him. Kuragin had held his hand out and shouted at his attacker to stop. 'In the name of Ulric, man!' he had screamed. 'Don't you remember me? I helped your son!'

The man's eyes stared ahead, but seemed to look right through him, as though he were staring into another, monstrous world where only madness prevailed.

'My son is dead, dead with all the rest of them.'

Kuragin had raised his sword, but the wild-eyed man came on, slashing indiscriminately with the jagged shard. He had lashed out at Kuragin, and Petr had struck back, instinctively. His blade cut the man open from his breastbone to the top of his throat. Blood sprayed from the wound, a slick mist of red befouling Kuragin and his assailant. Petr had pushed the man away, then watched him die. He knew he would not be the last that must fall beneath his sword.

And there was one more cost that he now had to bear. The fires that had begun in White Barrow were now spreading across Erengrad. Kuragin looked up, following the path they had taken through the city. Sat high upon the hill was the Kuragin House, his undefended fortress. Smoke was pouring from the towers and turrets, a choking cloud of black rising against the amber glow of the morning sun.

Petr Illyich Kuragin sat and watched his home burn, watched as the fire consumed his childhood and his youth, memories of his parents and his dead brothers charring into ash.

'You were right, Dimitri,' he whispered. 'May the great gods grant this sacrifice was not all in vain.'

IN TIMES OF peace Mirov would have been a small village, barely more than a hamlet in the shadow of Erengrad less than twenty miles to the north. But the time for peace was now in the past, and, perhaps, the future. Mirov had been transformed into a vast transit camp, almost a town in its own right. A sprawling carnival of tents, equipment and fighting men greeted Stefan as he rode down the valley.

He rode at an easy pace towards the encampment, keeping his horse close abreast of Schiller's, watching the bustling life of the camp unfolding before him. The sound of metal upon metal rang in Stefan's ears: soldiers honing their craft, smiths crafting fresh blades upon the forge. The camp was a sea of constant movement, long lines of men passing to and fro along the paths between the tents; teams of horses hauling long, heavily loaded wagons towards a marshalling point, the earth below the wheels churned to an ochre slurry. From afar the bustle of the camp looked chaotic, like a nest of restless termites. But Stefan saw the pattern and the purpose of an army preparing for war. It felt very much as though he was coming home.

'Sounds like between us we've more or less wiped out the beastmen,' Schiller commented. 'Our commander will be well pleased with the day's work.'

'Commander? Who would that be?' Stefan asked.

'Gastez Castelguerre,' his companion replied. 'The best soldier I've ever had the privilege to serve under.'

'Sounds almost Bretonnian,' Stefan said.

Schiller turned to look at Stefan, then laughed. 'You sound surprised,' he said. 'I told you. We're a rag-bag, mongrel army if ever there was one. Castelguerre is a Bretonnian, as are most of his men. I'm from the Kislevite borderland, despite my name. But we've men from all over the Old World here. Even from the Empire, you'll be relieved to hear.'

Now it was Stefan's turn to laugh. 'Actually,' he said, 'I'm from Kislev too.'

'Really? Where from?'

Stefan hesitated, then spoke the name of the village that had been obliterated from the map.

He expected Schiller's reaction to be as blank as Elena's, but the young man's eyes widened momentarily in recognition. He repeated the name.

'Odensk. I know of that place.'

'Knew of it,' Stefan corrected. 'I don't think anything much is left now.'

Franz Schiller nodded, gravely. 'That was the last time they got anywhere near Erengrad.' Stefan felt his body suddenly tense, muscles tightening in his stomach. 'What do you mean,' he said, slowly. 'What do you mean by "they"?'

Schiller reined his horse in and reached across and laid a hand upon Stefan's arm.

'I'm sorry,' he said. 'I assumed you already knew this. The murdering scum who destroyed your village are back on the soil of our motherland. A battalion of mutant Norscans is leading the dark army's march on Erengrad.'

Stefan shook his head. 'No,' he said, 'I didn't know that.' Fragmented memories of his home tumbled through his mind. He said a silent prayer, and hoped that somewhere his father was looking down upon him.

They rode on, and soon came into the camp itself. The air rang with the sounds of voices, of swords in practice for combat, and of smiths and armourers at their work. Franz Schiller led the way through the ordered rows of the canvas city, towards an enclosure roped off from the rest of the field. Once they had tethered their horses, Schiller left them and walked off alone towards an unmarked tent that had been pitched at its centre. He returned a few minutes later.

'There'll be food and drink ready for you soon,' he promised Stefan. 'But the chief wants to speak to you first. Her highness as well.'

'Her highness?' Stefan asked.

'I think he means me.' Elena grinned shyly at Stefan as she followed Schiller towards the tent. Her cheeks flushed with a hint of what could have been pride, embarrassment, or a little of both. 'I'm known differently in these parts,' she said.

Gastez Castelguerre sat at a low table inside his tent, studying a map of Erengrad. The shields and battle standards surrounding him gave some clue as to rank, but otherwise the tent was plain and unadorned. A steady drip of condensation fell from the canvas roof, forming a puddle by his right arm. The battle commander looked up briefly from the map as the entrance flap was lifted back and Franz stepped in, Stefan and Elena at his side.

'These are the travellers,' Schiller announced. Castelguerre glanced up, and appraised his visitors with a measured stare. 'I can't exactly say that you were expected,' he began. 'When the merchant train crossed the border without you we feared for the worst.' He frowned. 'But you are no less welcome for that. Nor less needed.'

Stefan took the Bretonnian's offered hand and shook it firmly. He reckoned Castelguerre for a man of about forty, his muscled frame just beginning to thicken with age. His dark hair was starting to grey, but his eyes still shone with the vigour and the hunger of youth. It was a look that Stefan had seen in the eyes of the priest, and Otto Brandauer before him. He knew this was a man he could follow into battle.

Castelguerre turned to Elena and bowed, slightly stiffly. 'And by what title shall we know you, your ladyship?' he asked.

'Elena will do fine,' she replied. 'It's served me well enough thus far.'

Castelguerre coughed, awkwardly. 'That's fine by me, too,' he said. 'You'll find we don't have much time for airs and graces around here. But I didn't want to get off on the wrong foot. You see,' he explained, 'you have a reputation that rides before you, Elena Yevschenko.'

'A good one, I trust,' Elena responded, amiably.

'An important one,' Castelguerre replied, his tone contrastingly sober now. 'A very important one indeed. And you,' he said to Stefan, 'you must be the Stefan Kumansky that Otto told me of.'

'I am,' Stefan said. 'But I have to tell you Otto is dead. Andreas Kornfeld too.' He watched the commander's face cloud with sorrow. 'I'm sorry to be the bearer of such tidings,' he added.

Castelguerre ran a hand across his brow, then pounded the table once with his heavy fist. 'Gods be watchful, their deaths shall be atoned!' he thundered. He drew down a deep breath. 'They were valiant comrades, both. Loyal soldiers for our cause.' Castelguerre paused, struggling with his grief. 'Otto thought highly of both of you,' he continued. 'Highly enough to let the hopes of countless peoples rest upon your shoulders. He would be glad indeed to see you safely here.'

'The journey to Erengrad has yet to be completed,' Elena observed. 'I have achieved nothing as yet.'

Castelguerre nodded. 'Indeed,' he said. 'Come, sit down,' he told them. 'There is business to attend to. Business that brings us together here.'

He beckoned Stefan and Elena forward, towards the scroll spread out in front of him.

Stefan looked down upon a map of Erengrad.

'From what we have been able to observe, the city is still holding out,' Castelguerre said, reading Stefan's thoughts. 'Or at least parts of it. Until we reach Erengrad itself we cannot be sure how bad things have become. But this much we know: the hand of Chaos is strong there.'

'Franz talked of enemy hordes marching on the city as well,' Elena said, anxiously. 'What of that?'

'We cannot be sure of their numbers,' Castelguerre told her. 'But they are many.'

'Invaders from Norsca and beyond,' Stefan said.

'Yes, they are the vanguard. But there are others, too, risen up as if from thin air. It is as if Chaos has nurtured an army of mutant souls, sleeping unnoticed in our midst, waiting for this, the moment of their calling.'

'We witnessed something like it in Middenheim,' Stefan said. 'Ordinary men, turned suddenly into mindless murderers. Their leaders were known as the Scarandar. It was they who killed Otto.'

'The Scarandar, apostles of the transformation,' Castelguerre said. 'Servants of the Dark Lord of Change, and of his chosen one, Kyros. Chaos has learned from its failures of the past. Learnt the lessons of Praag, for sure. The Scarandar are the invisible enemy. They can appear and disappear seemingly at will. Kyros knows a city like Erengrad will not succumb easily. Solid walls and an iron will are enough to defeat most attackers. But if he can get inside the city, eat away at it from within, then eventually the outer shell will weaken and crack.'

He paused, his expression thoughtful and solemn. 'Well,' he went on. 'At least that's his plan. We know the situation in the city is perilous, to say the least. The Norscan-led army is intended as the hammer that wields the final blow.'

'But–' he gazed up at them, and smiled. 'There is another, opposing force, equally resolute. A brotherhood of men such as Otto, Andreas and myself. A brotherhood pledged to defend with our lives the alliance that still binds the Old World. We have been waiting for Kyros to strike. And this time we'll be ready.'

Castelguerre lowered his eyes. 'I must make certain my comrades' sacrifice was not in vain. I must ensure that you

reach your birthplace together with the Star, Elena. Otherwise
we may all be lost.'

'I'm ready,' Elena replied. 'Ready for whatever the day of
battle may bring.'

Castelguerre frowned. 'I would be happier if you were
nowhere near the battle at all,' he said. 'But we cannot delay
your journey home by even another day. That means you
must cross the battle lines. I'll have to give some thought to
that.'

He paused, deep in contemplation. 'I'm sorry,' Castelguerre
said at length. 'I am forgetting that you are also our guests.
You must be hungry, and weary after your travels. I've talked
enough.' He stood up, and pulled back the opening to the
tent. Franz Schiller stood waiting outside.

'See that our comrades are given all they need,' he said.
'Tomorrow,' he told Elena, 'you will return to Erengrad. The
time for talking is all but done.'

STEFAN WALKED THE length and breadth of the camp after he
had eaten. His body ached for sleep, but he knew his mind
was not ready for rest, not yet. Every inch of space was filled
with fighting men and their trappings of war. The smells that
greeted him were the familiar smells of the battle eve. Smoke
and burning meat; leather, gunpowder and fresh polished
steel. Grease and sweat; smells of fear and of hope.

He walked through groups of cavalry and infantry, men
skilled with the bow and those, like himself, who would
stand or fall by their sword. Men finishing what might be
their final meal, immersed deep in conversation or, some,
already asleep. Most of them were strangers to him, but a few
he recognised from other battles, other wars. These he met
with a nod of recognition, in each greeting the silent
acknowledgement that it might be the last time in this life
that their eyes would meet. He exchanged few words with any
of them. Gastez Castelguerre had been right. The time for
talking was almost over.

Almost, but not quite. Retracing his steps, he came upon
Bruno sitting alone outside his tent, drinking wine from a
stone flask. There may never be a better time for this conversation, Stefan reflected. He walked quickly towards Bruno
and, without further word, sat down beside him.

Bruno looked round and handed Stefan the earthen flask. 'Present from Franz Schiller,' he said. 'Good stuff.'

Stefan drank, a long draught of cooling liquor. He took a second mouthful of wine, then handed the flask back.

'Do you think we'll see battle tomorrow?' he asked.

'I've been talking to Schiller,' Bruno said. 'He's sure of it. Their scouts report the enemy army converging on Erengrad from the north-east. Castelguerre's plan is for us to try and cut them off before they have a chance to breach the city walls.' He paused and took another drink. 'It won't be easy, though. Schiller's guess is that the numbers favour them by at least two to one.'

'We've come through worse,' Stefan observed. 'You and I.'

Both men turned at the sound of voices raised and steel biting on steel. Tomas Murer and Alexei Zucharov stood face to face, swords in their hands, squared up as though for combat. Every few seconds Alexei would strike out and Tomas would attempt to parry the blow, all the while running a good-natured commentary between them on the swordplay.

Bruno laughed. 'The perfect teacher and pupil,' he said.

'Indeed,' Stefan concurred. 'I'm not sure which is which, either.'

'Well, at any rate,' Bruno went on, 'they seem to have buried their differences.'

Stefan looked at Bruno. 'Perhaps it's time that we buried ours,' he said.

Bruno met Stefan's gaze, and forced a smile. 'Long past time in fact, I think,' he agreed.

'You know,' Stefan said, 'I've been watching a different man since we came through the forest. Unless I'm mistaken, there's more than one wound you've seen healed.'

Bruno sat quietly, deep in thought. 'There's something – something I've been blaming myself for,' he began. 'Blaming myself for a long time.'

'Since Stahlbergen?' Stefan asked.

'Yes,' Bruno said. His voice was cracked, heavy with emotion. 'And there's something I need to tell you about. Something I need to put straight.'

Stefan thought back to the time in the Grey Mountains, to the moment when the glory soured and heroism turned to tragedy.

'The woman,' he said. 'You did what you could do to save her. You were just too late, that's all. It would have been the same for me. The orc killed her.'

'No,' Bruno said, so softly his voice was barely audible. He closed his eyes, and let his head fall. 'No, that's not how it was. I killed her, Stefan. The knife was meant for the creature, but as soon as it had left my hand, I knew.' His voice dropped to a whisper. 'I knew I had killed that woman.'

Stefan sat letting the words sink in. The silence between them seemed suddenly to swell and fill the space around them. 'The thing is,' Bruno went on, 'I know now that it truly wasn't my fault. I killed her, and I can never undo that.'

'But you can lift the guilt you've been carrying,' Stefan said.

'I did my very best for that woman, inside that cave. I did my best, but I made a mistake. I made a mistake and she died,' Bruno said. 'Do you believe that?'

'Yes,' said Stefan. 'I made a mistake too. I could have come to your aid. I chose not to. That's the guilt I have to live with.'

Bruno gazed up again at the figure of Alexei Zucharov. He smiled, but the smile held some bitterness. 'It's ironic,' he said to Stefan. 'I suppose it's thanks to Alexei Zucharov that I'm here at all.'

'What are you saying?'

'He saw what happened at Stahlbergen, Stefan. He knew all along I caused that woman's death.'

'You're saying he used that against you – forced you to ride with us on this journey?'

Bruno shrugged. 'If he did, then it's turned out for the good in the end. There were daemons of my own that I needed to face.'

Stefan sat quietly for a moment. Something in the revelation about Zucharov troubled him deeply. 'Just when you think you know a man, he can surprise you,' he observed at last. 'And not always pleasantly.'

Bruno shrugged. 'He's a driven man,' he said. 'You told him you needed me for the mission. Alexei did whatever he thought he needed to achieve that end. It's in the past now.' He ran his hands through his hair and exhaled, deeply. 'One way or another, it feels good to finally lift that weight off my shoulders,' he said. 'It's like a part of me that was dead, coming back to life again.'

Stefan squeezed his comrade's shoulder. 'It gives me joy to hear that, old friend,' he said. 'We're going to need every last ounce of your fortitude and bravery on the morrow.'

'Then it's a good thing I have two good hands to lend!' Bruno declared.

'A very good thing.'

Bruno reached again for the wine flask, then paused. 'We can't promise ourselves never to make mistakes, can we?' he said.

'No,' Stefan agreed. 'We can only promise ourselves that we will learn from them.'

'And that learning never stops, does it?' Bruno smiled, picked up the flask, and put it in his pocket. 'This is good wine,' he said. 'I ought to find Franz, and share a little of it with him.'

Stefan nodded affirmation. 'That's a good idea.' He waved away Bruno's offer of a last drink. 'Go, find Franz,' he said. 'And the gods go with you, Bruno Hausmann.'

He watched Bruno go, picking his path through the forest of canvas. It seemed that he had grown taller, and his footsteps become lighter, all in the space of those few minutes. An old friend had returned.

He sat for a while, watching Alexei and Tomas at their sparring. More than once, the older swordsman got the better of his opponent, even managing to knock the blade from Zucharov's grip. The bigger man simply roared his approval, more than happy to be outdone. And Stefan was happy enough with his solitude. But he was not alone for long.

'Mind if I join you?' He looked up, and saw Elena standing nearby. Without waiting for a reply, she wriggled down onto the grass by his side, another flagon in one hand.

'More wine?' Stefan laughed. 'I've just told Bruno I've had my fill.'

'Well, you haven't,' Elena said, emphatically. 'I never drink alone – except when I am alone, of course.'

'Of course,' Stefan agreed. He took the offered flagon and drank. A mouthful of pungent Brandtwein stung the back of his throat. 'Good stuff,' he volunteered, hoarsely.

Elena drank a long draught of the Brandtwein straight down. 'What about him?' she asked, pointing in the direction that Bruno had gone in. 'Have you made your peace?'

'Yes,' Stefan said 'Or maybe it's more that Bruno has found his peace. Either way, we've said what needed to be said.'

'That's good.' Elena took another draw from the flask. 'Well,' she said, defensively, 'why not? Isn't it drink and be merry, for tomorrow we die?'

'I hope not,' Stefan said. 'But there's little doubt that many of the men in this field are seeing the stars for the last time.'

Elena thought for a moment. 'Ah. So this is the bit where you say to me something like, "Elena, I know you want to be brave, but for your own sake we must keep you away from the fighting tomorrow." Yes?'

'No. I've done what I can to get us this far. As for tomorrow, well–' He stared across the massed ranks of Castelguerre's army. 'That's up to you. Your decisions have proved to be as good as mine.'

'Oh.' It was hard for him to tell if Elena was surprised or disappointed. 'Well,' she went on at last, 'if you're interested, Castelguerre has arranged for me to ride under the protection of Franz and his men.'

'I'm glad of that,' Stefan replied. 'I'm saying I trust your decision. Of course I'm interested in what happens to you. You are very valuable. Valuable to Erengrad and – who knows? Maybe valuable to the whole of the Old World.'

'Valuable… to you?' she asked him.

'Yes,' Stefan said at last. 'To me, too.'

She spread her arms out by her side and lay back on the lush grass, staring up at the sky. The last wisps of cloud had been blown away. It was a clear, cool evening and the stars shone out from the heavens like iced crystals floating upon the night air.

'This is wrong, isn't it?' she said wistfully. 'The skies on the eve of battle should be full of storms and torment. This is too – too perfect.'

Stefan sat in thought for a few moments longer, then stretched out beside her to share the view. 'Let's enjoy it while we can,' he said. 'Try to savour the sight as though it were our last.'

They lay side by side, tracking the slow, steady motion of the heavens in silence. Eventually Stefan pointed to the sky in the east and said: 'Do you know what that one is?'

'The constellation? No. Tell me.'

'That's the Sword of Jewels,' Stefan said. 'Legend says it was worn by Taal when he slew the Hounds of Chaos and freed the world from captivity. And there,' he said, 'to the left, you see? That's Ulric's Staff.'

'Sometimes I dream of the stars,' Elena told him. 'And of the other worlds far away, beyond the sky. Do you believe there are such places?'

'Yes,' Stefan said. 'Maybe other worlds just like this one.'

'Strange thought,' Elena murmured. 'I mean, that there might be two other people, just like us, at this moment looking down upon our world from somewhere up there!'

'Strange indeed,' Stefan agreed. Elena twisted round and propped herself on her elbows, turning her face towards Stefan's. He could smell the wine, warm and sweet on her breath. 'Do you think those other worlds are at war too?' she asked him 'Do you think the struggle continues, even in the heavens?'

'I don't know,' Stefan replied. 'But somehow I imagine that it does. Not just here, but everywhere. A struggle that has always existed. And always will.'

'That sounds like a battle that can't ever be won,' she said, quietly.

'I'd rather think of it as a battle which we must never lose,' Stefan replied.

Elena sighed. 'I suppose that's why we're here,' she said. 'Why we've all risked our lives to get me to a wedding with a man I've never even met, let alone loved.' She paused, letting her thoughts run on. 'But what if,' she continued, 'what if Castelguerre secures Erengrad for the alliance, drives the forces of Chaos out? Doesn't that mean that there would be no need for this marriage?'

Stefan didn't know what reply he could make. For all that he knew, it was a question without answer. 'I don't know,' he said eventually. 'What is it you want me to say?'

Elena moved closer to him. 'I'm not made of stone,' she said. 'You could try sweeping me off my feet.'

Stefan hesitated, then reached out and laid his fingers lightly against the nape of Elena's neck. Her skin felt like cool silk under his touch. He cupped his hand, gently. As he pulled her towards him, he knew that she would not resist.

CHAPTER EIGHTEEN
The Battle for Erengrad

PETR KURAGIN BENT low over the body of Martin Lensky, trying
to staunch the blood flowing from the arrow wound to his
chest. It was useless. The ostler was dying. There was nothing
more Kuragin could do to save him, nor to stem the tide of
blood washing down through the city.

Lensky's breath had been coming in swift, tight spasms as
he fought for oxygen, fought for life. Now his breathing suddenly slowed. His eyes opened again, staring up at Petr
Kuragin.

'Erengrad is lost,' he said, weakly. 'The city will fall.' He
started to cough, hollow and dry, the rattle of death already
in his throat. Kuragin lifted a beaker of water to the wounded
man's mouth and dribbled a little liquid between his lips.

'The bricks and the mortar may crumble and fall,' he told
him. 'But that is just a shell. Erengrad is more than that.
Erengrad exists as a place in our hearts, and in our souls.
Whilst there are men with spirit such as yours, Martin Lensky,
then Erengrad can never die.' He looked down at the ostler,
took his hand and felt for the vital pulse. Somewhere deep
inside him, life held on by the slenderest of threads. Kuragin

lifted the bloodstained blanket and drew it up around Martin Lensky's shoulders. Gradually his shivering subsided a little.

'May the gods watch over you,' Kuragin whispered.

Footsteps drummed hard on the stone steps of the cellar. Two of his men appeared at the foot of the stair, their buckled and bloodied armour testament to the fierceness of the fighting raging above.

'Time to pull back, sire,' the first said. 'The rebels have all but overrun the quarter.' Kuragin raised his eyes and regarded the man quietly. He could see the agitation in the guards' eyes, the urgency of escape written into their weary faces.

'Pull back?' he said at last. 'Pull back to where?'

The second guard took a step forward. 'There's rumoured to be a pocket of militia, well-fed and well-armed, holding out in the south of the city,' he said. 'If we can break though the cordon of scum that have blocked off the quarter, there's a fair chance we can make it through.'

'We have to leave, sire,' the first man repeated. 'Now.'

Kuragin thought about it. His own wounds had left him feeling light-headed, dizzy. The words tumbled around his numb, aching head. Rumours. Pockets of militia holding out. He suddenly felt very, very tired. He didn't feel like running any more. And of one thing he was sure. He would not fail Martin Lensky again, not whilst he yet lived.

'Go with my blessing,' he told them. 'Take as many of the other men as you can muster.'

'What about you, your lordship?'

Kuragin stood up, with some difficulty, and drew his blade from its inlaid silver scabbard. He lifted the sword up, so that it glinted in the thin rays of sunlight penetrating from the street above. 'I still have this,' he told them. 'And I still have Erengrad in my heart.' He beat his fist twice upon his chest. 'I'm not done yet. Go on, leave me,' he insisted, seeing the two men hesitate. 'Something tells me I have business to finish here.'

STEFAN DRIFTED OUT of sleep into the waking day, roused by the sounds of life around him and the bitter chill bite of the morning air. He stretched one arm out behind him. The grass at his side was smoothed flat, but empty. The events of the night before were still fresh in all his senses, but of Elena there was now no sign.

He got up, dressed, and breakfasted off what he could find, mostly nuts and scraps of overripe fruit. There was food enough stowed within the camp, but it was mostly destined for Erengrad, should they ever reach their destination. Provisions for the men on the ground were adequate, but spartan.

Once he had eaten, Stefan picked his way amongst the canvas awnings of the makeshift camp, searching for his companions. The day had dawned cold and bright, but now dark clouds had drawn a curtain across the sun and the sky hung heavy with the promise of rain. Stefan shivered, drawing his cloak tighter as he went on his way. He came upon Tomas, buckling on armour that Schiller had given him. Stefan called out a greeting, which Tomas returned with a familiar nod of the head. He seemed to have sloughed off years in a few short weeks, and now, standing tall in his hauberk of fine-meshed mail, he looked far removed from the stumbling drunk they had dismissed in Altdorf. Stefan had been wrong about Tomas, and was happy to acknowledge it.

Alexei Zucharov had eschewed all offers of armour from their hosts. When Stefan found him he was standing in a clearing on his own, stripped down to his shirt despite the cold, practising his sword strokes yet again. But this time there was no joking, no horseplay. Battle might have been a game to Alexei, but if so then it was an all-consuming one, a game to the death. Stefan watched Zucharov's blade scything the air in fast, almost impossibly powerful sweeps. At moments like this, it was difficult to imagine any foe, mortal or otherwise, standing against him.

Stefan repressed a sudden, inexplicable shudder and hailed his comrade. Alexei looked up and acknowledged him without pausing from his work.

'You'll at least carry a shield with you into battle?' Stefan asked. Alexei stopped and shrugged, sweat soaking through the thin cotton of his shirt. 'I don't know,' he said. 'Will you? What you gain in protection you lose in speed. A shield adds unnecessary weight.'

'Maybe so,' Stefan agreed. 'But this isn't a street brawl we're going into. Axes and spears can make short work of flesh and bone.' He lifted one of the shields, running his hands over its irregular, leaf-shaped edge. 'I'll take some protection, I think,' he said. Zucharov shrugged again, and tossed his sword casually from one hand to the other. 'That depends,' he said. 'Depends whether you're there to defend, or to attack.' He grinned at Stefan. 'I know what I intend to do.'

Stefan felt a hand on his shoulder and turned to find Bruno at his side. If Tomas had grown in stature on their journey, then Bruno, since the Forest of Shadows, had shed a burden. He looked stronger and healthier than he had for months.

'No need to ask you where you stand on armour,' Stefan commented, noting the burnished breast plate strapped to Bruno's chest. Bruno laughed. 'Sharpened steel doesn't agree with me,' he said. 'I was reminded of that by our beastman friends.'

Stefan looked down at Bruno's left arm. The bandage had gone, but he still carried it stiffly. 'Will it be all right?' Stefan asked.

'Good enough,' Bruno affirmed. 'As long as I remember my limits.'

Somewhere towards the heart of the camp, a bugle sounded.

'What's that?' Zucharov asked.

'Summoning the men-at-arms,' Bruno said. 'Castelguerre is about to make his address.'

'We should hear this too,' Stefan said. 'Come on.'

They joined the mass of men crowding towards one end of the field, jostling each other for a better view of their commander. Stefan worked his way towards the front with Bruno and Alexei at his side. Once they had found their vantage point, he scanned the faces standing round them. There, not far from where Castelguerre was due to speak, he finally saw Elena, standing by Schiller's side. It took Stefan a moment to recognise her, strapped into light armour and with her hair pulled up beneath the cusp of a steel helm. Elena looked around and their eyes met. They exchanged a silent greeting, warm, but with a distance that seemed to come from both of them. Something had changed since last night, even if neither of them were yet ready to acknowledge it.

'Here's Castelguerre,' said Bruno, nudging Stefan in the ribs. Stefan pulled his gaze away from Elena as the bulky figure of the commander mounted the steps of the platform. A loud cheer rippled across the mass of men as Gastez Castelguerre climbed into view. Castelguerre stood in silence for a few moments, allowing the applause. Then he raised one arm aloft, calling the gathering to silence. He scanned the massed ranks, as though making contact with each and every individual, and forging an unspoken bond. Battle-hardened though he was, Stefan felt his pulse begin to race.

Castelguerre's voice rang out across the shimmering field of armour and steel.

'Today we stand at the precipice,' he told them, 'Today we defend not just Erengrad, but all that is good, proper and just. If we triumph on the field of battle today, we shall have inflicted a wound upon our enemy such as he will not easily forget. But if we fail–' He paused, looking across the ranks again, letting the moment sink in. 'If we fail, then the curtain of darkness may start to fall across all of the Old World.'

Stefan watched the faces of the men standing nearby in the crowd; comrades known and unknown. He saw the expressions on their faces: excitement, elation, fear and foreboding as the burden of duty began to bear down upon them. Their faces reflected what was in his own heart. Those were his emotions, too.

'Some of you will return victorious from the field of battle today,' Castelguerre continued. 'You'll return with heroes' tales, and a valour which will long outlive the span of your mortal lives.' He bowed his head, as though in prayer, then looked up once more. 'Some of you will never return. For you, the gods have decreed that this shall be your last dawn. If so, then meet the Fates with equanimity. For yours shall be a glorious end, long remembered in the histories of the Old World.'

Stefan glanced at his comrades. Bruno, impassive but resolute. Tomas, staring down in quiet contemplation of the hours to come. Zucharov, his eyes ablaze, already anticipating the taste of victory. And as for him, what fates awaited? Stefan closed his eyes briefly, and the Forest of Shadows closed in around him once more, whispering of things he had not yet seen. Somewhere ahead, the road forked. He opened his eyes, and nodded an affirmation to his friends. The future was waiting for him.

'For the victorious amongst you I have one final word.' Castelguerre continued. 'Drink from the cup of victory, but do not drink too deeply. Ranged against you on the field of battle you will find all manner of men and beasts. Some will be horrible to the eye, some, perhaps, may appear wonderful.

'Do not be tempted to plunder the bodies of the dead. No swords, no shields, helms or bows. Not the smallest ring or trinket. The poison that has shaped your foe exists in every fragment of his being. Let it lie. Let it rot with them in the cold earth.' Castelguerre raised himself up. His piercing stare seemed to reach into the soul of every man standing before him. 'Do not, I beg of you, let Chaos claim you by stealth.'

A fat drop of rain fell from the darkening skies, striking Stefan upon the face. A second followed it quickly, then a third and a fourth. Bruno gazed up to the heavens then turned towards his comrade.

'The gods are weeping, Stefan,' he said.

'Aye,' Stefan agreed, quietly. 'Let us hope it is for joy.'

THE THUNDER OF hooves and metal upon the shaking earth built steadily towards a crescendo inside his head. Varik leant back in the saddle, drunk on the sounds and smells filling his senses. He watched the mighty army driving forward, clouds of ochre dust rising in their wake. For the moment he was Varik no longer: he was Nargrun, Nargrun the mighty, Nargrun the invincible. The primeval lust for blood coursed through his body, and he was relishing every delicious moment of it.

Looking down upon his army – strong, mighty, unyielding in purpose – it seemed inconceivable that any force of man could stand against them. They would reach Erengrad before noon. Then, at last, the tide of blood would surely flow.

His scouts had already brought back news of the mercenary horde gathering at Mirov. The alliance was pinning its hopes upon preventing the might of Kyros from breaching the walls of Erengrad, rather than trying to defend the city from within. So be it. Let them add their blood in tribute to the tide. He did not fear battle, and he did not countenance defeat. It would be as it was the last time he, Nargrun, joined battle on Kislevite soil. The soldiers gathered at Mirov would have no more chance of stopping them than the villagers of Odensk, those many years ago.

Varik reined in and turned his horse to look back at the army spilling across the barren plains of Kislev behind him. Most wore clear allegiance to Kyros and his master, the Great Lord of Change himself. But the other gods – Khorne, Nurgle, and Slaanesh – had paid their tribute as well, their servants swelling the ranks of the great army of death. They might serve different masters, but, for this day at least, all were joined in one common cause: to strike at the sickly body of the Old World where it was weakest, here, on the western edge of Kislev.

He had already decided to kill Rosporov and those loyal to him at the first opportunity, regardless of whether the count kept his promise to deliver Erengrad. One way or another, he would be redundant by the time they had breached the city gates. Worse than redundant; whilst he lived he would remain a threat, a schemer with claims upon the patronage of their Dark Lord. Rosporov's death would leave only one pretender to Kyros's throne.

Besides, Varik reasoned, if Rosporov had succeeded in taking the city from within, might he not be tempted to claim the prize for his own? How could he be sure that the crippled nobleman would hold to his side of the bargain, and not attempt to bar the gates of Erengrad when the conquering force arrived?

He could not be sure. And so he had planned for this contingency also.

Behind the massing ranks of mounted knights and footsoldiers, a line of covered wagons carried the provisions of war: food, weapons, and armour. Three of the wagons were loaded with barrels packed with the most precious commodity of all, silver fire-dust from the merchant traders of Cathay. Enough to blow the gates of Erengrad apart, and reduce the surrounding walls to rubble. Rosporov might betray him, but the purging fire would surely not. And if the count was as good as his word, well then, Varik still saw no harm in stamping his mark upon the city.

But, before that, there was another death that he – they – would take pleasure in above all others. Somewhere amongst the stinking horde that would lay their puny might against

his, Kumansky waited for him. Images from a near and distant past flickered in his mind: the wretched peasant-boy in
Odensk, the knife hidden in his hand, and the arrogant
swordsman in the tombs of Middenheim, the mercenary
who had taken him to the very Gates of Morr.

Stefan Kumansky. Nargrun might not recognise him now,
but Varik surely would. Two burning insults would be
avenged as one. And, before he died, Kumansky would know
who it was he had dared to defy.

PETR KURAGIN WAITED until there was nothing more he could
do for Lensky. Then he covered the face of the dead man with
the bloodstained blanket and went from the cellar out
towards the street above. He emerged into a city that he
barely knew. The air was heavy with the acrid stench of burning: wood, molten tar and the sickening sweet smell of
charred flesh. People picked their way through the smoke-
filled streets, their cries of anguish and rage filling the air. It
was no longer a matter of friend versus foe; there were no
sides now. The wretched survivors of the rioting fell upon
each other indiscriminately, lunging at each other with clubs
fashioned from twisted iron bars, fragments of wood, or anything else that came to hand. Many of those left without
opponents turned upon themselves, tearing at their hair and
clothes with their bare hands. One such man, his eyes blown
wide with madness, saw Kuragin and rushed at him, wielding
a lethal axe. Kuragin sidestepped the madman's blow, then
cut him down with a single stroke of his sword.

He knelt at the fallen man's side. He had been old; old
enough almost to have been Petr's own father. Kuragin laid a
hand upon the body and said a silent prayer. To think that
Rosporov, casting the seeds of insanity throughout the city,
could have brought Erengrad to this. To think that he, Petr
Kuragin, could have been brought to this. To be able to strike
down his own kind, almost without thought or feeling. Petr
Kuragin tried to find his sense of shock and shame, but his
emotions, like his bruised and battered body, were all but
exhausted.

He was shaken from his gloomy reverie by the sounds of
marching feet: a company of men approaching from the far
end of the street. Kuragin stood and peered, bleary-eyed, into

the smoke-hazed gloom. They numbered twenty or more, all wearing identical black sashes tied across their bodies. At their head a man in military garb, a plumed and crested silver helm set upon his head. For a moment, Kuragin wondered whether the militia had not indeed broken through from the south of the city. For a moment, the hope that had stubbornly refused to die burned in his chest once more. Then, as the troops got closer and the smoke from the fires briefly thinned, he recognised the leader. It was Count Vladimir Rosporov.

Kuragin looked into the face of the man who had driven the city over the brink of madness. He was heavily outnumbered by Rosporov's men. In a few moments he was going to die, but, by the wrathful gods, he would extract a price first. Somewhere from deep inside himself, Petr Illyich found a last reserve of strength to draw upon. A last, deep-buried well of adrenalin to fuel his dying deeds. He stepped into the middle of the street and stood, feet set square and apart so that his presence could not be missed. Then, sword raised aloft, he hailed his nemesis.

'So, the fake citizen would now be a fake warlord, would he?' he bellowed. 'Come on then, Rosporov! Test your mettle against this steel!'

Rosporov clearly hadn't seen Kuragin before he stepped from the shadowed side of the street. Kuragin had the pleasure of seeing his opponent's face momentarily register fear and surprise, as the Lord of Erengrad reared up before him, sword in hand. But within a moment Rosporov had composed himself; the mask of noble hauteur settling upon his features once more. He drew out his own sword but fell back, allowing the men around him to take the lead.

'You see the true enemy of Erengrad before you,' the count shouted at them. 'He has the blood of the people on his hands. Bring him to my justice!'

The armed men surged forward. Kuragin scanned their faces. One or two he thought he recognised, but these were not simple townsfolk whose ideas had been twisted by Rosporov's serpent tongue. Their faces, sepulchral and hungry for yet more slaughter, belonged to creatures long since lost to Chaos. There would be no reasoning with them.

Petr Kuragin charged at Rosporov and his men. His blood was fired with the righteous fury of every good soul that had perished since that long night had begun. He screamed out his rage, and the rage of Martin Lensky and countless others like him. He fell upon the black guard, reaping a furious harvest with his sword; soon the street was running with blood.

But they were too many. Gradually their swords found their mark as the blows rained down upon the Kislevite noble. Kuragin urged himself to fight on, but his strength was fading. A blade sliced across his face, narrowly missing his eye. Another blow knocked the sword from his hands. Suddenly he was on his knees, struggling to stay upright, the cobblestones beneath him now slick with blood. Another blow, then another and another. Kuragin heard a voice cry out in pain and desperation: his voice. The smoke and figures above his head seemed to darken and dissolve, then he toppled forward, face down in the street.

He was unconscious for only a few moments. A flask or bucket of water thrown across his face brought him back to the terrible reality. The Scarandar clustered around him, looking down upon his body, slavering like animals. Their breath reeked with the stench of the charnel-house. Then the crowd parted and Rosporov appeared amongst them. His face was blank, inscrutable, seemingly untouched by the horror that had consumed the city. He reached down and ripped open Kuragin's tunic at the collar. Petr tried to lift an arm to fight him away, but found that his arms no longer moved. Rosporov fastened his fingers upon the chain around Kuragin's neck, and tugged. He pulled the silver icon free and held it up to the light, inspecting it with quiet satisfaction.

'You should have listened to me when I was prepared to be reasonable,' he said at last. 'Your futile gesturing has only delayed the inevitable.'

'Go rot in the Pit of Morr,' Kuragin spat at him.

Rosporov laughed. 'I'm sure I will,' he said. 'But not just yet. You, I think, will be first to make that journey.'

Kuragin struggled to lift himself up, to find some way yet of striking back at his adversary, but he was pinned down by at least half a dozen swords, and his body was beaten and broken. He coughed, a painful, wracking cough, and blood filled his mouth.

'Kill me if that's your intent,' he said. 'I've nothing more to say to you.'

Rosporov stepped closer to Petr, close enough for him to smell the lavender-scented polish upon the leather of his boots. Rosporov lifted one foot and brought it down upon the side of Kuragin's face, crushing it against the ground as the black-sashed soldiers of the Scarandar looked on.

'Oh, that's my intent all right,' Rosporov affirmed. 'But I think such an event deserves a better audience. Don't you?'

IT WAS NOT until they had saddled up and were riding from camp that Stefan finally caught up again with Elena. She was riding alone for now, no sign of Schiller. Both she and Stefan were buckled into their armour and carrying shields bearing the crest of the double-headed eagle. Riding side by side into the gathering storm they could have been comrades-in-arms or lovers. Stefan was no longer sure which was true.

'This is the first time we've spoken since last night,' he began. Elena smiled and laughed, but her laugh sounded brittle and anxious. 'Let's hope it's not the last time as well,' she said. Stefan looked across at her, trying to measure her mood.

'Are you all right?' he asked. Elena nodded, but her expression was more ambiguous. 'I think so,' she said. 'You tell me. Am I all right?'

Stefan took her hand briefly as they rode. 'You'll be fine,' he said. 'By the end of the day you'll be home.'

Elena laughed again, this time with some bitterness. 'Home? Erengrad? I suppose that's what I shall have to call it.' She pulled back from Stefan's grasp and wiped her hand across her face. 'What about us, Stefan?'

'I don't know,' Stefan replied. 'You've been avoiding me all morning. There hasn't been a chance to talk.'

Elena cast her eyes down. 'It isn't you I've been avoiding,' she said. 'It's me. I don't know what I'm supposed to do, supposed to feel any more. But what happened last night was very real for me, Stefan. You must believe that.'

'I do believe it.'

'But this is real too,' Elena said, indicating the sea of riders around them. 'Last night was about me and you. But this is about me and Erengrad, and Kislev and–'

'I know,' Stefan said. 'I understand.' Yet in truth, he did not fully understand. He felt as though he had at last stepped beyond a line he had never before allowed himself to cross. In his heart he knew that to be with Elena was one world. A world that part of him yearned to taste again, and perhaps remain a part of forever. But being here, amongst the army riding to save Erengrad, belonged to another world. And he did not know whether those two worlds could ever truly meet. Somewhere up ahead, he reminded himself, the paths must divide.

'We are in the care of the gods,' he told her, raising his voice against the growing clamour. 'If we offer our prayers they will deliver judgements. But I believe in my heart that, whatever their judgement, the gods will look kindly upon Elena Yevschenko.'

Elena smiled, this time without taint of bitterness or sorrow. 'And upon you, Stefan Kumansky,' she said.

Franz Schiller rode up abreast of them, flanked on each side by Bruno and Tomas. He hailed Stefan and bowed his helmed head in deference to Elena.

'I suggested to your comrades that we might ride together,' he said. 'I hope you've no objection.'

'None at all,' Stefan replied. 'Indeed, you honour us.'

Franz nodded. 'The honour's mine,' he said. He looked to Elena. 'Your ladyship,' he said, 'I've assigned a dozen of my best men to escort you. Once we near the battle–'

'I know,' Elena interrupted. 'Once we near the battle, they'll try and keep me out of harm's way.' She smiled at Franz and the others. 'I am beginning to understand,' she said. 'I'm important.'

'That you are,' Franz affirmed. 'Very important indeed.'

All five spurred up their horses, picking up the quickening pace of those around them. Stefan cast his gaze about for Zucharov. Although one of the tallest men on the field, there was still no sign of him. 'Have you seen Alexei?' he asked of Franz. Schiller nodded in affirmation.

'He wants to be first to the kill. He insisted upon riding with the spearhead,' he said, and laughed, incredulously. 'Almost as if he's worried he might miss out!'

'I'm sure there'll be plenty to go round,' Bruno observed, coolly.

'That there will,' Schiller agreed. 'But he's a fearsome man, your Zucharov, no?'

'Let's put it this way,' Stefan said, 'I'd rather be with him than against.'

The massed ranks of horsemen rode north-east, across thin scrubland mottling the earth beneath them a pale, malnourished green. After a while the bushes gave out and they were left upon the open plain, the barren land stretching out flat before them. In the far distance Erengrad was visible now, a jagged line of smoking towers against the horizon. And there, upon that same horizon, a blurred smudge of charcoal grey, indistinct but visibly moving, like a low cloud of insects converging upon the city. With every moment that passed, the mass ahead of them seemed to grow larger, more numerous. Fanfares rang out across the ranks, raising the alarm.

'It's them,' Schiller called out. 'The Chaos army.'

This is it, Stefan thought. He drew a deep draught of Kislev air, cold and deceptively pure, down into his lungs, and prepared to ride towards the future.

CHAPTER NINETEEN
Black Leaves Falling

THE FORCE LED by Gastez Castelguerre met the army of Kyros five hours after dawn, three leagues south of the city of Erengrad. Rain was falling from the skies as the enemies converged, lashing down upon ally and foe alike. The land that was to become the field of battle was quickly awash, a mass of churning, liquid clay.

Stefan knew that Castelguerre meant to cut across the path of the Chaos hordes, to slice through their ranks and sever the head of the army from the rump of troops following behind. The enemy force trapped between Castelguerre's men and the city walls would be too weak to threaten Erengrad alone. Castelguerre would then turn his forces first upon the larger body of men and mutants remaining on their south-western flank. Superior in numbers they might be, but split off from their leaders they would be no match for the allied force.

That much Stefan understood. The plan was sound enough. But as he looked upon the vast expanse of enemy troops now massing ahead of them, he could not help wondering whether it was not they themselves who would be cut off. Now the time had come when they would find out.

The distance between the two armies was eaten away with each passing second. So far the Chaos force seemed to have taken no account of Castelguerre's men. In a sudden and decisive moment, all of that changed. As Stefan pressed his horse forward the air around him seemed to fill with the sound of a thousand sighs. The sky above darkened momentarily, then shafts of fire started to fall amongst them, flaming arrows dropping from the heavens with the rain.

Many of the shafts fell harmlessly upon the ground, or were deflected away by mail or steel plate. But, amongst the deluge, others inevitably found their mark. Despite the rain, fire was spreading quickly from the arrowheads, flames catching hold even upon armour. Stefan watched as dozens around him fell from their horses, struggling to rip the blazing shafts from their flesh. Many more who did not die from the arrows perished upon the ground, crushed into the mud beneath the horses.

A cry ran along the lines of mounted riders, picked up and passed from one to another.

'Shields!'

Stefan lifted his shield high in the air, then brought it tight up against Elena's and others close by. The leaf patterns now found their purpose, the sculpted metal edges mating as part of a larger pattern, bonding together to form one huge, over-arching shield above their heads. The burning rain beat down upon them in torrents, but the steel canopy held firm.

'Keep moving forward!' Stefan shouted to his comrades. 'We'll be amongst them in moments.' As they passed inside the ring of fire marked out by the range of the arrows, they lowered shields and drew swords ready for combat. Stefan said one last, silent prayer before battle was joined. He prayed for his brother Mikhal, at home in distant Altdorf, and prayed that their reunion would come to pass. He prayed for Elena, that she might complete her quest unharmed. He prayed for his comrades, for Bruno, Alexei and Tomas. And he prayed for Franz Schiller and all men of good heart who rode out on this day. Prayed that they might see out the day, to revel in the glory of another dawn. But he knew that the gods could not spare them all.

The opposing force was no more than a spear's throw in front of them. Stefan stared ahead, expecting in some way to

see the taint of Chaos written clear upon the faces and bodies of the enemy. But all he saw were hundreds upon
hundreds of fighting men; men mounted upon armour-clad
steeds, infantrymen on foot treading the perilous path
between the horses, archers desperately trying to find space to
launch their deadly weapons skywards. Friend and foe mingled in one confusing melee, a tumbling dance to the music
of Morr.

Soon the air was full of the sound of men screaming and
steel crashing upon steel. Stefan stole a moment to look
around for his comrades. Bruno and Tomas were still close
by, turning their horses in to strike at the enemy ranks. Elena
was already drifting far out of sight, flanked by Schiller's men,
moving away from the sea of steel now raging all around. He
shouted her name a final time but his voice was drowned in
the battle storm. Now he could have only one focus. He must
fight to stay alive.

He looked up to see a knight, a youth with flesh so pale as
to be almost translucent. The rider bore down upon Stefan,
sword already poised to strike at his head. For a moment they
were looking directly at one another. The black, unblinking
eyes of the other rider radiated a cold evil, yet there was
something else in that fragment of a moment that Stefan saw,
a ghost of some other life that this boy might have led before
Chaos claimed him.

The blow fell, fast and heavy. Stefan parried it with his
shield, then forced his attacker back, throwing the ghostly
warrior off-balance in the saddle. Before the Chaos knight
could recover, Stefan had struck again. His sword ripped
through the knight's milk-white flesh below the mail corset.
A well of dark ruby blood sprang from the wound. The knight
raised his sword arm ponderously a second time, and Stefan
hacked it off below the elbow. The knight tumbled from his
mount into the tangled mass of fallen men below.

Now it has begun, Stefan thought. And now he began to
make sense of what the world had now become, the world
where there existed only life, or death. He marked out his
enemies amongst the surrounding throng, announcing his
presence with his unforgiving blade. Most of the enemy force
could have passed for mortal men, only the insignia of the
curled serpent upon their armour betraying their allegiance.

But, amongst them, Stefan saw the altered ones, those upon whom Chaos had clearly lain its hand. Men, or those that once been men, now become monsters. Grinning, slavering beasts with fanged jaws that dripped an acid bile. Creatures with the bodies of men and the heads of snakes or horned rats. There were beastmen too, amongst them; a few had prevailed to reach the field that would now become their grave. Stefan tore into them all, without care or discrimination. Whatever they had once been, wherever they had come from, he knew what they now were. And he could not rest until he had destroyed them all.

Ahead of him now was a group of Norscan warriors, lashing out with double-headed axes at anything carrying Castelguerre's colours. The sight stirred bitter memories in Stefan; he pulled back on the reins, trying to force his horse through the fighting, towards them. As he did so, someone – or something – landed upon his back. Muscular arms encircled his torso, arms more akin to giant claws than human limbs, plated with a shell-like armour. Stefan tried to punch his way free but found his own arms pinioned by his side, unable to move. The crab-like pincers were closing, squeezing the air from his chest. Just when it seemed his lungs must burst he felt a sudden impact punching into his back. The pincer limbs flexed then flew apart like a broken spring. As Stefan turned around he had a brief glimpse of the disintegrating shape of something like a giant insect slithering to the ground, and Bruno close behind, his sword tarnished with a putrid yellow gore.

'Watch your back,' Bruno suggested, breathing hard.

'I'm glad you were there watching it for me,' Stefan shouted back. He drew air back into his lungs, and shook off the shattered fragments of dung-brown bone. 'Glad, and thankful,' he added. 'It's good to have you back.'

ACROSS THE SEA of combatants, on the other side of the battle, the warlord of Kyros sat astride his horse, impassive, watching the ebb and flow of strife. For now he was Nargrun no longer. He was Varik: Varik the schemer, Varik the manipulator; Varik the orchestrator of men. He watched the battle unfolding as he might watch the movement of pieces upon a gaming board, weighing the loss of life on one side against that of the other with a cool diffidence. The opposing forces were perhaps both greater in number and better organised than he had first anticipated.

He recognised their commander – Castelguerre – as an old enemy of his master. He, too, was a member of the secret Old World cabal that sought to oppose and defy Kyros. So be it; he could meet his mortal fate here on the fields of Erengrad. He, Varik, would dispose of the gin-sozzled Bretonnian bandit just as he had despatched the others: the priest in Middenheim, and the meddlesome Brandauer in Altdorf.

That the forces of Chaos would ultimately prevail over their adversaries he had no doubt. The implacable forces of attrition, transformation and decay would allow of no other outcome. But, more immediately, it was vital to his own interests that the battle for Erengrad did not slip from their grasp. He knew that Kyros would grant him no further reprieve if it did.

He straightened, rigid, upon his mount, his eyes closed. Inside of him, the separate factions of his dual being struggled for supremacy. Varik sensed the animal rage of his shadow-self boiling to a crescendo inside of him, baying for release. Nargrun the Vengeful, Nargrun the Merciless. The Norscan had no interest in strategy or the checks and balances of power. His was the way of blood, and the purging power of the sword alone. Varik savoured the pleasing sensation of that power held at bay, tethered and teased like a beast in a cage.

But now the time for release was at hand. It was time for Nargrun to join with the battle and seek out his prey. He threw back his head and uttered a long, howling cry, a cry to rouse the furies of all whose souls had been touched by darkness; a cry to strike fear and despair into the hearts of all those who still prayed for the triumph of the Light. He whipped his horse on and surged forward, ploughing into the sea of humanity that lay ahead.

TOGETHER WITH BRUNO, Stefan fought his way steadily across the enemy line. The rage of the battle increased as the rain hammered down from the skies. The dead fell upon the dead, and the once barren plain became a graveyard of flesh and steel. And yet the fighting did not relent, but seemed to burn with an ever greater intensity. In the distance, through the haze of battle, Erengrad, too, was burning. The walls of the city stood intact, but there was no visible sign of any soldiers along their length. The defenders of Erengrad, if any remained, would make no contribution to the battle that raged beyond the walls. The city would be won or lost upon these blood-soaked fields.

Franz Schiller came into view, leading a group of men from the far edge of the field, trying to drive a wedge through the main phalanx of the Chaos army and sever the head of the beast from its body. As Stefan looked on, Castelguerre's lieutenant was surrounded from behind by a larger force of Chaos knights, half-human creatures mounted on grotesque, mutated steeds; horses with flesh like the armoured hides of dragons. Stefan shouted a warning but his words were again drowned out in the deluge.

'Come on!' he urged Bruno, pushing his horse forward. Grey-furred infantrymen with faces narrowed into rodent-snouts thrust spears towards them as they advanced. Stefan decapitated three of the creatures with a single sweep of his sword, and ploughed another two into the mire under his horse. The rest of the skaven fled in panic, clearing a path amongst the carnage for the two riders to pass through.

Two of Schiller's men were already down, and the odds against him were now at least three to one against. And these opponents were no cannon-fodder. Stefan watched in dismay as the black-armoured knights of Kyros pressed on, their heavy axes splitting flesh from bone in a relentless killing storm. They fought like grotesque mechanical marionettes, blind and unthinking, with no apparent regard for their own lives.

Franz Schiller was fighting back with a fierce desperation. His sword strokes were finding their mark, but still his adversary did not fall. Finally the black warrior found the room to swing his double-headed axe. Schiller's reactions were fast enough to save his life; the axe aimed for his neck hammered into his breastplate instead. But the force of the blow was enough to unseat him. Schiller lurched back in the saddle and toppled from his horse onto the ground.

The Chaos knight regarded his fallen foe with indifference, positioning his axe to strike a second, fatal blow. Schiller rolled to one side and gripped with both hands upon the booted leg of his opponent, trying to pull him down. In the same split second, Stefan aimed his sword at the jointed armour-plate above the knight's elbow and hacked the arm bearing the axe away.

Before he could draw back to strike at a second knight, he saw another rider coming up fast from the right. Tomas Murer's sword flashed bright as he tore across the Chaos knight's path at a gallop. His blade cut the knight across the neck, just below the rim of his visored helm. The knight clutched at his throat and crashed forward in the saddle, sending his brutish steed careering away out of control.

Looking round, Stefan saw that Franz had regained his feet and was riding up behind Bruno. The leader of the Chaos knights appeared to pause, staring directly at Stefan for a few seconds. Then he turned his mount around and was gone, his warriors following in his wake.

Whatever the reason, Stefan was glad of the respite. He had lost all track of how long the battle had been raging. It might have been minutes; it felt like hours. His whole body ached, and his face and hands were covered with cuts where enemy weapons had come close to finding their mark. The odds for survival were not long in such a world.

His comrades regrouped around him, Franz Schiller having found another horse to replace his fallen mount. 'Are you all right?' Stefan asked him.

'Yes,' Franz affirmed. 'No small thanks to you.' He raised his arm in salute to Tomas.

'What of Elena?' Stefan demanded. 'I thought she was with you?'

'She's safe,' Franz assured him. 'She's riding with Castelguerre's personal guard. If any of us reach the city, then she surely will.'

Stefan looked around, taking stock of the battlefield. Up above, the storm had cleared. Winds dragged the clouds apart, and sun flooded the bloodied plains of Erengrad. Light flickered off the buckled metal of fallen shields, scattered like silver petals upon the earth. In each direction, for as far as the eye could see, a battle to the death was being fought. In the distance, Castelguerre's standard could be clearly seen framed against the silhouette of the city, still pushing deep into the

enemy lines. In response, a second wave of flaming arrows
was launched skywards, falling like burning rain from the
heavens.

'That's madness,' Bruno said. 'They'll be killing their own as
well as us.'

'They won't care about that,' Schiller told him. 'They can
afford to lose two for every one of our men that falls.'

'Then someone needs to deal with that,' Stefan said.

'Agreed,' Franz Schiller said. 'Will you join us?'

Bruno and Tomas nodded. 'Count us all in,' Stefan replied.
He marked the direction of the arrows. 'They're coming from
somewhere over there,' he said, pointing north-west of the
city walls. 'Let's waste no more time.'

The riders set off at a gallop, towards the heart of the
enemy command. Many of the foes that dared to stand
against them were either trampled underfoot or despatched
by scything blows delivered from horseback. But, by sheer
weight of numbers, the soldiers of Kyros still took a heavy
toll of Schiller's men. At least half a dozen were pulled, dead
or dying, from the saddle, and still more were struck down by
the fiery brands launched by the bowmen. Through it all,
Stefan and his comrades rode on. There could be no turning
back.

Ahead of them now they could see the archers' emplace-
ment. A low trench had been dug into the clay, a pit filled
with a score of bowmen arranged around a vat filled with a
bubbling, steaming liquid. The bowmen were loading and
firing a constant barrage of arrows aloft, pausing only to dip
their darts into the vat. Each arrow pulled out crackled with
an evil yellow-green fire.

As Stefan and the others bore down the alarm was raised.
Half of the archers trained their bows directly at the
approaching riders. A flame-tipped shaft screamed past
Stefan's face, close enough for him to feel its heat. He looked
round to see a second arrow strike one of Schiller's men
square in the face. The knight fell from his horse, followed by
others battling to extinguish the flames spreading across their
bodies.

'Morr only knows what infernal substance that is,' Stefan
shouted. 'It seems to burn through armour as though it were
straw!'

'Aye,' Schiller agreed, breathlessly. 'And Morr help us if we don't overrun that position soon!'

An arrow struck Stefan in the chest, piercing the light armour of his breastplate. The ring-mail of his corset had saved him from further harm, but flame was already rippling out from the punctured armour, eating through the metal. Stefan pulled a hand away from the reins and tugged the arrow free before damping the flames with his gauntlet. The enemy position was all but in range now. He wrung one last burst of speed from his mount, launching it above and into the archery pit. Too late the archers scrambled to regroup. Too late; for Stefan and his comrades were amongst them now.

Stefan leapt from his horse and set about the soldiers in the pit in a fury. Most of the defenders had side-arms, but none were a match for the swordsmen now in their midst. He slew one archer as the man prepared to fire, his sword slicing through the longbow in the same arcing stroke. A second defender wielding a dagger fell upon him, but Stefan wrestled the man to the ground then plunged his sword down upon his opponent.

The battle within a battle was swiftly won. No more fire would rain from enemy lines. Franz Schiller wiped the blood from his face and marched purposefully towards the steaming cauldron. 'Let's be rid of this diabolic brew,' he declared.

'Wait a minute.' Bruno tugged at Stefan's sleeve. 'What's going on over there?'

He directed Stefan's gaze towards the far side of the archery pit, where a train of covered vehicles were being hastily driven back towards the enemy line, away from Schiller's men and the fighting.

'I don't know,' said Stefan, quietly. 'But our arrival seems to have worried our friends with the wagons.'

'Something they're anxious to protect?' Schiller suggested.

'Maybe,' Stefan concurred. He pulled a longbow free of a fallen adversary. 'Let's see how they like a taste of their own, anyway.' He dipped an arrow into the smouldering vat and waited for the eerie fire to flare at its point before notching it into the bow. Bruno did the same with a second bow, and others followed their lead.

Franz Schiller grinned as he launched his arrow. 'With the compliments of Gastez Castelguerre,' he yelled. Within moments at least a dozen flaming darts were arcing through the clearing skies towards the retreating wagons. Many fell upon the advancing foot-soldiers of Kyros's army. The infantry were left where they lay to burn, but every arrow that found its mark upon the wagons produced a storm of activity as men rushed to extinguish the spreading flames.

'Forget about the soldiers,' Stefan shouted. 'Concentrate your fire on the wagons themselves.' He reloaded his bow and aimed it skywards. He closed his eyes and said a prayer. It was a prayer to the memory of his father; a prayer that his soul might this day be avenged.

Stefan opened his eyes and let fly the arrow in concert with the others. The flaming darts climbed towards the heavens, then seemed to hang, momentarily suspended, upon the air before falling like avenging angels upon their enemies. Two or three at least fell into the very heart of the cluster of wagons. A cry went up among the men trying to marshal their retreat, and many turned and fled.

Stefan was on the point of reloading his weapon when the sky turned a blinding gold and he was thrown back upon the ground. As he fell, a roar like the breaking of a thousand storms split the air, and the earth trembled as though the world itself was being shaken apart. Thinking he was under some new attack, he scrambled to his feet, ready to defend himself. He was greeted by the sight of a great cloud of black and orange fire rising into the sky where the wagon train had previously been. Nothing surrounding it was left standing.

He stood with the others staring in silent awe at the sight. It was an elemental monster; the all-consuming ball of flame had destroyed everything within their immediate view. It was a while before any of them spoke, and then Franz Schiller said quietly and simply: 'That will alter the balance of the day.'

As the fireball evaporated into the heavens and the shaking in the earth subsided, a new rain began to fall. A black rain of ash, charred flakes that were now the only remains of the force of men and mutants that had been standing before them. As the ash settled, a cloud of choking smoke like fog drifted in towards them across the battlefield.

Stefan shook his head, still in awe of the display of power that might otherwise have been unleashed upon the defenders of Erengrad. Finally he turned away, and joined the others recovering those horses that had not already fled in panic. 'Now,' he said at last, 'we have to finish this.'

A group of riders emerged out of the smoke on their flank. Stefan tensed, ready for any new twist in the battle, but the tension turned to relief as he recognised Elena in their midst.

Stefan reined in and turned his horse back towards hers. Her face was smeared with the dark soot that had fallen from the air, and there was a small cut beneath one eye that would almost certainly leave a scar. For all that, it seemed to Stefan that she had never looked more beautiful. It was a realisation that lay surprisingly heavy upon his heart.

Stefan rode to her and took her hand between his own. 'I'm very glad to see you,' he said.

Elena smiled back at him with an easy warmth. 'And I you,' she replied.

She gazed around, acknowledging Bruno, Franz and Tomas. Stefan could see she was exhausted, driven to the point of collapse. She was keeping herself going by sheer determination alone.

'No Alexei?' she asked, forcing her words out. 'He's not–'

Stefan shook his head. 'Not as far as I know. He was last seen riding to the front, in Castelguerre's wake. If any man has survived this day, then surely Alexei has.'

Elena closed her eyes and took a deep breath, as though trying to suck strength back into her body. 'The ball of fire was some display,' she said at last. 'I've never seen the like of it, not even in my dreams.'

'Nor I,' Stefan concurred. 'My guess is it was some incendiary substance. Let's be thankful the end was not as Kyros had intended.'

'Thankful indeed,' Elena agreed. She gazed up above her head. The charred flakes were still floating down all around them, dark, fragile wraiths against the slowly clearing sky. 'Like leaves falling,' she commented. 'The black leaves of war.'

'In that case,' Stefan said 'Let us hope this is the autumn that portends unending winter for the forces of darkness.'

Whatever Elena's reply, Stefan never heard it. He heard another voice – Bruno, or Tomas maybe – shout a desperate warning. And, as the pounding of hooves filled his ears, he caught a glimpse of the figure in black armour, a giant on horseback bearing down upon him.

Stefan turned to face the attack, but not fast enough. His saw the shield, a huge expanse of convex steel, the crest of the coiled serpent embossed upon it. Then something – the shield itself, or the flat of a broadsword – struck him diagonally across the chest, and he was thrown from his horse onto the ground.

In the confusion of the next few moments as he lay bleeding upon the wet earth, only Stefan's experience told him what must be happening. His attacker had ridden past him; the sound of the hooves upon the ground receded, stopped, then grew louder once again. *He's turned around,* a voice in Stefan's head told him. *And now he's coming back to kill you.*

Stefan staggered to his feet and drew his sword, all too aware of how poor his chances were against a heavily armoured foe on horseback. As his vision cleared he saw the monstrous figure bearing down upon him. The face beneath the helm was masked behind a visor. The creature closing upon him roared, an animal scream which dripped with hate and rage.

In that same instant there came a second, answering cry. Stefan looked round to see Tomas Murer cutting across the attacker's path at speed, sword held aloft in his outstretched hand. In that moment all Stefan could think of was Tomas practising his swordplay with Alexei Zucharov. How, against the odds, he had somehow managed to get the better of the bigger, stronger man.

The two riders collided, flesh upon bone and steel upon steel in a single, sickening crash. For a second it looked almost as though Tomas and the Chaos knight were embracing, so close and so still did they seem to hold together upon the field. Then the Chaos warrior pulled his sword clear, and the blade dripped red with blood freshly drawn. With his other arm he swiped Murer away, and Tomas tumbled from his horse like a discarded rag doll.

Even before his comrade struck the ground, Stefan was running. He must have shouted for Bruno to surrender his horse to him, because suddenly the saddle was empty and Stefan was vaulting up. All the time he felt the eyes of the Chaos warrior upon him, fired with a hungry hatred that, Stefan sensed, burned for him alone. Fear not, he vowed, for you will have your fill of me now.

He turned Bruno's horse about and charged full on against the creature that had struck Tomas down. The two horses closed upon one another. At the moment of intersection Stefan swung his sword, and held his shield braced to receive the answering blow. Metal met metal and a shuddering jolt ran the length of Stefan's body. He had just enough time to see the visored helm of his adversary as the warrior thundered past, already wheeling around to launch another attack.

Stefan took rapid stock of his situation. He still had his sword, but the blade had come off the worst from the last exchange, and the cutting steel was now pitted and bent out of true. His shield had probably saved him from greater harm, but it too had taken damage, and had been ripped open from its centre almost to the far edge. So far he had suffered no wounds, but he knew already that this was no ordinary adversary. The warrior bearing the serpent crest was stronger than any mortal man he had encountered, bigger and heavier by far than Stefan.

Stefan pulled his horse about. His opponent had already begun his charge, heading directly at Stefan at a furious pace. The Chaos knight had now swapped his sword for a heavy, steel spiked mace which he swung from his left hand as though it were a toy. But Stefan knew it was no toy. If it made contact it would smash his armour like the shell of an egg. Stefan raised the pace of his horse until it matched that of his opponent. Once again, the two riders closed upon one another with frightening speed. Stefan jinked to the left, taking up a position identical to the first pass. He saw the Chaos knight swap the mace to his right hand, ready to strike.

Stefan watched the gap between them narrow. Sweat drenched his body and his muscles tightened to steel knots. One second too soon, or too late, and he would be dead. And he would get only one chance at this. At the moment before the riders met, Stefan tugged back furiously on the reins, steering to the right, across the path of the oncoming horse. The Chaos knight lashed out with the mace but could not connect. As Stefan passed behind him he stabbed home with his sword. The blade missed his enemy's body but lodged itself amongst the fastenings of his breastplate, dragging him back.

The sword was almost pulled clean from Stefan's grip, but he held on, two-handed, for grim life itself. His opponent's horse reared up, wild-eyed; foam flecking the corners of the creature's mouth. The Chaos knight hesitated, torn between catching hold of the reins and trying to strike at Stefan with the mace. The indecision cost him dearly. Before the Chaos warrior could regain control, Stefan channelled all his remaining energy in one last desperate burst. He hauled back upon the still entangled sword, and dragged the knight from his horse.

Stefan sprang from the saddle. His opponent was already rising from the ground, but Stefan's speed gave him the upper hand now. He launched a well-aimed kick at the Chaos knight's head, sending the warrior sprawling back into the mud. Before his adversary could rise again, Stefan had the tip of his sword at his throat. He pushed it home firmly, pinning his opponent upon the ground.

Stefan's lungs pumped in spasms as he fought to find his breath. He knew that his strength was all but spent. He must finish this, finish it now. But first, first he had to know. He lifted his sword away from the knight's throat and on to the helm, and prised the visor open. A scarred, milk-white Norscan face stared back at him through a single, unblinking eye. He seemed to register Stefan, and his expression filled with loathing.

Stefan did not recognise his enemy, but something akin to memory stirred within him. An instinctive memory, a memory that smouldered deep, and painful. A memory that would not let him rest. The Chaos warrior seemed to see the unease written on Stefan's face, for at that moment his expression changed and he smiled, a smile borne of a lifetime of cruel plunder. His lips moved around a single word: 'Odensk.'

Stefan felt something well up inside of himself, something burning, and sorrowful. An ache that he had never been able to lose now suffused his whole being. As he lifted his sword over his opponent, a picture of his dead father came into his mind. He visualised him as he never had before, at rest in a distant place. Stefan looked down again, into the single eye of an enemy who would know no second resurrection.

Now it was he who smiled.

He expelled the breath from his lungs, releasing at last a howl born of old, unending anguish. He drove his sword down, deep into the throat of the Norscan. As the light fled from the single, baleful eye Stefan cast his own gaze aloft.

'It is ended, father,' he said. 'May you rest in eternal peace.'

WITH THE WARLORD dead, Stefan's first thought was for Tomas Murer. But, by the time Stefan had pushed his way through the crowd gathered around his fallen comrade, it was already too late. Tomas would never now taste the fruits of victory that his valour had helped win, nor would he ever again look upon another dawn. He had died where he had fallen, face down upon the bloody soil of Erengrad.

Stefan cradled his comrade's head in his hands, but Tomas's eyes were already as cold and as dead as his father's, all those years past in the grey dawn light of Odensk.

'The blade cut through his heart,' he heard Bruno's voice saying. 'There was nothing we could do for him.'

Stefan drew down the lids of Tomas's eyes and lay his head back upon the ground. 'They have taken our brother from us,' he said, 'but they cannot take our memories of him. Tomas will live forever in our hearts. He shall never grow old.'

He felt a touch, light upon his shoulder. Stefan looked up and saw Elena standing over him, Franz Schiller and two of Castelguerre's lieutenants at her side.

A great weight seemed to lay upon her shoulders, but with it a quiet dignity he had not seen before. 'Apparently,' she said, 'the situation in the city has deteriorated.'

'The battle here has swung in our favour,' Schiller explained, 'but we've had word that the city itself could fall to the rebels at any time. If Elena Yevschenko is ever to return to Erengrad to claim her birthright, then it must be now.'

Stefan got to his feet, slowly, his gaze upon Elena. Tears were welling in her eyes. 'This is the end for us, too, isn't it?' she said.

Stefan took her hand. 'When I lead you through the gates of the city it must be as Petr Kuragin's bride,' he replied.

Elena forced a laugh that choked into something like a sob. 'We don't even know if Petr Kuragin is still alive,' she pointed out.

'No,' Stefan agreed. 'But we must complete our journey with faith in our hearts that he is. For all of our hopes are rested in him,' he said. 'And, in you.'

Elena let go Stefan's hand. She seemed about to pull away from him. Then she turned, and looked directly into his eyes. They moved together into a lingering embrace. Stefan clasped her to him, drinking in her warmth and her scent, trying to sift them away them like treasure inside of himself. 'Maybe we could–' he began, but Elena cut him off.

'Don't say it,' she implored. 'Don't say anything. Just be with me now. Stay by my side until the journey is ended.'

Stefan held her for just a few seconds more, then pulled away. Franz Schiller and his men stood facing them, waiting.

'We're ready,' Stefan told them. 'We can leave at once.'

CHAPTER TWENTY
The Poison in the Stream

EVEN BEFORE STEFAN Kumansky had plunged the killing blade into the body of the emissary, Kyros had sensed the tide of war begin to turn against his servants. The image of the fire-powder flash had seared itself upon his soul at the moment the merciless, blistering wave of flame swept across his forces, decimating his army at one fatal stroke. Kyros sensed their deaths as he might sense sand slipping from between his fingers. Individually, like single grains, their loss did not matter. But as hundreds ran into thousands, as the fire and the battle raged, the Chaos Lord knew that victory upon the field would not now be his.

He had granted Varik a final chance, a final redemption. Again his emissary had failed him. There would be no further failure. There would be no further redemption. Kyros dwelled upon his acolyte's final agonies with a cold impassivity, a silent observer upon Varik's passage from life into death. Varik was of no further account to him now; he was just another grain of fallen sand.

Of more account was the fate of Erengrad. Whatever happened now inside the city, the attempt to storm it from without would be lost. No sleight of calculation could disguise that. Part of him had expected as much; did not his own master pour scorn upon the crude orchestrations of the children of Khorne? Brute strength alone could always be undone by guile.

Kyros was servant to a subtler, more powerful god. Tzeentch, the Lord of Change, dark master of transfiguration. Long after the rage of war had been spent, the engines of Tzeentch would still be turning, invisible to the mortal eye. Defeat was apparent, but it was only a mask. Behind that mask, Kyros knew, one such magnificent transformation bided its time, waiting to be revealed.

ALEXEI ZUCHAROV RODE through the desolate fields of battle, picking a path through the bloody debris of slaughter. His own sword had paid fulsome tribute to the toll. He had long since lost count of how many of the enemy – men, mutants, orcs and even beastmen – had fallen beneath his blade that day. And yet, somehow, no matter how many the final tally, it was not yet enough. He had plundered freely from those he had vanquished, but the spoils had been meagre. A ring, a locket cast in bronze, a battered ceremonial dagger. None of them were worthy of him.

Something inside still smouldered; restless, yearning. A hunger which would not be sated, no matter how many foes he despatched. Alexei knew that he could not rest until it had been satisfied. And he knew, too, that, somewhere upon the field of battle, resolution awaited.

He had been far away from the wagons when the detonation lit up the sky. He had felt the fury of the fires upon his skin and the earth shuddering beneath him, and had guessed the course that the battle would now run. He rode amongst the vanquished now. The knowledge fortified him even as it sapped the strength of his enemies. He felt all-powerful, immune from harm.

Smoke from the explosions drifted down across the battlefield like an autumn fog, tainted and impure with the wicked stench of death.

Zucharov knew how quickly the course of a battle could alter. It was no surprise to him that the meshing, desperate crowds of barely an hour before had now all but disappeared.

The battlefield around him had become almost empty, eerily quiet in the false twilight.

Zucharov reined in his horse and turned around, performing a full circle to survey the remnants of the battle. Nothing stirred within his field of vision. Then, slowly, almost imperceptibly at first, a rider emerged through the haze, riding slow out of the enemy line like a ship cut adrift upon an ocean. Zucharov drew his sword and wiped the crusted blood from the blade until it gleamed anew. The steel was still sharp and fresh; like him it did not seem to tire. He was not done yet, not done by half.

The other rider sat statuesque and slightly lopsided upon a towering black stallion. By now he must have seen Alexei, yet he kept riding directly towards him at the same, slow pace. Whoever he was, he seemed either oblivious or indifferent to Zucharov's presence. As the servant of Chaos drew closer, Alexei saw his face for the first time. A face disfigured by images and runes that twisted and writhed with each animation of the creature's features. With a jolt, Alexei realised that every inch of the Chaos warrior's face was covered with what seemed like moving tattoos.

Zucharov was seized with a sudden unshakeable certainty. This was the moment of resolution he had been searching for. He touched the hilt of his sword to his lips.

'Do not forsake me now,' he whispered. He sensed destiny unfolding. He would not let it slip from his grasp.

THE BATTLE THAT raged beyond the walls of Erengrad had turned a decisive corner. The Chaos horde still remained in number, but increasingly, they looked a spent force, leaderless and without direction.

As the tide had swung, so the black alliance had crumbled as old, warring hatreds resurfaced. Skaven turned against beastman; the followers of Khorne against those of Slaanesh. The greatest number, soldiers of Tzeentch in the service of Kyros, turned against all their former allies without discrimination, bitter in their quest to find blame for their failure. Some still marched towards Erengrad, hopeful yet of conquest or even sanctuary. But most now knew the city for what it would surely prove to be: their tomb. They fled in ever growing numbers, away from the city, back towards the north, the avenging legions of Castelguerre's army at their heels.

Stefan and his comrades were riding east, a fast-moving squadron with Elena Yevschenko at its heart, bound for Erengrad, their final destination. As they got closer, the great city began to reveal its scars. Fires burned unchecked upon many of the ramparts. From inside the walls, ominous plumes of dark smoke snaked upwards into the now cloudless sky.

Stefan had been wondering how they should breach the city walls; whether forces loyal to Kuragin and Kislev would have managed to hold the gates, or, conversely, whether they would have to fight their way in. To his astonishment, he realised that the threshold could be crossed unopposed. The great gates lay open, unguarded, a gaping fissure in the mouth of the city. And, through that fissure, men, women and children now streamed, refugees fleeing Erengrad for whatever fate might await them beyond.

The trickle of refugees became a flood as they neared the walls. Soon it was impossible to ride any faster than walking pace, so dense was the human tide flowing against them.

Elena gazed down upon her people with horror and alarm. 'Where are you going?' she asked. 'Why are you abandoning your homes?' Few even looked up at her. Most of those who did met her with a dismissive shake of the head. 'We have no homes,' one woman told her. 'We'll take our chances out here.'

Stefan was trying to decide what this meant for the state of the city within. When his questions, too, met with no response, he sprang from his horse and plucked a man at random from the exodus, blocking his path.

'Who is defending the city?' he asked. 'What has happened to the militia?'

The man looked up at Stefan with weary, bloodshot eyes. His expression spoke indifference and disdain, but an instinctive deference still brought him to reply. 'No one is defending the city,' he told Stefan. 'There's nothing left to defend. And we haven't seen the guard since the sun last set.'

'Cowering in their holes,' another added, bitterly. 'Cowering or running, tails between their legs, soon as they got the chance.'

'What of Petr Illyich Kuragin,' Elena demanded. 'Do you know of him? Has he been seen?'

'Know *of* him,' the first man replied. 'But don't know where he is now. The Kuragin mansion was razed to the ground, along with all the other fancy palaces?' The man shrugged. 'Dead or dying, I expect. The count's calling the tune now.'

'The count?'

The man began to struggle free of Stefan's grasp. 'Rosporov,' he said, and spat upon the ground. 'You may judge his kindness by what you see around you.' Finally, he shrugged Stefan off. Within moments the man had disappeared, lost and anonymous amongst the flow of human misery seeping away from the city. Stefan turned to Elena.

'Rosporov. Does that mean anything to you?'

'I've heard the name,' Elena replied. 'From what I can recall, I don't suppose they'll be dedicating a Temple of Shallya to him.'

'I doubt it too. Time may be short if we are to find Petr Kuragin alive.' He turned to the others. 'I've vowed to Elena that I will be at her side until this is done, for better or for worse,' he said. 'None of you is under that obligation. There is still work to be done out here; the battle is not yet won. No less credit would fall to any of you if you chose to stay outside the walls.'

Bruno smiled. 'I've never seen Erengrad,' he said. 'It would be a shame to come this far and not have that pleasure.'

'That goes for me, too,' Franz affirmed. 'Count us both in.'

'I'm heartily glad to,' Stefan said. 'Gods grant only that we are not too late.'

BLOOD PUMPING HARD through his veins, Alexei closed upon his adversary. He was nearing the heart of the storm that had come to define his very existence. A storm that raged along the thin line between life and death, between failure and glory. Every sinew of his body was attuned to this moment. He was riding to meet his nemesis, to do combat with what lay within the shadows, and emerge victorious.

Zucharov positioned his sword for the opening strike and braced himself against the answering blow that would surely follow. Then, in the instant before the two riders met, he

entered a space and a silence that was at the centre, the very
eye of that storm.

Time and distance seemed to slow to nothing. Alexei found
his thoughts suddenly turned upon Natalia, upon the letter
to his sister that lay, unfinished, inside his pocket. Upon the
words of farewell that day in Altdorf. What was it he had
said? That he wouldn't always be around to look after his little sister? The other rider loomed ahead, seeming languid,
almost magnificent in his progress towards him. Could it be
that this was the journey from which he, Alexei, would not
return?

No, it was impossible. He was invulnerable. This day, at
least, he could not be defeated. Today the gods favoured only
one champion.

Thoughts flew away as time speeded up. The other knight
had not drawn his sword, nor even raised a shield. He neither
positioned himself for attack, nor seemed to move to avoid
it. It was as though he was deliberately leaving himself open,
defenceless.

Alexei cursed his opponent. Raise your sword! Claim your
supremacy and we will see who prevails! He could not
believe he was to be denied the sweetness of victory by an
opponent who offered no resistance.

Just before their paths crossed, the tattooed face turned,
and the knight looked directly into Alexei's eyes. The look
seemed to mock him; taunt him with a secret knowledge.
Alexei focused his anger, and swung his sword two-handed
through the air into the body of his opponent. The knight's
horse folded beneath him; the rider crashed to the ground
and did not move.

Alexei circled his fallen opponent twice, watching for
signs of life; some trickery of Chaos that would foreshadow
the real attack. He was stunned and vaguely disappointed to
find the contest ended so quickly and so decisively in his
favour.

When it became clear that the fallen rider was not going to
rise, Zucharov dismounted. His careful eye spied the wrought
steel plate still rising and falling upon the knight's chest. The
creature still lived. This was not over yet.

The knight lay exactly as he had fallen, face down upon
bare stony ground still heavy with rain. Alexei crept closer,

sword poised, then, very slowly, turned the body of the fallen warrior over with his foot.

The ravages of Chaos had wrought an evil transformation upon what had once, probably, been a mortal man. The knight's body had grown beyond normal bounds in size and proportion, with a leathery skin sketched across a grotesque musculature. Although there was no sign of any wounds upon the body, Alexei could only assume that the knight had been injured earlier in the battle. For this was not an opponent he would have expected to defeat with such ease.

Close to, the patchwork of runes and pictures etched upon the creature's face was even more wondrous to behold. More wondrous, and more terrifying. As the creature's lips moved soundlessly around unspoken words, the figures painted onto his flesh came alive before Alexei's eyes. It was like looking down at the battle in microcosm: he saw knights on horseback clashing, great armies falling like waves upon the shores of battle. Alexei stopped closer, then recoiled in shock. For in one of the tiny, moving figures, he momentarily recognised himself.

Zucharov stepped back from his prey. 'This is nothing but witchcraft!' he shouted. He drew back his sword, ready to put an end to the monster's existence, and with it the trickery that had befouled his mind. Just before he struck, the knight turned his head and stared up at Alexei through eyes that glowed like the embers of a dying fire.

Alexei had the unnerving sense of an opponent who, though defeated, yet had a power over him which he could neither match nor comprehend. Suddenly shaken, he lifted his sword to despatch the killing blow. Just before the sword fell, he saw the look upon the mutant's face change to an expression not of fear, nor even one pleading for life.

It was an expression of relief, and of release; as though a heavy burden was about to be lifted. For a moment, Alexei could have sworn, the knight smiled. He wants to die, he realised.

'Then may your wish be granted,' he snarled, suddenly incensed. He brought the sword down, driving it into the other's body with all the force as he could muster. The light in the creature's eyes faded and died. Life fled his enemy with one, final sigh of breath expelled.

Alexei stood motionless above his defeated enemy. He felt no satisfaction. It was as though he had been cheated, cheated of the glory that should have been his by right. He began to think that his instincts had proved false; this was not the moment he had been seeking, not the eye of the storm. On a whim, he kicked out at the dead body of his enemy, venting his anger and disgust. The sleeve of one arm rode up, and suddenly Alexei was angry no longer.

Something set upon the dead knight's wrist had attracted his eye. It was an engraved bracelet, a band of gold so bright it might have been spun from the very sun itself. Zucharov stared, captivated by its beauty. He had never seen its like before. It seemed impossible that so wonderful a thing might be found upon the body of a soldier of Chaos, but his eyes surely did not lie.

Alexei crouched down to look closer. The bracelet was inscribed with runes, and all around its outer edge, with words. It was a language he neither understood nor recognised, perhaps the elvish tongue, or maybe some foul script of Chaos.

As he gazed at the bracelet, he knew that he had to possess it. This, he realised now, was his treasure; his prize. He would not be denied it.

He pulled the short knife from his belt and held it ready. He would take his prize, even if he had to hack the hand from its arm to do so. He bent forward, and gently touched his fingers against the finely chiselled gold. It felt cool beneath his touch. To his surprise, it slipped cleanly from the knight's arm into his grasp. He lifted the golden band free of the body and raised it in the air, turning it one way and then the next beneath the sun. It felt light, lighter than the lightest armour, yet the gold was thick and sturdy between his fingers.

He squeezed his hand closed, and slipped the golden band over his wrist. He stood up, slowly, and looked about, taking stock of the surrounding world.

'I am invincible,' he said.

THE DEVASTATION INSIDE the walls of Erengrad was worse than Stefan could ever have imagined. Smoke billowed from the proud towers, and many of the jewelled spires of the once mighty city had been toppled. Flames raged across anything that could be burned, and rats had the run of whatever kingdom remained.

Elena looked around her, aghast. 'There is no way back from this,' she whispered. 'Star, marriage, come what may. No way back from this.'

'Yes, there is,' Stefan insisted, determinedly. He hadn't come this far to see Elena give up hope now. 'Cities can be built anew,' he said. 'If the spirit of the people is with you, there's nothing that can't be achieved.'

Franz Schiller shook his head slowly, in disbelief at what he was seeing rather than in disagreement with Stefan. 'True enough, Stefan,' he said. 'But what I see, the spirit of the people does not fill me with hope.'

They had abandoned their mounts at the edge of the city. Once within the walls, progress on horseback had become all but impossible, so thick upon the ground was the human debris all around them. They saw people laughing, and people crying from fear and from rage. People fighting each other, locked in combat to the death for no remaining reason. People bent upon their knees on the ground, praying for an end to come. Stefan had grown accustomed to facing the ravages of Chaos and its aftermath, but this was something different. Never before had he seen a people so turned in upon themselves in their rage and their despair; so instrumental in their own destruction.

'Morr's tears,' Bruno exclaimed. 'It looks like a city at war with itself.'

Stefan nodded. That was exactly what it looked like. The dark gods would be laughing long and loud at the ruination that they had engineered. He swore to do everything within his power to ensure that their laughter rang hollow before the day was ended.

They made their way through streets ankle deep in refuse and ordure, through air choked with the dust of crumbled buildings. For the most part, they found they were ignored. The desperate souls that milled around them seemed lost in their private madness; others who still held to their sanity were bent upon escape from the city.

Those few that stopped to challenge them as they forced their way through the tide sensed something in Stefan and

Elena that caused them to back off. 'Do we frighten them?' Elena asked.

'I doubt that,' Stefan replied. 'I'd wager most of them are beyond frightening after what they've been through.'

Elena looked at Stefan, and fingered the silver chain around her neck. 'Could it be the Star?' she asked. 'Perhaps, even incomplete, the two parts hold some warding power that's keeping us safe?'

'I don't know,' Stefan admitted. 'But whatever it is, let's hope it continues to work.'

ONCE FASTENED UPON his wrist, the bracelet no longer felt light. In the instant that he passed the glittering band over his hand it seemed to grow heavier until it might have been fashioned from lead, not gold. But Alexei Zucharov barely noticed. What he was more aware of was his own body, the feeling of energy that surged through his limbs, erasing the pain of his wounds, invigorating his spirit. It felt as if his strength was being replenished from a bottomless cup. Soon his weariness, the exhaustion of recent battle, was no more than a memory.

That was not all that had changed. As he roved the battlefield, Alexei began to see the world through different eyes. The dead and dying lay all around, those loyal to Castelguerre side by side with the troops of Chaos. He no longer distinguished between them.

With sudden insight, Zucharov now realised that the greater battle, the battle that would rage for all eternity, was not between good and evil. Those were no more than arbitrary distinctions, devised by men for the protection of fools. The real battle, he now understood, was between the strong and the weak. The strong were those that had been born to rule; it was their provenance. And it was their duty to rid the world of the weak: the puny and the feeble who would drag mankind down with their imperfection. The strong must be freed of their shackles, free to rise up and take their rightful place.

Their rightful place at the table of the gods.

A throbbing pain deep within his wrist distracted him from his reverie. Zucharov glanced down at the bracelet. It looked just as it had before, but it felt as though it had somehow tightened. With his free hand, he reached across in order to ease the band further down upon his wrist. It would not move. Zucharov cursed, vexed that his will should be defied in any way. He tugged harder, and finally the band moved an inch or so. Alexei looked down again, and pulled up short, tugging back on the reins of his horse.

Upon his skin, where the bracelet had lain, a rainbow-coloured bruise or stain had appeared. Alexei rubbed the spot hard with his other hand. The mark did not disappear. He lifted the blemish to his face and looked closer. What he saw he did not believe, but again his eyes did not lie. Instead of a bruise he saw a tiny picture, printed as though with ink upon his living skin. As he watched, the picture resolved into a recognisable form. He was looking down upon his own image, his sword raised above the body of the fallen knight.

Shaking, Zucharov replaced the bracelet, moving it up his wrist until it covered the mark. Only when the tattoo had been completely obscured did he ride on. On towards the east, on towards the city of Erengrad.

SETTING THE DAEMONS of madness loose upon the city had been one thing, drawing the anarchy back under his control was proving to be quite another. Vladimir Rosporov knew he no longer had command of the situation, and it was not an agreeable feeling. Doubts had begun to enter his mind, doubts even about the intent of Kyros himself. He spoke the blasphemy quietly, but he spoke it nonetheless.

For a while he had stood within touching distance of his dream. The entire city beneath his rule, bowed in servitude at his command. He was to have been the prince of Erengrad, regent for a new, dark age. Now that dream was ringing hollow. He began to wonder if the Dark Lord ever had any interest in conquering the city, whether he had not intended all along that it should be destroyed, allowed to tear itself asunder until only rubble remained.

Rosporov had fulfilled his vows; others had not. The victorious army of Chaos had never arrived. He would have bent the feeble-minded Norscans to his will easily enough. By employing their brute, animal force he could have brought the city to heel. But he knew now the Norscans would not be coming. None of them were coming. Kyros had abandoned him.

But, by the power of his will, he would yet prevail. Rosporov stared out from the rostrum at the sea of faces before him. A restless sea, a frightened, hungry sea of anger and confusion, held at bay by the black sashes of the Scarandar forming a cordon around the rostrum. This anarchy was his work, his creation. For a moment, Rosporov contemplated the thought with pleasure. But his creation could yet destroy him, too, if he did not find the means to subdue it.

The means, perhaps, was next to him upon the platform. Rosporov doubted whether Petr Kuragin would still have possessed the strength to stand, had the ropes fastening him against the iron frame not served to keep him upright.

Rosporov crossed the platform and seized his prisoner roughly by the hair, turning Kuragin's bruised and swollen face towards his own. Petr Kuragin stared back at him through half-lidded, vacant eyes. He had endured a beating that would have killed many men, but had proved as stubborn as he was stupid. Still he refused to cooperate.

But he *would* serve his new master, Rosporov was determined he would. One way or another, he would deliver him the people. And they would hand the prince of Erengrad his crown.

Moving to the front of the rostrum, Vladimir Rosporov addressed the people massed in Katarina Square. 'I bring you a gift,' he began. 'A gift of the man who has brought ruin upon your city.'

From out of the cacophony of warring voices that answered him, one voice could be clearly heard. 'We don't want your gifts,' it called out. 'We want food, we want warmth and we want shelter.' A ripple of assent ran through the crowd. Rosporov stood, his arms spread wide, at the edge of the platform. His voice took on a softer, more conciliatory tone.

'You shall be fed,' he said. 'You shall be housed. Now that the yoke of tyrants has been lifted, anything is possible. All I ask–' he paused. 'All I ask is that you bow in homage to me. I am your protector. Your lord.' He waited, with growing impatience, for the rabble to pledge their allegiance. To his fury, he heard Kuragin's name being chanted from somewhere within the crowd. Very well. If they wanted Petr Illyich Kuragin for their prince, they would have him. They would have their coronation.

He nodded to his lieutenants standing to one side. Two of the Scarandar climbed up on the platform. The first led Petr Kuragin forward, his feet still chained together. The second turned to a smoking brazier that had been set in the middle of the stage. From beside the brazier, Rosporov lifted aloft a ring of dull grey steel. The circlet was designed to fit exactly over the crown of a man's head.

Rosporov turned the ring into the air above Kuragin's head, savouring for a moment the fear registering in the other man's eyes. He held his arm motionless, and smiled at Kuragin. 'Let's warm this up a little for you, shall we?' He lowered the steel ring into the basket of burning coals, then turned back towards the now silent crowd.

'You shall witness the fate that befalls those that refuse my will,' he shouted at them. 'Are there any of you now who would defy me?'

For a moment, the only sound was a low wind blowing across the desolation of Katarina Square. Then a single voice in response. A woman's voice, strong and distinct.

'Yes,' the voice replied. 'I do.'

CHAPTER TWENTY-ONE
The Paths Divide

STEFAN WAS STANDING at Elena's side in Katarina Square as she spoke the words. The effect upon the crowd was electrifying. He had the feeling of a thousand eyes suddenly turning, seeking them out. Now he, too, was aware of the strange power that Elena had spoken of when they first entered the city. The silver chain about his neck began to grow hot against his skin, almost as though it were drawing raw energy from around them.

The effect upon Count Rosporov was more difficult to judge. He scanned the crowd, trying to identify the woman who dared oppose him.

'Name yourself,' Rosporov called out. 'Let us hear the name of she who would speak against the will of the people.'

'My name is Elena Yevschenko,' Elena said. 'And I speak *for* the people, not against them.'

If Elena had wondered whether her name would be remembered in Erengrad, she now knew. Faces in the crowd around them registered disbelief and awe. Some undoubtedly, were hostile, but the greater number amongst them seemed to sense that a corner had been turned in the grim

history of the city. Stefan heard the name being repeated endlessly, like a ripple flowing out across a lake.

Upon the rostrum, Rosporov's expression changed.
Arrogance and disdain started to leak away, replaced by
uncertainty.

Stefan looked at Petr Kuragin, standing in shackles at
Rosporov's side, guarded by two of the Scarandar. He could
only guess what torture the man had endured, yet his spirit
was still unbroken. At the sound of Elena's name echoing
across the square his face turned, and a glimmering of light
returned to his eyes.

'I applaud your insolence in returning here,' Rosporov
retorted. 'Or should that be foolishness? Your family have the
blood of Erengrad upon their hands. Their guilt is no less
than Kuragin's!'

The crowd parted in front of Elena as she moved towards
the platform. 'It's true,' she replied. 'We are guilty. Guilty of
allowing Erengrad to run to ruin. Guilty of allowing scum
like you to gain a foothold. Both our families are guilty of
devoting themselves to a petty family feud, whilst the city fell
apart around them. But I am here today to put an end to that
feud. To reunite our city.' She paused. 'The blood, Vladimir
Rosporov, is on your hands alone.'

A murmur spread through the crowd as they listened to
Elena's words. Reason began to prevail over the madness.

Petr Kuragin looked upon Elena's face for the first time as
she reached the front of the crowd. As their eyes met, Elena
nodded towards him just once.

Stefan fingered the knife in his pocket. There would be little chance of aiming a clean throw at the count before he
could move against Kuragin.

Rosporov turned to address Elena. 'The people have no
love of you, Elena Yevshenko,' he called out. 'What do you
have to offer Erengrad except for your excuses?'

Elena slipped the chain carrying the silver icon from
around her neck and held it aloft. 'I have this,' she said. A
gasp went up in parts of the crowd as the Star of Erengrad was
recognised. 'With it I pledge my life towards healing the
wounds that have scarred our city.'

'Empty words,' Rosporov scoffed. 'On its own the icon is
useless.'

'But it's not on its own,' Stefan said, now raising the second piece above his head for all to see. 'We have two parts of the Star, and soon we will have the third.'

Rosporov gazed out across the sea of faces, seeking out Stefan. Stefan met his gaze. 'Surrender yourself to our mercy, Rosporov,' he called out. 'Erengrad will never yield to you now.'

For a moment all was silent. Smoke curled from the brazier of burning coals, an emblem of the fire-ravaged city. Vladimir Rosporov took a step back, and took stock of the world taking shape around him. The tide of feeling turning against him in the crowd. The black-sashed soldiers of his Scarandar, there to die at his command. The beaten but still unbowed face of Petr Kuragin that stared at him with unremitting defiance. And Elena Yevschenko and her champion in the heart of Katarina Square. The would-be conquerors of Erengrad.

His own journey of conquest had all but run its course. Soon he must wake from his dream. But, in this last moment, he still held the dreams of thousands within his hands. All eyes in Katarina Square were fixed upon Count Vladimir Rosporov. He reached to his neck and lifted the third segment of the Star of Erengrad high into the air.

'This is what you have travelled so far to claim?' Rosporov turned the piece in the sunlight. He walked towards the brazier, then turned to face the crowds. 'This? It's just a worthless fragment.' He smiled, and let the icon fall into the flames. With his other hand, he pulled an iron from the fire and lifted the circlet of steel, already glowing red-hot, into the air.

'Now,' he said. 'It's time for our coronation.'

THE ACHE IN his arm where the bracelet pressed tight against his flesh had not lessened. Indeed, a pulsing pain now ran through Alexei Zucharov's body, rising through his arm to end in a steady hammer beat inside his head. And yet his entire being seemed to have been energised, filled with an all-empowering life, the like of which he had never experienced before. This was life, pure and undiluted. Everything else, he now realised, had been mere facsimile.

The tattoo upon his wrist was still growing. No longer contained by the narrow band of gold, it had begun to extend, upwards towards his shoulder, down towards his wrist. Alexei stared at it from time to time as he approached the distant city. Gradually, dimly at first, he was coming to know it for what it was. A mirror upon his soul, and the source of his power. The living pictures growing upon his flesh celebrated his past. Every deed, every life harvested by his sword was there. Over time, as the tattoo came to map his body, it would describe his future, too. His future, and the countless other deaths that that future held.

There might once have been a time when such a prospect would have appalled him, but Zucharov was struggling to remember it now.

So much seemed different. So much of his old life being sloughed off, like a snake shedding its old, desiccated skin. There were voices inside his head, talking to him. Some he recognised, others he did not. At times he thought he heard a woman's voice, calling him, calling him back. He struggled to find the name that would connect with a recollection that now seemed so distant. Natalia, yes, that was her name. Natalia. The name had been important to him, he remembered that much. But there was so much more to think of now. Zucharov shrugged the voice off, and thoughts of his sister fell away, fading into the deep well of memory that was the past, the old life.

Every so often Alexei looked up, towards the city. There, he knew, his purpose lay, even though its meaning had grown blurred and indistinct. But soon enough, his path would become clear. For there was another voice, sweet and insistent, rising and falling with the hammer beat inside his head now. He did not know it yet, but this was the voice he would learn to call his master.

He came at last to the city walls. People passed by him on all sides. Alexei regarded them coldly, without favour or pity. Most of them belonged amongst the weak, but it was weakness without importance or significance. They did not interest him. Most met his stare only briefly, then turned away. Those few foolish enough to stand in his path, he dealt with.

His head was beginning to clear. The cacophony of conflicts unresolved was slowly being sieved away. Purpose; clarity of vision; all was moving into focus.

Zucharov stopped, looked around him. He was inside the city walls but he did not know why. But the world was changing, that much he did know. It might take time, but like time itself, it could not be resisted.

In the distance, a bell tolled, faint but insistent. Alexei Zucharov located the direction of the sound and turned towards it. Progress was measured and steady; nothing in the bedlam unravelling in the streets around interested or distracted him. He paused only once, to glance at the tattoo spreading across his skin. He looked down, and watched the future being rewritten.

STEFAN HURLED HIMSELF towards the rostrum as Rosporov's men dragged Kuragin to the middle of the stage. Kuragin was struggling for his life, but beaten and weighed down by the shackling irons; he was lost. Rosporov held the ring of glowing steel aloft, and bowed in mock servitude.

'Behold the Prince of Erengrad,' he called out. 'Long may you reign in the pits of Morr.'

Stefan screamed out in fury, but his path was blocked by a cordon of Scarandar. Stefan set about them like a man possessed, scattering them with a flurry of blows from his sword. He knew he would not reach the platform in time. Rosporov knew it too, and the smile on his face was that of a final, bitter victory.

'Stefan, get down!'

Stefan had just a moment to turn and see Bruno behind him before his comrade aimed the knife over his head towards the stage. Rosporov was faster than either of them could have expected; he seemed to see the blade cut through the air, and pulled back from its path in time. The knife skimmed past Petr Kuragin and buried itself in the throat of one of his captors. As the Scarandar fell from the platform, Petr Kuragin dug deep for one final surge of strength. He brought his arms together and lashed out at the second guard, smashing the shackles into the man's face. As the guard staggered back, Kuragin leapt from the rostrum to freedom.

A roar went up from the watching crowd, and, in that moment, Rosporov's spell upon the people was broken. The Scarandar in their midst were better armed, but they were heavily outnumbered. The retribution of the people was swift and bloody.

Stefan now had just one point of focus. 'Take care of the Scarandar,' he shouted to Bruno and Franz. 'Rosporov's mine.'

The count was running towards the far edge of the platform. Whatever the mood of the people, there was no guarantee that he might not yet escape if he could lose himself within the crowds on the square. Stefan was determined that would not happen. As Rosporov prepared to jump clear, Stefan flung himself onto the platform, bringing down the smaller man. For a moment he had Rosporov pinned down, seemingly at his mercy. The count looked up at Stefan, his blue eyes radiating a cold hatred.

'I put a price upon everything,' he spat at Stefan. 'And, I promise you, the taking of my life will cost you dear.' Stefan had no desire to swap words with Rosporov. But, as he reached for his knife, a blow from out of nowhere punched into his stomach, sending the weapon spinning away.

Rosporov hit him again, hit him with a force that Stefan would scarcely have believed possible. Stefan reached for his sword, but Rosporov anticipated him. The blade was forced from his grasp. Stefan launched himself upon Rosporov before he could aim another blow. But this was no longer the slight, almost frail man of only moments before. Now Stefan found himself locked in a murderous dance with a fury who seemed to draw down fresh energy even as Stefan's exhausted body weakened. Rosporov's skewed, seemingly puny arm wound itself around Stefan's throat, and began to lock tight.

'Never trust your eyes to tell you the truth,' Rosporov taunted him. 'The world is full of deceptions.'

Stefan levered himself free of the choking embrace, only for the count to strike him a third time; a hammer-punch to the chest that knocked Stefan halfway across the platform. Now Rosporov had Stefan's sword. Smiling, he closed in on his victim.

Stefan twisted his body away as Rosporov scythed down with the sword, wielding the heavy blade as if it carried no weight at all. The steel bit into the wooden frame of the platform, an inch from Stefan's face. He aimed a kick at Rosporov and caught him square in the gut, but it seemed only to feed his manic rage. Stefan regained his feet. Rosporov aimed the sword again, and this time made contact. Stefan felt the

numb chill of the steel cut between his ribs. He staggered
back, blood already flowing fast where his hand was clamped
against the wound.

Rosporov surveyed his work with satisfaction and positioned himself to strike one final blow. Stefan looked around
him. The dagger was gone, Rosporov had his sword. He took
a step back and fastened both hands upon the only weapon
he had left.

The hot metal of the brazier seared his skin at the very first
touch, but, somehow, Stefan held on. As Rosporov swung the
sword a final time, Stefan dragged the glowing brazier from
the ground, and hurled the fiery mass of coals into the face of
his opponent.

For a moment there was silence. The air filled with smoke
and the pungent odour of burning flesh. The smoke cleared
to reveal Vladimir Rosporov still standing, his hands covering
his face. When he lifted his hands away the flesh was raw and
blistered, but the same evil light still shone, undimmed,
through his eyes. The mutilated figure started to move, turning, slowly, towards the front of the stage. Stefan took up his
sword from where it had fallen, and drove it up through the
air into Rosporov's body. The count toppled forward, into the
crowd. The people of Erengrad fell upon the body, beating it
with clubs, fists, anything that came to hand. Vladimir
Rosporov would not rise again.

The Scarandar had been put to the sword. Bodies of the
cultists lay all across the square where the people had taken
their revenge. Most of those that remained were upon their
knees, begging the protection of Franz Schiller's men. Most,
but not quite all. Three of the black-clad figures, the strongest
of Rosporov's guard, had fought their way clear of the crowd,
and were trying to escape. Stefan shouted a warning to his
comrades, but knew it was almost certainly too late.

The bid for freedom was short-lived. As the men reached
the outer edge of the square they were confronted by a figure
coming the other way. A figure with sword in hand, mounted
upon a towering horse.

'Sigmar's toil!' Stefan exclaimed. 'It's Alexei.'

Alexei Zucharov gazed down at the retreating Scarandar
with disdain. Unable to get around him, the three men
launched a last, desperate attack. Alexei brushed them aside

like vermin, then brought his own blade to bear like a butcher cleaving a carcass. The Scarandar fought for their lives, fought like madmen against the towering figure upon the horse. But they were facing a greater madness; an impassive, chilling madness that cared only to destroy, or else be destroyed. Zucharov lashed the Scarandar with his blade, impervious to any blows they aimed in reply. The screams of the Scarandar filled the square, and then subsided. Three bloodied bodies lay motionless at Alexei Zucharov's feet. The battle of Erengrad was at an end.

Leaning on Bruno for support, Stefan made his way over to Zucharov. 'By the gods, Alexei,' he declared. 'You certainly pick your moments.' He grinned. 'No complaints, this time.' He reached up his hand, offering his congratulations. Alexei did not take it.

'Running to save their skins,' he said, as if by way of explanation. 'They were weak.' His voice sounded distant and remote. He seemed barely to recognise either of them.

'Are you wounded?' Bruno asked of him. 'Do you need help?'

Slowly, ponderously, Alexei looked around him. 'I am strong,' he said.

'Come on,' Stefan said. 'Let's get you down off that monstrous beast.' He reached up a hand once more. This time Zucharov backed away, and, as he did so, Stefan caught sight of the gold band upon his arm, and the rainbow bruise that lay beneath.

'What in the name of–'

Zucharov quickly drew back his arm, masking the disfigurement. With his other hand he lifted his sword, and seemed about to swing it at Stefan. At the last moment, he froze, the sword hanging suspended above his head. He looked down from the horse upon his comrades, and a glimmer of recognition animated his features.

'Stefan,' he said, uncertainly. 'Stefan?'

'Come on,' said Stefan, urgency in his voice now. 'We're going to get you some help.' Alexei Zucharov looked down from the horse and shook his head slowly from one side to the other. 'No,' he said at last. 'I am strong.'

Zucharov turned his horse about and looked down upon his comrades. The light of kinship seemed to flicker briefly again in his eyes, then died. He moved his head, slowly, from one side to the other, as though in sorrow or regret, and picked up the reins of his horse.

'Stefan,' he repeated, and then: 'Goodbye.'

Stefan shouted out Alexei's name, but Zucharov was gone, the crowds parting in panic before the great horse as it gathered pace across the square. Stefan turned back to Bruno. 'We have to find him,' he said. 'I don't like what I saw at all.'

'We stand no chance of catching him on foot,' Bruno pointed out. 'Besides,' he glanced down at Stefan's bloodied tunic. 'There's more important things for you to be worrying about. Don't worry. He won't go far.'

WITHIN THE HOUR, Katarina Square had filled to overflowing. Word of Elena's return had spread through the ravaged city like wildfire, kindling fresh hope amongst the people. For the moment at least, expectation, not fear, hung upon the air.

Back upon the rostrum, Stefan turned towards Petr Kuragin. As he looked upon the bruised and bloodied face of his lover's husband-to-be, Stefan suddenly found he was without words, drained equally of strength and emotion.

'Are you all right?' he said at last.

Kuragin shook Stefan's hand as firmly as his own strength allowed. 'I'll live,' he said. 'What about you?'

Stefan touched one hand to his ribs where the wound had been freshly bandaged. 'I've had easier days,' he conceded. He looked around the square. 'What now?' he asked.

'Now,' Kuragin said, 'we must wake Erengrad from this nightmare.'

Elena joined them on the platform. Her expression suggested there was little to celebrate.

'After all this, they may have won,' she observed, bitterly. 'If Rosporov succeeded in destroying the last part of the Star, then all may still be lost.'

Petr Kuragin moved his head as far as he dared in a shake of dissent.

'No,' he declared, stubbornly. 'This must not have been for nothing.' Slowly, face contorted with pain, he climbed down upon his knees and began to sift through the charred debris scattered across the platform. At last he found what he was looking for. Petr Illyich Kuragin rose again to his feet, a smile beginning to light his battered features. In his hand he held the missing segment of the Star.

He brushed away the last of the ashes from the battered icon and rubbed it gently between his hands. 'Not destroyed,' he said, his voice still blurred and unsteady. He closed his hand around the silver fragment, the smile on his face broadening. 'By the gods,' he said to Elena. 'It's not even hot from the fire.'

He turned to face the crowds, holding the icon high above his head. Cheers, murmurs of astonishment and even applause began to ripple through the square.

'Like Erengrad itself, the Star may be tarnished,' Kuragin declared, 'but it will still endure!'

'The three parts of the Star,' Stefan said. He held out his segment, matching it against those held by Elena and Petr. The silver pieces appeared to fuse together into a single, seamless whole. Stefan waited, perhaps expecting something dramatic to follow. When nothing did, he felt vaguely foolish and disappointed.

'This good will cannot be trusted to last,' Franz Schiller warned, indicating the waiting crowds. 'You must declare your alliance before the people soon, or the tide may turn again.'

Stefan took a step back from Elena and Kuragin. This was going to be more difficult than he had imagined. 'Come on,' he said to Bruno. 'We should leave the stage to them.'

'Just a minute, please.'

Stefan met Petr Kuragin's gaze. 'I want to thank you,' Petr said. 'I understand it is mostly thanks to you that Elena has completed this great journey. All Erengrad is in your debt.'

Stefan felt awkward in the other man's presence, awkward and oddly aware that the Petr Kuragin of his imagination was much bigger than the man now stood before him. Although the stockier of the two, Petr was a full head shorter than he in height. Funny, Stefan reflected, how things are rarely as you expect them to be.

'It's not just down to me,' he replied, struggling for the appropriate words. 'Elena has shown valour of her own. It was her determination to be with you that has brought us here.' He began to make his way down from the stage.

'No,' Kuragin insisted. 'Please, hear me out.' He took hold of Stefan's arm. 'I am a man of many failings, but I will try with every ounce of my being to serve Elena, and to serve Erengrad. Do you believe that?'

'Yes,' Stefan said, truthfully. 'I do.'

'I know that Elena does not love me,' Petr Kuragin said. 'Why should she? This is duty, not love. We both know that. But I shall never give her cause to despise me, and – who knows – perhaps one day she may be able to find some love in her heart.'

Stefan waited. He knew no answer was expected of him. Kuragin looked at him for a moment, a strange expression on his face. Then he continued. 'For now, I think it is you that she loves, Stefan. Am I right?' He quickly waved away Stefan's protest. 'I'm sorry. I have no right to expect you to answer that. There is no need. Elena's eyes tell the story – yours, too.' He paused, searching for what he needed to say. 'I want to tell you I'm glad that you were there for Elena, Stefan. I want to give you my thanks.'

'Thank you,' Stefan said. A burden had lifted, but it had left behind a hollow place. Kuragin looked at him intently, and seemed to read his thoughts.

'Franz is right,' he said. 'We must make haste with the ceremony of the Star. But first, I think, you have your own ceremony to complete.' He nodded towards Elena, standing alone by the edge of the stage. 'Please,' Kuragin said.

Elena looked up, flustered, as Stefan approached. For a moment her face had worn a distant expression, as though her mind had been somewhere far away from Erengrad.

'So,' she said, as brightly as she could muster. 'This is good-bye then?'

'Yes,' Stefan said. 'The paths divide.'

Elena cleared her throat, her voice suddenly cracked and thin. 'I've realised something recently,' she said. 'Realised I'm not much good at dealing with goodbyes.'

'I don't know that I'm much better,' Stefan replied. 'I don't think there's an easy way with this.'

Elena dropped her head, and brushed a hand across her eyes. She looked up again, forcing a smile. 'Petr and I must consecrate the ceremony of the Star,' she said.

'Will you be our witness?'

Stefan stood facing her, battling with the forces inside of himself. All around them, on all sides of Katarina Square, the

sea of faces looked on, waiting, expectant. For one brief
moment he was oblivious to the thousand watching eyes.
Stefan Kumansky was alone once more with Elena, and alone
with his thoughts. His mind ran back to the night beneath
the stars at Mirov; to a moment in time so fleetingly grasped.
Would he have made the same choice, have taken that same
path, had he known for sure that it would run its course so
soon? Stefan had no need to dwell upon the question. His
heart told him what the answer would be. He took a step
back from Elena Yevshenko, and bowed low before her.

'Yes,' he replied at last. 'Yes, I will be your witness.'

Whilst Stefan looked on, Petr and Elena linked hands at
the front of the stage. In his other hand Petr held the Star of
Erengrad, complete now, and dazzling in the sunlight. The
clamour of voices rippling through Katarina Square suddenly
dropped away to nothing. Petr and Elena stood together at
the centre of a silent world. After a moment, Petr Kuragin
looked out towards the crowd. Towards the people of
Erengrad, his people, waiting for deliverance.

'Too much blood has been spilt,' he told them. 'Today we
come to mourn our children of Erengrad who have been lost.
But from today, too, the wounds shall begin to heal. With
your hearts, and with your hands, we shall rebuild our city
anew.'

He passed the Star to Elena and, between them, they lifted
it aloft in full view of the people massed around Katarina
Square. A sound rippled through the crowd, barely more
than a whisper; the collective intake of breaths. It was the
sound of a people offering a prayer for peace, and it was the
sound of hope.

'With this holy relic, I pledge myself unto thee,' Kuragin
intoned.

'With this holy relic,' Elena repeated, 'I pledge myself unto
thee.'

She turned towards the man who was now her husband.
'Not so long ago there would have been flowers,' she said, half
joking, half wistfully. 'The streets strewn with sweet garlands.'

'There will be flowers,' Petr told her. 'Even now, we sow the
seeds of their blossoming with our union.'

They moved closer, and their lips met in a single kiss. The
moment was stiff and awkward, but it had an unmistakable

effect upon the waiting crowd. A silence, absolute and total, fell across the square. Stefan, too, found himself drawn under some kind of spell, as though the Star were speaking directly to him. It spoke of unity, of peace, of an end to a generation of civil war. He felt a warmth growing inside of himself, a warmth that radiated from the Star itself. He knew that every other man and woman of Kislev that stood within Katarina Square was feeling it too.

Gradually, the city was turning back towards the light. The gestures were small – handshakes, conversation, a shoulder for the tears of the bereaved – but they were unmistakable.

'We live for moments like these, do we not?'

Stefan turned to see Gastez Castelguerre standing at his side. Stefan thought of Elena, and he thought of the journey that had brought him to this final place. He smiled. 'Yes,' he said at last. 'Yes, we do.'

'We are much alike, you and I,' Castelguerre continued. He appraised Stefan with a measured stare. 'I think our work here is done for the moment, don't you?' He took Stefan by the arm. 'Come,' he urged. 'Let's walk a while.'

Stefan allowed himself to be led away. Castelguerre was right, perhaps more so than he knew. His part in Elena's life was at an end now. Their story was drawing to a close, and a new chapter in her life with Kuragin – and the life of Erengrad itself – was opening.

Once they were clear of the crowds Castelguerre stopped and turned towards Stefan, his expression pensive, probing.

'There are not so many of us,' he said. 'Men like you and I, that is.' He glanced back towards the couple upon the stage. 'This is a great victory, but it has been won at a price. The world will not lightly bear the loss we have sustained.'

'You mean Otto,' Stefan said, 'and Andreas.'

Castelguerre nodded. 'With them gone, we are few indeed.' He paused. 'But we would always have need of men such as you, Stefan Kumansky.'

Stefan pondered the implication of the words. 'You're asking me to join your order?' he asked. 'To join the Keepers of the Flame?'

Castelguerre smiled, benignly. 'Yes,' he said, simply.

'And what if I say no?' Stefan countered.

'Then I'll content myself with having made you the offer,' Castelguerre replied. 'And I shall not ask you again.' He paused. 'But I do not think you will say no.'

Stefan's deliberations were cut short by a voice calling his name. He looked around to see Bruno approaching, looking troubled. Stefan made his excuses and hurried across to meet his comrade.

'What's wrong?' he demanded.

'It may be nothing,' Bruno began. 'But I'm hearing rumours about a rider running amok about the city, attacking people indiscriminately. Look, it might just be some garbled story, but–'

'But what?' Stefan demanded.

'The descriptions fit Zucharov,' Bruno said. 'It sounds as though he's lost his mind. Maybe he's ill, running with fever,' he added.

'Maybe,' Stefan murmured. The image of Zucharov, emerging through the smoking ruins of the city, filled his mind. Something in Zucharov had altered, but he had not looked ill. If anything he had seemed filled with a new, unnatural energy. Stefan heard again his comrade's last words to him: *I am strong.* The words and the image echoed in his mind like remnants of a bad dream.

'We'll find him, don't worry,' Franz assured them. 'My men will soon have the city sealed. He'll turn up before long.'

Stefan felt a touch upon his hand. 'What's happened?' Elena asked. 'Is everything all right?'

'It's fine,' he told her. 'Everything will be all right now. We've come through this, both of us.'

Elena looked towards Petr Kuragin upon the rostrum, then turned back to Stefan. 'I came to tell you I must go now,' she said. 'I need to–'

'Be at his side,' Stefan said. 'It's all right. I know. He needs you there, and you must go to him.'

She stood facing him for a few moments longer, the warmth of her smile tempered by a deeper sadness. 'We might have made something of a life together,' she said.

'I know,' Stefan replied. 'But that would have been another life. Along another path.'

She stretched out her hand, and Stefan held it in his own for the last time, before letting her go. As he watched her walk back across the square, he realised he was already looking at a different person; a young woman already carrying the burdens of office upon her shoulders. Somehow, Stefan suspected, she would carry them well.

'The war is won. Now they have to build a new peace,' Bruno observed. 'It won't be easy.'

'That it won't,' Stefan agreed. 'But Castelguerre has brought food to fill bellies, and men to rebuild walls. The rest – rebuilding hearts, and souls – the rest is up to them.'

Franz Schiller returned, talking hurriedly with Castelguerre. 'Zucharov has been seen,' he told Stefan. He hesitated. Now it was Schiller's turn to look troubled.

'What is it?' Bruno asked. Schiller paled. 'My men tried to stop him leaving the city,' he said. 'Three died in the attempt.'

'He's fled the city?' Stefan demanded.

Schiller nodded. 'We've lost him. I'm sorry, Stefan.'

'Well,' Bruno said, 'at least that means he can do no more harm here.'

'Here, no,' Stefan agreed. The thought did not console him much. What had Otto said, half a lifetime away back in Altdorf? Words that Gastez Castelguerre himself had echoed on the eve of the battle for Erengrad? Beware the poison that claims men by stealth. Beware the poison in the stream.

'Our troubles are still not yet ended?' the commander asked of him.

Stefan forced a smile, but it was tinged with the gnawing ache he suddenly felt inside. It was a feeling he knew of old, one which was not going to let him go.

'I fear Zucharov didn't heed your warning,' Stefan replied. 'I think he may be carrying the seed of darkness inside him.' He paused, remembering their earlier conversation.

'I'm not forgetting what we spoke of,' he said. 'But I cannot leave this unresolved.'

'I know,' Castelguerre replied. 'And my offer will still stand, whenever you are ready to accept it.'

Stefan turned back to Bruno. 'The journey's not finished,' he said. 'Not for me, at least. I have to track Zucharov down, Bruno. I have to find out. If this is some temporary madness, well and good. We'll find a way to bring our brother back to us.'

'And if it isn't,' Bruno asked, 'what then?'

'Then it can only end in death,' Stefan said. 'His death, or mine.'

'The world is wide, Stefan. He could be headed anywhere.'

'True enough,' Stefan agreed. 'I don't know where this journey will take me,' he told Castelguerre. 'Or for how long.'

'That doesn't matter,' the commander responded. 'When the time is right, we shall find one another.'

Stefan looked one final time to where Elena stood upon the stage. What should he call her now? Countess, princess, lady of Erengrad? To him, at least, she would always be just Elena. Perhaps they, too, would find one another once more. Perhaps their paths were destined to cross again. Perhaps. For now, there was another path, dark and uncertain, which he was destined to follow.

'I think Zucharov will try to disappear,' he said to Bruno. 'Disappear until whatever has taken hold of him has eased – or strengthened its grip. I think he will do as I would do, and return towards what he knows, towards home. But he won't be able to vanish without trace. Somewhere, sooner or later, I'll find him.'

'And I shall be there with you when you do,' Bruno said. 'I shall travel with you on that journey, Stefan. We shall ride together. Until the story is ended.'

EPILOGUE

DEEP WITHIN THE lightless, empty space that was the domain of Kyros, the Chaos Lord looked down upon the mortal realm, and sensed the balance of the fates as they shifted. Slowly but surely his prize had slipped from his grasp. Inside the city, as well as beyond the walls, the battle for Erengrad was now ended.

Kyros did not turn his face from defeat. He would drink it down, know its bitter taste and commit it to deep memory. For then vengeance, when it came, would taste all the sweeter.

And vengeance would come. The final victory would be his, as surely as the waves would return to fall upon the shore. All of this – Erengrad, Kislev and the blighted lands beyond – all of it had but one destiny. To be subsumed within the dominion of the Great Lord Tzeentch. The time of his coming might have been forestalled, but it would not be long denied.

Already, the picture was changing. Kyros now turned his gaze away from the gates of Erengrad, towards the shadowed deep of the forest and the lands that lay beyond, to the west. Towards the lone horseman riding hard for those lands, through the fields of the fallen dead. The speeding rider was not his to command and control; not yet. But the transformation had begun. Before long the dark flower would come to full bloom. Then a new champion of Tzeentch would walk the face of the world, and the world would know and fear his name.

Until then he must nurture his disciple, keep him safe from the spiteful intrusions of mankind. Kyros knew that Zucharov was being pursued, and in one of the pursuers he had recognised the seemingly unquenchable fire of an enemy that had already, time and again, stood in his way of his goal. For the moment, the hunter would become the hunted. But time was a river that flowed only one way. The flesh of all mortal men would weaken and yield. If Stefan Kumansky chose to pursue Zucharov, then let him. For he would be pursuing his own death.

Even as he set aside the conquest of Erengrad, Kyros was reaching out towards new, as yet unknown prizes. Prizes that would cast the loss of this miserable city into insignificance. The mortals could be vigilant, but their vigil could not stand forever. The fates would deal him another chance before long.

This day the battle had been lost. But it was just the first battle in a war that was only now beginning.

ABOUT THE AUTHOR

Neil McIntosh was born in Sussex in 1957 and
currently lives in Brighton. He has contributed
stories for the Warhammer anthologies,
White Dwarf and other magazines, as well as writing
for radio. Following a lengthy sabbatical, he
returned to writing fiction in 2000 with two stories
for *Inferno!* magazine. *Star of Erengrad* is
his first novel

More Warhammer from the Black Library

The Gotrek & Felix novels by William King

THE DWARF TROLLSLAYER Gotrek Gurnisson and his long-suffering human companion Felix Jaeger are arguably the most infamous heroes of the Warhammer World. Follow their exploits in these novels from the Black Library.

TROLLSLAYER

TROLLSLAYER IS THE first part of the death saga of Gotrek Gurnisson, as retold by his travelling companion Felix Jaeger. Set in the darkly gothic world of Warhammer, TROLLSLAYER is an episodic novel featuring some of the most extraordinary adventures of this deadly pair of heroes. Monsters, daemons, sorcerers, mutants, orcs, beastmen and worse are to be found as Gotrek strives to achieve a noble death in battle. Felix, of course, only has to survive to tell the tale.

SKAVENSLAYER

THE SECOND GOTREK and Felix adventure – SKAVENSLAYER – is set in the mighty city of Nuln. Seeking to undermine the very fabric of the Empire with their arcane warp-sorcery, the skaven, twisted Chaos rat-men, are at large in the reeking sewers beneath the ancient city. Led by Grey Seer Thanquol, the servants of the Horned Rat are determined to overthrow this bastion of humanity. Against such forces, what possible threat can just two hard-bitten adventurers pose?

DAEMONSLAYER

FOLLOWING THEIR adventures in Nuln, Gotrek and Felix join
an expedition northwards in search of the long-lost dwarf
hall of Karag Dum. Setting forth for the hideous Realms of
Chaos in an experimental dwarf airship, Gotrek and Felix are
sworn to succeed or die in the attempt. But greater and more
sinister energies are coming into play, as a daemonic power
is awoken to fulfil its ancient, deadly promise.

DRAGONSLAYER

IN THE FOURTH instalment in the death-seeking saga of
Gotrek and Felix, the fearless duo find themselves pursued
by the insidious and ruthless skaven-lord, Grey Seer
Thanquol. DRAGONSLAYER sees the fearless Slayer and his
sworn companion back aboard an arcane dwarf airship in a
search for a golden hoard – and its deadly guardian.

BEASTSLAYER

STORM CLOUDS GATHER around the icy city of Praag as the foul
hordes of Chaos lay ruinous siege to northern lands of
Kislev. Will the presence of Gotrek and Felix be enough to
prevent this ancient city from being overwhelmed by the
massed forces of Chaos and their fearsome leader, Arek
Daemonclaw?

VAMPIRESLAYER

AS THE FORCES of Chaos gather in the north to threaten the
Old World, the Slayer Gotrek and his companion Felix are
beset by a new, terrible foe. An evil is forming in darkest
Sylvania which threatens to reach out and tear the heart
from our band of intrepid heroes. The gripping saga of
Gotrek & Felix continues in this epic tale of deadly battle
and soul-rending tragedy.

More Warhammer from the Black Library

THE CLAWS OF CHAOS
Slaves to Darkness · Book One
by Gav Thorpe

AT THAT MOMENT, a dagger swept up towards Kurt's exposed armpit and he twisted quickly, catching it on his breastplate, his sword passing harmlessly over the Norseman's head. Horrified, his gaze moved from the clawed fingers gripping the knife, up a twisted arm that pulsated with exposed muscle and connected just below the northerner's ribcage. How could he have not noticed the man had a third arm?

THE ICY WINDS *of Chaos blow down across the civilised world, corrupting man and beast alike. When loyal Empire knight Kurt Leitzig is forced to choose between duty and love, a tragic chain of events is set in motion. The first volume in the Slaves to Darkness trilogy, an epic tale of high adventure by Gav Thorpe.*

More Warhammer from the Black Library

SILVER NAILS
Savage fantasy
by Kim Newman writing as Jack Yeovil

VUKOTICH WENT tense again, and Genevieve put her hand on his chest, restraining him. She felt his heart beating fast and realized her nails were growing longer, turning to claws.

She regained control and her fingerknives dwindled.

Vukotich was bleeding slightly, from the mouth. She had cut him when they kissed. A shudder of pleasure ran through her as she rolled the traces of his blood around her mouth. She swallowed, and felt warm.

SET IN THE *dark and dangerous Warhammer world, this adventure reunites some of his most popular characters including 'Filthy' Harald Kleindeinst and the scryer Rosanna Ophuls, Baron Johann von Mecklenberg, playwright and self-confessed genius Detlef Sierck and of course the vampire Genevieve.*

More Warhammer from the Black Library

ZAVANT
By Gordon Rennie

'YOU HAVE EXAMINED the corpse, no doubt?' Graf Otto rasped, looking at Zavant Konniger. 'What are your conclusions?'

Konniger set down his wine glass and composed himself before answering. 'Foul play has been committed, certainly. But it was not a robbery-turned-murder. The victim's killer left a full purse of gold behind him. And Altdorf's footpads and cut-purses may be a bloodthirsty lot, but I have yet to meet one who would make a habit of ripping out his victims' throats with his bare teeth.'

'Surely it is the work of some wild animal, then? Some beast loose within the city walls?'

Konniger paused, sensing that he was being tested. 'Animals kill for food. Whatever killed this poor unfortunate did so only for its own savage pleasure.'

THE OLD WORLD *is a dark and dangerous place, and even the towns and cities offer little shelter, for the evil that stalks their fog-shrouded streets is as deadly as it is elusive. Enter Zavant Konniger, the great sage-detective of Altdorf. Accompanied by his trusty halfling manservant, Vido, this most brilliant scholar must use his incredible powers of deduction to solve the most sinister mysteries of the day.*

More Warhammer from the Black Library

THE TALES OF ORFEO
by Brian Craig

*Tales of high adventure and mystery, recounted by
Orfeo the minstrel.*

ZARAGOZ

RIVEN BY POLITICAL intrigue, the countless petty king-
doms of Estalia are a dangerous land to travel through.
When he rescues a mysterious priest from brigands, the
minstrel Orfeo is drawn into a deadly power struggle
for the citadel of Zaragoz, where he is forced to use all
the power of his wits and skill at arms to survive.

PLAGUE DAEMON

IN THE WILDEST reaches of the Border Princes, the kingdom of Khypris is thrown into turmoil when barbarian
tribes descend upon its rich, fertile lands. Soldier of
fortune Harmis Detz finds himself fighting more than
mere human enemies when a cruel twist of fate sucks
him into a far more desperate endeavour – to find the
real source of evil that threatens Khypris.

STORM WARRIORS

WHEN A BAND of mysterious elves is shipwrecked on
Albion, the delicate peace of the land is shattered. Far
from being the innocent travellers they claim, the elves
pay allegiance to a more sinister power. Can King
Herla and the bard Trystan save the kingdom from the
whirlwind of darkness that threatens to tear it apart?